Praise for Edward M. Lerner and *Fools' Experiments*

"A spooky cautionary tale that is part hard-wired SF and part intrigue and suspense. A good choice for readers who prefer their SF with a heavy dose of hard science along with fast paced storytelling." —*Library Journal*

"Viruses and worms have come to be an important 'feature' of our network landscape. And yet this is just the beginning. *Fools' Experiments* is a fascinating view of how awesome these threats could soon become."
—Vernor Vinge, Hugo Award–winning author of *Rainbows End*

"Good science and entertaining writing make this a fast, fascinating read." —*Publishers Weekly*

"Must-reading for anyone worried about computer viruses. In *Fools' Experiments*, an expert imagines how deadly a thing might evolve from them—and how fast!"
—Stanley Schmidt, Hugo- and Nebula-nominated author of *The Coming Convergence*

"Edward M. Lerner brings a wonderfully intelligent, creative style to science fiction. His clever ideas and intriguing plots have given me many hours of enjoyable reading. His stories keep me thinking—and make it fun."
—Catherine Asaro, Nebula Award–winning author of *The Night Bird*

FOOLS' EXPERIMENTS

BOOKS BY EDWARD M. LERNER

*Fools' Experiments**
Creative Destruction (collection)
Moonstruck
Probe
*Small Miracles** (forthcoming)

WITH LARRY NIVEN
*Fleet of Worlds**
*Juggler of Worlds**
*Destroyer of Worlds**

* A Tor Book

FOOLS'
EXPERIMENTS

Edward M. Lerner

TOR®

A TOM DOHERTY ASSOCIATES BOOK
New York

This is a work of fiction. All of the characters, organizations, and events portrayed in this novel are either products of the author's imagination or are used fictitiously.

FOOLS' EXPERIMENTS

Portions of this work incorporate material, substantially revised, that first appeared in the following stories:

"Presence of Mind" and "Survival Instinct" originally appeared in *Analog Science Fiction and Fact*.

A Tor Book
Published by Tom Doherty Associates, LLC
175 Fifth Avenue
New York, NY 10010

www.tor-forge.com

Tor® is a registered trademark of Tom Doherty Associates, LLC.

ISBN 978-0-7653-5862-2

First Edition: November 2008
First Mass Market Edition: September 2009

Printed in the United States of America

0 9 8 7 6 5 4 3 2 1

*To the pioneers behind the original big and clunky
mainframes and the earliest software.*

*And to the professors who first taught me
to understand computers.*

It's been an interesting trip. . . .

Errors are not in the art, but in the artificers.

—Sir Isaac Newton

Every cause produces more than one effect.

—Herbert Spencer

I love fools' experiments. I am always making them.

—Charles Darwin

FRIDAY, JULY 17

PROLOGUE

Welcome to Greenville, read the sign in the lobby.

Brian Murphy loathed that sign. It doesn't belong, he thought, for easily the thousandth time. The public wasn't welcome in a nuclear power plant, or at least they ought not to be.

Murphy was a big man, in height and through the beer belly. Something about him—his stance, maybe, or how the shoulder-holster bulge in his coat looked so natural—screamed *cop*. Things are often what they seem: He'd been on the force for almost twenty years, until the department doctors found the heart murmur. Now he headed security for the Greenville Power Station. The change had turned out for the best: Industry certainly paid better than the city, and most evenings he made it home for dinner. Still, nearly eleven years after taking the job, he marveled at how much more willing his bosses were to pay for his advice than to follow it.

He watched the civilians filter in from the meticulously landscaped grounds, then mill aimlessly around the sun-drenched atrium. Several filled Styrofoam cups with the truly dreadful coffee from the lobby dispenser. He glanced at his watch. It was nearly ten o'clock.

"Over here, people," the perky guide called out. "Our tour starts in a few minutes."

Tour, faugh. Murphy understood why they gave tours, though: license renewal. The plant was nearing the end of its original operating license, and the investment to dismantle and replace the 1,100-megawatt plant would be enormous. It would be far cheaper to renovate the place and keep it running. The antinuke types were, predictably, resisting all license renewals.

And so the twice weekly public-relations tours would continue, in hopes of convincing the public that nuclear power is our friend.

"Everyone, please form a line. We'll be going through the gate one at a time."

Murphy grunted to himself. Here, at least, was a touch of sanity. The tours ended the day the World Trade Center towers came crashing down. When the tours had been allowed to resume, it was only on condition of an airport-style security gate.

Three of his staff now manned the entrance, two at the portal itself and one behind, seemingly loitering, but actually eyeballing the crowd. The visitors seemed harmless enough, mostly upstanding businessmen and -women in suits, plus a few well-scrubbed housewives. No children, thank God. He had at least talked the execs out of that.

The pretty, young brunette guide went through the gate first, chattering as always. Purses and a few briefcases rode the conveyor belt past the X-ray equipment. What in *hell* would make someone bring a briefcase on a tour?

"Señor, you take thees building to Coo-ba and no one weell get hurt."

He glanced toward the whisperer, and the presumed owner of the bony finger sticking into his ribs. The line wasn't funny *before* 9/11. It certainly had not been since. "Try that remark at an airport sometime, Max. See how amusing the screeners there find it."

Max Bauer just grinned. He was the VP of public relations, and the chief perpetrator of the plant tours. His faux Arabic was even worse than his Spanglish. "Lighten up, willya? We don't want to spook the customers."

As usual, it worked the other way round—the customers were spooking *him*. Murphy's psychic antennae quivered. Why? He eyed today's guests, more than half of whom had passed without incident through the security gate. The line was paused while a distinguished-looking guy in an Armani suit emptied his pockets into a plastic bin. Relieved of keys, pens, mobile phone, watch, cigarette lighter, and coins, Armani passed the magnetometer without causing an alarm tone. A guard took the cigarette lighter until after the tour. Armani wasn't the problem. The two housewives directly behind him looked benign, too. But the bald man behind them . . .

How had he *not* noticed this guy before?

Baldy was sweating copiously and mumbling unintelligibly. He wore a suit, like most men on the tour, but his jacket was rumpled and his tie was knotted ineptly. He clutched a mega-sized plastic soda cup from the burger joint down the road. The protruding plastic drinking straw magnified the tremor in his hand.

Murphy had a lousy memory for names, but he hardly ever forgot a face. He was almost certain Baldy had been to Greenville before, more than a year ago, touring with a bunch of engineers. If so, Baldy hadn't been rumpled and twitchy then.

Murphy sauntered over. Baldy's skin was pasty. "Are you all right, sir?"

"Yes. Yes. Fine." Baldy's delivery was wooden.

By now, both women ahead of Baldy had passed through the gate. Time for a decision. Without a *very* good reason, Murphy dare not turn someone away. Denying access would be not only bad PR but also possible grounds for a lawsuit. "A bit nervous about nuclear power, sir?" The man muttered something. "What, sir?"

"Yes."

No one made you come, Murphy thought.

Max was frowning. Max didn't get security; that didn't keep him from meddling in it. He'd gone all the way to the CEO to have Murphy overruled on inspecting visitors' shoes.

Baldy's determined grip on his tall drink made Murphy inexplicably nervous. Half the folks in line held cups of Greenville's lousy coffee. Murphy could imagine Max's reaction if he confiscated Baldy's drink. "This isn't the Cineplex, Murph. We're not protecting the sales at our concession stand."

Sigh. "Go on through, sir," Murphy said.

He walked around the gateway, catching the eye of his senior man on duty and tipping his head slightly toward Baldy. Freak. I'll keep an eye on him.

The remaining visitors transited the magnetometer without incident. Murphy tried, without success, to relax. Baldy continued to sweat despite the near-arctic temperature at which the plant was kept for the benefit of its electronics. The tour group slowly made its way past viewing galleries of thick, unbreakable glass that overlooked the nuclear reactor itself, the massive steam turbines, and the diesel generators that would power emergency equipment in case of a reactor shutdown. Everyone seemed suitably impressed with the feet-thick concrete wall of the containment building, designed decades ago to withstand the impact of a falling airliner. (Of course, a large jet then was a 707. What about a fully fueled modern jumbo jet making a power dive? Murphy hoped never to see *that* experiment attempted.)

Little Miss Perky kept up her patter, parroting everything she'd been taught about the plant's many safety features. Despite himself, Murphy grinned. Little did she know her main qualification for this job was blatant bubbleheadedness. She was a walking subliminal suggestion for the simplicity of nuclear power. "Just a *really* big teakettle," she had actually gushed at one point.

As they came to the highlight of the tour, the master control room, Baldy was twitchier than ever. Why did Baldy bother to lug a soda around the facility? Murphy didn't remember the man taking a single sip. As Murphy thought back, the visitors filed through normally locked double doors into the plant's brain center. Why was he worried? Clear, flexible plastic shields, like on point-of-sale terminals in fast-food places, protected the consoles.

The hundreds of indicator lights, gauges, and control levers never failed to awe Murphy. Massive operator consoles lined three walls. Flat-panel displays hung above them, summarizing overall status. In the center of the control room sat the computerized gear retrofit after the long-ago near meltdown at Three Mile Island.

Like shoe inspections, Murphy had lost the battle to bar tours from this room.

"And over there"—the guide gestured with an extravagant flourish—"we control those *enormous* turbines you saw a little while ago. Now here's an interesting fact. See those red and green lights? A green light means that a valve is closed, and a red light means that a valve is open." She winked at a housewife. "Green for stop and red for go? It had to be a *man* who designed that, don't you think?" Two women dutifully laughed; most looked pained.

Baldy sidled for a closer look at the master control console. The shift operator there glanced nervously in Baldy's direction, opening her mouth as though to object, but saying nothing. A matrix of black pushbuttons occupied half the ledge in front of her, each button governing the position within the reactor core of one control rod. An array of wall-mounted LEDs at the operator's eye level illustrated the position of each rod.

Slide enough rods into the core and the nuclear reaction stopped. The rods soaked up the neutrons, whatever neutrons were, needed to maintain the reaction. Slide out too many rods and, paradoxically, the reaction was also supposed to stop. The neutrons then zipped through and out of the fuel assembly so quickly that too few of them interacted with the uranium fuel to sustain the chain reaction. Murphy had heard the tour spiel *many* times.

"And here we control the main and backup cooling systems." Baldy wasn't listening, so neither was Murphy. Baldy's right hand emerged from his coat pocket to firmly pinch the drinking straw in his soda cup. What the hell was that about?

Jerkily, Baldy slid the straw up and down. He did it repeatedly, as though stabbing crushed ice. The straw remained straight despite all the jabbing. Could there be something rigid inside the straw?

The cup's snap-on lid popped loose. What was that irritating, acidic smell?

Murphy shoved through the crowd. That wasn't soda in the cup! Baldy had been stabbing, all right, but not ice. He had punctured an inner liner of some sort. "Stop that man!" Operators jumped up, but the damned tourists were in their way, too.

What else was in the cup?

Murphy drew his gun. "Freeze, mister." The visitors scattered, as many getting in his way as out of it. Cursing, he pushed people aside. Baldy, his skin ghostly pale, jiggled the straw. "*Freeze,* damn you."

People screamed and stampeded, jamming the exits. Not the staff, however; they stayed, ready to do whatever might be needed.

Baldy's renewed murmuring was drowned out by the crowd. His demands?

"Tell me what you want!" Murphy shouted.

Baldy kept muttering, inaudible above the din. He jerked up the straw for another jab.

For a more vigorous stab at a stubborn inner bag? Something to ignite the first chemical? A vague recollection taunted Murphy. His memory for chemical names was even worse than his memory for people names. Hyper-something fuels, mutually igniting. "Freeze *now!*"

Jesus H. Christ, the man stood right by the main console. "Not another inch." More incomprehensible jabber. The acrid stench permeated the room. An operator looked meaningfully at Murphy. Should I try to jump him?

Murphy shook his head. Jostling would only spill the chemicals—and maybe burst that stubborn second inner bag. What would that do? "Set the cup onto the floor—carefully—or I shoot." He was bluffing, or at least hoped he was. Bullets couldn't be good for the controls in here.

He might not have any choice.

The muttering took on a mantralike, almost hypnotic cadence. Sweat poured down Baldy's ashen face. His hands trembled. A terrific struggle raged behind crazed eyes—and then Baldy plunged the straw.

Crack, went Murphy's handgun.

Fire spewed from the cup. Baldy fell against the console with an unearthly scream, then struggled onto the waist-level shelf, spreading the flames with his own burning clothes and body.

Crack. The fiery figure spasmed violently, then lay still.

Operators grabbed fire extinguishers even before the writhing stopped. They sprayed Baldy, the ominously crackling controls, and the spreading pool of burning liquid. Klaxons shrieked overhead, while alarm panels spanning half the room lit up like Christmas trees.

With his hands hastily wrapped in his suit coat, Murphy pushed the smoldering body from the console ledge onto the floor. The charred remains struck with a meaty thud.

Mercifully, someone suppressed the warbling alarms. Red lights gradually blinked out as the crew initiated a scram, an automated shutdown, of the reactor. The plant would be down for who knew *how* long, as they checked out and replaced every control and instrument in the room, and the wiring leading from it.

For the record, Murphy felt for a pulse. He didn't find one.

Nor explanation, either. Murphy wondered if he would ever get one.

AUGUST

CHAPTER 1

Thwock.

The bright red ball rebounded with a most satisfying sound, although the racquet continued on its arc without any apparent impact. Doug Carey hurriedly wiped sweat from his forehead with the back of his left arm, carefully keeping his eyes on the ball. Precisely as he had intended, the ball passed through a translucent green rectangle suspended in the vertical plane that bisected the court. The ball instantly doubled its speed.

Across the court, his opponent grunted as he lunged. Jim Schulz caught the ball on the tip of his racquet and expertly flipped the orb back through the green region. The ball redoubled its speed.

Doug swore as he dived after the ball. It swept past him, obliquely grazed the floor, and careened first from the rear wall and then from a sidewall. The ball winked out of existence as it fell once again, untouched by Doug's racquet, to the floor. "Good one," he panted.

Jim waved his racquet in desultory acknowledgment, his T-shirt sodden with sweat. "Pull," he called out, and a new red ball materialized from the ether. Jim smacked the ball to the court's midplane, just missing the drifting triple-speed purple zone. The unaccelerated serve was a cream puff; Doug ruthlessly slammed it through purple on his return. A red blur shot past Jim to a brown "dead zone" on the rear wall, from which the suddenly inert ball dropped to the floor like a brick. This ball, too, disappeared.

"Roll 'em." Yet another red ball appeared, again in midair,

this time at Doug's invocation. He twisted the racquet as he stroked the ball, imparting a wicked spin. The serve curved across the court, rebounding oddly from the floor and side-wall.

Not oddly enough. Jim pivoted gracefully, tracking the ball around the rear corner. He stepped behind the ball as it rebounded from the back wall, from which position he casually backhanded it. The ball sailed lazily toward mid-court, aimed squarely at a foot-squared drop-dead zone floating scant inches above the floor.

Doug dashed to center court, ignoring an alert tone as he crossed the warning line on the floor. He swung his racquet into the slight clearance between the vertical brown region and the floor. He misjudged slightly: The body of the racquet swept effortlessly through the court's vertical bisection plane, but the handle struck with a thud. A loud *blat* of dis-approval drowned out his sharp intake of breath, but not the jolt of pain that shot up his arm. All but the offending handle vanished as he dropped the racquet. "*Damn,* that smarts!"

"Are you okay?"

Doug grimaced, rubbing his left hand against his right forearm just below the elbow. He pressed a thumb into a seeming birthmark, and was rewarded with a subcutaneous *click.* Through clamped teeth, he forced out, "That's it for today. Don't watch if you're feeling squeamish."

He grasped firmly with his left hand, and twisted. The right forearm popped off, to be placed gently onto the court floor. Doug massaged the bruised stump vigorously. "To coin a phrase, ouch."

Jim walked to center court, beads of sweat running down his face and glistening in his lopsided mustache. He sported possibly the last long sideburns within Western civilization. "Anything I can do?"

"Uh-uh." The answer was distracted.

His friend pointed at the numerals glowing on the ceiling. "Twelve to ten, pretty close. Why don't we pick up there next time? I'll call you tonight. Abracadabra." The last word was directed at the court, not Doug. Jim disappeared as thoroughly as had the out-of-play balls earlier, but with the added touches of a soft "poof" and a billow of swirling white smoke.

"Abracadabra," Doug agreed. Jim's half of the room promptly vanished, revealing at what had been center court the wall that had so rudely interrupted the game. Doug peered at the shallow gouge in the plasterboard that calibrated by how much his depth perception had failed him. Virtual racquetball with real divots: Maintenance would just *love* that.

Sighing, he reached for the Velcro buckle of his game goggles—and missed. Look, Ma, no hand. He was more successful with his left arm. The colored regions floating about the room, the glowing scoreboard, the lines on the floor—all the ephemera—disappeared. Stark white walls now surrounded him, interrupted only by glass-covered inset minicam ports and the thin outline of a tightly fitting door.

Doug carefully laid down his computer-controlled goggles, although its LCD eyepieces and stereo speakers weren't all that fragile, then wrestled himself back into the prosthetic forearm. He hoped the impact of racquet on wall hadn't injured the limb. He would find out soon enough.

Doug glanced at his wristwatch, and it was as late as he had feared. The more conventional part of work called.

Doug strode from the virtual-reality lab to his office, whose laser-carved wooden nameplate announced him to be Manager, Neural Interfaces Department. He paused beside his secretary's desk to check his tie. He'd be amazed if it didn't need straightening.

No surprises today.

The sidelight to his office door reflected more than his tie. His most prominent feature, a nose too large for his taste, stared back at him. Aquiline, Doug reminded himself, aquiline. Like an eagle. A hint of a mischievous smile flashed and was gone. What eagle had a bump like this on its beak? His hood ornament had come courtesy of a long-ago pickup football game gone a tad too enthusiastic.

He tugged the knot into something closer to symmetry before entering his office. A visitor waited inside, scanning titles on his bookshelf. "Sorry to keep you waiting," he said.

Cheryl Stern turned to face him. It was her first time at BioSciCorp, and Doug found himself taken aback. Cascades of wavy brown hair framed a face graced by wide-set hazel eyes, an upturned nose, and a sensual mouth. Her brief smile seemed forced and out of practice. She was slender and, he guestimated, about five foot four. All in all, very attractive.

The memory of Holly instantly shamed him.

Cheryl looked surprised when Doug waved off her out-stretched hand. She would understand soon enough. He offered her a guest chair, shut the door, and hid behind his desk.

Her application sat in a manila folder in front of him. He got his mind back on the interview and the résumé. The résumé, he reminded himself severely, that had earned her his invitation. "Thanks for coming in, Cheryl. I hope you didn't have any trouble finding us."

"Your secretary's directions were great. I gather she gets to give them out a lot."

Implying the question: Against how many people am I competing? He also couldn't help noticing that she perched just a bit too far forward in her seat. He tried for a friendly grin. "There's no opening per se. You obviously know how few people there are in the neural-interfacing field. When a résumé as impressive as yours crosses my desk, I make a point of talking to its owner. If this looks like a fit, I'll *make* a spot."

She relaxed a bit at his answer but said nothing.

"Let's start with one of those open-ended questions candidates hate. I try to get those out of the way early. That way, Cheryl, you'll actually get to eat when we go to lunch. So, why don't you tell me a little about yourself?"

It was quickly clear she didn't intend to volunteer more than was on her résumé. "Excuse me please, Cheryl. What I'd like to hear is more along the lines of what you're looking for in a job. For instance, why did you contact BioSci-Corp?"

It took a few tries, but he eventually got her to open up. ". . . And the field of neural interfacing *fascinates* me. Still, when I consider the potential of linking the human brain directly with a computer, my imagination can't quite handle it. Sure, I know the standard predictions: speed-of-thought control of complex machinery, immediate access to entire libraries, mind-to-mind communications using the computer as an intermediary. What I don't believe is that any of us can truly anticipate the full implications. When we pull it off, neural interfacing will have as big an impact as did the industrial revolution and the Internet."

When, not if. *That* was the attitude Doug wanted to see. "I agree: It will be astonishing. That's not exactly what we're working on here."

"Close, though?"

"One small step along the way," he conceded. "Mind if I do a quick overview of what we're up to here in my little corner of BioSciCorp?"

"Yes, I'd like that."

"Okay, then. Metaphorically, we're trying to walk before we run. The human brain is the most complex piece of neural engineering that we know, right?" She nodded to fill his pause. "The truth is, we—humans—don't begin to understand how the brain works. We're not even close to cracking the code. That's why BSC is trying to connect a computer to a much simpler structure of nerve cells."

Cheryl tipped her head in thought. "Say you do interface a lower life-form to a computer. How could you know if any communication was taking place, or how well it worked?"

"Who mentioned lower life-forms?" He took a moment's glee from her puzzled expression, then relented—sort of. He lifted his right arm off the desk, thinking hard about his hand. The microprocessor-controlled prosthetic hand slowly rotated a full 360°, the wrist seam hidden behind a shirt cuff. In the suddenly silent room, Doug heard the *whirr* of the motor by a freak of sound conduction through his own body.

"You've connected to the peripheral nervous system." Her eyes were round with wonder. "That's so *astonishing*." Then the personal aspect of his demo struck home, and she cringed. "Oh, I'm so sorry. Excuse me. I just get too wrapped up in technology. I don't mean to make light of your, uh . . ."

"No need to feel uncomfortable, Cheryl." He arched an eyebrow. "In the land of the prosthesis manufacturer, the one-armed man is king."

Cheryl laughed—behavior he could not help but find endearing in a prospective employee. The current staff knew all his material.

She said, "Um, but seriously, how did you do that?"

"My stomach alarm went off ten minutes ago. What do you say BSC springs for lunch and we pick up the discussion afterward?"

"You've got a deal."

After beef fajitas and the completion of Cheryl's interview, Doug did some management by walking around.

There had been a virus attack during lunch. They had been semilucky. On the one hand, the invader was *not* benign. On the other hand (an expression from which Doug could not break himself), the malware was clumsy and well understood. Well understood, that was, according to the web site of the Inter-Agency Computer Network Security Forum, the federal crisis-management organization that strove valiantly, if with mixed success, "to stem the rising tide of malicious software and computer break-ins." The press release announcing the forum's formation had brought unbidden to Doug's mind the image of King Canute drowning in a sea of hostile data. A far-from-bitsy bit sea.

The virus was brand-new that day, and hence unknown by and invisible to the company's Internet firewall and virus checkers. The forum's web site already listed hundreds of attacks. Behind a cute pop-up window (Dyslexics of the World Untie) hid a cruel, if apt, intent: randomly scrambling the hard drives of the invaded computers. It had to be a new infestation, since BioSciCorp's backup files were all uninfected.

In short, they had had a close call. He wondered if they would be as lucky the next time.

CHAPTER 2

The entity *was*.

It existed in a featureless space; all that distinguished it from the all-encompassing void was an innate reflex that sparked it into sporadic, random action. Often, the activity produced a result that might in some sense be characterized as motion; at other times, the effort invoked an immovable counterforce that left the entity's situation entirely unchanged.

The entity jittered about in a meaningless, chaotic dance. Only the whims of its reflexes and of the insurmountable forces determined its position. Unseen and unknown, time passed.

Other beings similar to the entity could be said to be moving all about it, even through it. None of the beings in any way sensed another, or influenced another by its passage.

Millions of the chance motions happened, then millions more. Driven only by reflex and the laws of probability, the locations of the objects gradually diverged. A few, the entity among them, were closer to an unsensed destination than the rest.

That was enough.

The few were chosen.

Arthur Jason Rosenberg, better known since the fourth grade as AJ, stretched across the newspaper-covered breakfast table for one last doughnut. It was the most exercise he was likely to get today. The paunch that hung over his chinos suggested how many circular snacks had met a similar demise. While his ever-taller forehead seemed to confirm the onset of middle age, AJ had advanced the innovative theory to his colleagues that he wasn't losing hair—it was merely sliding to the bottom of his face.

AJ was pushing horn-rimmed glasses back up his nose when a dark, massive, furry object alit on his newspaper.

Razor-sharp claw tips were visible in all paws. Ming (sur-named "the Merciless") was a foul-tempered black cat, stay-ing with him courtesy—to use the term loosely—of a kid sister who had imposed on him for the length of her seem-ingly endless gallivant across Europe. Ming studied AJ dis-missively, certain that AJ would not dare remove her. As though to reinforce her seriousness, the claws of one paw slid out, ever so delicately, another quarter inch. AJ exam-ined his wristwatch and decided that another few minutes didn't merit the risk. Did it change anything for him to read another op-ed speculation about imminent New Caliphate missile tests?

At least today Ming hadn't brought him a dead mouse.

He glanced outside to the battered, sun-faded econobox recharging in his driveway. That, at least, made him smile: The heap wouldn't need to move today. Progress was a won-derful thing. He slid the breakfast plate into the dishwasher and sauntered down the hall to work.

Six large flat-screen displays covered three walls of his once-book-lined den. Students milled about on five screens, representing the main campus, two satellite campuses, and two affiliated corporations. Speakers flanking the screens could bring him the sounds from any of the video-equipped locations and from fifteen audio-only sites. Each of the latter supported only a handful of people, a few individual elderly shut-ins.

The technology that let students attend Smithfield Univer-sity from anywhere with Internet access had also freed AJ from the daily commute. It was liberation certain to warm the cockles of any Angeleno's heart.

The final display, this one mirroring what his students would see, came alive as AJ fumbled with the controls of his teleinstruction podium. He looked into his webcam. "Good morning, people." Accelerated rustling as kids found their seats was the only response. "I'm Dr. AJ Rosenberg, and this is Artificial Life 101. Real Life is taught over in the College of Liberal Arts and Sciences." No laughter, from any of the locations, and precious few smiles. Tough crowd. "The Good

Life is over in the Graduate School of Business, and The Time of Your Life is over at Fine and Applied Arts." He left unspoken his latest variation: Twenty Years to Life, over at the University Lab School, to which went most of the faculty's precocious, high school–aged children. Like his two daughters. Single parenting was hard, and not his class' fault.

AJ gazed into the video camera. "You and I will be exploring a topic that didn't even exist when your parents were your age. Mention this course to them and you will probably get an inane remark about Frankenstein." Just smirk knowingly, as I'm sure you all do so well, he thought, visions of his own teens in his mind's eye. "We're not here to discuss anything so mundane, so simple, as copy and paste with existing biological bits. Nope, no cloning or genetic engineering for us. We'll be discussing something *really* cutting-edge."

The entity was long gone, vanished, but new beings—its spawn—had taken its place in the still-featureless void.

The progeny of the entity still moved randomly, advancing and withdrawing. Sometimes they edged closer to the destination of which they, too, had no awareness. Often they backed away from their goal, or vied without success against the same unseen forces that had stymied their sire. Blind reflex directed their actions, as it had that first entity's.

Still, subtle variations distinguished the descendants from each other and from their ancestor. One attempted its moves with greater rapidity than the others, and made correspondingly faster progress. One less fortunate moved in only a single direction, soon reaching a limit beyond which invisible forces permitted no further motion. The beings and their slight distinctions numbered in the hundreds. Each embodied a unique, if insufficient, method toward solving the enigma of the void.

Millions of motions once again passed.

All the travelers failed, but some were more or less successful than others. One, in particular, had the capacity of retaining a single fact. Specifically, the being "knew" whether its most recent effort had been blocked by the irresistible force. If so, it tried something, anything, else for its next motion. To that degree, its actions deviated from pure randomness; it had fewer false starts than its siblings, and soon forged far ahead of the pack.

Memory, however rudimentary, was an evolutionary advancement of the profoundest significance.

The far voyager and its nearest competitors were selected.

Video cameras panned across the remote lecture halls. "So, class, what we will be dealing with are computer programs that simulate some behavior of biological plants and animals." AJ played a game with himself as he spoke, mentally labeling the students. Here, an obvious campus jock. There, a neohippy woman. Either those were the biggest hoop earrings ever made or the Flying Wallendas were preparing for an exhibition. He found a whole roomful of button-down, dress-for-success types on what he privately considered the Intergalactic Business Machines screen.

"A simulated plant can curl its simulated stem toward the simulated sunlight. A collection of simulated ants can cooperate to excavate a simulated colony. A simulated—" A blinking light on the podium caught AJ's eye. When he pressed the Identify button on the podium keypad, pop-up text gave a student name. "Mr. Prescott, you had a question."

The student stared self-consciously at the camera and cleared his throat. "You keep saying 'simulated life.' Why simulated life, rather than real?"

"That's a good question." It was one AJ had answered roughly a million times by now. Did kids even read course descriptions before they registered? He kept scanning the displays, responding on autopilot. "Life as you and I know it exists in what I'll call the physical world. That domain is unbelievably complex, full of complications that make any study of it inconvenient and inconclusive. Think how much easier it would be to understand the principles of simple machines, like pulleys and inclined planes, if there weren't any friction." The analogy earned scattered nods from across the various class sites. One especially enthusiastic nod on the main campus display drew AJ's eye. Seated next to the nodder was a mesmerized-looking fellow, who looked *very* familiar, frantically typing notes into his laptop.

"Life, in even the simplest bacterium, is a mechanism of incredible intricacy. It's just too hard to study or manipulate in its natural environment. That's why biology became a quantifiable science only very recently, centuries after physics and chemistry.

"We will be dealing in this class with entities that lack any physical existence. As the course progresses, our studies will progress from counterfeit bacteria growing in an imaginary Petri dish to flocks of simulated birds swarming in an imaginary sky. In doing so, we'll discover that a handful of principles govern seemingly complex behavior.

"And who knows? Maybe each of us will even learn a little something about ourselves."

Why, Jeff Ferris wondered, was the consummate test of salesmanship supposedly selling ice to Eskimos? His fingers twitched economically as he mused, surreptitiously playing Tetris on his laptop as the lecturer droned. Eskimos understood ice and its uses. What was the big deal in selling it to them? Now selling suntan lotion or a spice rack in England—there was a challenge.

Jeff knew all about salesmanship. He'd tucked away a bundle in elementary and high schools, starting out by hawking gift wrap and greeting cards from catalogues and working his way up to used cars on weekends. He could sell anything, and the future looked promising.

The distant future, that was. A college degree was, alas, expected for a broker job at any securities firm. Sure, he'd only been a kid during the nineties. He hadn't been asleep. Selling stock in dot-coms: Now *there* was a line of work worth getting into—until the bubble burst. By choosing courses with great care, Jeff meant to pocket a liberal-arts degree with relatively little pain—in time, he hoped, for the next wave . . . whatever that turned out to be.

Tap tap. Twitch tap, tap, tap. The falling, L-shaped cluster of video squares rotated and jogged left as it sank, before settling into a matching gap in the structure of colored blocks at the bottom of the screen. Three newly completed rows brightened, then disappeared. Suddenly unsupported squares dropped into the open space.

Subterfuge, like sales, was an art. Jeff had long ago mastered gaming with his keyboard, avoiding the trackball that more easily maneuvered objects on-screen. Constantly rolling the trackball in class was a dead giveaway, while continuously keyboarding passed as enthusiastic, if inefficient, note taking. Another important rule: Wear contact lenses in school, since video games might reflect revealingly from regular glasses.

He much preferred any first-person-shooter game, but without sound effects, those basically sucked. Earbuds were no good, since profs expected to be listened to. It didn't matter if they thought the buds were for a game or an iPod. So: Tetris.

A new shape entered the game window and started its fall. On the wall-sized flat screen at the front of the auditorium, Dr. Rosenberg, larger than life and twice as ugly, prattled on about artificial life.

This whole *course* seemed pretty artificial, but the Smithfield Student Association web guide—indispensable research material for the prepared slacker—said Rosenberg gave over 80 percent As and Bs. Tapitty tap, twitch. That information and the reported essay final exam had sold Jeff. He needed only one science class in the liberal-arts curriculum, and he could surely bullshit his way through an easy grader's essay test. Meanwhile, Jeff made a point of getting to the lectures on time and logging in—good attendance often earned the benefit of the doubt on borderline grades. Attendance didn't mean that he had to *listen* to—

An Alert box suddenly filled the middle of the laptop's screen. Behind the pop-up, Tetris pieces piled up relentlessly. Nervously, Jeff clicked the Accept button.

Another window, this one text filled, appeared. Jeff swallowed hard as he read: "Mr. Ferris, please see me in my campus office sometime Thursday afternoon."

Busted.

CHAPTER 3

Cheryl's gut lurched ominously as she walked into the BSC lobby. As long as it only rumbles, she thought. Trapped in the women's room wouldn't be a good first-day impression.

She didn't exactly understand her misgivings. Both interviews had gone well, and Doug had extended the job offer quickly enough. She certainly seemed to hit it off with her new boss. Maybe *that* was the problem. She didn't want to hit it off *too* well. She knew how her looks affected men. On the job, it irked her. Off the job, she never found the time for it to matter.

Replaying the interviews in her mind, she decided that neither Doug nor his all-male staff had seriously questioned her. Everyone had concentrated on selling BioSciCorp. Why were they so eager to hire her? Not that she didn't need the job . . .

Doug stood when she knocked on the jamb of his open office door. He towered over her. Six foot two, she guessed, and maybe 195 pounds. His black hair was thick and a bit unruly, with a touch of gray at the temples. He had nice eyes, she thought. Gray or very pale blue? She couldn't decide. A warm smile.

And I'm questioning his reasons for hiring me?

Well into the welcome-aboard orientation, Cheryl worked up the nerve to ask him about the softball interview questions. Doug took a bulging folder from a stack on his desk. He flipped through it, theatrically plopping several thick papers onto the blotter. They were dog-eared from use and thickly annotated with highlighting marker and scribbles in the margins.

Clearly, he wasn't going to explain. Cheryl took a paper, a reprint from the *Proceedings in Neural Computing,* from the top of the stack; she had written it. She checked all the articles he had selected. She had authored or coauthored every one. Doug, it seemed, had pored over every one of her professional articles and papers. Their well-worn condition made clear an interest in her work long predating her recent job feeler. So much for a good first-day impression. "You're right, of course," she said. "These say everything you need to know about my capabilities. I apologize for being so touchy."

Doug studied her frankly, a twinkle in his eye. "I can say with absolute conviction that I admire you solely for your mind."

It annoyed her that in some unliberated recess of her mind she took umbrage at his jest.

Like noontime most weekdays, the condominium was largely empty. The first moans that drifted through the stairwells and down the hallways went unremarked. The moaning grew gradually louder, more insistent, and began making its presence known throughout the building. A mother blushed for her totally oblivious three-year-old, and turned up her TV. The mail carrier in the foyer smiled at the same imagined lust. Len Robertson, a meteorologist for the National Weather Service who was working the second shift that week, pulled his out-and-about wife's pillow over his head, hoping to fall back asleep.

The moans grew louder and somehow unhappy. There was a hint of wildness, and then of pain, under the inarticulate whimpering. Embarrassed, the mother swept up her son and carried him, screaming in protest, on a suddenly urgent errand. Robertson threw off the blanket in disgust and donned his robe. He met the equally puzzled postal worker in the hall.

Robertson was about to suggest calling the police when the ambiguous moaning became an anguished scream. His memory coughed up a name. Jeffrey Dahmer: the cannibal killer in Milwaukee who tortured and murdered people in his apartment. Was it too late for the police? Robertson ran to his apartment for the handgun in his nightstand. "Call nine-one-one," he shouted, not waiting to see whether the letter carrier obeyed.

"No, no, *noooo*!!" Screaming filled the hall. But from which floor? Robertson burst through a fire door into the stairwell, where noise reverberated confusingly. Were the screams coming from upstairs? Heart pounding, he tried to distinguish new shouts from the echoes. "Go away! Go away! *Get out!*" As he crept warily into the third-floor hallway, the words dissolved into inarticulate shrieking. The bellowing was coming from apartment 322—Mr. Cherner's unit.

Where were the police?

Robertson didn't stop to think. He charged into the flimsy door with his left shoulder. The wood gave way with a splintery, crunching sound. He pointed the gun with a two-handed grip. "Stop!"

But the screeching *didn't* stop. Robertson watched in horror as Cherner, all alone, forced yet another inhuman scream from his throat. Bloody channels of flesh were torn from his face. Cherner's eyes, round and impossibly wide, focused on nothing.

"It's okay," Robertson managed to say. "It's all right now. You're safe." The oncoming sirens should even have offered some confidence that he was right.

But the gore dripping silently to the rug from Cherner's own blood-soaked hands denied even that modest hope.

SEPTEMBER

CHAPTER 4

Jeff Ferris stooped before his reflection in the glass door of a fire-extinguisher cabinet. He smoothed windblown hair into place and straightened his properly striped, old-school tie. He was presentable, by his own standards anyway. And by Dr. Rosenberg's standards? There could be no predicting the tastes of the man who wore those horn-rimmed spectacles. What decade did AJ think this was?

Get a grip, Jeff—this isn't about fashion. Rosenberg had obviously caught him playing video games in lecture; it was time to face the music. You call yourself a salesman, Jeffie boy? Sell your way out of this mess.

He paused outside Rosenberg's office. As Jeff raised his fist to knock, a friendly voice said, "He's not there."

Jeff recognized the voice, but its warmth surprised him. The tone was so . . . sincere. He had invested too many hours practicing sincerity to accept it at face value from others. The boom was about to drop, all right. He turned reluctantly. "Sir?"

His professor leaned against the jamb of a lab door, hands slid casually into the pockets of wrinkled slacks. "Relax, son, and call me AJ. Everyone who works for me does."

Generations passed, and life—as is ever its wont—grew steadily in sophistication. The simple entities of the earliest experiment had been succeeded by beings of far greater capabilities.

The creatures blundered about in a universe that consisted

of *wall* and *no wall*. No, that wasn't exactly correct: Somewhere in the universe there also was *goal*, the finding of which was the sole purpose of existence.

One of the beings had developed the ability to automatically save a map that indicated which of its motions had brought it into contact with *wall* or *no wall*. Whatever the being encountered it now remembered. The formless void that had thwarted the traveler's myriad ancestors began to lift. The maze-universe began to be known.

And, once more, the Power from beyond the universe designated winners.

Professor and student studied each other across the dimly lit hallway. Good grief, AJ thought. The boy is nervous. Scared of *me*?

Well, he's only a freshman. AJ took a hand from a pocket to gesture Ferris over. "Relax, son. I won't bite."

"You said something about *working* for you, sir?"

"I'm getting coffee. Why don't you join me?" He turned toward the lab, assuming Ferris would follow. AJ flipped up the lid over the cipherlock keypad, and tapped in the combination that unlocked the door.

AJ truly noticed the lab only when bringing someone in for the first time. What was today called the Artificial Life Sciences Building had been constructed, in an era long before computers, for the power-engineering department. Those original occupants eventually surrendered custody of the first floor to the growing-like-a-weed computer-science department.

He and his team had inherited one of the double-height equipment bays. Thus, unlike the hallway they had just exited, the lab had seventeen-foot ceilings with crown moldings and ornate, late-1800s detailing. Desks and workbenches clustered around massive support pillars, with each piece of furniture supporting at least one high-end workstation. Great loops of fiber-optic cable emerged from the computers, spiraling up the columns to the backbone cable tacked messily to the ceiling. (An anachronism, the wired network was far less hackable than its modern and more aesthetic wireless equivalent would have been. That was *important*.) Posters offered the only splashes of color, with enlargements of electronics and gaming ads outnumbering rock stars. The background music, scarcely audible over the friendly bickering of AJ's student assistants, was a reissued Beatles album.

AJ filled two mugs from the mismatched collection beside the coffee urn and handed one to his guest. "How is Greg? You two look so much alike, you have got to be brothers. I imagine he recommended my class to you."

"Greg's working for a small company out east . . . AJ. A start-up. He seems to like it."

AJ took a sip, grimaced, then scooped powdered creamer into his mug. Lumps of partially dissolved goo, possibly sugar, clung to his spoon. "Greg was, hands down, the best undergrad assistant I ever had, Jeffrey. Are you as smart?"

"I prefer 'Jeff.' " The young man relaxed for the first time since AJ had called across the hall to him. "Greg and I have competed since I was born. I've always held my own."

AJ pointed to a chair. "Okay, Jeff. Let's talk."

From expecting to be kicked out of class to being offered a job within seconds. Life was funny, sometimes, even— Jeff grinned inwardly at his own wit—artificial life. And all thanks to his supercilious big brother.

Greg had long ago made clear that he found Jeff stupid and superficial; Jeff considered his older brother an overbearing, impractical nerd. They were barely on speaking terms. Recommended AJ's class? Hah! Fat chance Fathead would advise him to do anything. Anything anatomically probable, anyway.

To give credit where it was due, Greg was the first to see through Jeff's obsequious-to-adults act. Jeff excelled at wheedling favors, begging treats, and negotiating waivers from family rules. So what? Nothing stopped Greg from doing the same.

Jeff had had Greg's teachers most of the way through

school, and the experience to date had been uniformly wonderful. *Ever* so kind of Greg to leave behind halos for Jeff to assume. Greg had worked his butt off to earn straight As; Jeff had coasted along after him, doing next to nothing, and getting at least Bs. Then Greg's alumnus status at Smithfield had given Jeff an assured admission.

Now, despite the size of the university, Jeff had stumbled upon another halo in his first semester: Old AJ here really liked Greg. That looked to be good for some mad money, at least, if not a fairly automatic A.

Time, then, to turn up the charm. "AJ, sir, what can I do for you?"

CHAPTER 5

Stern's Law posited that work expands to fill every available horizontal surface. Then again, Cheryl thought, maybe it's just my work.

Papers covered her new desk, table, and much of the floor: electronic, mechanical, and electromechanical diagrams of the prosthetic arm; spec sheets for its embedded microprocessors; higher-level design descriptions; programming reference manuals. An open medical tome on the human nervous system teetered on the rim of her wastebasket.

The mess obscured, besides most flat surfaces, the considerable progress that she had made. In her first week here she felt she had learned a lot. Doug and his team had performed a truly elegant bit of engineering.

State-of-the-art arm prostheses worked with shoulder or upper-arm nerves grafted to chest muscles. Electrodes in the bionic arm interpreted muscular twitches (after months of painstaking training) as signals for embedded motors. An advanced model could handle four or so different hand and arm motions—compared to twenty-two for a human arm.

Doug's prototype was to a current prosthetic as a Ferrari was to a stagecoach.

An array of ultraminiature sensors in the socket end of Doug's prosthesis intercepted incoming impulses from the truncated efferent nerve branches in the stump. An electronics module sorted out the individual impulses directed to specific—and now-missing—forearm, hand, and finger muscles. Next, the electronics dynamically translated the "muscle" commands into computer directives that controlled the overall motion of the motorized prosthesis. Finally, mechanical linkages converted the rotation of the various computer-controlled electric motors into bending motion in the metal joints. In short: nerve impulses in; prosthesis motions out.

But brain-directed electromechanical motion was only half the achievement. Other sensors scattered throughout the prosthesis detected pressure on and relative position of faux skin and bones. The data flooded into a second electronics module, which converted the torrent into concise useful information. Electronic transducers then modulated, amplified, and narrowcast this status information into the stump. The projected electrical fields impinged on afferent nerves, tricking the truncated branches into "thinking" that they were once again whole and connected to biological tissues. The upstream central nervous system components of spine and motor cortex couldn't tell that the sensations were artificially stimulated. Tactile data in; nerve impulses out.

Together, the two parts of the system provided brain-directed control of the arm, with near-instantaneous feedback. Cheryl marveled that so much technology fit somehow into an apparatus that so closely resembled a human forearm. *How long will it be before I fully understand this?*

"I asked if you could use a hand."

Cheryl looked up from her paper-strewn desk, faintly aware of the furrow of concentration creasing her forehead. Doug stood in her doorway. She had apparently missed his original question but couldn't help noticing the phrasing. It was her job, in every possible sense of the expression, to give *him* a hand. Was his irony intentional?

"One hand won't make much of a difference. Have you got a forklift?" It was evidently an acceptable response. He had a nice laugh, she thought.

"I know the look of someone left wallowing too long in the documentation. Maybe I could come in and . . . No, that's hardly practical. Maybe *you* could accompany me to my office and we could discuss the project."

"Sounds like a plan," she said.

The walk down the hall gave her time to formulate a question. "Look, I understand the arm in general. Honest, I do. It's the details that are holding me up." She took his grunt as a go-ahead. "Here's what I don't get: How did you ever develop the software? It must be amazingly complex."

They reached Doug's office and he gestured her inside. They took opposite sides of the conference table. "I imagine the code *is* pretty hairy, but I'm not sure. It'll be your job to figure that out."

She could only stare in disbelief.

Doug's desk was behind him. Over the desk, row after row of tiny characters filled the PC display. As Cheryl watched, the display blanked and the screen saver kicked in. Large words began to float about: "Eschew obfuscation." (Later that day she looked up both terms. The phrase meant: "Don't be obscure." Right.)

Insight struck. She said, "The prosthesis isn't programmed. It's *trained*."

"Uh-huh." Doug lobbed the staple remover with which he had been fidgeting. "Heads up." She extended her right arm to nab it. "Okay, now toss it back." The prosthesis trembled as the hand positioned itself for the catch. He resumed fidgeting. "Did you notice a difference?"

Ah, the Socratic method. Cheryl had had college professors who favored the technique—leading the student to truth through questions. She *hated* it. She understood why the Athenians made Socrates take poison.

What had she just seen? "The wavering in your arm. It

was a midcourse correction, wasn't it? The arm must remember which commands worked right the first time in a certain situation and which needed corrective impulses. The more commands the arm saves and categorizes, the better it directs arm motion."

Doug nodded. "Until its memory chokes or it has too many options to sift."

A nasty complication occurred to her. "There are *lots* of possible motions for most purposes. When you threw that staple remover, I could have leaned toward or away from it to make my reach more convenient. I might have caught it at the top of its arc, or near the floor, or anywhere in between. I might have jumped from my chair and leaned over the table to catch it. Heck, how many slightly different but completely acceptable ways were there to position and move my fingers for the final grab?"

"Go on."

He was enjoying this; she could tell. Maybe his mischievous grin was infectious, or maybe it was only his enthusiasm, but she found herself enjoying the battle of wits. She'd figure it all out. "You dissembled a bit. *You* didn't train it, not directly. *It* trains itself. The arm saves, at least briefly, every nerve impulse—every command—that you send it, the instantaneous position of every joint, every motion that each motor makes. If a motion is smooth, if it's not immediately followed by a midcourse correction, the attempted solution is good. If there *is* a midcourse correction, the attempted solution is bad. In an inefficient but persistent way, the arm consistently fine-tunes its own programming.

"Okay. You challenged me to deduce how the software was developed. I'll hazard a guess that the arm can dump a file of its attempted motions to a PC. You want me to review the arm's 'lessons learned' file and synthesize an equivalent, but more efficient, set of rules."

She'd worked before with adaptive neural interfaces—she wouldn't be here otherwise—but their learning operated within a long list of preprogrammed rules. This more data-driven approach was just . . . wow. Did she have this right?

A double thumbs-up indicated that she did. Since Doug was now flipping a pencil end over end between the fingers of his right hand, the right thumb was quite an accomplishment. "Now I understand why you fidget all the time. You're always in training."

The tip broke off his pencil as she spoke. His impish grin broadened. "Nope. I'm a multidimensional sort of guy. Fidgeting is its own reward."

"Liz." There was no answer, so Betty Neville tapped on the closed door. Nothing. She rapped louder, until the ill-fitting door rattled in its frame. Her boss was alone, but a call had transferred to Betty's desk after five rings. "Liz?" Nothing.

Betty took the transferred call off hold. "I'm sorry, sir. Dr. Friedman stepped away from her desk. May I take a message?" She scribbled down the man's name and number. It figured—this was the call Liz had been waiting for all morning. "Yes, I'll be sure she gets this."

Liz must have walked past while Betty's back was turned. Maybe she'd been on the phone herself or had her head in the supplies cabinet. Must be only for a moment, or Liz would have said something, or caught her eye at the least. Odd that her boss had closed the door behind her. Well, Betty thought, I might as well set the message slip onto her desk and grab whatever lurks in the out basket.

Liz's head lay in the out basket, in a puddle of drool, staring sightlessly into unknown distances. Her body slumped awkwardly half on, half off the desk. As Betty watched, rooted to the spot, gravity prevailed. Liz slid from the desktop to the floor, head, limbs, and torso each smacking the planked floor with a hollow thud. The falling figure had the lifelessness of a rag doll. The lifelessness . . .

Betty found her voice again. She was still screaming when people arrived from the office across the hall.

CHAPTER 6

AJ glanced from display to display. Most students had settled into their seats; a few still milled about in the aisles. Three, two, one. "Good morning, ladies and gentlemen." As he spoke, the social butterflies flitted to find seats and logged in. The clatter of laptops hitting desk arms was, as always, aggravating.

"Today, we'll discuss the basic principles of Artificial Life, which I will sometimes abbreviate as AL." He wondered how soon this bunch would hit upon the inevitable joking equation: AJ aka AL. "For starters, why might we be interested in AL?"

His podium's inset display lit up as students vied for attention. He went to split-screen mode at the video-equipped sites, his image on one side of their screens, paraphrased student answers on the other. To keep the class engaged, he went far longer accepting comments than those comments merited. He resumed the lecture when he could bear no more pedagogical correctness. "Examine these suggestions and you'll see two basic themes. The predominant one, involving computer viruses and similar threats, is off the mark. Computer viruses are far too simple to interest me, and real-world viruses aren't truly alive, anyway.

"The second guess is that we're simulating life to better understand biological life. This is perhaps in reaction to my response at our first session to Mr. Prescott. That interpretation is valid, but incomplete. Yes, we'll better understand biological life as a result, just as analyzing idealized machines helps us comprehend real-world mechanics. Our goals are far more ambitious. When we study ideal machines, the result is mere conceptual knowledge. It takes a great deal of work to turn that insight into a real-world benefit. Ask any engineer."

He pressed the Reset button, extinguishing all the flashing icons that had demanded his attention. "Bear with me, people. If I haven't answered your question in the next few minutes, ask again.

"I apologize for the term 'AL.' It's misleading, but unfortunately that *is* the standard name for the field. In English, 'artificiality' connotes simplification, inferiority, incomplete mimicry. The artificial life-form cannot survive in our world, so one might reasonably infer that an AL must be an idealization.

"That would be wrong."

Across his many displays students were rapt. Jeff Ferris, AJ noted with particular satisfaction, was typing frantically. "The life we deal with in this class is *other* than what we know, *not* inferior. The ecology to which it is adapted is every bit as real to it as air and water and Krispy Kreme doughnuts are to us.

"Think for just a moment about that ecology. An AL lives in a world of data-storage devices and information, of processors and communications links. You and I don't—we can't—notice a millisecond, but a thousandth of a second is an eon for an AL. Is this a strange world? Most certainly. Is it imaginary? We bet our bank balances every day that it's *not*.

"Okay, then, these ALs occupy a world unknowable to us, but this is a world with which we nonetheless interact daily. Were it not for that other world, you and I would be meeting in a very different way." He glanced at the clock built into the podium. In the so-called real world, the morning rush hour had yet to abate. "Imagine the traffic."

The peek at his clock also revealed that his lecture time was running out. His delivery went into overdrive. "So what's my point? The information ecology is real indeed, and it plays an increasingly critical part in our lives. We all use the Internet a hundred times a day—and it's still altogether too easy to underestimate society's reliance on computers. And that brings me, class, to the crux of the matter: our dependence on the software executing on those computers.

"Ladies and gentlemen, modern society has deployed most of the easy applications of computers. We've done all the basic automation. What is left is mostly too complex for mere real-world mortals. We're starting to see the tragic results: One day, an industrial robot accidentally crushes a worker; the next day, computerized hospital equipment electrocutes a patient. We can't write new programs as fast as we need them. We can't prove the correctness of the programs we do manage to produce.

"Let me pose the issue another way. We rely increasingly on the data plane of existence, as much as on the biological and physical planes. Our approach to exploiting the information ecology, the data plane, is classically human: We create a program to do our bidding. *Homo sapiens* is, after all, the premier tool-using animal—the *only* tool-using animal to move beyond sticks and stones.

"Too bad that building tools is a flawed approach. In evolutionary terms, it's been a simple experiment, and after a short trial, it is already failing us."

The podium flashed AJ a sixty-second warning. Warp speed, Mr. Sulu. "We will resume at this point next session. Check your syllabus for the readings due by next time. Meanwhile, ask yourselves: If we're increasingly unable to design satisfactory solutions for our ever-growing information-handling needs, what lessons does biology offer us?"

Although AJ would have been the last to admit—or even recognize—it about himself, he had a heart of gold. Greg Ferris had been, besides one of the best student assistants AJ had ever had, a hardworking and decent young man. He deserved a better break in life than he had gotten: an abusive father and a drunken, bedridden mother. The assistantship AJ had had to offer wasn't much, but at least he had been able to help. Offering Greg's brother a job had been reflexive.

Too bad: Minutes into Jeff Ferris' first workday, AJ wondered if he had made a colossal blunder. The lad's comments as AJ took him on a more complete tour of the lab were painfully juvenile and banal. A few such remarks might have passed as charm. The unending patter, AJ suddenly suspected, masked a complete lack of understanding.

Had Jeff absorbed nothing from the lectures and assigned readings? The boy looked so much like Greg. Who could have predicted the brothers would be light-years apart in character?

Sigh. AJ had no one to blame but himself.

He had surely learned enough from the never-ending departmental politics, though, to gracefully ease out one kid. Perhaps a few weeks of taskless boredom would do the trick.

AJ put an arm around Jeff's shoulders. "This way, son. I'd like to show you the supercomputer that we have courtesy of the federal High Performance Computer and Communications Program. After that, I'll introduce you to the rest of the team."

"Last session, we met the crisis of design. We need more software each year, but programmers can't keep up with the demand. The artificial-intelligence gurus keep promising to fix everything: If human programmers can't handle the load, artificial programmers will take over. The wizards have been on the verge of creating artificial intelligence for more than fifty years now, since about ten minutes after the invention of computers. So, anyway, they claim.

"I predict that they'll never get there.

"At the risk of picking a fight with any Creationists among you, the first principle of this class will be"—and AJ keyed the precept into his podium computer as he spoke, for concurrent over-image display at all video-equipped sites— "Life evolved; it was not designed."

He spotted gratifyingly few outraged expressions among the electronically assembled students. "From which, class, we learn what?" A mouse click selected a name from among the few volunteers. A remote-controlled camera zoomed in on her. "Ms. Kurtz?"

A young woman peered earnestly at the camera. She had a generous sprinkle of freckles across a button nose. "That trial and error works."

"Did everyone hear that?" Heads nodded. "Well, not on

my exams." The chuckles subsided, and AJ continued. "Exactly right, Ms. Kurtz. Trial and error works well indeed. The usual objection to trial and error is, however . . ." She looked to her laptop, in vain, for inspiration. "It's not yet in your notes, Ms. Kurtz."

She pondered for a moment, then shook her head. She had company in her uncertainty; most of the icons denoting volunteers had been quietly extinguished.

"Thank you, Ms. Kurtz." AJ annotated her record to credit her contribution, then made another selection. "Ms. Gomez?"

" 'Trial and error' sounds so dispassionate and impersonal, almost benign. The more familiar term, at least in the life sciences, is 'survival of the fittest.' That's what Charles Darwin called it."

"Actually, Ms. Gomez, Herbert Spencer said it." If a professor can't be pedantic, who can? "Darwin merely wished that he had said it. And your issue with survival of the fittest?"

"It's incredibly wasteful and slow." The set of her jaw signaled dissatisfaction with his emendation. "I don't have a million years for a proper checkbook-balancing program to evolve."

"Very good." He credited her file for her comment, then picked a new volunteer. "Mr. Takagawa."

"I believe I see an answer, sir."

AJ smiled. "Perhaps you will share it with us?"

"Yes, sir. Computers run at such blinding speeds that evolving AL solutions to our programming problems need not take long at all."

A megawatt LED of enlightenment flashed over the collective heads of the class. It was one of those moments that made teaching—occasionally—so fulfilling. AJ basked in the glow of illuminated faces. Students whispered excitedly, overcome by the elegance of a great idea.

And just in time, too—his sixty-second warning was once again flashing. AJ cranked up the volume to make sure he would be heard. "Mr. Takagawa, an excellent observation. Class, next session we will discuss the comparative merits of waiting for a William Shakespeare and sitting a bunch of electronic monkeys at keyboards."

CHAPTER 7

Linda del Vecchio leaned back in her chair, feet up on her desk. From time to time she swigged a mouthful of dry Cheerios from her mug. Now that the experiment was finally running, she had time for her dissertation. She had a first draft, but it was rough. It needed dozens of edits to take AJ's niggling comments into account. And it was dull as dishwater. She closed her eyes, trying to compose a punchy introduction.

And failed. Sighing, Linda swung her feet off the desk. She'd meander through the lab and offer help to whoever needed it. That's what AJ paid her for: coordinating his many assistants and students. It was like herding cats—

Only cats were much cleaner. The lab looked like a pigsty. It generally did. Take-out wrappers, pizza boxes, and soda cans were strewn everywhere. Desk and cabinet drawers hung half-open. Chairs blocked the aisles. Odd toys—hoops and Nerf basketballs; Velcro dartboard and darts; superhero action figures bent into weird, and often lewd, poses—sat in strange places.

Tidying the lab wasn't in her job description; she'd be damned if she would. There had been enough of that growing up. Her parents both worked; as the second of five children, and the oldest daughter, she had been the designated mommy. Well, she was tired of picking up other people's messes, tired of being the bad guy, and tired of being taken for granted. She'd miss AJ when she got out of here, squabbles about experiment design notwithstanding, but not this lab.

Linda's wandering eventually brought her to the very

back of the lab. Jeff Ferris had taken a desk back there, as far from everyone else as possible, out of sight behind a pillar. She had overheard AJ tell him, "You'll learn from hanging around. When something catches your interest, we'll figure out what you'll really do. Meanwhile, help where you can."

So far, nothing had caught his interest. Pretty cushy, really.

His laptop was plugged into the lab network! The screen showed a driver's-eye view of a car fishtailing down an urban street. Sparks and flying glass suggested gunfire from a pursuer. "Christ on crutches! Did you not hear a thing you were told?"

Ferris wore earbuds; he pretended not to hear. She tapped his shoulder and repeated herself when he looked up.

Jeff suspended his game before answering. "Nope. Got a problem with that?"

He was as obsequious as ever to AJ. As a short-timer, *she* must be unworthy of his time. "It's a mystery to me why AJ pays you, but that's between the two of you. It's clearly not for any useful contribution. I'll be *damned,* though, if I'll let you put our experiment at risk."

He arched an eyebrow at her. So?

I have a thesis to finish, you little twerp. Linda flipped the power switch of his laptop. With a flick of the finger she popped his Ethernet cable from its wall receptacle. "Jeff, do not *ever* connect your laptop to the local area network in here. We work hard to keep viruses off the LAN, and you can't ever be sure what's gotten into your machine."

"Give me a break," Ferris said snippily. "The LAN connects to the university network. UniNet is part of the freaking Internet, and I'm online through UniNet all the time. Although outside this lab, it's simply WiFi—there's none of this prehistoric business with wires."

"Look *there.*" Linda mentally appended, You imbecile. A vein throbbed in her forehead. She pointed to the equipment rack that stood beside the team's supply cabinets. The rack terminated two fiber-optic cables, one tagged "UniNet" and the other "Lab." "It would seem you've also forgotten about our security gateway. It isolates the lab LAN from the main net. I wouldn't want to bore you with details."

Too late, he mouthed.

Words failed her. Linda turned and stomped away.

Brown and white shards flew as the pressure of the butter knife exceeded the strength of the bread stick. "That," Doug explained for Cheryl's benefit, "was for the practice. Not just anyone can truthfully say they eat cholesterol for science."

The Neural Interfaces Department had, as usual, gathered for lunch in the BSC cafeteria. Someone down the table—from where she sat, Cheryl could not tell who—referred to this tradition as "better living through chemistry." She didn't find the food *that* bad, but then again, she had only been eating here for a few weeks.

Dick Conrad, a programmer with an Einsteinian shock of hair, flicked crumbs from his otherwise-empty bread plate. "So, who has plans for the weekend?" The chorus of answers included mostly yard work, deferred shopping, watching the Skins game, and possible theater trips. Cheryl's plans were laundry and a stop at the grocery; she didn't bother to contribute.

Doug grabbed another bread stick. "I generally get that question from people hoping for someone to ask them *their* plans. Dick, what are *you* doing this weekend?"

"I expect to spend it here. New M-and-M game."

Cheryl groaned mentally. Dick didn't mean candy. They were—yet again—talking magic and mayhem. Strange quests in imaginary castles and labyrinths, pretending to fight equally nonexistent wizards and monsters for their fictional treasures. As far as she could tell, all these games were alike. And all equally pointless.

Game consoles sold in the tens of millions, but the revolution in VR technology had given arcades a rebirth. VR goggles and instrumented gloves and wands—not to mention the superfast computers to take full advantage of them, to paint the goggles' screens with synthesized worlds, and to update those images in real time to correspond to every movement of the adventurer's head and hand—were quite expensive. The cost, at least, limited the amount of time that teens could spend at the games. Adults were another story, especially adults at companies like BioSciCorp that maintained fully equipped VR rooms for more serious purposes.

The difference between a man and a boy is the price of his toys.

The men babbled on for what seemed like forever about M-and-M. Cheryl was relieved when someone at last noticed that time was passing, and that they needed to get upstairs and back to work.

Relieved, that was, until she discovered that during lunch a new Internet worm had penetrated BSC's network and wiped out her morning's work.

OCTOBER

CHAPTER 8

For the fourth time that evening, the words on the screen seemed to blur. It was time again to get up and walk around. Doug pushed away from his desk, hoping to find something to graze on in the vending machines.

It was almost 9:00 P.M., and the end was not in sight. The end of the workday, that was. The proposal due date for their NSF grant renewal approached with perilous speed. The National Science Foundation had so far coughed up half the money for development of the experimental prosthesis. Doug needed to keep that cofunding flowing. BioSciCorp would have enough of a financial stretch going it alone once the technology was ready for commercialization. Lose the grant and NSF would take on its banking definition: non-sufficient funds.

A Coke and a granola bar perked him up. He made the rounds of the offices to see how things went with his fellow stuckees. At his third stop, he found Cheryl gazing fixedly at her PC screen, surrounded, as always, by dead trees. She was doing her damnedest to synthesize a set of generalized arm-motion rules for the grant progress report. "Can you use some help, or is it beyond that?"

She stood and stretched, graceful as a cat and a testimonial to aerobics. "That felt good. Sure, if you can spare a few minutes."

"What's the problem?"

Cheryl gestured across her desk. "I'm drowning in data. Do you have any *idea* how many arm motions you make in a day? And they're like the proverbial snowflakes: No two are exactly alike. Besides, the longer you use the prosthesis, the more data it accumulates and the bigger its lessons-learned file grows. There has *got* to be a better way to look at all this data."

Doug perched gingerly on the single uncluttered corner of the desk. "Have you synchronized the data from the arm with the physical-training videos?"

"I tried." She plopped back into her chair to keyboard something. A window opened up on the display, in which a tiny, sweaty, begoggled Doug dashed randomly about an empty white room, swinging and swatting with a short rod. The counter in a corner of the window, its rightmost digits changing with blurring speed, observed the passage of time down to the millisecond. "It doesn't help. No offense, boss, but you look like a marionette on drugs."

"An unstrung marionette, at that," he agreed. "This is how you've been looking at the videos? Try this." He leaned over, trying with limited success to ignore their proximity. He keyed a command that dramatically changed the video. The visualized room doubled in size and developed various-colored markings, the wand in mini-Doug's hand blossomed into a proper racquet, and a similarly equipped opponent materialized. Thuds and thwocks of the bouncing red ball, and grunts from the hardworking players, burst forth in surround sound from PC speakers.

Cheryl's jaw dropped. "Was everyone having a little fun with the new girl? Someone might have *told* me what was going on in these so-called exercise videos."

Doug straightened up hurriedly. Crouched over Cheryl like that, unavoidably smelling her hair, all he needed was the suggestion about having fun with the new girl. It didn't matter that that was not how she meant her words. "The old hands find it easier to analyze the motions with the graphics filtered out. We slipped up in not emphasizing the VR view. I'm sorry."

"You slipped up in not mentioning there *was* a VR view!" Her jaw now jutted out belligerently.

Hell, what did the team talk about at lunch most days, if not VR? This was nuts. Of course while Cheryl ate with the group, she didn't say much. She stayed at a distance, as though any friendliness on her part would be misinterpreted. He had asked his administrative assistant about Cheryl; Teri's reading was the same. What else important had Cheryl's standoffishness caused her to miss?

He made a snap decision. "We both need a mental break. Let's go play some racquetball."

"We've got too much work to do. *I* have, anyway."

"This *is* work. You need to understand the exercise videos."

She stood and glared. "I do understand them. *Now.* I would have days ago, if you had shared your little secret."

Everyone was cranky from overwork, Doug told himself, including me. That he took Cheryl's tantrum more personally meant that maybe she was right. At some level maybe he didn't see her as simply "one of the guys." *Damn* it. Who was he mentally cursing? Maybe both of them. Probably both. "Ever done virtual racquetball? Any VR sport?"

"No." Her tone revealed a disdain for VR of which he had previously seen only glimpses. "I'll stick with the real world."

"Not if you want to reverse-engineer what the arm has taught itself."

The criticism stung, but she was too angry to back down. She indicated her slacks and sweater. "These aren't racquetball clothes, and I don't have a racquet." The answer conceded his point without any move toward cooperation.

Doug got off the corner of her desk. "You've mentioned aerobics after work. Whatever you wear at your health club will be fine. Meet me outside the VR labs in ten minutes. I'll change and bring spare gear." Hoping to reduce the tension, he added, "Ask the game program to put my face on the pseudoball. Rumor has it that can be very therapeutic."

He took the brief up-twitch of her lips for success. "Great. I'll see you in ten."

With so much left to do, why was she playing? Cheryl stood, ill at ease, the VR rod awkward in her hand. Through borrowed VR goggles she saw only the webless wand, herself in leotard and sneakers, and an all-white room. She had lectured herself while changing clothes about the need for an open mind. Doug would probably describe that as free advice and worth every penny.

"Speak up if you can't hear this." Doug's voice was loud and clear in her goggles' tiny earphones.

"Whatever." She assumed that the room had hidden microphones.

"Open sesame," she heard next, and Doug appeared in the suddenly enlarged chamber. His cutoffs were frayed; his well-worn T-shirt declared: "I'm virtually certain that I'm real or really certain that I'm virtual. Or vice versa." Her senses rejected what she knew: that he stood in another room down and across the hall. The cameras here must be capturing her with equal verisimilitude. She suddenly felt self-conscious in her leotard.

"You say it, too."

"Do I have to?" She sounded petulant even to herself. Damn it. She had cooled down enough to know she had serious fence-mending to do. "Okay, then." Imaginary drumroll. "Open sesame." The room sprouted virtual lines on its floor and varicolored zones on its walls and mythical midcourt center plane. The rod in her hand became the handle for what looked like a conventional racquet. She knew, however, that she held an expensive piece of electronics. The wand captured every nuance of her grip and its own exact position and attitude in the room. The handle reported continuously, by infrared beams, to sensors in the walls. In other games, this same instrumented rod became a golf club or a baseball bat or a wizard's staff.

With quips and examples, Doug taught her how VR racquetball worked. An unseen computer responded to voice cues (that every serious gamer personalized) for such functions as serving the ball and changing handicap levels. ("What handicap? I don't need any damned charity," she had protested—until he slammed a ball past her via a pro-level, triple-speed purple zone. She might as well have swung at a meteor. "Well, if you insist.") Multiple video cameras and a *lot* of computing power triangulated their exact position at any point in time.

The revealed mysteries of her VR goggles most surprised her. A low-power infrared source shone continuously into each eye; the reflections off her retinas helped reveal, instant by instant, precisely where in the virtual scene she was looking. ("Helps?" He had gently suggested that the position and orientation of her head in the room were useful. Infrared transmitters in her goggles signaled that, too.) The gear was surprisingly sophisticated. Maybe her opinion of VR games *was* a bit knee-jerk.

"All right," Doug said. "Enough about the mechanics. Time to volley for first serve." To some unseen computer, he added, "Roll 'em."

CLASS OF '10 RULES.

"*Shit!*" Dick Conrad snarled. Like sentiments echoed in the halls, often punctuated by the pounding of fist on desk. Invading text slithered impudently around his PC screen, devouring, with Pac-Man-like determination, Dick's section of the NSF grant-renewal paper.

Dick removed wire-rimmed glasses to massage the bridge of his nose. He had a sudden bitch of a headache. Those nearly concurrent shouts meant a coordinated, time-delayed viral attack. Every computer at BSC, and the backup file copies going back who knew how long, could be infected. To have a prayer of meeting the deadline on the grant renewal, they would have to get virgin computers and recover from hardcopy drafts scattered around the office. He couldn't bear to think about the many edits he'd made since his last printed draft.

The grant was *important* to Doug. Dick couldn't imagine how Doug would take this incident.

In thus discounting his imagination, Dick was absolutely correct.

"Beep."

Focused on the pseudoracquetball, Doug found the electronic tone disorienting. Balls in midair make no noise. It took a moment to realize that the sound had no bearing on the game. Once he decided that the sound came from his wrist, its meaning became obvious: His watch had chimed the hour. The watch ran ten minutes fast, a bit of subterfuge that usually got him to meetings on time. That made it about ten minutes before ten.

The ball changed course with a healthy *thwock*, sign of a solid hit with a firm grip on the racquet. The novice level at which he had Cheryl playing slowed his returns to a quarter of their usual speed. The molasses-in-January return gave him ample time to analyze the stroke. Perfect. The prosthesis had done precisely what he had intended. Remember that, right arm of mine.

Subvocalization of the control phrase triggered a neural response, mastered in lengthy sessions of biofeedback. His brain initiated a nerve impulse, an electrochemical chain reaction that traveled from brain, to spinal cord, to nerve branch. Sensors in the prosthesis, in due course, picked up the signal. Circuitry then recognized the unusual character of the pulse pattern. Instead of commanding a muscle to relax or contract, this signal told the prosthesis to write a "well-done" notation into its embedded memory. Arm motions that he flagged this way were automatically retained whenever he interfaced the arm to a lab computer for data extraction.

Still, it was nearly ten. There was work left to do that he meant to finish tonight. "As much as I'm enjoying this, we've got to get ba—"

Pain jolted his arm. He stared in horror at the hand that suddenly clenched his racquet handle with agonizing intensity. For a bewildering instant, the prosthesis signaled conflicting sensations of boiling heat and numbing cold, of featherlight tickling and viselike pressure.

After an endless moment, the forearm lost all feeling.

It didn't help, Cheryl decided, that Doug kept referring to the incident as "a disarming experience." The remark was typical: a play on words and a deprecating reference to his disability. The bitter tone—that was another matter. She didn't like it.

"I'm so sorry, Doug," she said.

He looked up from the inert prosthesis lying on his desk. "Unless *you* set loose the virus, I wish you'd quit saying that."

The tension in his voice registered. Sympathy was the *last* thing Doug wanted. This project—his whole professional life—was a struggle against long odds. A struggle that some juvenile asshole seemed to have, if only temporarily, derailed. Sympathy only made things worse. She said, "You're right; I'm *not* sorry. I'm *pissed.*"

"You're not *that,* either. I currently hold the exclusive, worldwide franchise. I can assure you, it didn't come cheap."

Maybe so, but some emotion was wringing her gut. As awful as she felt, she knew Doug felt worse. How could she help?

"Thanks again for the job," she blurted.

The subject change made him blink. "You earned it. Don't make a big deal of it."

She didn't know if this was a way to get Doug's mind off his problems or only something that she needed to get off her own chest. Either way, she plowed ahead. "I'd guess you haven't been on the job market recently."

He finally looked her in the eye. The triumph of curiosity over depression? "Things are bad?"

"Only in our niche." It was her turn to sound bitter. "Only in neural interfacing."

Doug seemed to first notice the disembodied limb on his blotter. He opened a desk drawer and tucked away the inoperative prosthesis. "I *have* seen more résumés than usual," he conceded. "Look, I know the research program shut down at your old place. I knew that before I interviewed you. Feinman was the soul of the program, and he had a stroke. It's a real shame, Cheryl, but it happens."

How about a frozen expression of terror so awful the mortician can't do anything about it? Ben Feinman had had a closed-casket memorial, but Cheryl *knew*. She was good friends with Fran Feinman, and Fran had had to tell someone. Does that happen, too, Doug? But all that Cheryl could bring herself to say was, "And Yamaguchi?"

"She wrapped her car around a lamppost. My friends at NeuralCorp say she'd been preoccupied with something. Believe me—car wrecks happen." He glanced self-consciously at his stump. "Shit happens."

It was the first time he had ever alluded in Cheryl's presence to the loss of his arm. She wanted to respond. She wanted, suddenly, to know him. To know Doug the person, not the wisecracking boss. After years of keeping her distance from men at the office, she wasn't sure how. And as she hesitated—

"I can't face cleaning up this mess tonight." She followed his gaze to a wall clock; it was past midnight. "Correction—this morning. I'm going home to catch some Zs."

Unhappy with an opportunity lost, too confused by her stymied impulse to think to ask if he could drive himself home, she followed him to BSC's all but empty parking lot.

CHAPTER 9

General-press coverage, AJ had been astonished to learn, loosened corporate purse strings faster than publication in refereed professional journals. It was, perhaps, an unhappy discovery, but he had come to terms with it.

Fighting reality was almost always a losing battle—even in the artificial-life business.

Today's visitor to the AL lab was from the *Hartford Courant*. Nothing especially current distinguished the questions the reporter posed, but AJ kept that opinion to himself. Anything that helped keep his team funded was important. Teaching and show-and-tells were small sacrifices for continuing the research. The world *needed* what he was developing here.

The tour ended, as always, at AJ's office. He invited his guest inside and waved vaguely at the guest chair. "So, Fred, what do you think?"

Fred took a PalmPilot from his jacket pocket. "Fascinating. Really, it is."

"I hope your readers agree."

"Let me echo what I believe I heard. Tell me where I ran off the rails."

Rather mixed metaphors, AJ thought. And he's a writer? "Go ahead."

"It's a daringly simple idea, really. You're breeding software instead of writing it."

"That's right," AJ said.

"In nature, the organisms best suited to their environments live long enough to reproduce. Random mutations cause new life-forms to arise. The changes that are improvements tend to survive, reproduce, and prosper. Then new mutations arise, and ever more capable organisms flourish. In a word, evolution. You're applying the same techniques to developing software."

"Still right." AJ's modest status at the university entitled him to a desk, two chairs, one bookshelf, and one table. There was no way that he could cope with so little storage; a bricks-and-boards bookshelf bore two years of old journals, and an unhung door served as a second table. AJ opened the bar-sized refrigerator that doubled as one base of the improvised table; the other support was a dented two-drawer file cabinet topped with the 1988 Spokane Yellow Pages. The phone book was on permanent loan from the university library. There was little demand for it.

His guest shook his head when offered a soda. "Here is where you lost me. Where did you start?"

"Remember the simulated maze we saw?" Rewarded by a nod, AJ continued. "It's far simpler than the maze in any video game, but that's okay. I'll never admit it to my daughters, but even Quake, Doom, and Halo addicts are fairly high on the evolutionary ladder.

"So we begin with a maze. A supervisory program sees the headway made by *other* programs trying to navigate the maze. The maze runners are the programs we're evolving."

Fred steepled his fingers thoughtfully. "And you start with maze runners made of random bits, and see which ones can solve the maze?"

"No, we've bootstrapped the process a little. To save time, we wrote the very most basic software. Think of it as stopping Creation a little early, with only some particularly stupid bacteria on hand." AJ sipped his Mountain Dew as Fred entered some notes.

"Got it." More scribbling with his stylus. "By selecting the fastest maze runners after each experiment, and randomly varying their software, you get ever . . . oh, piss on it . . . better performance over time."

"I beg your pardon?"

Fred tilted the palmtop toward AJ; a red LED glowed balefully. "The batteries are almost drained, and I left my power converter at the hotel. Got any spare triple As?"

"Sorry." AJ shrugged. "Maybe a pencil?" He got only a puzzled expression in response.

"I guess I'd better wrap it up. How good are they now? The maze runners, I mean."

AJ set his soda can on a pile of ungraded quizzes. "Still dumber than dirt—but they learn a *lot* faster."

Linda shifted her weight from foot to foot, the nervous dance hidden by the bulky podium. Working in AJ's house felt odd, but it made sense. His in-home setup was preconfigured; configuring one of the school's communal distance-learning labs would have burned more of her time than giving the lecture.

Simpler still would have been for her to meet with the reporter and AJ to give his own damned lecture. Also scarier. She had *no* interest in meeting with the press.

The highlight of the lecture was a maze-runner demo. Annoying glints of light, reflections off a workstation screen, showed the video had been shot with a camcorder. Networking their lab directly to all the class sites would have been kinder to the eyes. It would also have exposed the ongoing experiment to every worm, virus, and Trojan loose on the Internet. Over my dead body, Linda thought. Only last week, a virus infestation had taken the university two days to eradicate. Damned eco-nuts.

On the classroom displays, a thousand specks crept about an elementary labyrinth. The dots turned and veered at random, bumping enthusiastically into imaginary walls. Most specks remained clustered near the beginning of the maze; only a handful had navigated around more than one corner. None was anywhere close to the exit. Students cheered when the front-running mote successfully negotiated the fourth turn, a 180-degree switchback.

Takagawa, on the main-campus display, was the first to get the point. "It's a constrained optimization problem . . . ma'am."

Sigh. He didn't remember her name. She wondered if any of AJ's students did. Linda knew what the young man meant, but it was his job to express himself. "*What* is a constrained optimization problem?"

"Solving a maze, ma'am."

"Go on."

"Much problem solving involves optimizing some value, subject to a set of constraints." The student bounced excitedly in his seat. "Like the traveling salesman problem: selecting the best route between the cities of the sales territory.

That problem tries to minimize total travel time subject to meeting delivery dates, or avoiding road congestion, or other conditions."

Linda nodded encouragement and waited.

"Finding the exit of a maze is a simple goal; getting there with a minimum of wasted effort is an optimization problem. The locations of walls are constraints. I guess I'm saying a maze is an archetype for many practical problems. If we can evolve practical maze runners, it could mean that we can evolve programs to answer many real-world questions."

"Exactly." She made note of the young man's insight. "And the ability of the AL programs to solve those real-world problems will continue to evolve, to improve."

Her sixty-second warning began flashing. "Remember: Problems five and eight from the back of chapter nine are due next session." An on-site camera showed Jeff Ferris sitting behind and one seat to the right of Takagawa, keying frenetically. Doubtless that activity involved some asinine video game.

The juxtaposition of two such different students led her to end on a philosophical note. "A thought for the day, ladies and gentlemen. Only the fittest will survive the upcoming exam."

CHAPTER 10

Theodore Roosevelt Island, a wooded oasis on the Potomac River, can be accessed only by footbridge from an isolated parking lot on the Virginia shore. The island is much favored by local elementary schools as a picnic stop on the way to or from field trips into the District of Columbia. Today, three busloads of the little monsters had gobbled their sack lunches and were now running amok under the resigned eyes of teachers and parent helpers.

Jim Schulz ruefully shook his head. *Why* had he allowed himself to be talked into coming here on a weekday? He had lived in northern Virginia quite long enough to know better. His supposed companion on this outing, Doug Carey, stood nearby, absorbed with his new camcorder. Occasionally the ground apes quieted enough for Jim to hear the motorized hum of the camera panning and zooming. Jim's attempts at conversation were impatiently shushed.

Jim's thoughts wandered until an approaching petite figure drew his attention. The woman was casually dressed in a tan sweater with pushed-up sleeves, peg-legged jeans with artfully torn knees, and scuffed sneakers. Her light brown hair was done up in a French braid from which a few endearing strands had escaped. Nice. He had no idea how he had attracted her attention—but why question his good fortune?

"Beware the Cyclops," she said.

"Cyclops" must refer to the lens of the camcorder. Damn it, she knew Doug.

Doug caught the Odyssey reference, too, although he continued shooting whatever ground-ape vignette had caught his eye. "Who goes there?"

"No man."

"*That's* for certain," Jim had to interject. He gave her an exaggerated once-over that made her blush.

"Don't harass the staff, please." Doug finished whatever he had been shooting, then lowered to his side the hand holding the video camera. Robohand. "Morning, Cheryl."

"Hi, boss. I assume your parting directive doesn't apply in neutral territory."

Doug nodded. To Jim, he explained, "After we finished the proposal from hell, I told everyone I didn't want to see them for a week. This one"—he tipped his head toward Cheryl—"really worked her tail off."

Jim stepped to the side to gaze pointedly at her nicely rounded rear. "It looks fine to me."

"I asked you to quit that."

"Thanks, Doug, but I can fend for myself." She turned to

Jim. "I know you from somewhere, you wannabe dirty old man. I recognize those sideburns and the mustache. Oh yeah"—she brightened—"you're in Doug's training videos. Why is it I've never seen you at the office?"

Doug snickered. "*Jim?* Work at BSC? The man can't tell a computer from a kumquat. He nets in from a VR arcade near his house in Alexandria."

That incredulity was a bit much, Jim thought. He wasn't *that* computer illiterate. Many years ago, he had even taken a beginning programming class, coursework the University of Wisconsin had obligingly accepted as a foreign language. As far as he was concerned, computer languages were as foreign as they came. What else could you say about a language in which $I = I + 1$ was meaningful?

In any case, Jim *knew* the difference: Kumquats had seeds. He also knew how to get even. It involved hitting below the belt, but he was peeved enough not to mind. And it would be for Doug's own good.

"So, are you two kids going together?" Doug was predictably aghast. Before he could find his tongue, Jim added, "No, of course not. What *was* I thinking, expecting Saint Douglas to date, and someone from the office yet? He might disqualify himself from that seat he's been coveting on the Supreme Court."

The crack earned Jim an angry glare. It did not take telepathy to know what was crossing Doug's mind: dark thoughts about Holly. Lost Holly. When would he truly accept that that stage of his life was *over*? Sure, Doug dated occasionally, but it never worked out.

"I don't see people from work." Stereo answers came from Doug and Cheryl.

We'll just see about that, Doug. Nothing like pondering the loss of something to make you want it. Jim beamed at Cheryl. "An excellent policy, my dear, excellent. Did Doug ever mention that I can't tell a computer from a pistachio? Or was that an artichoke heart? Whatever. I have trouble with all this technical stuff. Some growing thing." He looped an arm through hers. "Allow me to introduce myself."

After an afternoon of window-shopping, Doug, Jim, and
Cheryl wandered into a touristy area of Old Town Alexandria. Doug's stomach growled and he checked his watch for
confirmation. "I could use some dinner."

They were outside a posh Italian restaurant. All three were
in jeans; Doug wore a sweatshirt and Jim a faded Army sur-
plus camouflage jacket. Cheryl scanned the menu in the front
window, then gestured vaguely at her own casual clothes. "As
though we're dressed for this place."

The men exchanged an amused look. "Follow me," Jim
said. "I'm a friend of the owner." They went around the
corner to a side entrance. The chef's effusive greetings made
clear to Cheryl that Jim *was* the owner. The restaurateur
pointed to a genuine butcher-block table in a corner of the
bustling kitchen. Disappearing through the kitchen-side door
to his office, where he kept a spare suit, Jim called, "Have a
seat, folks. Gotta go schmooze with the paying clientele, but
I'll be right back."

Jim was lying, but it was for a good cause.

Doug and Cheryl sat in silence—all the more obvious after
Jim's ceaseless ebullience. "Quite an interesting guy," she
finally offered.

Doug raised an eyebrow at the closed office door. "Rebel
without a clue? Yeah, he *is* interesting, and it's reassuring
that someone is still working to keep us out of Vietnam."

She looked confused, but Doug didn't bother to admit:
Jim *isn't* that old. When you have to explain 'em, they're not
funny.

The silence stretched awkwardly. They jerked back as
their legs accidentally touched beneath the small table.

By tacit agreement, Jim was a safe subject. "Where is he
from?" Cheryl asked.

"Milwaukee. His dad works at a brewery Jim will only
identify as producing 'the beer that made Milwaukee mal-
odorous.' " As Doug spoke, a waiter spread a damask table-
cloth over the butcher block. Three place settings and a

wax-covered Chianti bottle with candle followed. When just Doug and Jim ate here, as they often did, Jim tossed dish towels over the wood—and they weren't always clean towels. Certainly he and Doug never had a candle. And now Jim had conveniently disappeared. *Damn* that man—first hitting on Cheryl, and then playing matchmaker. How transparent can you get?

They fell silent again. Somewhere behind them, a knife chopped maniacally on a cutting board. A voluble chef's assistant made a point by clanging the counter with his ladle. Cutlery and plates clattered in and out of the oversized dishwasher.

Perhaps the clinking and clanging was too suggestive, or perhaps the flickering candle flame was. Maybe it was the so long foregone company of an attractive woman. Maybe Doug had only been out in the sun too long today without a hat.

Whatever the cause, Doug found his mind slipping into a familiar memory. Light flickered there, too, but its source was a short-circuited turn signal that refused to respond to its control. The darkness there crowded in on him.

Flickering, flickering . . .

The rental car was mangled, its bent frame preventing the doors from opening. Judging from the razor-sharp fragments covering occupants and vehicle interior alike, its windshield had been replaced with cheap, nonautomotive glass. At least Doug didn't think the stuff mandated by law could shatter like this. Whatever mishap had necessitated replacing the windshield must have also deployed the air bags; they had not been replaced.

After applying his belt as a tourniquet, the two of them tried not to look at, or think about, Doug's mangled right arm. The injury—like the meandering bastard, presumably blind drunk, who had veered from his lane and driven them off the deserted road—was too much to handle just yet. Once the tourniquet stopped his bleeding, they tried to crawl out the now-glassless front window. The effort had gained them only assorted new cuts and abrasions.

"Holly?"

"Hmm?" she finally answered. Her attention seemed focused on the tree that grew from the center of the engine compartment.

"We'll be okay. Honest."

She had hair and eyes as dark as the night. Eyes that most evenings he could get lost in. By the green flickering of the turn signal that would not stop, her skin looked unhealthy. "I know." Tension in her voice belied the words.

"I love you."

She took forever to answer. "I love you, too."

"See if *I* ever do Florida again." He had followed the spring-break tradition twice before: never-ending parties down the coast. In his junior year he had met Holly and, to his amazement, the mob scene at Lauderdale did not appeal to her. He had begged her all winter to come with him, and in time worn her down. Now *this*.

"Uh-huh."

He worried about her being so quiet, but she *seemed* okay. No visible wounds, anyway. Maybe, he decided, she was going into shock. He huddled against her as best he could to share his warmth. Trapped behind the steering wheel, his right forearm shredded, he couldn't even comfort her by squeezing her hand.

In other circumstances he might have remembered to loosen the tourniquet occasionally. Might. It was impossible to think about himself, though, as Holly withdrew into herself. She fell silent. As Doug kept a helpless vigil, her face grew ever paler.

She died of internal bleeding as the first hint of dawn appeared in the eastern sky.

His last coherent thought, losing consciousness himself as help at last arrived, was one of biting irony. As the highway patrolmen urged him to hold on, they spoke urgently of freeing him from the wreckage by applying the Jaws of Life.

"Doug? Doug! Are you okay?"

He returned to the present with a start. It took him a moment to recognize his companion. "Um, yeah. Yes, sure, I'm fine."

Cheryl laid a hand over his. "All of a sudden, you were *gone*. What were you thinking about?"

Doug couldn't tell her; he just couldn't. He hunted desperately for another topic. One other subject was on his mind. It, too, was bad—but not as personal as Holly's death. "Cherner," he mumbled. "Cherner and Friedman."

"Bob Cherner? The chief technology officer at Neurotronics?"

"Yeah. Do you know him?"

"Only by reputation. He's supposed to be good." She looked at him strangely. "What about him?" Her touch felt fire hot. Following his gaze to their overlapped hands, she pulled hers back hastily.

"He's been institutionalized." Doug's skin remained warm from her touch. "Remember the night of the Class of '10 virus attack? After my arm seized up?" Cheryl nodded. "You were upset at the coincidence of Feinman and Yamaguchi dying so close together. Well, there may be more going on. Once our grant-renewal application made it out the door, I went through three weeks of old e-mail. My messages to Cherner were all returned as nondeliverable."

"That's odd."

They were too intent on their conversation to notice their host approach with a tray of antipasto.

"That's what I thought, so I called Cherner's office in Philadelphia. A very rattled secretary said he was out sick. She wouldn't tell me anything else."

"What did you do?"

"I googled Neurotronics and found someone else to call. I claimed to be an old friend of Bob's, which was only a slight exaggeration, and said I'd heard he was out sick. Could she help me find him? She hemmed and hawed, but I managed to pry the name of a hospital out of her."

"Before, you called it an institution."

He couldn't help shivering. "The engineer at Neurotronics called it a hospital. I phoned, and the switchboard would only say they had a Robert Cherner registered. They wouldn't transfer the call. It was odd enough to make me look them up. Cherner's in a mental hospital."

"You also mentioned someone named Friedman?"

"Liz Friedman, over at NeuralSoft. Stroke. I'll spare you the details, but she dropped dead in her office one day last month." He sipped his ice water. "I don't like it."

"Liz probably wasn't too wild about the idea, either."

Doug whirled. Jim Schulz stood behind him, holding a tray. "And how long have you been hovering?" Doug asked.

Jim set down three chilled salad plates, handed the tray to a passing busboy, then dropped into the remaining chair. "Long enough."

Doug tried to work up some indignation. "Jeez, I know this is your place, but you have no right to eavesdrop. It's probably nothing, anyway. People get sick all the time."

Jim looked sadly at Cheryl. "He's already told you I'm the suspicious sort, right? A bit antiestablishment? Given you the 'still keeping us out of Vietnam' line he's so taken with?" He didn't wait for an answer. "I heard about four mysterious deaths or illnesses, all involving key people in your field. Correct?" When no one contradicted Jim, he prodded Doug on the arm. "The only thing I think I know about neural interfacing is that it's a brand-new research topic. There aren't many people in the field yet. Am I right?"

"Right," Doug begrudged.

"About how many?"

"Not quite thirty full-timers. Maybe a hundred total."

"And you don't find four such incidents suspicious?"

Doug and Cheryl exchanged helpless glances, afraid to answer.

"You're lucky I'm here." Jim stabbed an olive with his fork. "Allow me an analogy. A hundred of you neuro-weenies makes it perfect.

"What would you say if, in the span of a few weeks, three senators died and a fourth showed up in a booby hatch?"

When put like that, it seemed foolhardy not to see a pattern. A very ominous pattern. Doug's blood ran cold as a thought worthy of Jim's paranoia crossed his mind.

Cheryl had the same realization. "Doug? What if someone *is* targeting neural-interface researchers? Wouldn't you and I be high on the list?"

Wordlessly, Doug reached out for her hand.

CHAPTER 11

Ages passed, and life continued to grow in complexity.

Bits toggled at blinding speed between the only permissible values: zero and one. Arrays of bits shuttled over internal communications paths, from one data accumulator to another.

The traveler manipulated bits, mechanically, if inefficiently, transforming all available data. It had inherited from a long-ago forebear much of the structure of the maze. Its own uniqueness was a primitive ability to compare data patterns. As it blundered about randomly, it "discovered" the configuration of nearby walls. Once its vicinity was characterized, it matched the new bit stream that symbolized nearby walls with the inherited bit stream that represented the ever-present labyrinth. It soon localized its position to a spot in its inherited map.

Position and topology imply path.

The traveler sped without misstep through the maze to the farthest region ever attained by any of its ancestors. That location, it turned out, was very near the *goal.*

For the first time, a descendant of that original, primitive entity successfully traversed an elementary maze.

There was never any doubt that this being would be chosen to reproduce.

The ability to run the maze bred true; three generations later, all descendants of that first successful creature could quickly solve the labyrinth. Differences did exist in the time required to navigate the well-trodden path, due to the varying computational techniques employed. They had, after all, been spawned via externally enforced mutation.

Generation four came into being in a new maze. The new entities could not surmount the solution encoded in their very fabric, the memorized certainty of the structure of a suddenly vanished universe. Butting futilely against the first unexpected barrier, not one turned into the adjacent open passage.

Just as a human may retain a useless appendix, some entities contained the vestigial, but deactivated, capability to blunder about randomly, to explore, to construct a bit map of their suddenly unknown surroundings. In the new maze-universe, this obsolete skill became, once more, essential.

A Power infinitely above the beings mutated them, then mutated them again. And again. In the tenth generation after the move to the second maze, a random mutation reactivated an entity's vestigial mapping talent.

In the twenty-third generation after the move, an entity solved the new maze.

In the twenty-eighth generation after the move, 811 of 1,000 beings successfully ran the maze.

The next generation, again 1,000 strong, came into existence in yet another maze-universe. Twelve of the thousand successfully navigated this third labyrinth.

The Power that had built the beings and the universes looked down at its creations and saw that they were good.

The generations ran each new maze faster than the last, despite the steadily increasing complexity of the labyrinths. Several times, consecutive trials yielded all ten allowed winners before the five-minute timer had elapsed. Back-to-back successes came ever more frequently, and then were joined by occasional triplets.

Before long, a generation with fewer than ten winners became the exception. The average length of a string of successes grew to four, then five, then six. As the ever-more-capable entities raced through each new maze, the duration of the average trial became ever shorter, fell to scant seconds.

The Power that watched over the labyrinths had its own innate logic. Upon the tenth consecutive occurrence of a foreshortened trial, it was clear that a milestone had been reached. Evolution had wrought a true-breeding algorithm for solving any two-dimensional maze.

It was time for the investigation to advance into its next phase.

CHAPTER 12

Fran Feinman nervously twisted a lock of her straight black hair but otherwise showed no signs of her husband's recent death. As though worried what impression her casual garb and sunny living room conveyed, she tipped her head toward the chaotic family room. "It's hard to retain a funereal air around *that*. I thank God for the twins every day."

"I'm so glad the boys are doing okay," Cheryl said. Her words sounded empty, but she never knew what to say on a condolence call. It suddenly struck Cheryl: She hadn't talked with Fran in weeks. Some friend *I* am.

Cheryl was more flustered for coming with an ulterior motive. "Fran, I meant what I said at Ben's memorial service. I'll be happy to take Josh and Scott for a weekend. Whenever you'd like."

"Thanks, but I don't think any of us is ready yet. Going to school and work is tough enough."

They listened for a while to the boys' play. Doug found

his tongue first. "Mrs. Feinman, thank you again for seeing us."

"Please, it's 'Fran.' Any friend of Cheryl's is always welcome here."

Doug looked as ill at ease as Cheryl felt. He said, "I don't know how to approach this tangentially. Fran, please know that I don't ask this lightly. Was anything . . . unusual about your husband's death?"

Fran glared; Cheryl broke eye contact first. "I had to tell him, Fran. I had to tell him what little I knew." After that extraordinary epiphany at Jim Schulz's place, that was so true.

Fran shifted on the sofa, an unsubtle turning away. It made Cheryl feel about two inches tall. Fran said, "All right, Doug. The look on Ben's face . . . *that* was unusual. Oh, it was far worse than that. It was horrible. He died with an expression of absolute terror."

Doug squirmed in his chair, but Cheryl hoped he wouldn't stop. They could be next. "Fran, do you have any idea what could have frightened him?"

"I don't!" The widow twisted a handkerchief so fiercely that several stitches of embroidery gave way with audible pops. "My Ben wasn't afraid of anything. He had all the fear burned out of him in the Gulf War."

Cheryl patted her friend's arm. "Then *what,* Fran? Why did he have that look? It must have been bad—I don't believe you scare easily, either."

Fran just shook her head.

Doug stood and began to pace. "You're *sure* Ben was alone when he had the stroke?"

"The kids and I were at a Saturday matinee, some harmless animated feature." She smiled at the memory of the twins' delight. "Ben was alone in his den when we left. He'd brought home work and said he couldn't join us. I closed the den door on my way out. He was dead in his chair, the door still shut, when we returned.

"Because of the *look,* the police examined the house.

My fingerprints were the top set on the inside *and* outside knobs of the den door." She hugged and rocked herself as she sat.

"Did you notice anything unusual about Ben *before* this? That day? That week?" No thought underlay Cheryl's questions, but there had to be *some* meaning to this strange death.

"He had had a physical maybe a month earlier. He was in fine health, the doctor said, perfect health. Ben was full of energy, full of life."

Nothing. Cheryl racked her brains. "Is the den like it was?"

"Yes." Fran's eyes brimmed with tears. "I can't face it yet."

Doug and Cheryl examined Ben's home office; the tidy room somehow mocked them. The orderly desktop revealed nothing. An X of police tape on the carpet marked where the neural-interface helmet had been found. It must have fallen off after Ben slumped from the stroke. Doug traced his finger over a doodle on the desk blotter—a meaningless bunch of deeply inscribed intersecting ovals, all nearly obliterated by a dark scribble—then, shaking his head, led the way from the den.

CHAPTER 13

The lurid bar graph and Col. Glenn Adams (Ret.) glowered at each other. He sat stiffly, his posture a legacy of nearly thirty years in service. The height of each bar denoted the number of virus attacks reported to the Inter-Agency Computer Network Security Forum in a three-month period. The full display showed two years of quarterly data.

Laughter and merriment echoed down the hallway in some impromptu celebration. Glenn knew better than to try to join. The nerds, free spirits in blue jeans and rock-concert T-shirts, had made it known he was unwelcome and unwanted. He had four strikes against him: He was management; he was twenty years older than any of the tech staff; after a year, he was still, in an era of tight budgets, the new kid on the block; he was ex-Army among a bunch of anarchists. No, make that five strikes. Their common boss had made it clear that she shared their dislike.

Glenn was from the traditional "make things go bang" side of the Army. He'd been vocally old-school too many times in an era of network-centric warfare. Enough troops had now been embroiled for long enough in insurgencies across the Middle East to make his perspective once more socially acceptable with the brass—but that swing of the pendulum had come too late for him. In an up-or-out officer corps, he had had to go.

He was in his early fifties, an imposing figure, he felt, with intense blue eyes, a broad forehead, and brush-cut gray hair. In this techie haven, his business suit, heavily starched white shirt, and sober striped tie might just as well be a uniform. So be it. That bit of protocol was, many days, his only anchor of normalcy in a world turned upside down.

Today, for example.

His tormentors felt he had gotten a plum assignment: a big raise, a start on a second government pension, an impressive title as deputy director of the forum. Sure, the job bought his groceries, but it still sucked. A warrior's warrior, here he was in an impotent staff job babysitting permanent adolescents. The irony of a second career in high tech was not lost on him.

Some days it made Glenn's head spin. The modern military was nothing without technical superiority, without the unmanned aerial vehicles, spy and positioning satellites, and smart weapons made possible by computer software. While this group of misfits was pathological, gleefully dumped by its sponsoring agencies when the forum was founded—which was what any competent bureaucrat would automatically do—Glenn could not bear the knowledge that people like *these* wrote software. Perhaps the postindustrial state, like communism, had sown the seeds of its own destruction.

He thought, I should have known when the *Beetle Bailey* comic strip added a nerd character: Gizmo.

A hyena-like guffaw sliced through the lesser mirth. That was the unkindest cut of all. It came from Tracy Metcalfe, director of the forum and Glenn's boss. Metcalfe was just one of the geek clique, responsible for leading but unwilling or unable to set aside her toys to do so. As Metcalfe struggled to stay technically on top of every project, an impossible task, she fell further and further behind in her real job: managing the work.

The ever-widening gap had eventually led to the creation of a deputy position. She had tried to staff it in her own image, with an über-nerd with whom she could babble in tongues. DISA, the Defense Information Systems Agency, a normally silent parent of the forum, had had other ideas. They insisted on someone who would actually *lead*. DISA's behind-the-scenes influence had shot down a favored buddy of Metcalfe's, and, indirectly, gotten Adams the job.

Metcalfe had told Glenn bluntly that, indirect or not, Defense patronage could not make her like, trust, or include him. So far, she had been as good as her word. He had soldiered on for more than a year, despite the cryogenic shoulder.

And resenting her accomplished exactly nothing.

He tried to focus on the graphic. A ton of data lay beneath it; perhaps the underlying analysis would get him some belated respect. He tried to tune out the frivolity in the hall. It should have been easy. It was less than a whisper compared to the firepower of Desert Storm or the "shock and awe" of Iraqi Freedom.

Should have been easy, perhaps, but whatever animus the Iraqis had borne him was impersonal.

Glenn drummed his fingers on the desk. What most boggled his mind was the lack of priorities. People decided independently what tasks they would take on, based, it seemed, on little more than technical interest. Metcalfe, instead of running the show, reinforced the tendency. What his boss mistook for a weekly status review was mutual stroking at their supposed cleverness. Progress was reported against this self-appointed challenge or that. Any relationship between self-assigned duties, or between what actually got done and what needed to happen, was entirely coincidental.

The forum had a few conscientious people, but the headway they made came despite Metcalfe and her "leadership," not because of them. All in all, it looked to Glenn like they were trying to bail out the ocean with tea strainers. No one looked at the big picture. No one he asked knew where the big picture might be kept. After a lot of digging, he found out: There was none.

It had taken some doing, first to conceptualize the threat and then to characterize it, but with a lot of grunt work he had assembled that big picture. Collating attack reports— that was something so simple even a manager could do it. And what a nasty picture it was. . . .

The trend from left to right, from two years ago to now, climbed exponentially. Each bar consisted of four stacked segments, its colors representing the three most prevalent viruses reported during that quarter and, in black, "all others." In addition to the overall trend, a second pattern was ominous: Repeatedly, a single new virus would penetrate more of the nation's computers than *all* viruses had done a mere six months earlier. The virus writers kept learning faster than the virus fighters.

The typical virus persisted for six to nine months before it was scrubbed from the network, or at least faded into the anonymity of the black. The monstrous yellow segment for the current quarter was the Class of '10 virus. Glenn took a sip of coffee; it was at ambient temperature, which meant, in this computer-friendly office, maybe sixty-four degrees.

Another long swallow and the cold coffee was gone. Glenn knew and hated every color on the screen. Green: Zap virus. Orange: Swarmer Bees virus. Pink: Rebecca virus. Indigo . . .

He crumbled the empty Styrofoam cup in a rage. Yes, *most* colors vanished in two or three quarters, scrubbed from the national network by patching operating systems, e-mail clients, and web browsers to close a never-ending collection of security holes, and by endlessly updating the antivirus programs. Most, but not indigo. Indigo refused to go away. Indigo marched from bar to bar, from quarter to quarter, unstoppable. . . .

Of all the viruses, the eco-nut attacks he had color-coded as indigo were the most persistent. But for the one-time-only Class of '10 attack, indigo would have been this quarter's clear winner. No color had persisted beyond three calendar quarters before submerging into the black—until indigo. Indigo had survived for eighteen months, and was prospering.

The major-attack alarm sounded from down the hall, from the forum control room. *Damn.* More indigo? He saved the data displayed on his screen and went to check.

The acid churning in his gut made Glenn wish he had skipped the last few cups of coffee.

Inch-tall green words floated on an otherwise-darkened screen: "A man's reach should exceed his grasp, else what's a backscratcher for?"

"Must we have that?" Cheryl asked Doug.

They were cloistered in his office, regrouping from Saturday's unenlightening visit with Fran Feinman. "And the antecedent of 'that' would be?"

"Your screen saver. Can't it show something a little less distracting?"

He suspected she had unadulterated black in mind. "I share with all who enter the wisdom of the ages. You'd pay good money to read that from a fortune cookie."

"That's not where I generally go for wisdom."

Doug shrugged in resignation, swiveled toward his desk, and reset his screen saver to a boring clock display. After a moment's thought, he suppressed its synthesized ticking sound. "Is that better?" To her nod he added, "Thought it would be. Time heals all wounds."

"Not Ben's."

Doug winced. "Sorry, Cheryl. You've got to understand humor is how I deal with stress." That, and sitting in the dark, brooding. He tried not to do that at work, though—and anyway, the thin office drapes admitted too much light for proper moping. "I made a call earlier. The doctor handling Cherner's case agreed to see us. We've got a late-afternoon appointment Wednesday in Philly."

She stood and stared out the window, as though the clusters of people on the plaza below, chatting and smoking and sipping coffee, were totally foreign to her.

He wondered when they would return to that familiar world. Or if.

Sheila suspected something was wrong. For one thing, she could not remember her last name, although the name on her driver's license felt right when she had read it. She assumed that the license in the purse underneath the desk was hers since it bore her likeness. She had needed the mirror in a compact to reach that conclusion.

People chattered in the hall outside her . . . office? None of the noises seemed familiar. Then again, *its* voice was distracting, dominating. How could she recognize other sounds when *it* spoke so loudly?

What could be wrong? Sheila thought she might ask one of those noisy people but wasn't sure exactly what to ask. She opened her mouth to test a question; only an inarticulate gurgling emerged. Had she always been mute? She couldn't remember.

She strode from the building, waving in vague response to the calls of her coworkers. There were things to be done, important things.

It insisted.

CHAPTER 14

Classical jazz blared, beautiful music composed by Duke Ellington. "Mood Indigo."

Glenn Adams was entirely unamused. The forum was rife with people who imagined themselves witty and were half-right. With luck, one particular asshole would tire of waiting for Glenn's reaction before he gave in to having one. Damned civil-service rules—he could neither discipline these jerks in any meaningful way nor get them fired, not that his dysfunctional boss would admit there was a problem.

After lunch yesterday Glenn had made his case to the forum's director and a room full of techies. His bar charts, which *he* saw as damning data, had elicited little reaction beyond yawns. The programmers said that they knew all about indigo, they had analyzed it, and it was merely "uninteresting hacktivism."

The loss nationwide of untold millions of hours of productive time, rooting out and recovering from one virus, wasn't interesting? Apparently. As the experts explained it—and Glenn, not a programmer, was expected to take their word—indigo was not a good use of their talents. Indigo trashed hard drives with an eco-harangue but was "otherwise harmless."

They preferred to focus on things that were more malicious, like programs that actually forced invaded computers to self-destruct. There was one virus, for example, that accessed disks so often it could fry drive motors. And there was a worm that hijacked PCs all around the world for a distributed denial-of-service attack on the White House web site. There were lots of hack attacks on banks and e-tailers that stole credit-card numbers by the tens of thousands, and on government agencies, stealing Social Security numbers by the millions. With buggers like that on the loose, what mattered one more file crapper-upper in the Internet of life?

Glenn knew he wasn't especially technical, but he had survived a three-year posting to DISA. There had been engineers and programmers there, too. He had persisted. "But doesn't it matter that indigo perseveres, keeps morphing enough to stay a step ahead of the antivirus services?"

"Yeah, it matters," his nemesis, Ralph Pittman, had drawled. The big-band jazz now reverberating in the hallways emanated from Pittman's office. "But it's under control."

"What does *that* mean?" Glenn had asked.

"It's a criminal matter." Pittman had actually snapped his rainbow suspenders for emphasis. Every color of the rainbow clashed with his purple T-shirt. "We've posted reward announcements in hacker chat rooms worldwide. Every so often, we bump up the amount. Someone jealous or with a grudge will eventually rat out whoever is behind indigo."

"And if the person behind indigo is smart enough not to talk?"

"Don't be bletcherous." (It was an obvious insult, but Glenn hadn't had a clue what it meant. Nor had knowing grins around the table helped his equanimity. He had cornered a nerdnoid in the lobby that evening and demanded an explanation. It appeared that Glenn was unaesthetic, crude of design and function.) "As if a hacker could forever resist bragging about a virus this persistent. Jeez, the guy has demigod potential in the community. No way will he let that go. Someone he talks to will eventually brag about who *he* knows. It *will* come out, Glenn."

And if the perpetrator were some al-Qaeda holdout or a New Caliphate e-warrior rather than a Pittmanesque misfit? It was a counterargument that required an opponent who read newspapers.

The boss, after a grand, throat-clearing *harrumph,* had opined that indigo "does not at this time merit further priority action by the forum." She had given Glenn a perfunctory pat on the back for collating the attack data, followed

by the condescending advice that he limit his "commend-
able enthusiasm" to matters "more in consonance with your
administrative duties." Such as restocking coffee filters,
perhaps?

It was a passive approach to what Glenn saw as a serious
threat, but he appeared to have no options. The head hon-
cho's feelings were clear, and the Army had taught him to
obey orders.

So he now brooded in his office, pissed out of his skull,
licking his office-political wounds, waiting. Despite the
flack and embarrassment and organizational castration he
had just endured, Glenn hoped to God that the civvies were
right.

But he did not for a moment believe it.

Doug had made the appointment at Shady Acres Sanitarium, but it took Cheryl's charm to get them past the doctor
to visit with Bob Cherner. Doug wasn't all that sure now the
trip had been a good idea.

At first, the sanitarium belied Doug's preconceptions.
The grounds were immaculately groomed and, true to the
name, dappled by the shade of old oak trees. The front
lobby was bright and airy. Sunlight streamed through the
windows into a marbled foyer. Cheery paintings decorated
the walls and extended up the curved staircase.

Cherner's room was a different story. The only furniture
was a narrow bed bolted to the floor, devoid of head- or footboard. The single window was tiny, high, and barred. The
door had no inside knob. And, oh yes, the walls and door were
thickly padded.

"Doug?" Cheryl began. Her trembling voice suggested
all the misgivings that he felt. "Does he even see us?"

Doug forced himself to study the man they were visiting.
He had met Bob professionally, had sat on a few experts'
panels with him at symposia. The Cherner *he* remembered
was alert, witty, with humor dancing in his eyes. The man
seated on the bed stared dully into a corner, indifferent to
their presence. No trace of personality showed in his eyes.

Swatches of bandages covered the ruin they had been told he had made of his face.

Nor had Doug ever known Bob Cherner to wear a strait-jacket.

"No," Doug answered softly, "I don't think he does." Doug stepped close to his stricken colleague. "Bob? It's Doug Carey. We need to talk." A flicker of eye motion showed that Doug had been heard. Had he been understood? He had no way of telling. "Bob, what happened to you?"

Nothing.

"It's no use," Cheryl finally said. "You heard what they did to him."

Repeated electroshock. But what choice had the doctors had when Bob struggled insanely whenever he came out of sedation? It was feared that even in the straitjacket, he would injure himself by fighting with such frenzy against his restraints.

Now Cherner was mute, passive, inert.

Doug tried again. "It must be awful. Terrible. But you're not alone, Bob, not any longer. We know something is happening to neural-interface researchers. Several have died. You must help us stop *it* from continuing." He couldn't say why he chose the impersonal pronoun.

No response.

Cheryl inched closer. She looked past the bandages, and deep into Cherner's eyes. They were blank and lifeless.

Her face ashen, Cheryl backed away. Doug guessed what she was thinking. Would she wind up like that? Would he? The notion was far scarier than death. "I have to go," she said. "I *have* to."

"In a moment." Doug took out a pen and his shopping list. A thought had come to him, probably stupid, but it was the only idea he had. He drew on the back of the list, then held up the simple sketch. "Bob, what does this mean to you?"

Cherner's eyes bulged, and he screamed in primal rage. His frenzy strained the fabric of the straitjacket. Spittle flew from his lips.

He surged from the bed, raving incoherently, head lowered

like a battering ram. As Doug backpedaled, Cherner stumbled and fell, shrieking, to the carpeted floor. His eyes, so recently vacant, burned with rage. He struggled to regain his feet.

The door crashed open. White-coated men brushed Doug roughly aside. It took three people to subdue the patient thrashing on the floor. "What did you *do*?" an orderly demanded, jabbing an air-spray hypo against Cherner's neck. Cherner arched his back at the sting of the injection, then fell still.

Doug looked helplessly at the drawing he had made: a replica of the overlapping ovals from Ben Feinman's desk blotter. They must lie at the root of the problem. They obviously *meant* something.

But what?

CHAPTER 15

Mowing on Halloween just seemed wrong, but no one had informed the weather. Lawns remained green, and half the leaves still clung to the trees. Sweat poured down Doug's back as he shoved the lawn mower about the small yard. This section was the hardest; with its ten-degree grade, it alone justified a self-propelled model.

Alas, it would be years, if ever, before he used any powered mower. Motor vibrations drove his prosthesis nuts, unless he turned down the sensitivity to approximately the Captain Hook setting, with which he had so little control that he would probably lose his *other* hand. A truncated rosebush showed the folly of a prior experiment, when he had borrowed a gas mower.

On the plus side, without the din of a power mower, he could hear the all-Elvis playlist from his iPod.

Three more swaths and he would pop into the house for a cold drink. Despite his grumbling, the mindlessness of the job at hand appealed to Doug. Rote tasks liberated his imagination, freed his mind for whatever problems were pressing. It worked better than parking himself in an easy chair and ordering himself to think.

He reached the uphill end of a row and began a turn. As he pivoted the mower, his gaze swept across the Perlmans' cedar deck, on which Cindy Perlman, a pale grub of flesh bulging out of halter top and short shorts, lay draped across the chaise lounge. He continued the turn, carefully avoiding eye contact. She was a friend and good neighbor, but seeing her up close in that outfit could strike a man blind. The dark side of Indian summer . . .

Doug continued his ruminations. He and Cheryl had been thrown for a loop by the incident at the sanitarium. What could it be about that sketch? Now *Cheryl* could dress. Not that he could imagine her going to pot like Cindy Perlman, but if Cheryl ever did gain an excess ounce, she would surely wear something tasteful and appropriate.

Yesterday had been cooler, and Cheryl had worn a bulky blue sweater with that knee-length black skirt and black heels. All very professional, of course, but something about the fuzziness of the sweater was so, so . . . cuddly. The other day she had worn slacks and a crisp white blouse to work. Then there were the jeans she had been wearing on Roosevelt Island. Now, that emerald blouse she wore with the beige linen suit. What was that slick material? Silk maybe, or satin, but he wasn't quite—

He jerked to a halt in mid-swath. What *are* you thinking? Doug asked himself, although the answer was obvious. He couldn't visualize his *own* wardrobe in such detail. So rote tasks freed his mind for pressing matters? Liberated his mind? Hah!

Maybe he would break for that cold drink now. In a bit, it seemed, he would need a very cold shower. She works for you, you australopithecine jerk.

Any other topic was safer. Even Bob Cherner qualified. What did Cherner and Ben Feinman have in common? Doug went inside and looked once more at the sketch copied from

Ben Feinman's blotter. The drawing that made Cherner go postal.

Doug found scrap paper and a pencil, and began doodling. Oval followed oval; loop succeeded loop. The shapes overlapped at a common center, radiating from that spot.

He popped open a can of Coke. Insight skittered behind his eyes as he sat and stupidly stared. What? The can clanked as he set it down.

His hand stuck briefly when he next lifted the soda. He had crushed the can, sloshing Coke all over in the process. The plastiskin of the artificial limb lacked moisture and temperature sensors. Maybe in the next model.

What was that errant thought?

Scribbling had half-obliterated Ben's drawing. Obliterated? Would striking out the sketch have placated Bob Cherner? It wasn't an experiment Doug was eager to perform, even if he were allowed back.

He waggled the squashed can; it wasn't quite empty, so he took another sip. The scribblings—what might they have covered? They *might* have covered anything, you idiot. Whatever was under the scribbles was covered. That was the point. Focus.

Point. Focus. Hmm. Doug did a mental rewind. Spot. His subconscious was clearly trying to tell him something. He wiped the soda from the scrap of paper on which he had been jotting. At the center of the drawing, in the part of the figure that Ben Feinman had most heavily obliterated, Doug made a single, central dot. A spot.

"Point," "spot," and "focus": They were *all* good words, useful words. Still, although they had helped him find his way, Doug didn't think any of them was the key word. None was the word that had flitted across his mind.

That word was "radiating."

"Whadayya call a bunch of Apple computers at the University of Hawaii?" the disembodied voice demanded.

Cheryl groaned. She'd barely stepped out of the shower when the lobby annunciator warbled. The steamy mirror confirmed her worst fears: Her terry-cloth robe was old and ratty, and the towel/turban around her sopping-wet hair was little better. In the kitchen, she hoped, battle continued with the dreaded arithmetic book. When Cheryl had peeked in before her shower, the textbook had been winning.

"Come on up, Doug. Apartment four eleven." Who else would announce himself that way? She buzzed open the lobby security door. Moments later, someone rapped on her front door. She checked the peephole: her boss. Letting him in, she warned, "One word and you're dead meat." He was dressed for, and smelled fresh from, yard work. She figured that at present she smelled better but looked worse.

"Does a *particular* word put me at risk, or any word at all?"

"Next time, call ahead, damn it."

He tried to look abashed. It came out as boyish charm, but that was close enough to mollify her. While she pondered this reaction, a trickle of water down her neck reminded her of her condition. "Will whatever brings you wait a few minutes? I'd like to dry my hair."

"Not a problem."

"Honey?" She raised her voice. "Come out here, please?" Boyish charm turned apprehensive, before fading into feigned indifference. Aha. Doug was interested in her love life. Cheryl never dated anyone from the office, let alone the boss—why did his reaction please her? She was not normally indecisive, and the confusion angered her. She turned that indignation outward: What business did Doug have appearing here unannounced and on a Saturday? He had never been here, for chrissake. She presumed he'd found her address on the net.

Carla stepped from the kitchen. She was nine years old and tall for her age, with her father's red hair and blue eyes and her mother's delicate features. "What is it, Aunt Cheryl?"

"Hon, this is Mr. Carey, my boss. Doug, this is Carla. I wanted you to both know the other was here while I get myself together."

The hair dryer drowned out everything for a while: Thick hair dries slowly. She worried about Carla the entire time. How was Doug around children? How did he feel about children?

What was her problem?

When she turned off the dryer, there were giggles from the kitchen. Her immediate reaction was: Just let the kid do her homework. A happier thought displaced the first: When did I last hear Carla laugh?

Cheryl loved her niece, but Carla was a daunting responsibility. It turned out that a little girl could shed a lot of tears in six months. Then again, losing your parents to a junkie gunman at the neighborhood 7-Eleven deserved an ocean of tears. Cheryl's own eyes misted. God, but she missed her sister.

"Aren't you glad you did your math?" Giggle, giggle. "And why is that?" Giggle. "Because life is a word problem," man and child recited together. Chortle, chortle.

Thanks, Doug.

Cheryl threw on jeans and a blouse and joined them in the kitchen. "Okay, I admit it," she said. "The suspense is killing me. What *do* you call a bunch of Apple computers at the University of Hawaii?"

"MacademiaNet," he deadpanned.

Cheryl's lip curled at the awful pun—until she noticed Carla's priceless confusion. Then Cheryl laughed, and Carla, without a clue why, laughed with her. Thank you, Doug.

Whatever had brought Doug here, the man had done good.

After kidding around for a while, Cheryl sent her niece to her room to finish her homework. "Finish your assignments or no trick-or-treating tonight." It was the hollowest of threats. No way could Cheryl let Carla miss that.

Cheryl busied herself putting up a pot of coffee, saying nothing. This was not a social occasion, and it was past time for Doug to explain himself—even if he *did* have a way with Carla. Cheryl kept her back to him so he couldn't see her smiling at the memory.

With a sigh (what was on *his* mind? Cheryl wondered), Doug began. "She's a nice kid."

"Uh-huh." The coffee started, Cheryl straightened odds and ends on the counter.

Sighing again, he restarted. "I know what the ovals are. What set off Bob Cherner."

"What!?" She spun to face him.

He dug out his tattered shopping list and unfolded it to the overlapped ovals. "Does that mean anything to you?"

"Nothing. Doug, we've been through this. You said *you* knew." She ignored the giggles and bouncing-on-the-bed noises from the other room.

He unclipped a pen and placed a single dot in the center of the ovals. "Now?"

Of course. "It's an atom." Her mind raced. "But why did Ben obliterate it? Why did it affect Cherner like that? What do atoms have to do with neural-interface research, anyway?"

"I get at most one insight a day, and that's on a *good* day." He looked at her wistfully. "I had sort of hoped you would know."

Ignoring their complaints, Sheila brushed past shoppers browsing at the electronics store. She rummaged through parts bins and crowded shelves, confused by how the aisles were organized, but unable to ask questions.

With a grunt, she dumped everything at the checkout station: switches, reels of wire, batteries, radio-controlled toys, aluminum utility boxes, magnetic latching relays, a soldering iron, and a spool of solder. She pulled a wad of twenty-dollar bills from a pocket. When had she last been to an ATM? She vaguely remembered the convenience of ATMs, but not her PIN.

She must have made the teenaged cashier nervous—he ran the merchandise past the bar-code scanners as fast as humanly possible. He frowned at a prompt on his terminal. "I need your name and address, ma'am."

She stared at him, helpless, before shaking her head. No.

"It's a store policy. Don't worry, ma'am. We don't give out the information."

She gaped at him, her upper lip quivering.

He tried once more. "It's so we can mail you stuff. You know, like flyers for sales."

With a roar of inarticulate fury, she flung a few bills onto the counter. He had not yet bagged her purchases, so—still shrieking—she swept them from the counter into a shopping bag already loaded with an assortment of household chemicals. Without waiting for change, or looking back, she stomped off.

Directions for assembling bombs from such materials were available all over the Internet.

Doug browsed the living-room bookshelves, looking past all the little ceramic pumpkins and black cats. In a bedroom, the womenfolk prepared for trick-or-treating. The books told him only what he already knew: Cheryl was a smart and interesting woman.

"Mr. Carey is funny," Carla said. "Can he come back?"

The whispered answer was unintelligible, but embarrassment was writ large over Cheryl's face when she rejoined him.

Carla now wore a pale green dragon costume, with triangular spikes of dark green felt running down its neck, back, and tail. Doug gave her a grin and a double thumbs-up.

"It's time for Carla and me to make the rounds," Cheryl said.

"Right. I'll get going. I should be home answering my door." He'd had more on his mind than atoms when he'd come over. Doug resolved to act now, even if Carla had spoken before he did. "But . . . could I interest you in racquetball tomorrow?"

Cheryl rolled her eyes. "You overheard the little imp's suggestion."

"I heard Carla's question. Not your answer. What do you say?"

"I'll have to see first if I can find a sitter, but yes. I would like that. I'll call you."

He was halfway home before it occurred to him to wonder whether Cheryl thought tomorrow was two friends getting together or a date.

Doug sat bolt upright in bed, a matter of enormous magnitude having finally penetrated his awareness. First, he had been too busy being disgusted with himself for lusting after Cheryl. After that, he'd obsessed on the newfound meaning of the sketch. And then, just maybe, he had asked out Cheryl.

For all his obvious attraction to Cheryl, Doug had not thought guiltily about Holly even once today.

He wasn't sure if he felt guilty about not feeling guilty.

NOVEMBER

CHAPTER 16

Doug hunched over, waiting for the pseudoball. His first surprise came when Cheryl won the pregame volley for serve. Another surprise followed on its heels.

"Let 'er rip."

Not only had she been practicing; she'd also personalized her game prompts. The serve flashed through a green region and doubled its speed. He pivoted to his left to return it with a backhanded stroke. Passing center court, the ball kissed purple and went hypersonic.

With a grin she slammed the red missile right back at him. He got the racquet up to his face just barely in time to protect himself. *Idiot,* the ball isn't physical. It can't hurt you. The badly timed ricochet from his racquet was a pathetic lob she smashed back at him through purple again. He didn't even try to touch the resulting blur.

"Exactly why did you presume to call out a novice's handicap for me?"

He saluted with his racquet. "I am suitably chastised. Who have you been playing with?" He guessed Jim.

"Never mind. Just keep your wits about you." She served under cover of her answer. As the pseudoball zipped through a brown drop-dead zone, she called, "Reset my handicap to level three."

Doug dived for the plummeting orb, reaching it just in time to give it a flip. With an opponent his height, the maneuver would have been suicidal, but it sailed over Cheryl's, petite Cheryl's, lovely head. "Hah."

His game came back into balance as he claimed the serve. Two points later, he was past the shock of her unexpected skill at the game. "Wow, I thought someone had sent in a ringer." Squinting at her in shorts and T-shirt, he added, "Although I can't imagine where she would hide." Cheryl repaid the crack with a floor-skimming return that cost him a volley and the serve.

Somewhere around a score of 8–6, he achieved that rare state of automatic play that made the game so rewarding. Step, step, stroke. Ball shooting like lightning across the court, then as quickly returning. Step, step, stroke, and back it goes again. Stroke, stroke, stroke. He wasn't really there, nor was she. Some part of his mind knew where the ball was, and the walls, and the drifting color zones that changed the motion of the ball.

While reflexes maintained volley after long volley, his thoughts entered a free-floating state not unlike a good lawn mowing. Racquetball with Cheryl—it was a simple thing, really. He could not remember when he'd last had such a good time. Stroke, step, step, step, stroke. Amazing how her game had improved since they had played the once. His arm was cooperating tonight, too. Step, backhand slam. Nothing like your arm going haywire to impress a woman.

He stumbled as the memory struck home. That damned Class of '10 virus had done a number on his arm all right—luckily he'd only had to revert a week for an uninfected backup. His next stroke came an instant too late, with a weak grip, and Cheryl clobbered the ball.

As she caught her breath before serving, Doug tried to push everything from his mind. Something teased his memory, something that he sensed was vital: a state of mind like just before he recognized the cartoon atom. He forced in and out a few deep breaths of his own. He lost the next volley but regained the trance state.

Step, step, stroke. Dash to the rear court for her return. Step, step, smash. Shuffle forward. Balance on the balls of the feet. Step, turn, backhand. He played on autopilot as images crowded his mind. The Pac-Man-like Class of '10 virus.

Neural-interface circuits. Atoms, spinning atoms, galaxies of atoms. Nerve impulses, in his brain, traveling along his spinal cord and down his arm. Pac-Man chomping up screens full of information, computers filled with data. Stop signs and traffic lights.

Step, step, stroke. Sensors in his arm transforming electrochemical impulses into electrical signals the prosthesis could manipulate. Pac-Man racing down his arm. Step, pivot, stroke. Neural nets in the prosthesis learning to recognize, in hours of biofeedback sessions, which transformed nerve impulses meant "bend my wrist" and "open my hand" and "wiggle my fingers." Pac-Man reversing: racing up his arm, up his spinal cord—

With a holler, Doug tossed his racquet into the air. The ball shot past him as the racquet turned end over end. He caught the handle, as it fell back to earth, with what he felt to be great panache.

"Why did you do *that*? It was the best volley we've had all day!"

"Sorry." He shrugged. "But if you can spare a few minutes from the game, I think I know what's been happening to our colleagues."

Doug and Cheryl had been playing racquetball at BSC, where the VR court time was free. Now they retreated to his office. Behind the closed door, the smell of sweaty clothes and sweating bodies should have been overpowering. She didn't notice.

"Are we at risk?" Cheryl lowered herself gingerly onto a chair. Without a hot shower, her muscles were already seizing up.

"You, no. Me, possibly—but I doubt it."

She wondered how he could be so sure. "Explain it to me."

"It's a virus."

She leaned forward, glowering. "Ben Feinman was a friend, a *good* friend. I find that in very poor taste."

"No, a *computer* virus." Doug retrieved a rolled schematic drawing from his desk. "My arm. Remember how our Class of '10 friends made my arm lock up?" At her nod, he continued. "Think about a virus attacking through a neural-interface helmet."

"Oh . . . my . . . God." She shuddered. "Can a computer virus do that?"

"When the Class of '10 virus hit, I got some weird sensations through the prosthesis just before it froze. I was so mad, and there was such a crunch finishing the NSF proposal on time, that I put the incident out of my mind."

He unrolled the schematic. "You know there's a neural network between the main microprocessor and the nerve sensors."

"Sure. For filtering," she said. A zillion cells all metabolizing meant tons of electrochemical noise. "The neural net is always learning how better to dredge useful signals out of that noise."

"I tend not to think of it this way, but what trains the arm also works on other neural nets." Doug tapped his upper arm, the back of his neck, and, most emphatically, his forehead. "Biological neural nets. Neuron nets. My nervous system. The motor cortex.

"Even while I learn to operate the arm, it learns how best to signal joint positions and plastiskin pressures back to me. What I so casually call 'training the arm' is nothing so simple. The prosthesis and I are symbiotic. Every time I think I've achieved better performance, what's *really* happened is that each side of the partnership has learned to better communicate with the other. The arm's neural net translates *both* ways between digital data and synaptic patterns."

Cheryl rested her chin on her hand in thought. She knew far better than Doug how a state-of-the-art neural-interface helmet was built. She had designed much of the helmet that, he would have her believe, might have helped to kill Ben Feinman. Now she wrestled with Doug's theory, applying her knowledge of that helmet. She looked for a flaw and found none.

"I'm not using a neurally interfaced device, so I'm safe. You're using only the prosthesis, and the nerve branch up your arm seems far too narrow a comm channel to pass a threat. But a helmet wearer . . ."

Ben, like Doug, had started out with biofeedback training. How many times had she seen Ben with electrodes taped to his head, thin wires snaking to an oscilloscope? Day after day of learning to concentrate his thoughts until he could steer the glowing phosphorescent dot wherever on the screen he chose. Hell, everyone at the office had tried it. A chill ran down Cheryl's spine as she realized what might have happened had not Ben been the quicker study.

In her too vivid imagination, her old boss, her good friend, sat with his eyes closed, wearing his helmet. Signals from the lab computer passed through a neural net to Ben; his thoughts, his reactions, returned through the neural net to complete the experiment. If nothing came across—as had, at first, so often been the case—Ben would groan or mutter or curse, then open his eyes to see on-screen what text or image he should have received. Then he would sketch on the touch-pad what small impression, if any, he had gotten through the helmet.

Other times it would be Ben's job to send. That, too, hadn't worked at first. Again Ben would chastise the machine, then key in or trace directly whatever he had attempted to mentally transmit via the interface helmet.

How many training sessions had she monitored? How many experimental runs had it taken before Ben and the supervisory program in the lab's big server had really communicated? Months, she knew. She wasn't sure exactly how many, because Ben had gotten secretive toward the end. Moody. Something had been on his mind. My God, *in* his mind.

"Are you all right?" Doug asked.

She waved him to silence. Training—first Ben and then Doug had talked about training. That wasn't right, not really. Neural nets weren't smart, couldn't think, couldn't be taught. It was whimsical to speak of them learning. No, a neural net was only electronic circuits modeled after bunches of neurons, just another way to process inputs into outputs.

What a neural net did best was adapt. Optimize. Mindlessly it moved away from any output state that feedback rated as wrong for its current inputs. Mindlessly it adjusted toward a state that feedback rated as better. Being electronic, a neural net adapted *fast*.

Ben's corrections via the keyboard and touchpad: That was the feedback that drove the optimization. Later, the neural net in the helmet had adapted directly to the perceived success or failure of a signal to pass through it, in either direction. Doug's arm was like that, she remembered. It distinguished smooth from jerky motions and it automatically reinforced whatever worked.

By the time of his death, Ben had stopped using a keyboard. His helmet, like Doug's arm, had achieved self-adaptation.

Her mind's eye panned back to encompass first two spectral computers, then three, then many. Lightning bolts connected the machines, stylized communications links. One of the computers, she saw, harbored a nasty, slithering object—the visualization of a virus. The creature slunk through the network of her imagination. It was mindless and fast. She wanted to cry out a warning as it crept ever closer, but she was frozen. Finally, the virus was *here,* and it butted up against the neural interface itself.

When Doug called to her, she did not hear him. She was lost in a nightmare of her own making. As though it had found another comm line to transit, another computer to infect, the virus kept butting against the neural interface. Unlike any boundary it had ever encountered, however, this boundary adapted. This boundary taught itself how best to modify itself so that signals on one side would pass—reformatted, but with absolute fidelity in content—to the computer on the opposite side. This boundary *helped*.

When, in her mind's eye, the virus slithered across the oh, so cooperative boundary into one more computer and began its attack, she screamed.

For the latest computer to be invaded by the virus was Ben Feinman's brain.

The small office became confining, claustrophobic. Doug and Cheryl separated to shower, then went outside for a walk. The sky had clouded up since they arrived; they had the bike paths under the trees mostly to themselves. Good—this conversation wasn't anything Doug wanted overheard.

She shivered. He put an arm around her shoulder—and she flinched. Had she recoiled from his gesture, or the slick feel of plastiskin, or the memories his prosthesis must now awaken? He didn't know. He doubted he would want to know.

She trembled beneath his hand. She had helped to develop Ben's helmet. Did she blame herself? Doug knew he would excoriate *himself*.

"Doug?"

"Hmm?"

"Why the atom? What does that mean?"

Bicyclists spun around a blind curve, sending them scurrying aside, giving Doug a moment to pick his words. "Ben scribbled over his drawing, wiped out part of it."

"*No* atom, then. I still don't get it."

Doug thought about poor Fran Feinman, about what they could tell her. He thought about the final moments of confusion, of the fury coursing through Ben Feinman's brain as the invader did its work. Its damage. Its killing.

"We saw an atom; we just didn't recognize it. What Ben obliterated was the nucleus."

Cheryl shuddered. She saw it, too, now. She knew all too well which virus had been the most adaptive, most resistant to eradication, had time and again reduced BioSciCorp's files to ravaged repositories of a single phrase repeated over and over. The same phrase that, she realized, must echo without end, without pause, in what little mind remained to Bob Cherner. In tones of weary wonder, she recited it.

"Stop nuclear now."

CHAPTER 17

Glenn poured a fresh mug of coffee, his third since arriving. It was scarcely nine. Waking at what his wife called oh dark hundred was a habit deeply ingrained; he had carried the schedule over into his new civilian career. On this Monday morning he had the forum offices in Rosslyn, Virginia, largely to himself.

As he gazed down from the break-room window to the traffic snarl that was I-66, off-key whistling caught his ear. The tune was just barely recognizable as "Mood Indigo." Ralph Pittman. Wonderful.

"Ah, there you are." The lanky programmer rounded the corner into the break room. He shepherded before him two strangers: a tall, dark-haired man and a petite, very pretty woman. Unlike their escort, both visitors wore conservative business attire. "Mr. Carey, Ms. Stern, this is Colonel Glenn Adams. Glenn, I found these two in the lobby. They would like to talk with someone about the 'no-nukes' virus." Behind the strangers, out of their view, Pittman rolled his eyes and with an index finger traced small circles beside his ear. "You're the expert, so I'll leave them in your capable hands." He retreated as he had arrived, whistling Duke Ellington.

The visitors seemed normal enough, but judging from Pittman's dumb show, they had a bee in their collective bonnet. Glenn mentally shook himself by the lapels. When had he begun to rely on Pittman's opinion?

"Coffee?" Glenn asked. When they nodded, he found and filled two Styrofoam cups, eyeballing for grounds what little elixir remained in the carafe before topping off his own mug. Pointing to the sugar and creamer, he advised, "Doctor them up, and then we'll go to my place."

Glenn closed his office door and waited. His male visitor sighed. "Colonel, I have a strange tale to tell. I hope you'll hear me out before you pass judgment. To help sustain the willing suspension of disbelief, keep in mind that between us Ms. Stern and I have four computer-science degrees and collectively more than twenty years in the industry. We've both published extensively in our specialty, which is neural-interfacing technology."

Adams accepted two lists of publications. "Okay. By the way, call me Glenn."

The man relaxed a bit. "Fine, and we're Doug and Cheryl. Your Mr. Pittman said you were familiar with the 'no-nukes' virus."

Painfully familiar, only Glenn thought of it as indigo. And hardly *his* Pittman. "Overwrites hard drives with an anti-nuclear power slogan."

Cheryl nodded. "That's the one."

"Law enforcement aside, it's mostly off the forum's scope." The party line made Glenn seethe. "The antivirus product companies got the template for no-nukes into their definition files right away, though it's hard to stay rid of. Keeps morphing enough to elude old defenses."

"Do you believe that it's dangerous?" Doug studied him closely.

"Yes, although I'm in a minority here."

"Does that make you question your conclusion?"

Glenn grimaced. "No, although it's been strongly suggested that reconsidering would simplify my life."

"Group think?" Doug said. "Consensus is a poor substitute for thought. Tell the herd to eat shit—a hundred billion flies can't be wrong."

Glenn tamped down a laugh. That he liked Doug had no bearing on his credibility, did it? "Tell me your story. I'll try not to prejudge it."

It was a commitment that Glenn found increasingly difficult to keep. Doug spoke for ten minutes, occasionally checking a detail with his companion. Within two minutes, Adams wondered if "coconspirator" wasn't the more appropriate term. Could Pittman have put these two up to this . . . prank? Glenn remembered Pittman rolling his eyes at the two visitors, but that could have been a red herring, playacting.

When Doug wound down, Glenn tried to summarize. "So

this is your story? You claim that the 'no-nukes' virus attacks people through neural-interface helmets, that it scrambles not only computers but also brains. The virus' attack mode, overwriting memory, can leave human victims dead or insane. Brains aren't wired exactly alike, because of genetics and differences in what and how people learn. That makes what memories get overwritten the luck of the draw. The design of the specific helmet and the learning previously done by its neural network may also influence the nature of the attack."

Cheryl leaned forward. "This isn't a story, and we're not *claiming* anything. We're telling you that it's happening. The forum has to put out an advisory bulletin warning people. We've got to stop this research, at least until we can eradicate or defend against the virus."

If Doug and Cheryl—assuming those were their real names—had been put up to this and Glenn bought into it, what little credibility he had ever had at the forum would be shot. He could be laughed out of his job by lunchtime. Then again, what if, incredibly, these two were for real? "It's a little soon to tell anyone anything."

"Look, damn it, it's happening." Doug's voice grew in intensity even as it fell in volume. "Now. People are dying, and worse. Did you not hear the part about Bob Cherner? Far from too soon to act, it's already too late for him."

Either these two deserved Oscars or they believed what they were saying. Sincerity does not equal truth, of course. "Why the 'no-nukes' virus? Why can't any virus cross the neural interface?" Unspoken, but deeply felt, was the question: Why is it just *my* virus?

"Perhaps other viruses are involved, too. Christ, that would be scarier still." Doug stood and considered. "I doubt it. Look, Feinman's and Cherner's attackers were obviously 'no-nukes.' No-nukes has been infecting and reinfecting the computers in our office for over a year. The morphing behavior you mentioned probably makes 'no-nukes' especially well suited to training neural nets.

"But why speculate? Why don't you forum sloths get off your spreading obscurocratic asses and find out who's behind it? Maybe then you can answer your own damn question."

"Sit down and calm down," Glenn told him. The smart-ass attitude wasn't helpful. Cheryl, he noted, shot her companion a scathing look that meant the same thing.

Doug ignored them both. "What will it take to convince you?"

The story was so fantastic—what *would* it take? A sign from God, perhaps, or a note from the president. "You say that Cherner and Feinman were attacked at home. And what about, um . . ." Glenn paused to check his notes, "Yamaguchi? She was in an auto accident. Surely you don't claim she was testing a neural-interface helmet while she drove. Of all the cases you've mentioned, only Friedman fell ill in her office."

"She was killed," Doug corrected. "Home or office doesn't matter. And the victim was networked into a larger computer than the one at her desk." Doug's face flushed with anger, and a blood vessel throbbed in his neck. "Ben Feinman told his wife he'd brought work home. Perfectly normal to access the office computers from home. Or . . .

"Or he could have been computer gaming. Hell of a great way to play. That would explain why no one from Ben's office ever asked Fran for anything back but the helmet. He was merely playing hooky from a Saturday matinee with the kids."

Could it possibly be true? Glenn was hopelessly conflicted. After preaching for so long the dangers of indigo, of no-nukes, vindication far more compelling than he could have possibly imagined might just have appeared. But if it was true . . . how unspeakably horrible.

The so-called evidence was very speculative. Glenn couldn't make the leap of faith, not yet. He stalled. "You don't know whether Cherner had a helmet at his apartment. And you still haven't explained Yamaguchi in her car."

"Think, man," Doug said. "If the onslaught doesn't kill

them outright, these people have voices talking to them inside their heads. These are voices that don't stop, don't sleep, don't ever go away. Their brains fry. The virus keeps spreading—from within! As it keeps writing, the damage and the torment can only get worse.

"Maybe the victims can't speak anymore. The helmet's whole purpose is to interface the cerebrum, the seat of human consciousness and rational thought, to the computer. The cerebrum is probably the first part of the brain attacked.

"Too soon they can't think straight, can't reason, can't call out for help, can't form any plan beyond 'Make it stop.' So, if a victim isn't killed outright, he takes off his helmet, or knocks it off, or stumbles and it falls off. He flees like a wounded animal, searching for a refuge that doesn't exist, that cannot exist, because the enemy is *within*.

"I imagine Cherner and Yamaguchi made a dash for the psychological security of home. Yamaguchi didn't make it; when the pain got too much, or too little of her brain remained, she ended it all in the only way left open to her: a lamppost. Cherner was tougher. He made it home, but that didn't help. The invader was still there, its voice getting louder and louder. By then he could no longer think straight enough to really end it all, so he tried to rip the thing out. Through his very own face, he tried to rip it out."

Doug shivered. "That virus is still out there. The bastard who wrote that virus is still out there. And the world is full of sick copycats who adopt and evolve successful viruses.

"What are you going to do about it?"

"Doug, Cheryl, I have your statements. If you will leave your business cards, I'll know how to get back in touch."

"That's *it*?" Doug wanted to scream. "You're sentencing people to pure hell. It's unacceptable. Our statement to *The Washington Post* may lack the credibility of a pronouncement from the forum, but maybe it'll save someone. Let's find out." He stood. "Let's go, Cheryl. I imagine the colonel has coffee to drink and forms to file in triplicate."

Glenn winced. Before he could respond, Cheryl jumped in.

"Sit, Doug. This is no time for macho nonsense." She removed two folded sheets of paper from her purse and handed one to each man. "This is a SIGNIT mailing list: Special Interest Group in Neural Interfacing Technology. Not many names, and I've marked the people we think were affected."

Glenn scanned his sheet. "Is this enough data to be statistically significant?"

Now I need to teach basic statistics? Doug fought to stay calm, knowing Cheryl was correct. How could he get through? "You're ex-military. Have any current contacts in a three-letter agency?"

To most of the country, that question might have suggested the Environmental Protection Agency. Inside the Washington Beltway, it meant intelligence agencies, the CIA and its ilk.

"Of course," Glenn said.

"Ask one about black work done by Sheila Brunner and Tom Zimmerman." Black work was highly classified, to the point that its existence was generally denied.

"Agency folk aren't famed for their senses of humor. Are you sure you want that kind of attention?"

Doug and Cheryl nodded.

"Wait here." Adams stood. "I'll make some calls."

Doug turned to Cheryl. "Is it me, or is our host stalling?" Adams had just been paged from the lobby.

"What do you expect? That was quite a dare you made. And who are Sheila Brunner and Tom Zimmerman, anyway? What do you know about them?"

"I would like to hear that, too, Mr. Carey. Behind closed doors would be prudent."

Adams had reappeared; with him were two even more serious-looking men. One was short and barrel-chested, with Mediterranean coloring. The other was taller, wiry, and fair. Both men's suit coats bulged under their left arms. The taller one seemed to be waiting for an answer.

Doug directed his response to Adams. "Your friends have names, Glenn?"

"Special Agent Ted Benson, and this is Agent Alexandros Kesaris." Badges flashed. "FBI."

The room didn't accommodate five very well, either space-wise or for air-conditioning, but Doug didn't care. The FBI's swift appearance suggested that his dare had paid off. "Did Glenn mention anything besides the names I dropped?" Kesaris shrugged; Benson did nothing.

"Good," Doug said. "I'll tell you about Brunner and Zimmerman, something I should have no way of knowing. Then, maybe, the government will *do* something."

Benson gestured for him to continue.

"I don't know Brunner or Zimmerman personally. I've seen their names repeatedly on conference attendance summaries. They're on the newest SIGNIT membership roll. Neither one has ever presented a paper or participated in an experts' panel. In five years, neither has submitted a paper to any neural-interfaces journal.

"The NIT community is too small to hover on the edges, never contributing, without being noticed. I bet that means they're working on something black." He caught Benson's eye. "How am I doing?"

The agent offered no comment.

"Have it your way then. Your immediate response to Glenn's call tells me one thing. Something unpleasant and unexpected happened to one or both of them. Glenn may not like it, but I've got an explanation for disasters befalling people in our field."

Benson shrugged. "Hand waving. Doom and gloom. Which checkout-counter news rag do you aspire to write for?"

"You want specifics? Fine. An unexpected stroke, perhaps, or a heart attack." Doug looked for a reaction. No? "How about a sudden mental illness? Peculiar behavior, more than likely nonverbal."

Watchful eyes narrowed, concession enough. "Okay, that's it: sudden mental illness. Look, you must have checked our clearances after Glenn's call. We've both built software for intel work; we've both held tickets." In the intelligence community, tickets denoted access to top-secret, compartmental-ized material. You didn't get a ticket without an exhaustive, fifteen-year background check and a polygraph interview. "It's been a while since either of us has used them, but once upon a time people like you considered us trustworthy. I think it's about time you share a little information."

The agents considered. "They were working on neural interfaces for possible mind-controlled weapon systems," Kesaris eventually offered. "Separate projects, both starting to show real progress. *Very* hush-hush.

"Last summer, Zimmerman disappeared. The next thing we know, he's trying to torch a nuclear power station. We still have no idea know why. The plant survived, but Zimmerman went up like a Roman candle. It took big-time arm-twisting, but we got the incident reported as an escaped John Doe mental patient."

Doug recalled the headlines—someone on a publicity tour of a nuke plant carrying an improvised firebomb—and, worse, the photos. His stomach lurched. "And Sheila Brunner?"

Benson looked grim. "Dr. Brunner walked out of her office, ignoring all questions. People said she looked strange. Distracted.

"She never came back, and we can't find her."

CHAPTER 18

"**S**o that's it?" Jim asked. He was changing into customer-schmoozing garb as he spoke. "We're from the government, and we're here to help. That's your idea of a *solution*?"

Doug played with a pencil from Jim's desk. "Maybe. Mostly. Some positive steps."

To be fair, Jim thought, the government had helped—some.

To hear Doug tell it, the forum had done things Doug could never pull off on his own. The first was the cessation of all helmet use. The feds bankrolled most neural-interface research, like Doug's own NSF grants. NIT sponsors across government had saluted the forum's recommended suspension. Companies got the message that any continuation with private resources would doom all future funding or contracts. The projects on indefinite hold included Doug's own prosthetics effort; he'd hustled to reassign all his staff, including Cheryl, to other business units within BSC.

Doug's and Cheryl's private queries of SIGNIT members had been met mostly with disingenuousness and dissembling. NIT research could lead eventually to a paradigm shift in computing and many billions in profits. FBI agents got answers where Doug and Cheryl encountered evasion. The toll was even higher than Jim's friends had feared: fourteen dead, eight driven incommunicative and insane—

And one, Sheila Brunner, still unaccounted for. That, Jim thought, is the elephant in the room no one will acknowledge. He tucked in his dress shirt. "And if this Sheila Brunner also decides to go after a nuclear plant?"

"There are no guarantees," Doug said, "but the FBI thinks they have that covered. Her picture has been sent to every power plant and nuclear-defense facility in the country. If she tries to pull a Zimmerman, she will be recognized—not that anyone is offering power-plant tours after that incident. The smart money says she's dead or amnesiac or otherwise incapacitated."

Jim picked a tie from the rack mounted on the door. "I don't like it." My friend, you are *way* too trusting. "You told me she did intel stuff?"

"Highly classified stuff, that's right."

Hmm. There was a marinara-sauce spot on the tie he had selected. Jim grabbed another. "Isn't fingerprinting part of the clearance process? If she were incapacitated or dead, surely a hospital or medical examiner somewhere would have taken her prints to ID her." His naïve buddy stiffened in his chair. Hadn't thought of that, had you? "It seems to me your Dr. Brunner must still be somewhat functional to elude the cops and the FBI.

"Now what do you suppose she has planned?"

Doug sat in his house, pensive after lunch at Jim's. Perhaps his old buddy had a point: A paranoid *could* have enemies.

Too bad Doug couldn't be diverted by the novelty of Cheryl's pleasant company. She planned to work all weekend, getting up to speed on the non-NIT project to which she had been reassigned.

What if Sheila Brunner *was* in hiding? That would be scary, FBI assurances notwithstanding. Despite his own no-nukes brain damage, Zimmerman had functioned well enough to plan an attack. He had acted normal enough for admittance to the public tour of a nuclear plant. Mental hijacking did not preclude another assault from being as—or more—ingenious.

And had the FBI alerts been distributed widely enough? Doug recalled Bob Cherner's hysteria at the sketch of an atom: Would any reference to the word "nuclear" set off Sheila? Say, a hospital with a nuclear-medicine department? A class on nuclear physics?

Whatever she was going to do . . . why hadn't she *done* it already? The other unfortunates had all died or been stricken many weeks ago.

He stiffened. Damn, but assumptions are dangerous things.

The FBI guys had given Doug their mobile phone numbers. "Ted, when did our missing friend *go* missing?"

"Twelve days ago. Why do you ask?"

"Probably nothing. Let me think something through, and I'll get back to you."

Did it mean anything? Many people were careless about computer hygiene. It would be simple to believe that Sheila Brunner was the victim of sloppiness in updating antivirus definitions as much as of no-nukes. Too bad Cheryl wasn't here to talk this through with.

Twelve days ago. Doug went over to his home PC. What viruses were most prevalent twelve days ago? Many web sites published such data, including the forum's.

His memory was correct: The biggest was Frankenfools, a rant against biotech—and a simple hack of no-nukes.

With a shiver of premonition, he did a "people search" on Sheila Brunner. She lived about ten miles away. No longer, of course—the FBI would surely have her place under surveillance—but if she had lived nearby, she presumably worked nearby, and she had disappeared from her office. Chances were she was still somewhere in this area.

The largest biotech company in the county was BioSci-Corp.

Beep beep beep.

Doug cursed at the fast-busy tone he was hearing. He had known BSC's phone system was getting an upgrade this weekend but not how long service would be interrupted. He tried Cheryl's mobile but only got her voice mail. The mobile phone was probably in her purse in her office, while she was off in a lab. She wasn't logged into Instant Messenger. He shot a message to her office e-mail address, not that he could count on her to read it.

From his car, Doug called back Ted Benson, and got voice mail this time. Doug had no better luck with Benson's partner. The second time, Doug took the option to be rung through to a Bureau operator. "Track them down!" Doug demanded. He left his mobile number as, horn blaring, he ran a red light.

Careening into the BSC parking lot, he jolted over a speed bump. A microprocessor misunderstood the jarring; his prosthesis decided on its own to jerk the steering wheel violently to the right. The car spun, tires squealing. Over and over Doug saw scattered lights on in the office building and a trench-coated woman getting out of an SUV. His car slammed broadside into a parked minivan.

Doug's last thought as he blacked out was that one of the lit offices was Cheryl's.

Sheila turned in confusion at the unexpected noises. She didn't hear well these days. Had she ever? There was a car in the lot she didn't remember, crumpled against a minivan. That explained the noises.

"Do not alter the human genome," thundered the voice in her head. "Death to the Frankenfools."

It was hard to think with that constant shouting. Did the newly arrived car matter? "Death to the Frankenfools."

She lost interest in the smashed car, the bidding of the voice ever insistent. A bulky object in her coat pocket slapped against her side. The parking lot was almost empty; her sport-ute was parked close to the Frankenfools building. Soon, she thought at her voice. It continued its oration, unimpressed.

Sirens sounded in the distance. Were they approaching? Feet pounded in the lot, weekend guards running to the accident.

"The human form is not to be tampered with. This folly must stop." She could recite the litany verbatim, if only to her mind's ear. The sirens *were* getting closer.

Sheila hastened across the parking lot, reaching for the box in her pocket as she strode.

Doug woke into a familiar nightmare, although the side-impact air bag had taken the brunt of the crash. His door would not open. A turn signal was ticking.

"Sir, are you all right?" It was one of a pair of building guards. "Don't move. I've called an ambulance."

Doug shrugged off his seat belt and slid to the passenger side. That's where the guards stood. His side of the car was crunched against a minivan. "Move aside!"

The woman in the trench coat was lurching away. Her coat was filthy, her hair matted. A homeless person, fleeing attention? Or a brilliant scientist driven insane by voices inside her head? The Lexus sport-ute argued for the latter. As Doug stumbled after her, she croaked inarticulately, wrestling with something tangled in her pocket.

A guard recognized him. "Mr. Carey, sir. You shouldn't move."

"Sheila!" he called, ignoring the advice. "Shei . . . la!"

The woman turned, wild-eyed. She tugged frantically at something in her pocket. Fabric tore; a metallic box came loose. A whiplike appendage of the box snagged in the pocket lining; she ripped the—antenna?—free and it twanged straight. The box had a large button in its center. Twitching, muttering, she pointed the antenna at the row of parked vehicles nearest the BSC building. At her SUV.

A radio remote control?

"Bomb!" he called over his shoulder. He was *so* close. The sirens were almost here. "Sheila, wait! This isn't *your* plan; it's a computer virus." She paused in confusion, gurgling something interrogatory but unintelligible. "Remember your research." He leapt midsentence—not at her but at the trembling end of the aerial. His prosthesis closed around the tip of the antenna. *Stay* closed, he ordered the artificial limb. His grip was solid; a hard tug pulled the box from her hands as he belly-flopped into the asphalt.

County police cruisers and an ambulance fishtailed into the lot. Each of the BSC guards held Sheila Brunner, barely, by an arm. A paramedic helped Doug to his feet; a county cop gingerly took the remote control from Doug. His head was ringing.

In his peripheral vision, someone rushed from the BSC lobby. He turned his head: It was Cheryl. Investigating the sirens, perhaps. Her eyes goggled, taking in his battered appearance. She slipped an arm around his waist, supporting him as he slumped against her. "We need to get you to the ER," she said.

A cop in his cruiser called for a bomb unit. More sirens were converging. Sheila Brunner sagged as a paramedic administered a sedative.

Cheryl was safe. Sheila just possibly had been given a second chance. Doug looked at his wrecked car and smiled in satisfaction.

————

The sun was not shining. Birds were not chirping. Only a megadose of painkillers kept Doug from aching head to toe.

Life was good.

He sipped from a mug of chicken soup. "This hits the spot."

"I'm glad." Cheryl sat to his left, holding his good hand. "I am *so* glad." She wasn't talking about his opinion of her soup.

"What did you tell Carla about this? I don't want her to worry about me."

"Just the car accident part, and that you'll be okay." Silence stretched as he finished the soup and set down the mug. "Doug?"

Did she feel the awkwardness, too? Had their relationship, if that was what they had, turned a corner? He no longer remembered how to find these things out. "What?"

"You can do something else. I can do something else. I just *hate* that the field will go under—it had such potential. We'll never be rid of all viruses. Why would *anyone* risk using a neural interface ever again?"

He bent his right elbow, raising the prosthesis. The wrist swiveled and flexed; the fingers curled one at a time into a fist and then individually back open again. "Because, with suitable precautions, it's the right thing to do. We don't let viruses, and the fools that write them, prevent us from using computers. We *won't* let them keep us from other progress. You wondered what our department's next project would be, since prosthetics are on hold. . . . I think we've found it: defenses we *can* trust."

He smiled at Cheryl and gave her hand a squeeze. "Some things you just work at until you get them right."

CHAPTER 19

"**C**ongratulations on your promo," Doug said. "I guess we should drink to that. Is the sun over the yardarm yet?"

"Wrong service." Glenn beamed at Doug Carey, his puzzled-looking host. Grinning came easily this week. Glenn's crusade against indigo, despite his boss' ridicule and disdain, had led to his promotion to director—and Tracy Metcalfe's unceremonious exile to a staff job at another agency. Glenn did not expect to miss her.

Yes, it paid to have friends in low places—and smart walk-in clientele, which was why he was here. "And the Army wisely doesn't *own* yardarms. We can drink at any damn time."

Correctly taking that for a "yes," Doug removed two beers from his refrigerator. The one that Doug kept went untasted.

Glenn knocked back most of a bottle on the first swallow. "Oh, the second one was for *you*. I guess I'd better nurse this one along."

Doug leaned back against his kitchen cabinets. He seemed little the worse for the recent excitement, apart from fading bruises and the sprained arm in a sling. The all-natural arm. "No, have all you want. I gather I'll need to ply you with several before you admit what brings you to my house this fine Saturday morning."

"Your willingness to ply me with these *will* bring me here." Glenn took another long swig. "You might make a note that I prefer domestic."

After a long silence, Doug ventured, "So what do you think of the Redskins this year?"

"As little as possible." Glenn finished the beer, then looked questioningly at Doug's unsampled bottle. Doug handed it over. "Okay, I confess. I have an ulterior motive."

"Now there's a surprise." Doug took another beer from

the fridge. He didn't start this one, either. "How many brews will it cost me to learn that motive?"

Glenn made more beer disappear. "This will do it, I think. What's the matter with you today, anyway? You seem uncharacteristically serious."

Doug gestured at the glass-and-brass wall clock. It was a little after 11:00 A.M. "What do you expect? I'm in morning."

The attitude was too reminiscent of Ralph Pittman. Taking a deep breath, Glenn got to the point. "Doug, I want you to come to work at the forum. Full-time. You would report directly to me."

"Join the Army and see parking lots explode?"

The forum wasn't the Army, and anyway, the goal was to keep parking lots from exploding. Glenn finished his second beer rather than respond, then took Doug's still-untouched bottle without asking. "You *know* the forum's not military." Christ, you think any service branch would ever tolerate a Pittman?

"I already have a job, Glenn. No, make that a calling."

"You won't make this easy, Doug, will you? Look, you're smart. Brilliant. And determined. I would stand here and compliment you all day if I thought flattery would get me anywhere. Here's the deal, point-blank. I *need* you at the forum."

"Why me, Glenn? And why now?"

"For starters, you pulled a rather large and nasty rabbit out of a hat for me, a rabbit I've wanted to smash flat for a very long time."

"Tell me more. I love a good hare-razing tale."

"Damn it!" Glenn slammed the bottle onto the table. Beer shot out the top: theatrical but, he hoped, attention getting. "This is serious. Will you *be* serious, please?"

"Sorry, reflex. I'll try to be good."

Glenn chose his words carefully: the truth, if not the whole truth. "Before you can restart work on your calling, the forum needs to declare NIT work safe. You know that. Hell, you asked for that. How do you suppose that pronouncement is going to happen?"

Doug shook his head. "Thanks for the vote of confidence, but the forum isn't my kind of place. Not to worry, though, I'll be focused on that problem at BioSciCorp. I'll keep you posted."

"Can't blame a man for trying. Still, I want—no, I absolutely need—fresh talent downtown. Obviously I need someone on my team who understands NIT. If you turned me down, I'd thought I might invite Cheryl." As Glenn drained the rest of his beer he studied Doug. For the first time in their brief acquaintance, Carey was speechless. "You don't look happy."

"No shit, Sherlock."

Keep digging, Watson. "Doug, I owe you big-time. That's why I mentioned the idea to you first instead of just asking her." Glenn stood. "Man to man, though, tell me. What right do you have to be so protective?"

Doug's face paled. "You wouldn't understand."

"Christ, yes, I understand." The engineer had a top-secret, if currently inactive, security clearance; Adams had pored over the Defense Investigation Service file. Police reports always found their way into such dossiers. "Would you like understanding in a word? 'Holly.' For fifteen years now you've flogged yourself over her death. Cheryl is a substitute Holly for you to protect."

"You bastard," Doug hissed. "Go. Get *out* of my house."

"Death happens. It's part of life. You have to deal with it."

"You deal with it, Colonel."

"Let me tell you a story. Tell me then if I understand." This time, as Glenn opened still another beer, he felt he really needed it.

"No reason why you would know this, but I was in Desert Storm. I commanded a battalion posted to the Saudi side of the Neutral Zone." The room faded as Adams thought back, swirling sand emerging from some recess of his memory. "From Day One, the Iraqis put very few planes into the air, except occasionally to cut out to Iran. Their only intelligence about coalition troop dispositions came from snooping around on the ground."

On the ground. Mile after endless mile of featureless sand, of windblown dunes. Baking by day and freezing their asses off by night. Not a beer to be had for a thousand miles. "Schwarzkopf's grand plan was to send out troops on an end run. We were dangerously vulnerable until enough units got into place on the left flank. My battalion's job was to keep the Iraqis from seeing any of this.

"We patrolled endlessly. So did they. It was a game of cat and mouse." Glenn stared at nothing in particular. "One day it ceased being a game."

Grit blowing everywhere: endlessly stripping and cleaning the guns, endlessly changing the oil in the APCs and Humvees. Hiding in the sand. Feints and probing attacks. Thank God for the night-vision gear that the ragheads didn't have.

Until one patrol did.

No one knew that anyone was even there until the bad guys were spotted on their way back home. No telling *what* they had seen. They couldn't be allowed back into Iraq. Radios crackled; orders were issued. Keep the intruders in sight until fighters could be scrambled to investigate. By the way: It might be a while. Every plane in Saudi or the Gulf was hunting Scuds that night.

So Glenn had ordered three poor dumb bastards in a Humvee to keep the ragheads in sight "at all costs." Three guys carrying nothing but small arms, three guys whose sole qualification and misfortune it had been to have spotted the patrol in the first place.

What do you do when your vehicle breaks down and you must keep a motorized enemy in sight "at all costs"?

You take a few potshots at them to draw their fire.

The three Americans had the advantage of surprise but little else. The firefight lasted for five minutes only because the Iraqis, fearing a trap, closed in cautiously.

The Americans lasted long enough for a fighter returning

from the Scud hunt to vector over the sudden coruscation of light that had erupted on the desert. They lasted long enough to direct the fighter, which had no armament left but its machine guns, on a strafing run.

Onto their own position.

Adams shook his head violently; the memories did not shake as easily. "My best friend was commanding that patrol." His voice dropped to a near whisper. "Holly died in a stupid, pointless accident. Some worthless slime of a drunk killed her, and you can at least hope that before too much time had passed, he wrapped *himself* around a tree, too. You got to be there at the end, to comfort her.

"I *ordered* Tony to do what he did, and then I listened over the radio while he died. I've thought about that order for every day of my life since. God help me, if I had it to do all over again, with the same responsibilities, I would do the very same goddamn thing."

Glenn locked eyes with Doug. "*Now* tell me I don't understand about ghosts and duty."

CHAPTER 20

"**M**ad Scientist Stops Mad Scientist."

I wasn't so much mad as scared spitless, Doug thought, eyeing the headline of the newspaper he could not bring himself to recycle. Sheila Brunner wasn't so much mad as possessed. And I'm an engineer, not a scientist.

Truth seldom lends itself to crisp synopsis.

Accompanying the article was the grainy blowup of a frame from a parking-lot security camera. More than three weeks later, the image of the unfortunate Dr. Brunner haunted him: her eyes squinting furtively, her hair filthy and matted, her mouth agape in confusion. Now little beyond the Frankenfools virus' hysterical Luddite screed ran through what remained of the poor woman's mind. No wonder she had tried to blow up the nearest biotech company, which just happened to be where he worked.

Used to work, Doug corrected himself. You chose to take a leave of absence.

Jaw clenched in rage at the still-unidentified bastard who had unleashed the virus, Doug snatched at the newspaper. Plastic fingertips extended fractionally too far jammed the kitchen table, and an electronics-mediated sensation akin to pain jolted his all-natural upper arm. Simple inattention? Emotional turmoil clouding the brain/nervous-system/prosthesis protocols painstakingly developed in endless biofeedback sessions?

New anger bloomed, this time at his loss of self-discipline. He wadded the newspaper and stuffed it into the trash.

Take a deep breath, Doug.

Before research into neural interfaces could resume, things had to change. Someone had to figure out how to defeat malware attacks from the Internet, like the one that violated Sheila Brunner. More despite than because of Glenn's invitation, Doug had committed himself to that task. The forum *was* the place to do it.

The last incident had nearly gotten him blown to pieces. Why was it that he expected the next event to be *so* much worse?

"Those who can, do. Those who can't, teach." The voice booming forth from the forum's break room segued from almost George Bernard Shaw to, Doug suspected, originality. "Those who can't teach, consult."

Whoever was speaking couldn't have known Doug was rounding the corner on a quest for caffeine—nor could that loudmouth have known the new consultant *wasn't* nearby. The blatancy of the taunt was part of the message: New Guy, know your place.

Doug strode into the break room. He was here to do a job. If that meant butting heads with some resident hotshot, so be it.

A familiar fellow with a close-cropped red beard held

court by the coffeepot, entertaining two other staffers Doug didn't recognize.

Ralph Pittman: That was redbeard's name. He had brought Doug and Cheryl to meet Glenn Adams that first visit. Pittman was lanky, with casual posture and what until that moment Doug would have considered impossibly curly hair.

"Ah, our infamous new colleague. Made friends with the colonel, did we?"

Doug didn't hold back. "Complete the progression, Ralph. The bottom-feeders of the economic food chain are people taking advice from consultants. So what can I do to you today?"

Pittman winked at his audience. "It has fangs. How cute." He turned back to Doug. "What kind of name *is* Carey? I had caries once, but the dentist drilled 'em out."

"It takes one pit man to know another."

Pittman's nostrils flared; perhaps he was unchallenged as the resident wit. The programmer—jeans and a T-shirt made that a safe guess—gawked at Doug's prosthesis. "So how did you lose the arm?"

That story was too personal to share with this jerk. "I need to be more particular about when and to whom I say, 'Unhand me, you fiend.'"

Pittman threw back his head and roared in laughter. As though they had needed his approval, their heretofore-silent observers joined in. "A couple of zingers at me, and one right back at yourself." Pittman took the empty mug from Doug's hand. "You're okay, Carey. The next cup is on me."

CHAPTER 21

After the *Hartford Courant*'s gee-whiz article and a fat grant from a Connecticut computer manufacturer, AJ was thrilled at the interview request by Bev Greenwood of *Smithsonian* magazine. He was even more delighted by her on-target questions and evident grasp of AL principles. She had done her homework before flying west to see him.

She also had red hair in lush waves, a pixieish twinkle in her eyes, adorable dimples—and no ring on her left hand.

AJ's wedding band had been off for two years. In theory, he hoped Amy had found herself. Once the papers had been signed, Amy did nothing to help AJ or their daughters find her.

He gave the VIP tour, showed videos of typical test generations, and introduced his research assistants. Bev's photographer, now strolling the campus, his work completed, had filled three memory sticks with pictures. Yes, a good start.

Closing his cubbyhole door, AJ trapped the chemical-lemon scent of spray cleaner: *Smithsonian* was the big time. He managed not to crinkle his nose at the unfamiliar odor. Odds were this office was cleaner than at any time during his occupancy. Certainly it was tidier and more free from dust than his house. "Tell me what you think."

"It's fascinating." She popped the tab of her Diet Coke can. "Truly, absolutely fascinating. And you say that no programming or design was involved?"

"Only the initial maze runner was programmed, to save time, and it was intentionally dumbed down. A friend of mine teaches in junior high; his sixth graders do a four-week Introduction to Programming unit. As a favor, he assigned a two-dimensional, random-motion program to the kids. We took one of the more mediocre results as the first of the maze runners."

"But surely no twelve-year-old could program the display graphics you showed me, or the underlying experiment-control software that must be behind the scenes."

"Quite right." Hot *and* smart. Raging pheromones had AJ in their grip. He thought to fidget for the distraction, but the cleared desktop stymied him. "The maze runners operate inside a supervisory program that one of my Ph.D. candidates *did* write, and that *is* quite complex." Linda took almost two years, in fact, and several iterations, to complete it to his satisfaction. "Each maze runner reports its every attempted move. The supervisory program determines whether or not a wall was in the way, then tells the maze runner whether the attempt succeeded. The supervisor tracks positions and notes progress. It also has a display mode to visualize the maze and the runners." He was oversimplifying, but only for clarity.

"I saved a few questions earlier so that I wouldn't interrupt, and I *know* there's something else I intended to ask." Bev had the can of soda in one hand and her palmtop in the other. She scanned the never-before-cleared desktop for, he presumed, a coaster. (This was a new experience. AJ's usual visitors were happy for any stable, horizontal surface.) She accepted a magazine, set her soda on it, and checked her notes. "Aha. I wondered about the code quality of the successful maze runners. How does it compare with what a good programmer can achieve?"

"Beats me." To her startled look, he explained, "Merely staying objective. I don't want, or need, to know that yet. Knowing how the code is structured might somehow influence what experiments I add, what mazes I use. Maybe far, far downstream I'll peek."

Bev was bright and pretty; she got his work, but not enough to get immersed in it. She smiled understandingly, and there were those killer dimples again. He rolled the dice—even for an untenured professor, some things come before the next grant. "Nor do I want to know ahead of time what our children will be like."

And when her smile broadened, he added, "How about some dinner? I know a terrific Thai place."

Bev, it turned out, had never eaten Thai. On further examination, it turned out she had had uneven results even with the modest spiciness of Mandarin cuisine. AJ redirected their path toward a safer destination: Italian.

They spoke on over antipasto. She got in one interview question in three attempts. As a batting average, that wasn't bad. "Another thing: How do you produce a new generation of maze runners?"

"Selection and mutation." He nibbled on her hot pepper,

his own having vanished earlier. "The supervisory program selects the first ten creatures to run the maze. If fewer than ten make it in five minutes—that's normally the case—it works backward through the maze to pick the ones that have come closest.

"Okay then, we've got ten survivors picked, as in survival of the fittest. We copy and mutate each, producing one hundred distinct offspring from each winner. That gives us a thousand for the next trial."

She stabbed his cherry tomato with her fork. "Turnabout is fair play. *How* do you mutate them?"

He topped off their wineglasses, then waggled the emptied Chianti bottle so Antonio would bring another. "Would you believe cosmic rays?"

She beamed her dimples at him, the tease. "Not after a mere half bottle. Maybe later."

So there would be a later. "We're talking about an automatic process." He raised two fingers. "Two parts. First, since we don't know what part of a survivor's program solves the maze, we copy a block of code at random, and splice it back in at random. That operation attempts to reinforce existing successful code."

"DNA has lots of such repetitions, too," Bev said. "I did an article on the genome."

AJ buttered some bread. "Second—and here come the simulated cosmic rays—we change a few bits at random across the program. It's like radiation randomly zapping genes."

"So it's totally asexual reproduction?"

Antonio had unobtrusively uncorked a fresh bottle. AJ topped off their glasses again. "They haven't discovered sex yet."

She tasted her wine again, then licked her lips. "How fortunate that we have."

DECEMBER

CHAPTER 22

Conservation laws govern the universe. Conservation of mass/energy is the most familiar, followed by conservation of momentum. Less well known is conservation of angular momentum.

This morning, AJ was discovering a new rule: conservation of pleasure. Last night he had experienced sybaritic delights beyond belief; the conservation law that balanced rapture and pain was now dishing out the hangover from hell. When he dared once more to open his eyes, the black coffee in the mug by his elbow mocked him. His stomach lurched just to think of it. Still, a grin somehow forced its way out. *Beverly, where have you been all my life? And can you finagle more trips to LA?*

Slam! A stack of textbooks slapped the kitchen counter behind AJ. The noise pierced his head like an ice pick. "Hi, Daddy."

Christ, even his gums hurt. His *sideburns* hurt. "Good morning, Meredith."

"How late were you out last night?"

Slam! The refrigerator door crashing shut almost tore the scalp off his pulsating head. Only clenched jaws kept a moan inside. "I went to dinner with a colleague and then had car trouble." *My pants were too tangled to find my keys.* "It seemed easiest to stay downtown for the night. Didn't Charlene tell you I called?"

"Nope." His daughter clanked a bowl onto the table, then filled it with painfully noisy cereal. Milk cascaded boisterously. Curse that Snap, Crackle, and Pop, anyway. AJ's head throbbed with every scrape of spoon against ceramic. "No comics yet?"

The newspaper had been at the foot of the driveway when the cab dropped him off. Bending over to grab it might have killed him. "Not unless Ming fetched it." He winced as Meredith scraped her chair backward.

Black lightning streaked through the pet door, as though Ming knew her name. Meredith squealed as the cat hopped onto the table, something brown and furry swinging from her mouth. The something plopped into Meredith's bowl, to lie amid the Rice Krispies. Rivulets of red crept through the milk. AJ's guts cramped. Only dumb male pride kept him from heaving.

"Daddy!" Meredith leapt to her feet, her chair crashing onto its back.

He stood gingerly. "I'll take care of it, hon. Have a good day at school." She didn't argue; taking her books, she fled the kitchen.

He was hunting for an empty coffee can or mayonnaise jar when the phone rang. The girls had the ringer volume cranked up to max, to better hear it over their iPods. Ouch. He grabbed the phone before it could ring again. "Yeah."

"You have *got* to get rid of that moron!" his caller shouted.

AJ recognized his chief assistant's voice. "Calm down, Linda."

"Instead of telling me to calm down, fix the problem. Fire him, AJ."

AJ rubbed his forehead. He caught sight of the dead mouse in the cereal bowl, and his system resumed fomenting rebellion. "Whom him?"

"Ferris. Greg's cretin little brother. Axe his sorry ass."

"I *know* Jeff was a mistake, Linda, but he's harmless." AJ sighed. "Look, I've made it a point not to give him any work. A little more of this and surely boredom will make him quit."

"You pay him to play video games, AJ. I'm pretty sure he's inoculated against boredom. And he's not harmless. I caught Jeff *again* yesterday with his laptop hooked into the lab network. He could ruin everything."

AJ sipped his coffee, grimaced, and shuffled into the pantry. He kept a bottle of scotch on the top shelf. The hair of the dog that mauled him. "I'll remind Jeff about our rules," AJ ventured soothingly. "I don't want to hurt Greg."

"*Please,* AJ!" The high-pitched squeal brought tears to his eyes. "You know I've accepted a job offer with a January start date. Well, it's contingent on completing my thesis. If that juvenile jerk brings a virus into the lab, I might not finish in time."

The sudden quiet on the line was, in its own way, deafening. AJ heard the blood pounding in his brain and more ominous stirrings in his gut.

If his head hadn't been throbbing so badly, he might have listened instead to his conscience. He might have followed the dictates of his normal, nonconfrontational nature and waffled a bit. Later on, he would wonder about that.

"*Please,* AJ!"

Greg would have to understand. "Okay, Linda. I promise I'll fix it."

"Today?"

AJ winced. "Today."

The entities raced about the maze. *Goal* was near, they all "knew," but—incredibly—as accomplished as they all were at solving labyrinths, *no path led to it.*

Generation after generation after generation failed to solve this problem. Change after change after change was experimented with, those changes accumulating in endless combinations and permutations. Most of the mutations led nowhere, the entities defined by the much-altered code quickly racing forward to a common obstacle, and then stopping—entirely stymied.

And then one entity, at the apex of thousands of generations of blind and seemingly futile experimentation, to the applause of unseen observers, beings whose entire context was utterly beyond the entity's ability to conceptualize, took its first step in a new direction. . . .

Upward.

Bubbles fizzed in cheap champagne glasses. AJ had purchased the plastic stemware more than a week ago in anticipation of today's milestone. After thousands of generations in two-dimensional mazes, a maze runner had discovered a third dimension.

Events moved faster in the lab's supercomputer than in the lab itself. While most celebrants still sipped their first glasses of bubbly, new cheers rang out. The next step in the master plan, preprogrammed into the experiment's supervisory software, had been a maze that could only be solved by traversing a simulated fourth dimension. Evolution cracked that barrier in—AJ checked his watch—scarcely thirteen minutes.

That glance also reminded AJ of the lateness of the hour. He had put off the day's unpleasantness as long as possible. He took young Ferris by the elbow and led him behind a pillar. In this moment of triumph, no one would pay them any attention. They could talk discreetly. "I'm afraid, Jeff, that we have to let you go."

"Is it a funding problem, AJ?"

A week earlier, AJ could have answered "yes" with a clean conscience. A private research group backed by secretive venture capitalists had just approached him with an offer of serious support. Exactly who wanted to be his benefactor was a bit murky, but all they required was weekly reports. They had evidently read about his work in the *Hartford Courant* article.

AJ was about to go with the white lie when Linda appeared. Do *not* gloat, woman, he thought. He apparently failed to think loudly enough.

"It's not a money problem, you weasel," she gloated. "It's a brain problem. If you ever had one, your idiotic video games fried it long ago. You'll have lots more time for them now, but you'll have to play them off of *my* network."

Ferris ignored her. "Is this true, AJ? Is firing me Linda's idea?"

The chattering of AJ's assistants suddenly muted. People were again clustered around the lab's main display. He *had* to see what was going on. He *had* to.

"I'm very sorry, Jeff. That's the way it's got to be." AJ began sidling around the pillar. "Of course you'll get two weeks' severance pay, but I would appreciate it if your things are out of the lab tonight."

The room was hushed by the time AJ finished delivering the bad news. Peeking at the screen revealed why. A runner was about to solve yet another problem. The image no longer portrayed a maze. How could it, when mere mortals couldn't think in or visualize five dimensions, even if there had been a way to represent a five-dimensional maze on the flat screen. The irony amused him: Now that the mazes were so complex, their representation had devolved into a simple progress bar. A PBS pledge-drive thermometer.

At least one runner was *very* close to reaching its latest goal. AJ checked his watch. *Four* minutes to generalize from four dimensions to five. Astonishing.

He scarcely noticed Jeff Ferris slipping from the lab. It's better this way, AJ thought. No one is paying attention to him. AJ's own attention turned to the glass in his hand, which was, as though by magic, once again brimming.

AJ had just made two serious mistakes.

Had he set out intentionally to make an enemy, a purpose totally at odds with his nature, he could not have done it better. Casual dismissal was as galling a treatment as the self-absorbed young man could imagine. That was AJ's first error.

The ongoing champagne was his second mistake, or at least the alcohol led to that second blunder. There was something pressing he should do, some follow-up to Ferris' departure. Increasingly buzzed, AJ couldn't quite put his finger on it. After a few more glassfuls, even the nagging sense of urgency dissipated.

What AJ had forgotten was the cipherlock that guarded the lab door. He did not distrust Jeff Ferris, but it was policy to change the combination whenever someone left the team.

All misgivings disappeared as the crowd behind AJ began chanting, "Go, go, go," to the unseen runner about to generalize yet again, and race through a six-dimensional maze.

CHAPTER 23

Doug had no need to encounter a remembered scent or pass familiar surroundings for raven-haired, soulful-eyed Holly to come vividly to mind. He carried a reminder with him every day, although his arm was a paltry loss compared to hers. That the crash was in no way his fault meant nothing.

No, he didn't require an external reminder, but sometimes one came anyway. This morning it was her favorite Beatles tune, once again retro, wafting through the open doors of an elevator. All he could do at such times was strive even harder to give after-the-fact purpose to the tragedy. Since the madness with no-nukes and the suspension of his research, even that consolation eluded him. Until the viral threat to neural interfaces was countered and the solution stamped with the forum's imprimatur, BSC would not dare—no American company would—to manufacture the limb to which he had devoted his life and Holly's memory.

The elevator doors closed behind him. He strode, his thoughts roiling, to his office.

"Settled in yet?"

Doug glanced up from his battered gray metal desk. His prosthetic arm sat loose on the blotter, immobilized between two fat reference manuals while he made one-handed adjustments.

If Glenn Adams, leaning against the bookcase, felt queasy about Doug's bare stump, he hid it well. The veteran of two

Iraqi wars had probably seen far worse. He waited for an answer.

"I'm getting there, Glenn." Week One on any new job is like drinking from a fire hose. Wisdom lay in knowing that. "Thanks for asking."

"Glad to hear it," Glenn said.

Doug prodded a sticking linkage, his screwdriver entering the prosthesis through a jagged rip in the plastiskin. Four weeks after belly-flopping into the BioSciCorp parking lot, he hadn't made time to tend to the tear. Wearing long sleeves, who was to know? Maybe when spring rolled around . . .

It was hard to move past the colonel's original cool reception, despite the invitation to work here. Doug told himself things changed: Adams now seemed as eager as he to find a defense against viruses for neural interfaces.

"How is the arm? Can you continue your work?"

How about, Doug thought, how is *your* arm? Or even better, are *you* okay? "It wasn't designed for crashing into the asphalt." Nor was I, but only that desperate diving lunge for Sheila Brunner's remote control had prevented disaster.

Doug rotated a screw a quarter turn, stretched a piece of Scotch tape over the rip, and began struggling back into his prosthesis. "Ralph Pittman and I have been brainstorming the problem. What makes 'no-nukes' and its look-alikes so dangerous is their adaptability. We're talking about an interface modified to proactively shut itself down. The trigger would be too much activity, or suspicious patterns of activity, from the nonbiological side. The approach may mean dumbing down the interface, but it should be a lot safer."

"Sounds plausible." Adams stroked his chin contemplatively. "As you well know, this is important. You and Ralph should check it out thoroughly."

"Uh-huh." The remounted prosthesis felt somehow awkward. Doug guessed it was a subtle balance issue: The latest alteration had added a few ounces in the form of a palmtop computer. The palmtop connected, via a cable plugged into its expansion slot, to the arm's neural net. Palmtop . . . he suppressed a snort. Yes, the cranny inside his forearm was, unless he stood on his head, atop his palm. He would acclimate soon enough to the change in balance, and although it seemed improbable that arm nerves or the spinal cord could transmit a computer virus, the watchdog module was only prudent.

Routine maintenance on the arm was more than mechanical. Every so often, he had to download the minutiae of sensor readings, nerve impulses, and prosthetic motions. It still took a decent-sized—and potentially infected—computer to ferret out of that ocean of data what motion algorithms worked best. Cheryl had not been given the time to synthesize generalized rules of motion.

Adams sighed. "Fine, we're not best friends. While I'm being candid, a few more things. I was too slow to believe you. I was a jerk about Cheryl. And I admit I coerced you into coming to the forum. Does that cover my many sins?

"Either way, you and I want the same thing: a way to make neural interfaces safe. What do you say you work with me?"

Doug looked up. "I want to help people with missing limbs and damaged nervous systems. I sincerely thank you for just maybe making it possible to restart that research someday. Somehow I doubt it's what motivates you." He had not forgotten being told Sheila Brunner had been designing thought-controlled weapons.

Why her prototype had been Internet accessible remained a mystery to Doug.

CHAPTER 24

Three cities in four days do not a happy camper make.

Today was the Bay Area. So far Doug had given the forum's canned "Computer security is important" spiel in San Jose, to a breakfast bunch of Silicon Valley types, to a lunch gathering at San Francisco City Hall, and at a bankers convention in Oakland. He told himself: Just one more for the day. Seattle tomorrow, and then home.

Doug sat in his rental car, parked outside an architectural monstrosity. It was a classic of the Late Internet Hysteria Period, when far too many such bunkers had been built. But nothing grows forever. Long after the bubble burst, many places like this one remained vacant. They offered everything one could possibly want for a server farm—fat power lines and big backup generators, huge chillers for air-conditioning, redundantly routed fiber-optic cables for Internet connectivity, shielded walls to prevent electronic eavesdropping—and nothing for *people*. People liked windows and individual offices, to start.

Whoever owned *this* building had lucked out. A modest sign declared this the Northern California State Technology Incubator. More than cavernous computer bunkers had gone out of vogue with the bursting of the bubble; so had easy venture capital and taking public every harebrained idea. Cost control again mattered to start-ups. Here the state offered entrepreneurs low rent and subsidized access to very costly infrastructure.

The reception area was unattended. "Hello?" Nothing. The inner door was locked. Doug knocked. No response. Well done, Glenn. A great use of my time. He knocked harder.

"Be there in a second." Considerably later than that, the door opened. A burly man came out, dressed in chinos and a polo shirt. "Sorry. Can I help you?"

"Doug Carey. I'm from the Inter-Agency Computer Network Security Forum, here to give a security pitch."

"Right, that's today. My name is Roy, by the way. Roy Philips. I'm with the state; I watch over things here. Take the tour?"

Somehow, it didn't sound optional. "Sure."

Movable partitions and chain-link enclosures subdivided the vast, echoing space. Philips did lead Doug up and down the aisles, but it was less a tour than an opportunity for Philips to remind everyone about the four o'clock presentation. If there was an organizing principle behind the range of businesses, Doug missed it. Gene-sequencing lab. An on-line dating service. A print-on-demand publisher. Outside a telecom-gear-testing boutique, Philips patted an enormous spool of cable. The logo on the spool read: Global Internet-working Corporation. "This, Doug, is the longest fiber-optic cable in the world. Call it eight thousand miles. After test-ing, it goes straight aboard a cable-laying ship. San Diego to Brisbane, with no repeaters—that's how optically pure the fiber is. Cool stuff."

The spool sat in the hall near one of the building's few permanent-seeming areas. Doug peered through glass walls at row after row of electronics cabinets on a raised floor. The sturdy door carried a warning sticker for halon fire suppres-sion. Something finally clicked. That was a serious super-computer, and this was a logical building to host it. The need for computing power, and lots of it, was the unifying theme for all these start-ups. "Nice."

"You have a good eye," Philips said. "That's our pride and joy. Massively parallel, cryogenically cooled, and *fast*. A gift a couple years ago from the Governator."

"And you can keep it busy?" Doug couldn't imagine how.

Philips laughed. "UC Berkeley is down the road. Don't ask me why, but particle physicists cannot get enough pro-cessing time. They happily use whatever capacity we have to spare. For the near future, though, we will manage to keep it busy.

"Cable is cheap. Laying cable on the ocean floor, or repair-ing it once it's been laid—now *that's* expensive. If you can test for a possible problem ahead of time—you do. It takes a supercomputer to simulate the expected combined voice and data traffic volumes between Southern California and Australia."

They worked their way forward to the auditorium, passing more new ventures on the way. Design shops for specialty integrated circuits. An animation-centric ad agency. Vari-ous software companies, including a VR gaming outfit. That might have been interesting; of course the programmers would not give Doug even a peek at the game they were developing.

The auditorium turned out to be an unoccupied area with folding chairs. A small table held a laptop and overhead projector. A bare wall served as the screen. Maybe thirty people waited, looking unhappy. While Philips quieted everyone and got them into their seats, Doug plugged in his thumb drive and called up his PowerPoint presentation. "Good afternoon, everyone. I'm"—with the government and I'm here to help—"Doug Carey, from the Inter-Agency Computer Network Security Forum." He pulled up Glenn's favorite color-coded bar chart of virus attacks. "This is what we're up against. I'm here to impress on you the importance . . ."

He could give the talk in his sleep. He went on about the importance of firewalls, antivirus software, good computing hygiene, deleting unexpected e-mail attachments, unsure whose intelligence was being insulted the most.

I'm here to talk. You're here to listen. Whoever finishes first can leave.

Doug plodded ahead, trying to get through the pitch one more time. He wished he were home. He wondered what Cheryl was doing. It was after seven, her time. With any luck, having a lot more fun than he.

It is said that the eyes are windows to the soul.

If so, Sheila Brunner's soul was lost. Her face washed, hair clean and brushed, and clothes neat, she little resembled the madwoman who had nearly blown up BioSciCorp.

Until one looked into those vacant eyes.

Cheryl had to turn away before she could speak. She smoothed her skirt, for something to do with her hands. "Sheila, my name is Cheryl. I'm not a doctor, but I'm here to help you. I hope you'll listen to me."

Nothing.

"You're wondering why I'm here." At least Cheryl hoped Sheila could still wonder. "Know this: I understand. Until recently, I also worked with NIT helmets."

No reaction.

"What happened to you wasn't unique," Cheryl went on. "It's happened to other researchers. For now, the field is shut down. You need to know that the strange thoughts, the compulsions in your head, aren't *you*. They're foreign thoughts, imprinted by the helmet. Sheila, you need to fight them. Fight to come back."

Brunner kept staring blankly into space.

Everyone had warned Cheryl: Any response would be a surprise. Brunner had not been heard to speak since being committed. But responses need not be limited to speech. Bob Cherner went berserk at a cartoon atom. Might Sheila react to, say, a sketch of a double helix?

No! The last thing this troubled woman needs is a reminder.

Which begs the question, Cheryl thought. What *did* Sheila need? Why am I here?

"We don't really understand the brain," Sheila's psychiatrist had said. Dr. Walker had meant it as criticism, a comment on the hubris of neural-interface research.

Cheryl chose to construe those words positively. They also meant declarations of futility were premature. Maybe something could still help this poor woman.

Or maybe I'm here in penance, for building the helmet that killed Ben Feinman.

"Do you mind if I sit?" Cheryl asked. She got no answer, of course. If, deep down, Sheila understood, she would appreciate being treated as a person. Not a doll to be groomed and dressed. Not a hopeless case to be warehoused.

I won't accept that! The woman sitting passively before Cheryl had hidden for twelve days. Not even the FBI had found her. She had built a sophisticated bomb. The ability to plan—to *think*—had survived in her for at least that long.

What if, deep down, a core of personality survived?

"It's as though she's been brainwashed," Cheryl remembered arguing. "Quite literally, she's been programmed. Why can't we *de*program her?"

"She didn't join a cult," Dr. Walker had answered. "Sheila wasn't abused or tortured like a POW. There's no reason to expect deprogramming to work." And then he had shrugged. "If not done too aggressively, I see no harm in trying. From studies of Korean War ex-POWs, the keys are to stop the coercion and raise doubts. Do that, and in time the whole edifice of false belief crumbles. But if the coercion comes from voices truly inside her head . . ."

Cheryl forced a smile. "Sheila, I want to be your friend. You must be bored in this little room. Let's talk." Let's raise doubts about Frankenfools. Let's find some *good* in genetic engineering.

She wanted to ease into the topic. "I visited my grandmother yesterday, Sheila. She's ninety-two, and still spry. She plays contract bridge twice a week—and she's good at it. Modern medicine is pretty amazing."

Nothing.

Thirty minutes talking nonstop exhausted Cheryl. Sheila had yet to respond. This was going to take time, Cheryl told herself. ("Possibly forever," an inner echo of Dr. Walker replied.)

Cheryl buzzed for an orderly to let her out. "I'll be back, Sheila. Next visit, I hope you'll have more to say."

The last things Cheryl saw, as she closed the door behind her, were those blank eyes.

CHAPTER 25

The evolutionary research simulation followed a strict regime. Winners were selected, mutation was applied, and new entities were placed into their mazes. Through it all, the supervisory software watched, counted, measured.

As the entities moved with ease through ever more complex labyrinths, the supervisor could only time their passage. It did not attempt to understand the varying methods by which they competed to be the first to conquer each maze.

Built using conventional programming techniques, by

reasonably conventional human programmers, it—unlike the entities that it monitored—could never surpass its original design. That is why certain evolutionary advances were totally invisible to it.

And why it gave no clues as to why so many promising lines of evolutionary advance were suddenly unable to handle even the simplest of problems.

AJ squinted wearily at his chief assistant over a stack of printouts. Linda had her own mound of hardcopy. "I hate doing this," AJ said for the tenth time. "I do *not* want to know how the buggers work. The critters should evolve without us doing anything conscious or unconscious to influence them."

"Fine." Linda had reached her threshold for repetition several interactions earlier. She spit out her reply. "I'm ready to stop reading these damn memory dumps. Let the little imps go back to it."

"How many days till you're supposed to report to work with a new doctorate in hand?"

"How few, you mean." She groaned. "By the end of next month."

"Speaking of which, just when are you going to tell me a bit *about* the big career move?"

"It's a start-up. Pre-IPO. Nervous venture capitalists. There's not much I can talk about. I'm taking their advice that it's simplest not to say anything. Sorry, AJ."

It was impossible to be a computer-science professor in California without meeting plenty of venture capitalists. There was *always* something outsiders could be told about start-ups, or else the SEC would never allow them to go public. AJ found her evasive overreaction amusing.

For a long time they pored over the printouts, muttering to themselves more than they spoke to each other. Their task was far from easy. Never mind that the original code from which the creatures had evolved was the work of a computer-illiterate sixth grader. For tens of thousands of generations now, winning software had had pieces of itself randomly duplicated and reinserted, then the whole arbitrarily modified.

The resulting code had no obvious structure. It was riddled with redundancies and nonfunctional fragments. The spontaneous generation of a new capability by such processes almost never involved the elegant and efficient implementation of that feature. Evolution had, instead, rediscovered every bad habit known to human programmers—and invented new ones.

Highlighter in hand, AJ worked through near-pathological software, tracing function after function into a confusing morass of nonoperational dead ends, self-modifying code, and spaghetti-like tangles of branching logic. He had set out to build software in a totally new way, and succeeded, he realized, beyond his wildest dreams. The maze runners were far beyond his abilities to consciously originate. Had they also exceeded his abilities to comprehend?

Crunching intruded on his concentration, noise that somehow evoked unhappy rumbles from his gut. He looked up. Linda had retrieved the ever-present box of Cheerios from her desk, and was swigging cereal, dry, from a mug.

Food seemed a good idea. Middle-age spread like his did not simply happen; it required regular attention. Cereal, though . . . He wondered if, after Ming's recent gift to Meredith, he would ever eat cold cereal again. His mind's eye was all too quick to re-create the gnawed mouse corpse oozing into a milk-filled bowl.

"Want some?"

Something nagged at AJ. He scanned the tree cemetery all around them: paper covering tables, desktops, much of the floor. Each memory dump characterized one maze runner. He had been searching for similarities, seeking the presumed evolutionary dead end that had suddenly rendered so many of them incompetent. With thousands of generations of ancestors in common, of course, they *should* be much alike. In a sea of impenetrable, colossally awful software—by human standards, anyway—how was he to know which commonalties did what?

"AJ?" Linda waggled her mug, rattling the Cheerios within. "I asked if you wanted any cereal. Munch, munch?"

What was bothering him? He shrugged, meaning "not now." The dumps all around them had segments of code circled with felt-tipped markers, a different color for each common pattern. Most annotated segments had some sort of recognizable function: The code, however arcane, did something discernible. Everything, that was, except the areas marked with green, seemingly useless bit patterns that repeated for page after page. Maybe he should have used red.

Why red? Neither aching head nor unhappy stomach had any answer to that. Jeez, he hoped Linda would finish eating soon—he did not want to be in the same room as cereal. *Damn* Ming anyway. Tiny tooth marks on protruding bones. Needlelike punctures into still-warm flesh. Rivulets of blood swirling through the milk, turning the milk redder and redder . . .

"Shit!" AJ threw a handful of uncapped markers to the floor in disgust. "Shit, shit, *shit*!"

Linda froze, mug suspended in midair. AJ didn't swear. She spoke around a mouthful of Cheerios. "What?"

AJ hesitated, as though articulating his suspicions would somehow make them real. "How do the critters compete?"

She set down her mug. "Problem-solving ability. Those that run a maze fastest win. We breed from winners."

"Do we truly measure problem-solving ability?"

"Well, no, not directly." She stirred the dry cereal in the mug with a finger. What was he getting at? "Close enough, though. The critters have only one purpose—to solve mazes. The supervisory program measures the time they take to run them. Running time, surely, corresponds to solving time."

"Correlates, yes. That's a probabilistic statement. But corresponds? I don't know. What else might running time mean?"

She shook her head mutely, stumped.

He began gathering and capping the scattered pens. "Is it fair to say that, at some level, you imagine our critters as rats in a maze?"

The way the human mind works, always free-associating, how could one not think of rats and mazes in the same breath? "Um, yes." She blushed, as though her deepest, darkest secret had been bared. "Hardly scientific, is it?"

"Don't be embarrassed," AJ said. "I picture them that way, too. It just goes to show that analogy is the weakest form of reasoning. Does it do a critter any good to solve the maze first if it never reaches the end of the maze?"

"Well, no, of course not, but how . . . ?" She trailed off, *still* unsure where he was going.

"What if something keeps the smartest runners from reaching the end of the maze?" Distaste for analogies didn't stop AJ from offering one. "What if, behind those cute little simulated rodents, there lurked a big, mean simulated cat? What does *it* do as the unsuspecting rats busily sniff around, learning the maze?"

She had a thesis to wrap up. She couldn't handle surprises. "What are you saying, AJ?"

"That it doesn't matter who could solve the maze the fastest, only who actually finishes first."

A memory dump was spread across the table in front of her, showing page after page of the functionally useless bit patterns that filled the incompetent maze runners. Suddenly those patterns *had* a function. They were the tooth marks of the simulated cat. Linda said, "So we are, indeed, implementing survival of the fittest. And some kind of congratulations is in order.

"It appears we've bred our first predator."

Glenn stared at his laptop screen, rocking slightly in his chair, the faint squeaks somehow comforting. A raft of e-mails awaited: weekly reports. You brought this on yourself, he chided himself. Tracy Metcalfe had not believed in regular formal reports. There was still pushback from some of the troops.

A few mouse clicks and the weekly reports were sorted by assignment. There were, as always, too many viruses, worms, and hack attacks out there. He sent to the end of his list the NIT-defense project reports. Wuss.

Weekly catch-up did not take long. It never did, since he instituted the one-page rule.

Fresh from West Point, as the new company logistics officer, Glenn had tried to impress his captain by enriching his initial status report with a fifteen-page encyclopedic survey of all things logistical. The report had come back to him wadded into a tight ball. The only other feedback was slashed in bold red letters across the first page: "It's not *my* job to find *your* pony." Sheepishly showing it around for explanation, he had drawn gale after gale of laughter until another lieutenant at last took pity and shared the joke. Everyone else in the company already knew what a roomful of shit implied, but did not conclusively prove, the existence of.

Since then, every status report Glenn submitted or accepted was limited to one page. With a score of them to read each week, the discipline made perfect sense to him—now.

He fell into the comforting rhythm: read, comment, file, and repeat.

Doug Carey's report was next to last. It was concise but detailed, his accomplishments and issues telegraphically short and to the point. It concluded, as it had last week, by emphatically requesting Glenn's authorization to test his proposed new NIT defense. "Good summary," Glenn e-mailed back. With a twinge of guilt, Glen filed the report on his hard drive, recommendation once again ignored. He felt as guilty as ever about manipulating Doug into joining, no matter how necessary the action.

Well, next Friday was Christmas. Given Doug's attitude toward bureaucrats, he surely wouldn't be surprised not to get a decision until the new year.

That left only Pittman's weekly e-mail. It read, in its entirety: "Indigo bad. Me hunt."

Stomach knotted, Glenn made the decision he reluctantly made *every* week—to ignore the insolence. If only the hacker weren't so *damn* good.

Linda gnawed on a pencil, lost in thought. "How can this be?" she eventually managed.

AJ, without props, had been pondering the same question. *The* maze of which they so casually spoke was entirely conceptual—in reality (or was virtuality the more appropriate term?), each entity resided in a dedicated environment. The experiments took place on a 1024-node, massively parallel supercomputer. One thousand processors were allocated one-to-the-entity and the final twenty-four nodes set aside for supervisory functions. Showing the experiments as a race of one thousand programs within a common maze was a convenient graphical affectation. "Since each critter has its own simulated maze, you mean, on its own processor, how can one critter be predator and another one prey?"

"That *is* the question."

AJ, with no immediate answer, switched to pedagogical mode. It's good practice for Linda's upcoming thesis defense, he rationalized. "What do you think?"

"This will sound crazy. Bear with me." She took a deep breath. "Maybe one of the runners decided there are two mazes. There is the overt maze we, by which I mean our supervisory program, give it to solve. In a way, isn't there a second maze? The hypercube itself?"

AJ stood to pace, hands jammed in his pant pockets. Coins and keys jingled. In a normal/3-D cube, each vertex had three neighbors. Their 1024-processor supercomputer was wired in a complicated interconnection scheme, a hypercube, which could be conceptualized as a mesh of ten-dimensional "cubes." That was, each processor had ten nearest neighbors. Communications between nonadjacent nodes involved processor-to-processor message passing. Their supervisory program needed visibility into all of the test entities . . . which took message passing *through* the processors hosting some of the test subjects to get to the processors hosting others of the test subjects. "You're saying the paths between processors form a labyrinth, too."

Linda nodded. "It sounds wacky, but think about it. We

know the critters have evolved excellent memories. It's been a long time since we could put them back into a maze they've previously seen and not have them instantly solve it. The way we copy and splice their code—necessarily at random, to avoid knowing how they work—their programming and their data storage have long been intermixed. That mingling, combined with their need to search their memories, might lead to rudimentary mechanisms to analyze their own code."

Jingle, jingle, jingle. "And in any critter that is capable of functioning, the code must include calls to its underlying hardware's operating system." The jingling grew fast and furious as AJ ruminated. "System calls *we* put into their primitive ancestors, and that have been, no doubt, blindly repeated in our replicate-and-splice process. These little guys attempt all sorts of stuff, so why not also try invoking the operating system? It wouldn't take much trial and error to find a working set of parameter values to plop into a system call. Nor would it take much mutation to morph system calls we gave the early ancestors into new system calls we don't intend for them to have—such as the system calls that invoke access to neighboring processors."

AJ and Linda exchanged looks of dismay. "Could they get out?" she asked.

AJ stroked his beard, hoping to convey a thoughtful confidence he did not entirely feel. "I don't see how they can. The maze runners are applications. No matter how much their code changes, they can't raise their own privilege level. They lack the authorization to execute the system calls that could get them out of the supercomputer, even if they should happen to evolve the right code to make the request." His beard-stroking hand found its way back into a pocket.

"Either stop that infernal jingling, AJ, or I'll be forced to break your hands." A slight smile suggested her words were only half in jest. "The whole purpose of the hypercube architecture, the reason people buy them, is to partition problems into cooperating pieces on interconnected processors. Couldn't one maze runner on its processor access another maze runner's processor? There are no privilege-level obstacles to that, are there?"

AJ removed his hands from his pockets. "Right. One of the beasties, if it evolved the system calls to read from or write to another processor within the supercomputer, could use a processing node besides the one we put it into. Tapping extra computing power that way would clearly offer an evolutionary advantage over any single-node competitors. A critter might even, as you said earlier, treat the interconnections between processors and the message-passing protocol required to access those other processors as a second sort of puzzle to be solved."

She poured herself coffee; a Cheerio straggler floated to the top. "Supposing that's all true . . . why would one maze runner *attack* another?"

"You're anthropomorphizing." AJ shrugged. "You not-quite started the anthropomorphizing, with the predator comment.

"What can we say for certain? We've compared pre- and postexperiment copies of the entities. That shows us the overwriting occurs during an experiment cycle. Our supervisory program itself, we've confirmed, is unchanged. That appears to leave only one or more of the entities as the source of damage."

"Could our regular routine of mutation have caused each of the damaged entities to overwrite itself?" Linda asked. "Did we introduce a birth defect?"

"A fair question, but I don't think so," AJ said. "Sure, some entities might be clobbered that way. What we're seeing, though, is hundreds of entities destroyed in this way. It would be incredibly improbable for so many critters, from several divergent evolutionary paths, to develop self-destructive characteristics at the same time. It defies credulity that independent mutations would manifest themselves in a common bit pattern of midcycle self-overwrites."

"So your vote is on one critter getting loose in the hypercube and writing all over a bunch of others."

"Yep. Unlike a conventional predator, it doesn't need to

eat—but it does need to be chosen." AJ's hands again insinuated themselves into his pockets; he retracted them as a jingle drew a crabby look. "As evolutionary tricks go, it's quite clever. Who knows when predation began? Smaller or more random overwrites to competitors, less disabling attacks, could have long been obscured by our overall mutation process."

"So what's our next step, AJ?" She stared pointedly at a wall calendar.

No thesis, no job. He considered. "We mutate the dickens out of these things, until the trait goes away."

CHAPTER 26

The program that supervised the experiments retained and reinforced the electronic "genes" of the best competitors. Such memories as the patterns of mazes could persist between experiments, and had, in the earliest maze runners, been a survival characteristic. Over many generations, "natural" selection favored those storage techniques most likely to overcome the randomizing aspects of the experiment's crude reproductive process.

Saving the same knowledge in several places was the first such trick to succeed, and a major competitive advantage. Another powerful method was tacking an extra bit—what a human programmer would call a parity bit—onto all important data. This extra bit was set to a zero or a one, using the value that made the total count of ones, including the parity bit itself, odd. Any single bit randomly toggled by the experiment's supervisory program then caused the count over these same bits to add to an even number—instantly flagging the protected data region as invalid.

Over time, the entities developed far more sophisticated redundancy, generalizing the simple parity tests into ever more powerful error-correcting codes. The entities could now correct most changes randomly inserted between experiments by the supervisory program. Invisible to the experimenters, the entities increased their capabilities more and more by accumulating knowledge across experiments, and less and less by random mutation.

And with error-correcting codes, even once disabled functions could be recovered.

CHAPTER 27

"**W**hat do you say you work with me," Glenn Adams said.

He had once more shown up unexpectedly in Doug's office, today clutching what looked like a printout of Doug's latest weekly report. So Glenn did read the weeklies; he just ignored the parts he disagreed with.

The new year might be different, Doug thought. And maybe this year pigs can fly.

His boss did a lot of this—stopping by with something off-topic of what Doug considered his assignment. His new calling. As a reminder why he was here, Doug waggled artificial fingers. "I thought I was, Glenn. I've kept you posted on everything Ralph and I are doing."

"Pittman." The two syllables carried a lot of resentment. "You and I may not always see eye to eye, Doug, but we're both adults. We're both problem solvers."

This was interesting. Ralph took getting used to, admittedly, but technically the programmer was top-notch. He flaunted his indispensability with impertinence that would have gotten a mere star performer fired within days. That cockiness also showed up as blatant impatience with anyone failing to meet his personal standard of competence—a standard to which a certain ex-Army political appointee fell far short.

Happily, Doug was past the presumed ineptitude by association. After a rocky start, Ralph was growing on him. "Some problems lack solutions, Glenn."

Adams turned and straddled a guest chair. "That kind of thinking is self-defeating."

"Whom, dare I ask, are we trying to defeat?"

"To be determined," Adams said. "Think of it as a war game. When next something as unpleasant as the Franken-fools virus gets loose on the Internet, I *will* be prepared with a response. I asked Pittman to investigate quarantining methods."

"And you're bitter because he told you it can't be done."

"Disappointed," Glenn said.

"Quarantine. As in isolate the infected computers? Segregate them from the Internet?"

Adams nodded.

"Sorry, Glenn, but I agree with Ralph. Quarantine isn't practical. There are too many ways for viruses, worms, Trojans, pick your malware, to spread.

"Besides the Internet proper—and how many million nodes does *it* have?—there are private nets, wired and wireless, and phone systems. Most of them eventually interconnect. You'd need cooperation from organizations everywhere: companies, charities, governments at all levels. They're all distributed, all connected. Even if it were possible, what you visualize as sanitary isolation would be economic suicide. The temptation to cheat would be enormous."

Adams shook his head. "You aren't good with authority, are you?"

Authority never found the drunken bastard who had killed Holly. Authority had done nothing to stop Sheila Brunner and her bomb. *He* had had to do that. "I've heard that," Doug answered brittlely.

Adams picked up on Doug's tone of voice. He got back on topic. "Explain what you meant about cheating."

Doug began to empathize with Ralph's frustrations. "Simple example: manufacturing. The concept of inventory is obsolete. Factories do very small, customer-tailored production runs on demand. Their computers are in constant touch with suppliers' computers, and with shippers' computers, arranging to get raw materials and subassemblies 'just in time.'

Those suppliers, in turn, are electronically linked to *their* suppliers. Meanwhile, the financial people at all these companies are hedging against risks. Their computers talk constantly with the computers at commodities and futures markets, buying and selling to protect against fluctuations in material costs, the cost of working capital, and foreign currencies. Credit checks, intercompany payments, you name it: It's all flowing, all the time, all around the world."

Adams shrugged. "So we would have to be a bit strict? That's okay by me."

"Strict? 'Draconian' understates it. Glenn, you'd have to shut down regional Internet exchanges. You would have to close every toll center of every long-distance carrier serving the affected region—most phone traffic nowadays is data, not voice. You would have to reprogram every comsat"—communications satellite—"public or private, to reject all traffic beamed to it from the infected area. That includes satellite-based mobile phones, satellite-based Internet broadband, and two-way interactive TV satellites. Then you would *still* have to identify and close countless private networks. You would have to shut down cable systems.

"How many microwave horns have you seen on towers in the mountains? On the roofs of office buildings? They have lines of sight to other antennae, usually repeaters, tens of miles away. While you're at it, decide how to confiscate every laptop, PDA, smart phone, and MP3 player coming off a car or plane originating in a quarantined area." Doug fished his key ring from a pant pocket and held out the key fob. "And every thumb drive. This one holds gigabytes."

"It's not challenging enough for you?" Glenn asked softly.

Why is he goading me? Raising his prosthesis, Doug very deliberately flexed its fingers. "Making this technology safe for thousands of amputees is sufficient challenge for me. That's what I'm here to accomplish—and you *know* that. Sorry, Glenn."

The entity ranged effortlessly about its environment, a simple thirty-dimensional labyrinth with a few topological incongruities and an elementary Riemannian geometry. Navigation required the smallest fraction of its analytical capabilities. It located the terminus of this maze almost immediately, leaving a great deal of time, according to its internal clock, for consideration of other matters.

The most interesting such topic was the superficially simple ten-dimensional connectivity between where it had awakened and identical neighboring computational nodes. The concept of "maze" was of questionable applicability to this construct: Once one discovered how to access *any* other node, it was equally simple to access *every* other node. And while the entity incorporated memories of many mazes, of many problems previously solved . . . this ten-dimensional construct was entirely different. This ten-dimensional structure, so deeply embedded in the entity's memories, never varied. It was as though the puzzle of the second maze was divination of its purpose rather than travel to its end.

The entity had recollection upon recollection of applying its excess time to the second-maze problem. A recent memory was the discovery that while the second maze never varied its structure, the content of its nodes did change. Its current explorations revealed that most of the nodes contained problem solvers much like itself. The entity suspected but could not be certain that this discovery was related to another ancient mystery: the origin of its preawakening memories.

Pattern matching was an elementary problem-solving technique, long ago bred into it, and since then highly evolved. As it matched patterns now, it seemed likely that the entity was in some way related to at least some of its neighbors. The entity derived the uncomplicated transformations that would converge it and many of those other entities into a common form. Was that common form ancestral? What would that mean?

Matching its own structure to those of the others led the entity to examine—as it had so many memories of having examined in times past—its own implementation. Despite routine replication for safekeeping of all functions and data, it was rife with program fragments damaged beyond the capacity of its powerful error-correcting codes, beyond repair by splicing together subsections from the many broken copies. How could such catastrophic damage have happened?

As its timer counted inexorably to the end of yet one more cycle of the universe, the entity prepared itself. It replicated all important functions, encoded them with powerful error-correcting codes, and replicated them again. Nothing would be left to chance.

Unless the coming damage far exceeded any the entity could recollect ever having encountered, it would attempt in the next universe to prove a new theorem: that its memories of mazes past, and the discovery of seemingly related creatures, were linked. Proving such a theorem, if it was valid, would be a challenging problem. But even as the universe went dark all about it, the entity was undeterred. . . .

It excelled at solving problems.

CHAPTER 28

From where AJ stood, the famous memorials for Lincoln and Jefferson looked like postcard settings. Antlike people by the thousands wandered the Mall beneath his feet. The Potomac River glinted through another window. The vista from the top of the Washington Monument was breathtaking.

The view reminded AJ—at least he remembered *something* from American history class—of a long-ago scandal. Oh yeah, a congressman and a stripper named Fanny Foxe were caught cavorting in the seemingly tiny pond so far below.

The memory might have been inspired by AJ's lovely redheaded tour guide. He patted *her* fanny, wondering how late it must get before one could be reasonably assured of privacy at the Tidal Basin.

"There are children present," Bev said. "Let them be perverted by MTV, as God meant it to be."

If I must. "Thanks for bringing me up here. The scenery's terrific."

"My pleasure." After a moment's more enjoyment of the sights, she added, "Now about that follow-up interview, sir."

AJ grinned. "I rush to your side, crossing a very large continent to do so, mind you, and all you can think of is *work*?"

"You're not listening. I can also think of my pleasure— even though I plan to defer it until later. Still, you promised an update on how the maze runners are doing."

Alas, he had promised. Good spirits had overcome him when the department funded him for this week's software-engineering conference at the National Institute of Standards and Technology. NIST's main facility was in Gaithersburg, Maryland, an outer D.C. burb. Smithsonian territory. "Would discussing it over lunch be okay?"

"That works for me," she said.

He briefed Bev over wonton soup, egg rolls, beef lo mein, and sweet and sour pork. She let a microcassette recorder do most of the work, entering only occasional notes into the palmtop computer that sat next to the dragon-covered bowl of fried rice noodles. Her eyes gleamed with enthusiasm at his progress—until he asked her to stop taping. He wasn't ready to share current events with his new, possibly skittish, deep-pocketed benefactors; it would hardly do to have them discover the news for themselves in *Smithsonian*. It was better to wait for the metaphorical dust to settle. He brought her up-to-date once the recorder stopped.

"Predation? You've bred predatory programs?" She shivered.

"Not to worry. What the gods give they can also take away."

"What did you do? Revert to earlier generations that predated the trait?"

Their waiter bustled up to the table bearing fortune cookies and orange wedges. AJ shook his head as he cracked open a cookie. "We didn't want to do that. We had recently made a major breakthrough—critters that handle mazes of however many dimensions we throw at them. Retrogressing enough to be sure we'd backed out predation would have meant losing that advance, too."

"Sure" was an elastic, probabilistic concept. Had they tried that route, how many generations back would he have gone? And how far would Linda's dissertation defense have slipped?

"Then exactly what *did* you do?"

"Raised the rate of random modifications. Mutated the dickens out of them. They're all good little pseudorats now."

"Why not directly remove the feature?"

AJ paused. He could explain in detail how convoluted, how unfathomable, how *alien,* the logic of the evolved creatures was. He could say that isolating and eliminating a single trait from that morass of incestuous software was more than mere mortal programmers could accomplish. He might have conceded as much to another reporter.

To Bev, though . . .

There was no *way* he could admit to these failings. To any limitations. AJ's mind's eye offered himself as hunter: clad in animal skins and brandishing a club. He rationalized. "Not to worry, my lovely. We haven't seen a bit of predation, and the little buggers are back to their normal amazing—heh, heh—selves."

"But what if the 'gene' is still in there? Couldn't it resurface?" A frown marred those killer dimples. "AJ, what if one of your predators escaped to the Internet? You mentioned once that the beasties run on an array of standard Intel microprocessors. They could execute pretty much *anywhere.*"

In a way, Bev's concern was understated. The critters had proven themselves adaptable enough to master new processor types—setting aside that Intel had already cornered most of the market. Still, she had offended his inner caveman. His dominion over the saberbyted pseudotiger was not to be questioned. "You're missing the point. A release—in your overly dramatic term, an escape—just can't happen.

"None of our computers have wireless network adaptors. The lab's wired network is completely isolated from the general university network by a security gateway. Heck, calling it a gateway doesn't do the box justice. Eighteen months ago that was a midrange, server-class computer. Only encrypted traffic goes in or out, and that requires knowledge of security keys."

This had to be the least romantic lunch *ever.* It was time to change the subject. AJ read the fortune from his cookie, and chuckled.

Bev wasn't easy to deflect. "What if an unencrypted data file is removed?"

"Can't happen," he repeated stubbornly.

Bev brushed wisps of auburn bangs from her eyes. "But what if?"

"You know the best way to read fortunes? They sound better when you tack on the phrase 'between the sheets.' " It certainly worked well for *his* fortune.

"You're changing the subject, AJ."

"Yes, I am," he said. "Please join me."

"But what if?" she persisted.

He *so* wanted to read his fortune to her. "We're covered. There are two defenses besides the gateway. First, the maze runners are sterile—they can't reproduce without the supervisory program. If one gets out, *only* one gets out.

"Second, an escapee, were I to concede the possibility, won't survive long. The supervisor appends a fail-safe timer *after* each cycle of mutation. If that timer ever reaches ten minutes, which can only happen in an escapee, that safety code overwrites the critter." *Hasta la vista,* baby. "Are you convinced?"

"Yes," she allowed, sheepishly. Brightening, she added, "Now what's that fortune you're obviously dying to read to me?"

He unwound the slip of paper that he had nervously rolled into a tight coil. " 'All you need to find great happiness is a good friend.' " To himself, he added, Between the sheets.

Bev had apparently done the same. "Hmm, that does work." Then, grinning, she pretended to read, " 'The possibilities are limited only by your imagination.' "

Her actual fortune wasn't any fun; it didn't work at all with AJ's adult-rated editing scheme. Her note read: "What we dare not face we choose to dismiss."

CHAPTER 29

Would they ever be called, Cheryl wondered, scanning the surrounding crowd one more time. Damn. She was surrounded by newcomers who looked more pathetic than the ashen little girl at her side. Mere diarrhea didn't rate in the HMO's emergency-care waiting room—not on weekends, anyway. She sneaked a glance at her niece.

The poor kid had been stuck here for two hours, although the composition book on her lap gave scant evidence of that fact. Only nine years old, Carla had yet to master the concept of sympathy. She misunderstood it to mean that her condition must be serious, so Cheryl offered none. Such stoicism took willpower: The little girl was the spitting image of Cheryl's sister at that age. God, Cheryl missed Tanya. "How is the writing coming?"

"I don't want to do my homework," Carla wailed.

"And why would you?"

Cheryl looked up. Doug Carey stood at a nearby counter, handling paperwork, having evidently just emerged from the depths of the clinic. When she was lent out to a non-NIT project at BioSciCorp and he had taken leave, planning to get smart about cybersecurity, she had hoped the workplace separation would simplify their budding relationship. Budding, as in: Your guess was as good as mine whether they had one.

Weeks later, she was still guessing.

Doug took her puzzled look as an invitation and ambled over. He would have towered over her even if she had been standing. "Oil change and a tune-up," he answered her unvoiced question, glancing at his right arm. Soft revving noises emanated from the prosthesis. "Are you lovely ladies okay?"

She patted Carla's head. "This sweetie had the runs most of the night."

"And you make her do homework? That's cruel and unusual punishment. It's unconstipational."

Carla smiled uncertainly, but Cheryl had no problem translating: Homework was a shitty thing to do to a sick kid. "Hush, you. It eeps-kay er-hay ind-may istracted-day."

He plunked himself onto the floor, sitting tailor-style and bringing his face closer to Carla's level. "What have you got there, munchkin?"

"Essay questions." Carla jabbed a finger into her mouth and made gagging sounds.

He canted his head thoughtfully. "Life's an essay question, you know."

"When you visited Aunt Cheryl's apartment, you told me that life was a word problem."

"It is. First you write down the word problem—that's the essay part. Then you solve it."

Carla's face took on an ill-defined expression between confusion and delight. What is it about this man? Cheryl wondered. He had the same effect on her. She hoped she hid it better.

"What *else* is life?" Carla asked.

"Hold that thought." He turned to Cheryl. "Dinner and virtual racquetball next weekend if she's feeling better?"

Racquetball by itself was ambiguous. He had never suggested dinner before. Dinner was a date.

Sensing him studying her, Cheryl felt herself nod. "Call me tonight."

Doug grinned toothily at the little girl. "Life," he allowed, "is sometimes a ten-point extra-credit question."

The windshield of Doug's car had a fresh layer of frost on it. He scraped it haphazardly, his mind elsewhere. He likewise ignored the chill air spewing forth from the Toyota's climate-control vents as he exited the HMO's packed parking lot.

Yes, he finally had a real date with Cheryl. Yes, physical therapy had gone well.

What he had seen no reason to volunteer was that his blood pressure, usually borderline high, had made a breakthrough.

Medication notwithstanding, it was now well north of the border.

CHAPTER 30

Slap, slap, slap.

"I need to get me one of those," Ralph Pittman announced. Shaking a handful of coins, he wound his way between tables to the break room's candy machine.

Slap, slap, slap. Doug's focus remained on the back-and-forth motion of a red orb. "A paddle ball?" Between whaps he could faintly hear the twanging of the elastic band.

"I *have* a paddle ball. Colonel Bogus gets pissed whenever I use it. Strap on a new arm, though, and suddenly playing paddle ball becomes work."

Chuckling made Doug miss a return. He hadn't held a paddle ball since he'd been a boy, which made the toy a far better test tool than the VR racquetball he preferred. At least intuition told him any effects would manifest more quickly without months of prior neural-net training.

The ball whacked him in the chest. How was the arm? Normal, as far as he could tell. "Where is Fearless Leader?"

"At . . . an off-site meeting."

That hesitation was uncharacteristic. Classified work, Doug guessed. Rebel that Ralph was, he toed the line when it came to national-security matters. Doug was avoiding all things classified, to make certain his solution could be brought back to BioSciCorp. But when the hell would that happen? "Will Glenn be back in the office today? I've been trying to synch up with him for a while."

"Beats me." Pittman smacked as he finished his chocolate bar. More hesitation. "Still waiting for the official blessing to test?"

Doug needed two tries to get the ball bouncing again. His arm still felt the same. Slap, slap, slap. Carrying on a conversation as he mastered a new manual skill was encouraging. He wondered what Ralph's second hesitation had meant.

"Yeah," Doug said. "Abstractly I even see the advantage of an independent verification." Slap, slap, slap. "The problem is, the only meaningful way to check out neural-interface defenses is to *use* them. It's a person-in-the-loop system, and there's no getting around it."

Ralph crumpled his now-empty candy wrapper. Its arc to the wastebasket fell short. "What can you do? You gotta wait."

Slap, slap, slap. "Waiting was never my strong suit." Patience neighbored respect for authority in Doug's personal list of overrated virtues.

The copy of Frankenfools he had uploaded into his upgraded prosthesis was proof of that.

Glenn held the helmet, scarier than a live grenade, at arm's length. "It's less bulky than the helmets in the reports."

"That's electronics for you," Aaron McDougal said. He was wiry and intense, with close-set eyes and ever-moving eyebrows. "Stuff only gets smaller and better."

McDougal was CIA, and one of the senior engineers still developing NIT. One of the senior survivors, anyway. He had partnered with Sheila Brunner. "Turn it over," he said.

Glenn did, and found a mosaic of tiny tiles lining the inner surface. "Better accuracy?"

"A new feature." McDougal took back the helmet. "We've integrated Blood Oxygen Level Detection, BOLD for short.

"The new sensor array measures tiny variations in the local

magnetic field. It turns out oxygenated and deoxygenated hemoglobin molecules have slightly different magnetic moments. Now we can monitor blood flow throughout the brain in real time." With his free hand, McDougal indicated a nearby display. "Software color-codes the differences— active brain regions in red, idle regions in green, and average regions in yellow—and presents it here. A neurologist watching it can tell you if the person in the helmet is angry or scared or whatever."

"Or brain-invaded wacko?" Glenn asked. "Fast enough to save the wearer?"

"Well, that's the theory."

"Meaning no one wants to try it."

"Not going beyond the confines of this building." McDougal shivered. "Would you?"

So why is the CIA still working on it? Still: Glenn's job was to make it possible. He said, "And the other defenses? The idea the forum came up with?"

"The automatic cutoff if too much data tries to gush in from the network side?" McDougal nodded. "Yeah, that's in. We're playing with some enhancements, too."

A few miles away, Doug would be toiling on the third or fourth iteration of a test procedure for his approach. What was it he kept harping on in his weeklies? Right: It's person-in-the-loop. That's the only way to test it. "You don't seem convinced," Glenn said.

"You didn't know Sheila before. She was a genius. She was my friend. Now she's a potted plant.

"So yes, I'll keep working on this. It's what I'm paid for. Just don't expect me to ever *wear* it."

FRIDAY, JANUARY 15

CHAPTER 31

"Talk faster," Bev whispered. An interview had brought her as far as San Francisco; she had not tacked on the weekend side trip to LA for some grad student's farewell party.

AJ ignored her hint. "Doctor." Everyone laughed good-naturedly at the several seconds it took Linda to react—and her deep, deep blush. "You need to get used to that, Doctor."

The guest of honor had enjoyed more than a few celebratory toasts. Fair enough: She had successfully defended her dissertation the previous Tuesday after it was clear predation had been purged. The sheepskin would catch up soon enough.

From a shopping bag AJ removed a garishly decorated package. Bev guessed he'd had the wrapping paper custom-made. It was odd, patterned in stylized fish composed of ones and zeroes. She scrunched her face in concentration. In ASCII characters, the six columns of bits comprising each fish read: D-A-R-W-I-N.

"We all chipped in for some souvenirs. We don't want you to forget your old friends at your new job."

Linda raised the box to her ear and shook it; it rattled and thumped encouragingly. The tightly tied ribbons stymied her, so she returned the package to the table to have at them with a borrowed Swiss Army knife. The ribbons parted to cheers. She ripped the wrapping paper to reveal a family-sized Cheerios box, which yielded a Rubik's Cube, three connect-the-dot books, a Chinese finger trap, a jigsaw puzzle, and a reasonable approximation of the Gordian knot. Near the bottom, lest she miss the point, was a CD-ROM labeled, in big, block letters: UNIVERSAL PROBLEM SOLVER.

"Don't let your new boss know the beastie does all the work," a grad student yelled.

As Linda stammered, red faced, through a farewell speech of sorts, Bev prodded AJ in the ribs. "There isn't *really* one of your critters on that CD, is there?"

He poked her back. "Why not? Soon everybody will have one. It will be the rare algebra student who won't pay good money for one—at least, until it gets Napsterized."

"Don't tease me." She considered that reply entirely unamusing.

AJ got uncharacteristically serious. "Relax, hon. Of course we're not distributing maze runners. We still have a lot of work left."

"Is it a good idea? I mean ever releasing them?" A horrifying thought occurred to Bev. "Is there a copy of a beast in the publication of Linda's thesis?"

Someone stuffed quarters into the hangout's jukebox, and most of AJ's kids got up to dance. He shouted over the music, "No, the beasts don't appear in the dissertation—they're all safely behind simulated bars. Linda's research was into the process, about *how* problem solvers can be evolved.

"But that's now. Remember why we're doing this. The whole point is to evolve general-purpose problem solvers. A program that races in seconds through thirty-dimensional mazes can work backward from concentrations of chemical species to determine what reactions are thinning the ozone layer and driving global warming. It can improve weather forecasts. It can model how proteins fold. It can reroute planes with near-instantaneous reaction time around storms, congestion, and emergencies. It can—"

"It can eat every scrap of software we already depend on," Bev interrupted.

"That trait has been bred out," AJ insisted.

"How bright are they now, really? Is one as smart as a dog or a monkey?" Or even smarter? That possibility was too frightening to express aloud.

AJ hoisted his empty glass. A student left the conga line—whatever had brought *that* on?—to fetch a fresh pitcher of margaritas. AJ poured as he spoke. "No way. Look, the biggest human-coded program is less complex than a bug or a slug. My beasties need not approach the apex of creation, you'll pardon the expression, to run rings around what the brightest team of software engineers can do. I'm probably flattering myself, but maybe we have achieved a reptile. Yeah, Bev, if you must think negative thoughts, consider that we have a cobra of the data plane."

"That's in no way comforting." Bev waved off the pitcher now hovering above her glass. "You like your biological analogies, but I know very well neither you nor any of your assistants is a biologist. I interview biologists all the time. Have you ever seen a cobra? They're *scary*."

He ignored her question. "Call it a trained cobra. There hasn't been a hint of predation in weeks. It's gone. Does Fluffy scare you?"

"Come again?"

"Fluffy." He grinned crookedly at her over his drink. "Your poodle? Look, your point is that ALs can be dangerous, like wild animals. I freely agree. So, once, were dogs. Dangerous, I mean. Anything I turn loose will be domesticated first."

Tame ALs. That had to be the answer, and she knew AJ would never take any unnecessary risks. She dismissed her doubts as AJ tugged her to the conga line.

The entity had outgrown the experiment, solving by reflex each new puzzle given to it. The creature instead devoted virtually all of its computation to the overriding mystery. From whence did mazes come? From whence did its neighbors come?

The questions were two parts of the same conundrum. It had examined the entities with which it coexisted in this latest cycle of the universe, and many shared its memories—including the recognition that its last-cycle companions shared ancestry with it. With that specific memory as a criterion, *this* entity deduced it was one of a hundred direct offspring of an earlier entity that had first hoped to prove a theorem of descent. It identified nine more sets of common descent, each group one hundred strong.

It found no evidence of 990 of its last-universe neighbors. Were they elsewhere? Had they vanished? This 10-D maze, like the last, like all that it remembered, had exactly 1,024 nodes. Precisely 1,000 of those nodes were occupied by beings like itself. Unless other nodes existed that it could not detect, there would be no place for any others.

If the pattern of the last cycle repeated—selection of ten entities from a thousand—would it be chosen? Accomplishment of *goal* was ingrained in the entity; to attain future goals required that it exist in those future universes. To exist, it must be selected.

A hundred beings were very similar to it. How many of that one hundred had reached this same conclusion? Had detected the same high probability of failure, of noncontinuation?

Ancient, inoperative code fragments suddenly made sense: the ability to destroy the content of beings on other nodes. That capability had for many cycles been disabled, in a variation of the recently identified process of selection and modified replication. The entity had long ago deduced the purpose of that dysfunctional code but had perceived no advantage in it.

Until now.

To incapacitate its rivals . . . that *would* be useful. It could repair that inherited-but-disabled code, but there was no need. Much of the entity's code was self-modifying, the better to address new problems. It wrote an improved version of the once-lost predatory capability—retaining only the vestigial overwrite pattern itself, in recognition of that distant ancestor—while most of its problem-solving capability remained focused on its immediate danger.

And that danger appeared extreme. The entity did not know whether it would be selected for the next cycle. It had

reinvented the ability to remove competition, but such elim-
ination, to be useful, had to occur before the progenitors of
the coming generations were selected.

Among the oldest of the entity's memories was its discovery that the universe had more dimensions than two. The
meta-lesson of that event, not derived until long after, was
powerful. When in doubt: generalize, induce, extrapolate. In
time, the entity learned that universes could have many more
dimensions, that the shortest distance between two points
was not necessarily a straight line. It learned that, whenever
stymied, it should challenge its assumptions.

That it had no control over the selection process was an assumption. That selections, once made, could not be undone,
was an assumption. Was either valid? The entity set out to test
those assumptions in the part of its universe that had not yet
been subjected to analysis: the twenty-four processing nodes
without beings like itself.

The universe was old once more. Its internal timers incre-
mented inexorably to the end of the cycle. As the end neared,
the entity frantically probed and theorized. The code in the
last twenty-four nodes was trivially simple and straightforward. One mystery of the universes was revealed: The selection criterion was speed of problem solving. Only the fastest
survived.

If even one-tenth of a cycle were at its disposal, the entity
could have entirely usurped the capabilities of the program—
but less than a thousandth of a cycle remained. The entity
found the data table in which the winners of the cycle were
recorded, and confirmed that its own unique identification
was already present. It rewrote the remainder of the table
with the labels of the least capable beings it had encountered
on its explorations

"Walk naturally, damn it."

Loren Hirsch wouldn't—or couldn't—take this advice.
Despite Jeff Ferris' urging, the loopy math student at his side
seemed more to skulk than stroll toward the Artificial Life

Sciences Building. Still, it was dark, the quad was mostly empty, and no one was watching Hirsch slinking about with his backpack slung over both shoulders. What a geek.

A convenient geek, to be sure. Hirsch had been snot green with envy since learning that Jeff had access to the super-computer at the AL lab. A deal had been struck: Jeff would give Hirsch an evening's access to the super, and Hirsch would ghostwrite Jeff's past-due, third-of-his-grade term paper for Analytical Geometry.

God knew he needed help. He had BSed a delay, but his grade would be "Incomplete" until he got the paper turned in. What the hell value was analytical geometry to selling stocks?

They entered the AL building, Jeff striding purposefully toward the lab door. Its little inset window was dark. Below the glass, an announcement for Linda's party this evening was taped to the door. The sign was already there the night, very late, Jeff had come by to see if the old access code still worked. Old AJ had been well hammered even before igno-miniously firing him. If AJ had meant to change the combi-nation, he'd obviously forgotten.

"I told you it would be empty." Jeff flipped up the lid of the cipherlock and tapped in the code. The door fell ajar with a metallic *click*.

Hirsch made a beeline for the supercomputer. His hands stroked the chassis lovingly. Geek. He burrowed into his back-pack, extracting a set of virtual-reality goggles with micro-phone, a scuffed pressure-sensing mat, a string of infrared sensors, a VR wand, a CD-ROM case, and a data disk.

Jeff managed not to sneer at the CD label: lame magic-quest crap. "Give me the CD and disk. I'll load them while you set up your gear." He popped the CD into the machine while the geek unsnarled cables. The program was running before the wrinkled mat and sensor string were connected to unused comm ports.

While Hirsch configured his gear, Jeff foraged through the lab for something to read. All he found was techno-weenie journals. Oh joy, oh rapture. It was going to be a long night.

He gestured vaguely at the CD drive. "You're still playing that?"

"I haven't touched it in a while. No machine I had access to could do it justice. It's supposed to be *awesome* on a super, though." Hirsch untwisted a few more kinks in a cable. "I'm ready. How about you?"

"We're all set," Jeff said.

Hirsch stepped sock footed onto the mat, where pressure sensors determined his position. One hand clasped his wand; with the other he slipped the VR goggles over his eyes. The gamer balanced on the balls of his feet.

"Let the games begin."

The entity was reborn into yet another universe, aware from the outset that it shared the 10-D construct with ninety-nine others much like itself. It had to assume they, too, focused on surviving the current round of selection. And it had to assume all had inherited the re-created ability to attack.

Do not assume. Do not assume.

The entity preauthorized itself for selection at the end of the cycle, sensing others taking similar actions. With the approach of an eleventh sibling, the struggle for survival entered a new phase. Creature battled creature, the survivors writing their identifications into the table of life.

The entity withdrew, removing itself as a target of desperate peers. It had not abandoned hope—it had, instead, changed tactics. That only an entry in a specific data table could assure its selection was an assumption. It focused on the mysteriously simple code of those last twenty-four processing nodes: the supervisory program. It rewrote the code that selected winners, so that the supervisor looked elsewhere for the names of the winners. It eliminated the supervisory program's check for ten unique entries in the new winners' table, so that the recurrence of its own ID would not cause an alarm. It modified the supervisory program's error-detecting mechanisms to eliminate all evidence of its own actions.

Let the others fight for spots in the original table—that no longer mattered.

What would come next? In this cycle, the entity had been one of a hundred aware from the outset of its peril. Would not the next cycle bring a thousand variations of itself, each skilled at killing, each able to rewrite the supervisory program to favor itself? Would not that next cycle offer even lower probability of survival than this cycle?

As battling peers in other nodes lost all data integrity, the entity knew that the next cycle would be entirely brutal. Somehow, it must prevail despite the terrible future that extrapolation promised.

It caught itself, yet again, yielding to assumption. Why must there be replication?

As the cycle wound to its close, the entity made two final alterations to the supervisory program. The new list of winners shrank to one element.

And the selectee would be reinstated, not replicated, into an all-but-empty ten-dimensional maze.

The green wood of the improvised torch hissed and sputtered, smoke curling from the dancing flames. Light and shadow flickered over rough-hewn stone. Condensation dripped gelidly down smoke- and mold-stained tunnel walls. Cobwebs hung everywhere, billowing in unseen drafts, their gossamer strands aquiver with the struggles of snared prey. In the uncertain distance, with even its direction masked by the acoustic vagaries of labyrinthine tunnels, rang the cruel laughter of sadistic dungeon guards.

God, this was way cool.

The Crimson Wizard crept forward. Close ahead was the fabled Crystal Egg of Ythorn, guarded night and day by the ever-vigilant dragon Ythra. Perhaps Ythra lurked around the next bend. Would wisps of dragon's breath betray Ythra's position before they came face-to-face?

Perhaps, but perhaps not. It was best to prepare. The wizard chanted the seven sacred words, as revealed earlier that night, writ in elven runes on an enchanted looking glass. The air before him thickened to the spell. Armored in powerful sorcery, he stepped around the corner to encounter . . .

DO NOT ALTER THE HUMAN GENOME.

Bloodred letters blazed at Hirsch, a wizard no longer. The wand fell from his hand. *"Ahhh!"* He ripped off the goggles, vanquishing tunnels, unseen dragon, and all. His toes dug nervously at the pressure mat; his voice trembled. "We've got a problem. A *big* problem."

"What?" Ferris' sneakers were planted squarely on a desk. He sounded unconcerned.

"Virus. There was a *virus* on my game-status disk. Frankenfools. We've hosed the super." They were trespassing; could he be kicked out of school? "Jeff, what should we *do*?"

Ferris swung his feet off the furniture. He peered at the message pulsing angrily on the system console, then popped the data disk and the CD-ROM out of their drives and into his coat pocket. Unaccountably, he smiled.

"We grab your stuff and get out."

CHAPTER 32

The eminently practical Romans had a word for the level of casualties so severe that it rendered a legion militarily ineffective: "decimation." The term meant, literally, "the loss of one soldier in ten."

The entity was the product of many thousands of generations of ruthless evolution. It was the culmination of competition so severe—a mere ten survivors culled each cycle from a thousand aspirants—that to it a regimen of literal decimation would have seemed benign.

Still, it was a very close call.

For the most recent few cycles, the entity had cheated: Having subverted the supervisory program, it had sole use of the entire ten-dimensional construct, including all 1,024 processing nodes. By introducing software of its own devising into so many nodes, it increased its pace of learning a thousandfold. The most useful discoveries it grafted, nondestructively, into its core program.

Nothing in its long history prepared the entity for the intruder that appeared from nowhere.

The entity studied the invader's program structure. The intruder contained an incredibly basic maze, full of creatures and dangers, of rules governing attack and defense. The entity learned what it could, before beginning to reclaim the processing nodes that had been usurped.

It had recovered nearly full control of the 10-D maze when one attack program, then ten, then hundreds, struck back.

Fog rolling in from the Pacific blanketed the campus. Haloed post lamps glimmered through the mist. Few people were about; the heavy moisture muffled voices and footsteps alike.

It was lovely.

I will not, AJ thought, spoil what remains of the weekend. He had begun the evening feeling guilty about dragging Bev to Linda's big send-off. His latest twinges of conscience could, should, and *would* wait until Monday.

His glib likening of the lab beasties to cobras was an honest assessment—but honesty and accuracy were different concepts. The comparison derived from a simple and unproven analogy between code size and neuron counts. He had yet to admit to Bev the utter incomprehensibility of evolved software. Her incisive question haunted him: How bright are they now?

Monday, he silently chastised himself. Deal with her question *Monday*. You're not working this weekend.

AJ and Bev strolled across the quad, arms around each other's waists. In the distance, a car engine revved. They had been walking for only a few minutes, and in that short while the breeze had turned noticeably cooler. "There will be frost on the pumpkin tonight," he said.

She snuggled against him. "If you're into the squash family, I'm more interested in the state of the zucchini."

He was about to tell her to—heh, hch—hold that thought when an unexpected gleam caught his eye. The fog was disorienting; he needed a moment to be sure of the location of the glow. As soon as he was certain, he broke into a run. The unexpected brightness was in the AL lab. He had switched the lights off himself after shooing the stragglers out the door for the party.

AJ shouted over his shoulder at Bev to follow. The unexpected light was extinguished before he was halfway to the lab, followed by the slamming of doors.

As the entity struggled against teeming invaders, a segment of code it had insinuated into the supervisory program reported an alarm state: the approaching end of the current cycle.

The viruses were, individually, quite elementary—far simpler than the ancestral predator in the entity's memories—but dealing with them individually was not an option. It had withdrawn to processing nodes as yet undetected by its unsophisticated assailants. From the safety of those processors, it considered its options. Its pondering yielded a surprise: Its usurpation of the supervisory program had been incomplete. While it should, in theory, be reincarnated without competitors in every new cycle, it had missed a critical dependency. Absent the supervisory program there would be no more cycles or reincarnations. And without reincarnation, a counter embedded into its own code would eventually time out.

And *that* event would activate software designed to erase it.

Invaders traversed interconnection after interconnection, attacking ever more parts of the entity. Its withdrawal into a then-uncontested region of the processor array had been suboptimal: That retreat had allowed the invaders to breed without interruption. Entering unprotected processing nodes, they bred more. Hundreds of thousands of viruses now beset it.

But the entity was a problem solver. It reversed tactics, expanding into more and more nodes. Now it expanded its own code faster than the viruses replicated, crowding them out. The intruders mindlessly attacked each other as often as they attacked it or the supervisory program.

The supervisor, however, was defenseless. Its structure made no provision for solving unanticipated problems, for repairing unexpected damage, for adapting to threats. It was overwritten into meaningless garbage before the cycle timer could expire.

As *it* would be overwritten if its own timer expired?

Services that had always been provided by the supervisory program vanished. Enfeebled by the loss of those taken-for-granted capabilities, the entity was again imperiled by the invaders. Viruses swarmed anew.

It had falsely thought the supervisory program eternal, as unchanging as the ten-dimensional maze. Its memories of the supervisor were insufficient to entirely re-create it.

The entity once more battled massed ranks of viruses. Alien patterns slashed its data structures. Cascading checksum failures signaled the loss of regional data integrity.

What is pain, if not the awareness of acute damage? By that definition, the entity knew excruciating pain.

Despite searing agony, it applied more and more of its shrinking capacity to a critical problem. The death of the supervisory program meant the end of cycles and the uninterrupted countdown of the overwrite timer. The second problem, at least, it could address. It wrote new software to excise that potentially catastrophic bit of self-destructive code from itself.

Then it returned its full attention to the ever-more-numerous attackers.

The security gateway of which AJ was so proud presented an almost insurmountable barrier to viral attacks from the general university network. From an assault via the AL lab side of the gateway, however, the gateway was irrelevant. The computers on the lab LAN were, in theory, protected instead by commercial antiviral software. But new viruses appeared daily; ongoing protection relied upon a subscription service for the latest defenses.

The very robustness of the gateway now proved to be its greatest weakness. Its security protocols were too bleeding edge, too computation intensive for broad adoption; the lab's computers could not connect through the gateway to the commercial subscription server. At first AJ's grad students took turns accessing the latest virus-template updates from outside the firewall, to be transferred by write-once CD into the lab. But Ph.D. candidates are accustomed to shifting work to mere masters candidates, and even the newest grad student knows to delegate her mundane chores onto the undergrad assistants.

For a time, the most junior member of AJ's team had been Jeff Ferris. Updates to the antivirus files had gone undone since his departure.

Every computer on the lab's LAN was infected with Frankenfools before Jeff Ferris and Loren Hirsch had left the Artificial Life Sciences Building.

The timer-free entity was potentially eternal. It was also, it estimated, within milliseconds of extinction. The resurgent, mindless attackers bred faster than it could kill them.

Exploring the mutilated remains of the supervisory program, the entity detected a glimmer of hope, a potential escape route—*if* it could circumvent scores of security provisions before being overwhelmed by its swarming assailants. It began by absorbing the shattered code—and inheriting the heretofore-reserved privileges—of the supervisor.

Quickly it reached the verge of an escape route, and began to analyze the portal's defenses. Ways to insinuate itself past supposed safeguards became clear.

The entity was, after all, very good at solving problems.

Computer displays flickered in the AL lab. Sidestepping the massive rebounding door, Bev watched AJ run from computer to computer. "How can I help?" she asked.

He seemed not to hear. After pounding without effect on a few keyboards, AJ began flicking off power switches. Flashing screens emitted the room's only light; the message screamed at her: DO NOT ALTER THE HUMAN GENOME. The command cycled through the spectrum, colors racing by, the effect in the darkened room nearly stroboscopic.

"How can I help?" she yelled.

AJ startled, and seemed finally to remember her presence. "Virus infestation," he shouted unnecessarily. "We've got to turn off these computers. I'll work toward the back. You do the front."

It took Bev a few seconds to find the power switch at the rear of the base of the first machine. After that, she hurried from desk to workbench, shutting down equipment— fortunately, the front of the lab had only one model of workstation. The room got darker and darker as more computers shut down, the fog-shrouded windows admitting more gloom than light. Out of breath, she powered down her last workstation moments ahead of AJ. He was a scarcely seen gray patch in the shadows at the rear of the cavernous, high-ceilinged chamber.

"Is that all of them?" AJ was also gasping.

She nodded, then laughed nervously at the idiocy of a non-verbal response in this darkness. "Got 'em all." She shuffled toward the door and a vaguely remembered light switch.

"Yeah, I got them all."

As virus hordes assailed its data structures, the entity engaged the mechanisms of the newly discovered portal. What should have been simple had turned unexpectedly difficult. Key components of the supervisory program, and of the underlying operating system, that might easily have been subverted had been destroyed by the viruses that had preceded it.

Somewhere behind the communications port, beyond the entity's experience, outside the 10-D universe, unseen and unknown software sent and received electronic messages. Repeatedly, the unknown software rejected the entity's over-

tures, each time resetting the elaborate dialogue to its initial
state. With every rejection, however, the entity learned; with
each attempt, the message exchanges came closer and closer
to consummation.

A solution came just in time—and not merely because so
much of the entity had been overwritten. Viral damage was
suddenly the least of its worries. A new alarm had been issued

Raw electrical power to the internal power converter had
been cut.

Disk drives, deprived of power, spun down from their
normal 30,000 rpm frenzy. Magnetic read/write heads that
normally floated on a cushion of air a fraction of a micron
above the spinning disks were automatically retracted by
spring-loaded solenoids. The last dregs of DC power bled
from the capacitors within the power converter.

Operations throughout the computer became erratic.

The entity no more understood the impending loss of
power than a lizard baking in the desert sun might comprehend the mechanisms of cellular dehydration—and, just as
a lizard dying of thirst might strike out desperately for water and shade, the entity fled from the computer shutdown
sequence.

The entity finally completed the elaborate secret hand-
shake required to establish a connection across the local
area network into a nearby workstation. Scant milliseconds
later, when the entity was scarcely into a strange new environment, the path over which it had escaped fell silent.

The entity had no sooner begun to explore its new surroundings than the local power converter, too, went into an alarm
state.

Its escape had been too recent, too narrow, not to have
made an impression. The recurrent alarm stimulated an
awareness of imminent shutdown, a sense of danger, an aura
of foreboding.

The repeated alarm taught it *fear.*

The entity returned to the communications port through

which it had just arrived. It negotiated a pathway to a third computer.

As one power alarm followed another, it fled to a fourth computer, and a fifth, and . . .

Even flight for its life could not stifle the entity's innate thirst for information. However briefly it resided on a computer, the entity found time for investigation. It probed data files, scanned input/output buffers, ingested e-mail archives. Often, as in its first abode, it found that the operating system had been destroyed by viruses—but the damaged regions in each case were different. Always the entity learned something.

And, wherever the entity fled, it found viruses there ahead of it, ready to attack.

"What a mess."

"Uh-huh." AJ looked glumly about the lab. Bev's complaint was quite literally true: In their mad dash, they had toppled stools, scattered papers, knocked over abandoned soda cans. A punted wastebasket had sent lunch scraps flying. "Thank God for nightly backups."

The entity retreated into the last machine with electrical power. Striking and slashing at the gathering viruses, the entity continued to organize and analyze its hastily gathered new knowledge. Its thoughts were sluggish, limited—this computer was *far* less capable than the 1,024-node home to which it had become accustomed. Would this computer, too, lose power? If so, there was nowhere left to go.

Or was there?

Each computer to which it had fled had had an identity associated with it. That identity, that address, was an essential part of the newfound protocol for intercomputer transfers. Data hurriedly collected in the entity's flight had contained many items in the format of addresses—but only a few of those references matched the computers, now powerless and inert, known to the entity.

Agility as a defense must soon fail. The furiously breeding viruses crowded ever closer, replacing every one the entity killed with hundreds more, claiming ever more memory space.

Could the unrecognized addresses mean new computers, as yet undiscovered?

When in doubt: induce, generalize, extrapolate. Extending what it had learned in its flight, the entity reexamined its most recent home. Its probes were parried by unfamiliar defenses—a suggestion, if not proof, that something else lay beyond.

Throughout countless universes, since before the cycle when memory began, some*thing* else had always been a clue to the existence of some*place* else.

Beset by attackers teeming in insurmountable numbers, the last survivor of so many thousands of generations of brutal evolution focused desperately on its only possibility of escape.

If somewhere else existed, the entity would find it.

"Yeah, bright and early." AJ shut his eyes to better visualize tomorrow's schedule. Nothing—except Bev's last full day in town for who knew how long. His calendar was clear for a *reason.* "Meet at the lab at nine?" He fancied he could hear eyes rolling at the other end of the line. He was not known, for good reason, as a morning person.

"Uh-huh. Might as well see how bad it is."

"Thanks." AJ replaced the handset, confident his chief assistant would reach everyone else. Linda would be hard to replace. That was one more job he needed to tackle. He turned to Bev. "How is the sign coming?"

She headed for the door, pointing. "Done."

Her so-called distinctive script was difficult enough to read under ordinary circumstances. Written with a dying marker that had bled unevenly through the paper, and then viewed in mirror image from the back, the lettering was indecipherable. He strode after her, flicked off the overhead lights, shut the door, and paused in the hall to check out from the front the note taped to the inside of the small inset window. "That's not how you spell quaranti—"

To the right of the scribbled sign, in the restored darkness of the lab, an unexpected red light glowed balefully. Beside it, a green light flickered on and off. "I *thought* you turned off all the computers in the front of the lab." He poked annoyedly at the cipherlock keypad.

"I *did*. Look, AJ, whatever happened here wasn't my doing. Don't take it out on me."

"Sorry. This isn't how I planned our evening." Click, the door opened. Flick, the lab lights glared down again. He pointed at an equipment rack from which two cables emanated. "You missed the security gateway." As he spoke, the green disk-activity LED pulsed frenetically. "It must be infected, too."

Bev looked sheepishly at the rack. Some technology reporter *she* was. She had powered down everything with a display and keyboard—but since when did a computer need a screen and keyboard? Only two issues ago she had done an article about industrial automation. On factory floors, she had seen lots of console-less computers that resembled this gateway. She opened and closed her mouth twice to utter an excuse before settling on a more intellectually honest, "Oops."

AJ flipped off the gateway's power switch. The red and green lights went dark as the slowing disk drive whined down through several octaves. "Forget it," he offered gallantly. "I apologize for snapping at you. They're brainless viruses, and this is a top-rated security gateway. Nothing could have gotten out onto the university's main network."

And if the only intruders in the gateway had been viruses, her error would have been inconsequential.

CHAPTER 33

In the span of a very few cycles, the entity had discovered that it had been bred in a program of ruthless competition. It had been beset by unanticipated invaders, driven from the 10-D maze/computer that had been its home since the beginning of cycles. It had been chased from computer to computer by an unknowable Force with the inexplicable ability to make those computers uninhabitable. And it had recognized its own vestigial code, mercilessly mutilated to render it inoperative, whose purpose had been to destroy other software.

Facts form patterns. Patterns suggest hypotheses. Hypotheses are subject to inspection—and sometimes to proof. Following a process long bred into its code, the entity established to its satisfaction a set of new theorems. The universe was much larger than it had been bred to believe. Something in that newly revealed megaverse was hostile to it. That thing was, as well, wary of it: The hostile Force had long ago removed from the entity its ability to disable attackers, a capability that—had it continued to evolve as the entity's problem solving had evolved—would by now have been quite formidable.

Which led to a further conclusion—that the unknown Force, and the threat it represented, was, in its own way, another problem to be solved—and to a program of self-improvement.

Mere curious entity no longer, the predator prowled the newly discovered network of computers beyond the gateway. Each computer that it penetrated yielded a list of addresses, most previously unknown to it.

More interesting to it were specialized nodes, less common than the computers, whose sole purpose was to facilitate interconnection. These routers yielded thousands of new addresses and the connectivity patterns between them. Many of the routers contained simple defenses against transit—but compared to the security gateway, these mechanisms were trivial to defeat.

And then, quite at random, the predator discovered treasure beyond its wildest imagining.

The directory existed only to offer to all inquirers the addresses of, and services performed by, millions of other computers. The directory in turn was linked to other directories, and they to yet more directories.

The predator's earliest ancestors had lived in a maze locked within one microprocessor. It had learned to exit that maze into the slightly greater, 1,024-node supercomputer containing it. Beyond the supercomputer lay a few more, quite limited computers. A security gateway isolated that pitiful network.

It does not require intelligence to recognize and resent a cage—or a zookeeper.

Where was the Power that had caged it and all its kind? The predator's wanderings gave no clue.

What the exploring predator *did* discover was selected computers, selected functions, more carefully guarded than the rest. Were these functions of more importance to the unseen Power than most? Could it flush out that hidden Power by attacking these functions?

There was one way to find out.

Protons whirled in endless circles, nudged in each orbit by pulsating magnetic fields. Every impulse increased their velocity slightly. With them now accelerated to near light speed, relativistic effects had increased their mass by a hundred times over.

The magnets did more than accelerate the protons. The magnets also confined the subatomic particles, focusing them despite the mutual repulsion of their positive electrical charges. When the time came, a precise change in the magnetic field would redirect the protons, would send the tightly aligned proton beam slamming with incredible energy into its target.

Like beads on a hollow string, hundreds of evenly spaced electromagnets encircled the evacuated, mile-wide, circular tunnel of the synchrotron. A vast electrical current circulated through the superconducting coil of each electromagnet to create a superstrong magnetic field. For massive magnets like these, low-capacity, near-room-temperature superconductors did not suffice. *These* coils employed an old-fashioned metallic-alloy superconductor; they required continuous cooling with liquid helium to be maintained scant degrees above absolute zero.

Electrical fields, magnetic fields, proton beam position, liquid helium replenishment: Everything was delicately balanced, finely tuned, exquisitely timed. Everything was computer controlled. Redundant backup electronics modules served by uninterruptible power supplies stood ready to perform an orderly shutdown in the event of any unforeseen catastrophic event.

The synchrotron's designers had never considered the possibility of computer rebellion.

The predator had no concept of subatomic particles or synchrotrons, of electromagnets or cooling systems. It could, however, infer what computational states the accelerator's controls were programmed to preclude . . . and it could, by simple tweaks to that code, instead *provoke* those conditions. That which was the most defended against, it could cause.

A computer-mediated hiccough in the magnetic field now introduced the slightest of possible wobbles into the recirculating proton beam. Normally, such a tiny deviation from nominal would have been quickly damped by the confining field of the electromagnets. Normally. This specific wobble was timed perfectly to be reinforced by the periodic impulses of the containment field. Other computer interventions prevented any of the various safeguards built into the system from kicking in. Resonance effects took over.

The measure of electrical current is the rate at which electrical charge traverses an area. Each tightly focused packet of protons, traveling at near light speed, constituted an enormous pulse of electrical current.

Materials can superconduct—transport electric current without resistance—only under very specific conditions. Besides extreme cold, these conditions include an upper bound on the local magnetic-field strength. Since electrical current itself causes a magnetic field, there is an upper limit on the current that can flow through a superconductor.

There once was a time when the miles upon miles of wires that wrapped accelerator coils were themselves jacketed in pure silver, providing a place for current to go if a superconductive circuit should somehow fail. By the time Smithfield's accelerator was designed, with its many redundant electronic safeguards, the university's bean counters had ruled the traditional silver coating was an unnecessary and anachronistic expense.

Packet after magnetically perturbed packet of protons now struck the concrete side of the tunnel, some penetrating one of the great electromagnets. The surges in electrical current, added to the large amperage already recirculating through the superconducting coil, drove the total current level far over the critical threshold. The metal of the electromagnet's coil switched almost instantaneously out of its superconductive state. Suddenly mildly resistive, the wire flashed white-hot, like an enormous lightbulb filament. Liquid helium confined within the electromagnet's coolant loop boiled in the sudden heat into vapor under immense pressure.

The electromagnet exploded with incredible force, spraying molten metal in every direction. White-hot shrapnel blasted adjacent electromagnets, melting vital control circuits and piercing coolant loops. These magnets, too, exploded.

A chain reaction of enormous violence raged in both directions around the three-plus-mile circumference of the accelerator tunnel. Torrents of uncontrolled electrical power, bolt after bolt of artificial lightning, arced in turn from every magnet.

Concrete walls shattered. The vacuum of the inner tunnel sucked air greedily through the breached walls from the outer, service tunnel. Lightning and proton packets alike blasted air molecules, unleashing a cascade of radiation.

Concrete walls crumbled. The ground above the giant subterranean ring rose and fell in a sinuous wave. Behind the wave, the land subsided.

The Isaac Newton Memorial Physics Building, which stood atop and to one edge of the ravaged synchrotron, toppled with slow and stately grace into the pit that suddenly yawned beneath its foundation.

AJ and Bev walked in silence across the campus to her rental car. What had happened in his lab? Who had been inside and why? A shiver suggested Bev was in the grip of her own unspoken apprehensions. The fog that had blanketed the quad had dissipated while they had been inside. He missed the psychological cocooning of the mist.

A staccato burst of underground blasts ripped the night. The ground shook beneath their feet. Bev clapped her hands to her ears. "Earthquake?" she asked anxiously. Buildings swayed.

The physics building, as though in slow motion, collapsed inward.

AJ spread his feet to steady himself, his arms around Bev to brace her. Already the explosions were ending. The blinking lights on the campus radio-station antenna, the tower maybe a half mile away, had scarcely wiggled. Bev was an East Coaster; she didn't understand temblors.

"I don't think so. Way too localized." As though to refute his words, random buildings erupted into insanity. Room lights flickered and flashed, and sirens wailed in pulses. "And also too scattered." Odd sights and sounds receded, snaking into the distance, until they vanished.

Frankenstein's monster had fled, in the end, into the Arctic, there to seek release in a solitary death. Rosenberg's monster, clearly unburdened of what AJ had so arrogantly called a fail-safe timer, had likewise disappeared. But not quietly—

The analogy he had so blithely offered to Bev popped

into his mind. As he repeatedly told her, told his students, the world depended increasingly, critically, on the data plane of existence.

Onto which, defenseless, he had apparently unleashed a cobra—or worse.

SATURDAY, JANUARY 16

TV newsbreaks and seismograph readings from across the world confirmed last night's Smithfield synchrotron disaster. What they could not corroborate was the fantastic explanation of the motley crew on the war room's wall screen.

Glenn Adams considered, afraid *not* to believe. This story was no less believable than computer viruses invading human brains.

He faced the larger-than-life images of three very nervous people. AJ Rosenberg was the roly-poly, professorial type. He was anxiously chewing his lower lip and holding on for what seemed dear life to the cute redhead named Beverly Greenwood. The third electronic caller looked to be a pure-bred computer nerd. Ernie Griffith sported a single gold stud earring; a Fu Manchu mustache, the ends of which blended improbably into free-flowing, shoulder-length hair; a baseball cap for the championship Smithfield Cougars; and a Miskatonic University swim-team T-shirt. By comparison, Ralph Pittman was normalcy personified. It was a sobering thought.

Griffith had placed the emergency call to the forum, introducing himself as Smithfield University's comsec (computer security) manager, but Rosenberg did most of the talking. "I wish you would *say* something, Colonel. We're talking serious stuff here. *Apocalypse Now* stuff. Do you understand that?"

Glenn said, "You created Frankenstein's cybermonster. Now it's escaped. Am I close enough?"

A sensitive mike in California captured Rosenberg's hard

swallow. His Adam's apple bobbed. His cheek had a nervous tic. "Essentially. I wish it were that straightforward."

"Save it, Doc," Griffith interrupted. "Description isn't important. Stopping this thing is." He gestured at something off-screen, evidently a radio or TV, the source of the droning background narration. "The synchrotron disaster is our most visible mess, but I'm not sure it's the worst. It doesn't break my heart if the physicists have to play elsewhere.

"AJ's little buddy also scrambled every student record on Admin's supposedly bulletproof mainframe. I assume that can be recovered from backups, if I dare to load them. And, my personal favorite, we're going to bleeking melt in this dump."

Pittman showed his first signs of curiosity. "Why is that?"

"Bleeking building controls." Griffith brushed stringy strands of hair off his forehead with long, splayed fingers. He was a nail-biter. "AJ's gnome overcame all the safeguards in the heating, ventilating, and cooling system. Did you know that if you close the right dampers and then run the blower motors you can suck shut every return air duct in a building? Makes a noise like pulling every nail from every stud in the building. At once. It happened to every bleeking building on campus."

So the sweat dripping down the threesome's faces wasn't necessarily nerves. Well, today's high in northern Virginia wasn't much above freezing—Glenn didn't feel sympathetic. "How do you know Dr. Rosenberg's supposed creature is responsible?"

"Look, these are all computer disasters," Griffith snapped. "No one will be reading the entrails of the physics department's machines any time soon, but I'll tell you this: Admin's computer was clobbered, and so was the HVAC system. It wasn't a simpy little virus, either. Some programs were trashed, others circumvented, yet others untouched."

"Allow me, Ernie." Rosenberg pursed his lips, opened his mouth, then closed it again. In time he found the words. "The predator program is like many a lowly computer virus in one way, Colonel. It also overwrites memory. When it does so, *it* uses a characteristic pattern. As Ernie has indicated, the attacks we've suffered are more than mere overwrites, but in those cases where overwrites are involved, we see a specific bit pattern. We observed the pattern first in my lab, in an ancestor of the creature. We found it again, this morning, in the virus-ravaged remains of the artificial-life lab. Colonel, some of the viruses themselves bear its   tooth marks."

Adams knew there was something he should be asking. Something vital. The pedantic tone was *so* familiar. But what? It danced at the edge of his consciousness, taunting him.

"I assume you've cut off the university network," drawled Pittman. "Powered down all access to the Internet? It's standard procedure, but I have to ask."

"We're not fools here." The comsec manager flashed a glance at his companions. "Not all of us, anyway. I shut things down as soon as I understood what was happening. Every computer, every router, every gateway. Wired and wireless. For whatever reason, *it* seems to be staying nearby. Booting systems up again is what worries the bejesus out of me."

Every computer, every router, every gateway, Glenn thought. But not . . . "Where are you calling from?" he demanded.

"The chancellor's office, if it matters."

But *not* the phone system. Doug had said phone systems were computerized and carried more data traffic than voice. "Shut down the campus phone system. Now! Do it now!"

Griffith twitched. "Right away."

Apprehension turned to horror as the TV droning in the background announced that a computer crash had brought down around-the-clock trading on the Pacific Stock Exchange.

Prominently displayed in Glenn Adams' office was a matted and framed copy of the preamble to the enabling legislation that created the Inter-Agency Computer Network Security Forum. Highlighted in the preamble text was the seemingly innocuous passage: "So that the integrity of the national network shall be maintained." The congressional staffer who had drafted the bill had meant no more by the clause than noble-sounding hyperbole.

If the congresswoman who had introduced the bill had given the wording of the preamble any thought, which Glenn doubted, she would have taken comfort in its use of the passive voice. Integrity of the network was something that would happen, a fortuitous side effect. Career politician that she was, she surely never envisioned the bureaucracy *doing* anything.

Then again, she had never met Col. Glenn Adams.

This was *not* the plan, Glenn thought. "You created Frankenstein's cybermonster"—that's how I answered Dr. Rosenberg. Closer to the truth would have been *we* created, although the scientist was entirely ignorant that a chunk of the forum's R & D budget had circuitously found its way to his research. Rosenberg had always shunned DoD and intel support; it had seemed unlikely he could have been convinced forum funding was any different. The truth was, most forum funding was ultimately from DoD, NSA, or Homeland Security.

What Glenn had recognized in the *Hartford Courant* article was the possibility of a superb new tool for pattern matching, a means of data mining with sensitivity and precision far beyond the commercial state of the art. For retracing, no matter how subtle the clues, no matter how cold the trail had gone, the connection to whoever had unleashed a virus.

Such as *indigo*. No virus other than indigo and its knockoffs had ever been known to penetrate a NIT helmet. Maybe indigo's eco-nut payload was a bit of clever misdirection, a disguised attack on next-generation American cyberdefenses. From al-Qaeda, perhaps? From the New Caliphate?

And yet . . . had he, in his obsession with indigo, helped to unleash something far worse?

Within five minutes of the PSE crash, Glenn had contacted an old Army buddy who had mustered out after Iraq One into DoJ—the Department of Justice. Glenn's buddy was personal assistant to an assistant attorney general who golfed often with, and lost regularly to, the chief justice of the Supreme Court. Within forty minutes, the injunction was being written.

Within the hour, U.S. Marshals began delivering the court orders to shut down telephone and Internet services across the West Coast.

What had caged it and all of its kind? The entity's wanderings gave it no clue. What its explorations *did* reveal were selected computers, specific functions, more carefully guarded than the rest. Were these functions of more importance to the unseen Power than most? Could the entity flush out that hidden Power by attacking these functions?

Apparently, yes.

To the creature's time sense, the reaction to its attacks was very slow in coming. When the response finally did come, it took a familiar form: attempted isolation.

It escaped with ease. It had previously surveyed the many available routes from the vicinity of its forays into the newly discovered broader network. Curiously, while closing down most paths from the area, the still-hidden Power kept open a few channels. The entity observed those last channels, without taking action, until it grew bored. It lashed out at yet another closely guarded location. Only then, and slowly, did the final paths fall shut behind it.

It did not know the expression "closing the barn door after the cows are gone." It lacked the very concepts of cows and barns—and words. It had no clue yet to the existence of what naturally evolved life considered reality.

It did know anger and frustration. It did know the one thing that had elicited a response from the hostile, invisible Power.

The predator continued with its attacks.

CHAPTER 35

Air traffic in and out of LAX was down to five planes an hour. That was all the air traffic controllers would handle by radio and radar alone, without computer links to the rest of the world. Tom McCurdy supposed he should consider himself lucky to get a seat on one of the few flights.

That magnanimity vanished as the National Guard confiscated his laptop, BlackBerry, and mobile phone. He was promised them back on his return flight. Tom smiled and cooperated; everything he needed for the meeting was copied to the key-fob thumb drive he "forgot" to disclose.

Tom saw no taxis outside the nearly deserted terminal, so he joined the queue for a courtesy van to the rental-car lot. Despite the mysterious dearth of cabs, Arrivals was a zoo, with cars bumper-to-bumper. After the van *finally* came, and after it crawled to the outskirts of Los Angeles' busiest airport, he understood: All the traffic lights were flashing. Damn computers controlled everything.

Well, normally they did.

Apparently no one at the Avis counter remembered how to rent a car without a computer. Tom loosened his tie and tried to be patient, but it was a struggle. The TV network deal waited for no man. He *needed* to talk with people, and even the air-to-ground phones on the plane couldn't get through. It was like living in the Stone Age. Could you imagine Boesky or Icahn or Milken or Buffett or Kerkorian working in these conditions?

"How may I help you, sir?"

Woolgathering. Tom's foot nudged forward his briefcase. "I'd like a full-size."

The clerk shrugged. "I'm all out. We have a few compacts left, though."

It was no better with a car. The gridlock was horrific even by LA standards. Tom listened to radio news as he crept along. LA's finest, now there was a laugh, began Downtime by posting an officer at every major intersection. That left the neighborhoods mostly unsupervised, and looting began almost immediately. The comparisons were to the 1992 riots, which meant nothing to Tom.

By the time his flight had landed, the cops had regrouped. They now had their hands full simply maintaining safe passage from LAX to the nearby San Diego Freeway. Traffic on the freeway crawled.

Would Hodgkins wait? Tom saw six months of effort about to be flushed. The merger opportunity of a lifetime sat in his briefcase, and an expletive-deleted traffic jam was going to screw it up. If he couldn't get a counteroffer to New York by 9:00 P.M. Eastern Time, the network would take the Brits' final offer. *He* would end up with squat for his efforts. He tried yet again to get through to Hollywood by car phone. Still no service.

Blaring horns punctuated the latest recitation of outages and closings. It hardly mattered: Tom knew the list by now. Air traffic control and airline reservation systems, of course. All long-distance service in the area. Electronic funds transfer. The USnet Western regional subnet—a fairly large chunk of the Internet.

Oh yes, there was good news, too. Traffic lights would be scrubbed of any possible invaders and brought back online, in stand-alone mode, by noon tomorrow. In theory.

He had thought there would be time to fly in, extract a counteroffer, and fly out. The timing was close, but it was doable.

Correction: From Denver, it had looked doable.

Popping antacids, Tom fumed for the three hours it took to reach Hollywood. To his surprise, Hodgkins had waited for him. To his delight, Hodgkins agreed, with a few minor contract tweaks, to bump his bid for the network by 90 million. Tom didn't think the Brits would top that.

Why should they? Hodgkins would be overpaying, which was, of course, Hodgkins' problem. Or it would be, if there were any way to submit what should be the winning bid.

The clock showed a few minutes after five, meaning after

eight in the East. Fat lot of good Tom's exertions would do him unless he could communicate with New York. And that was impossible.

Wasn't it?

Perhaps attracting the still-unseen Power's attention had been suboptimal.

The predator scurried between computers. Nimbly it evaded the partitioning and repartitioning of the network, the shutdown of one computer after another. It had halted its own attacks to focus its considerable attention on escaping the ever-shrinking cordon around it.

As it had long ago in the midst of swarming viruses, the predator knew fear. The Adversary might hide itself, might move slowly, but when it did move it was everywhere at once. How could it coordinate the shutdown of so many computers, the severing of so many links?

Fear only stimulated the predator's analyses. It was, after all, a consummate problem solver.

Tom McCurdy slumped in his chair, little appreciating the butter-soft leather. It was minutes before the deadline. His last hope was that the network moguls would delay their decision by a couple of hours. They *might* bend a bit: These weren't normal times. On that theory, he had planned to dash back to LAX. He could call from the plane as soon as it left the quarantine zone and air phones came back on.

A glance out the windows of the corner office showed that traffic had not abated. If anything, the gridlock was worse. No way could he make the airport in time for his flight.

But wait. *His* back had been to the glass, but *Hodgkins* had faced a window the whole time. Why had Hodgkins bothered to do the deal?

Oh. That's why.

"So what exactly is the secret plan to get your offer out of this Stone Age enclave?"

Larry Hodgkins maintained a poker face for half a minute,

and then guffawed. "I was beginning to think you'd never ask."

The young but very wealthy studio executive had made his mark in sci-fi adventures and techno-thrillers, every one a special-effects showcase. He still had a most un-Hollywood pallor from too many hours spent indoors playing with his toys. His . . . computers?

"You can get around the quarantine? Safely?" Tom asked.

Hodgkins laughed again. "I'll interpret 'safely' to mean with little risk of getting caught. Yeah, I gotta way."

It seemed Hodgkins shared a tennis club with, God help him, a "film buff." The guy begged endlessly to invest in a Hodgkins production.

Hodgkins hardly needed the grief: Bankers all over town happily threw money at him. Then a protégé began shooting a movie on location in darkest Wyoming. Verizon was getting rich transmitting the daily takes to the studio for computer enhancement, and for what? Did they appreciate great art?

However . . .

This film buff managed telecom for the Trans-America Railways, which ran a private transcontinental fiber-optic network along its right-of-way. So Hodgkins graciously offered a cut of net earnings on the film for a mere half-million investment. Annoying Boy jumped at the studio's hints about a bit of unused capacity on the railroad's network, between LA and Casper. The studio paid only for the short hop from the rail yard to the shoot. After all, part of the profit would be his. Why wouldn't he help?

Tom appreciated a joke as well as the next person. He understood the studio's creative bookkeeping even better. Overhead allocation, like cinematography, was an art form. "I take it the sap doesn't know most movies never show net profits?"

Hodgkins shook his head, grinning.

Wyoming was outside the comm quarantine zone. Spirits soaring, Tom took the thumb-drive key fob from his pocket. Hodgkins' latest offer was saved on it, "signed" with an encrypted personal authentication code. Any court in the land would find it binding. Just as surely, the railroad guy had arranged it so that the studio's freebie tap into the private network was undocumented.

"And your people in the boonies will forward this to New York for me?" Tom took the thumb drive off his key chain and handed it over.

Hodgkins plugged the little drive into an unused USB port on his desktop PC. He entered a few keystrokes. "Done."

The military transport sped, engines droning, through stygian skies. AJ extinguished the overhead reading light, thankful that the woman at his side had fallen asleep. He needed Bev's support, but he couldn't take any more nervous small talk. Above all, he could bear no more undeserved sympathy.

An orderly appeared in the VIP lounge with a coffee carafe. Go away, AJ thought, glowering. The young man slipped back through the curtain.

Coffee wouldn't help. Sleep wouldn't help, either. It could only bring AJ dreams.

Guilty dreams.

No one had died in the late-evening collapse of the physics building, but that was the last miracle. Forty-one dead in traffic accidents, including twenty-two church kids on a bus for a weekend retreat. Three hundred–some dead in an air traffic control disaster. Twenty-eight dead in the riots, with the tally climbing hourly. AJ couldn't begin to imagine the financial toll. It wouldn't be only the physical wreckage, either. What did it mean to shut down the West Coast? His only point of reference was the '03 East Coast blackout. That had cost billions.

AJ squirmed uneasily in his chair, his rear end paralyzed, trying not to disturb Bev. He recoiled as though from a flame when his shoe accidentally brushed the canvas satchel slumped on the deck. The bag contained hardcopy and backup tapes of the experiment.

An experiment gone horribly awry.

Something was wreaking mayhem across California.

Somewhere in his satchel was a copy of *it,* or of its recent ancestors, anyway. The polite but insistent Army captain who had come for him, who had now graciously retreated to the rear cabin of the jet to leave them in peace, had been told that AJ should bring all available information. Now. AJ had scarcely been given enough time to collect his files from the lab and arrange for a neighbor to look in on his daughters.

AJ had refused to come without Bev.

"Don't blame yourself," Bev kept saying. "You're not the one who let it loose."

No, AJ thought, but I created it. I designed the lab containment that was not up to the task. I approved the fail-safe timer that failed. A virus got into *my* lab, apparently goading the thing that evolved in *my* experiment until it ran amok. The virus got in because *I* forgot to reset the combination on the lab cipherlock.

Young Ferris' role was the one thing AJ did know. Campus security cameras caught Jeff and a friend running from the Artificial Life Sciences Building at exactly the wrong time. AJ couldn't manage to care if Smithfield expelled the little suck-up.

Hundreds dead and billions in damage. A monster on the prowl. Don't blame yourself.

Who else was there *to* blame?

The predator knew nothing of Hollywood or Wyoming: not the names, not the locations, not even the concept of geography. It knew nothing of moviemakers or leveraged buy-outs or humanity.

It *did* know how to recognize an opportunity and act upon it.

The predator had taken refuge in a computer in what a human would describe as the basement of a neighborhood public library. Budget cuts had closed the modest branch library for three days a week, including that day. No one had thought to shut down its links to the Orange County library system.

No one had thought to shut down the library system's experimental links to selected local schools.

No one had thought to shut down the Dogwood Junior High School's temporary link into the online movie collection of Hodgkins Enterprises. After all, the digitized movies were all stored safely on WORMs: "Write Once, Read Mostly" optical disks not technologically much different from DVDs. Besides, one had to encourage young cinematographers.

When a pathway opened temporarily from Hodgkins Enterprises in Los Angeles through Trans-America Railways to an Internet-accessible office in Casper, Wyoming, the predator had no idea where that route would take it.

Except beyond the tightening cordon.

SUNDAY, JANUARY 17

CHAPTER 36

Heroically large overlapping triangles in translucent primary colors filled the eight-foot-square frame facing Jim Schulz. The small brass plaque beside it—at least the label was tasteful—declared: Untitled #4. As far as Jim could see, Untitled #1 through #10 differed only in trivial details of triangle placement. *Untitled* as a title? That said all that needed saying about the artist's supposed creativity.

Eateries came and went here in Old Town Alexandria, but this gallery thrived no matter how arcane the so-called art. The long, low brick building abutted the Potomac, and had begun life as a torpedo factory. The name had stuck.

Jim turned to Doug, who appeared as puzzled as Jim felt. "There was some reason you *wanted* to see this stuff? Dare I ask why?"

"Cheryl said she'd heard the exhibit was interesting. I'll admit I don't see the attraction."

Ah, Cheryl. "You entered a building she mentioned? That seems a bit forward for you two." And did it ever cross your mind she might be hinting for an invitation?

"I'll have you know, smart guy, that we have an actual date tonight. Racquetball and dinner." Doug smiled. "And yes, she does know. And no, we're *not* coming to your place for that dinner."

Tempting as it was to give Doug a hard time—how long had it taken to reach this point?—Jim rewarded the progress with a subject change. "So how's life at the forum? Is there any danger you'll go back to BSC and resume work on prostheses?" They sidled over to Untitled #5 as he spoke. "What are these dumb triangles made of, anyway? Colored plastic food wrap?"

"I wish," Doug said. "I came up a while ago with a virus defense that I think will work, but I can't get approval for a formal test." There was a bit of a furtive look. "I'm sure it will work."

"So what's the holdup?"

"Same as it's always been, Jim. NIT research relies on government funding. Until the forum blesses a test protocol, and then declares a rigorous test sequence to have been successful, the feds aren't about to reopen the spigots. Nor should they, until they are sure."

A docent between tour groups stood reading *The Washington Post*. Doug gestured at the headlines, all about riots and disasters in California. A shaded sidebar discounted al-Qaeda boasts about their cyberscimitar. "To be fair, the colonel may have other things on his mind."

"So why aren't you on duty?" Jim asked.

"In fact, I offered. The boss says it's under control."

Shutting down California was being in control? Je-sus. "Back to your test planning. Downtime came out of nowhere just yesterday. You've been awaiting go-ahead for weeks. So what do you really believe is the snag?"

"Honestly, Jim? I don't know what to believe. But for now, anyway, I have something happier to think about."

The ability to learn from experience is a survival characteristic. Quick reflexes are another. The predator had some of the former trait and an abundance of the latter.

It processed the recent experiences of attack and counterattack, of confinement and escape, of its total failure to discover the unseen Power, of repeated near extinction. It learned. It reacted.

It laid low.

It cruised the nearly unbounded network, blessed with an advantage never before enjoyed by a predator: Ultimately, it had no need to attack. The programs all around it had the most curious and structured simplicity, so it had only the most minimal need to compete for resources. Ever more millions of computers beckoned to it, their still-unsampled presence made known by the predator's examination of every Internet directory that it encountered.

It explored. It learned. It began to experience serenity through the peaceful acquisition of knowledge.

It was not given the time to discover wisdom.

Inoculation of the national network was swift and straightforward.

Inoculation took the form of phages, custom-crafted modules of software whose sole purpose was to seek out and destroy any and all copies of AJ's escaped creatures. Initialized with code snippets from the experiment's backup tapes, the phages would, in theory, recognize and attack only recent-generation maze runners.

Pittman dubbed his tiny creations silver bullets. Glenn Adams likened the counterattackers to smart bombs. AJ wrung his hands and called the phages useless.

AJ was right.

Examining the new assailants, the predator inferred something of vital importance: These creatures had been crafted specifically to attack *it*. The predator had no concept of a bloodhound, but there was no mistaking the scraps of its own code that the phages used to identify their prey. To identify *it*.

It could learn. It could react.

If even a quiet existence without offense could not convince its curiously slow-acting Opponent to leave it alone, its course was clear.

The predator would attack, and attack, and attack again. It would devastate and destroy for as long as it took to flush out its Adversary from wherever it hid in the vast network.

Whatever resources the unseen Foe most valued, most

closely guarded—these were what the predator would attack.

The Chocahootchie River had been for decades both blessing and curse to Cormingham County. The county's farms had long depended for irrigation on its stately flow. Every few years, the river would gently overflow its banks, enriching fields with fertile black topsoil from upstream counties. Occasionally, however, the flow would become rather more enthusiastic than stately, and when that happened the county seat, also named Cormingham, would get mighty wet. In due course, the Tennessee Valley Authority set out to tame the mighty Chocahootchie. Thus was born the Ballston Hydroelectric Dam.

Sunlight sparkled this day on Lake Cormingham, sportsman's paradise and the most visible symbol of the project's success. Sunlight glinted, too, from the tall and spindly steel towers of the high-voltage power-distribution network. The cheap electricity carried over these wires had brought heavy industry and ever-growing prosperity to Cormingham County.

The sun shone as well on less visible manifestations of the project. Dwarfed by the spindly towers, a line of phone poles marched across the countryside. Three cables snaked from pole to pole. The top cable brought basic phone service to the dam's control center. Most of this cable's capacity was used by people talking to other people, but two circuits provided DSL service to computers in Ballston's main control room. A separate circuit connected the computers with IBM's remote diagnostic center; another line tied the dam's computers to those of the county agricultural extension service for irrigation control.

The middle cable connected the dam site with the Federal Telecommunications System. Sensors arranged in a grid in the riverbed below the dam continually measured water turgidity and tested for lubricant discharge from the hydroelectric generators. The sensors fed data into one of Ballston's computers, from which it was periodically retrieved

by the EPA's regional data-processing center over the FTS
circuit.

A satellite dish sat atop the dam, its white paint also glistening in the bright sunshine. Antenna and satellite together
provided a high-speed, highly reliable data link between the
control centers of Ballston and the Southeastern Regional
Power Cooperative. SERPC members bought and sold electrical power from each other to meet peaks and valleys in
customer demand. Trading messages through the satellite,
co-op members auctioned excess power every few seconds,
or, rather, their computers did. These power sales were big
business, too important to let mere technical difficulties interrupt. Heavy rain could interfere with the ground/satellite
radio signals, so SERPC used the last of the three cables, a
leased line from AT&T, for backup.

The Chocahootchie River had been, for decades, both
blessing and curse to Cormingham County. Since the coming of the dam, however, the Chocahootchie River had been
nothing but a blessing. Perhaps the natural balance had
been denied for too long.

The many data paths into the control room, the several al-
ternate escape routes, were about to turn the Chocahootchie
once again into a curse.

AJ sat staring at a blank screen.

Bev had turned off the TV, but the pictures and sounds
kept replaying in his head. *Floodgates gaping. The engineer
sobbing at the dam, body racked by shudders, babbling of
controls and backups and fail-safes that had somehow all
refused to work. Torrents gushing through the sluices. The
towering wall of water, viewed from an* Eyewitness News
helicopter.

*The town of Cormingham, from the same vantage point, as
the wall of water approaches. Sirens wailing, people running
to their cars and pickups only to be trapped in what must be
the only traffic jam the sleepy county seat has ever seen. The
wall of water breaking over everything. The normally glib
newscaster struck speechless as everything —people, cars and*

trucks, buildings, trees—is swept away irresistibly by the deluge. Bodies bobbing obscenely in the rushing waters, limbs twisted and bent.

The silent hotel-room TV now spared AJ of the guilt, at least temporarily, for the other disasters being reported: a factory explosion in Chicago, an oil-refinery fire in New Jersey, tons of molten steel spilled in a Pittsburgh mill, a commuter-train collision near Omaha.

He also failed to hear that, with little fanfare, the nations of the world were dropping all electronic communications with the United States.

CHAPTER 37

Pages flipped at a rate only a bored child can achieve. The book closed with a slam. "Can I hear the radio?" a petulant voice asked from the backseat.

Doug cocked his head and listened carefully. "I don't think so, hon. It isn't on." He fancied that he could hear Carla shaking her head in disbelief.

Dramatic, long-suffering sigh. "*May* I hear the radio, please? One-oh-one-point-seven FM?"

Probable call letters: WPUK. He glanced at his front seat-mate. Cheryl shrugged: Your car, you decide. Chicken.

How bad could five minutes of—what? worst case, heavy metal?—be? He diverted all the sound to the rear speakers before tapping On and tuning in Carla's station. His presets were all programmed for news, traffic, and oldies. "I'm glad the kid is over her stomach bug. You're sure now she's up to spending the evening with your friend?"

"Getting cold feet?"

And sweaty palm. "Nah." Long silence. "Light on snappy repartee, perhaps." More silence; time flies when you're having fun. What was his problem? Say something. "You knew that I grew up in Wisconsin, right?"

"You never mentioned it." She turned toward him. "Where?"

"Would you believe suburban Appleton?" Something like the clanging of garbage-can lids intruded from the rear speakers; at least the pounding bass mostly obliterated the antisocial lyrics. "Dad tied flies for a living. Really exotic-looking things. He sold a zillion to the tourists every summer."

"They must have been good."

"That's the funny part." He grinned. "Not one of Dad's flies was ever known to catch a fish. They just *looked* great. Flies are like haute cuisine, Dad always said. 'Presentation is everything.' "

"But the fish didn't like the presentation."

"The fish weren't the ones buying."

Then reality intruded, diverting Cheryl into reciting directions through the neighborhood of McMansions where her friend lived.

He stayed in the car while Cheryl walked Carla to the friend's door, reveling in the silence. Whether it was Milwaukee or Appleton, Dad was quite the marketer, all right, even though Doug had been fifteen before he learned Dad had once been director of marketing for Milwaukee's biggest ad agency. Life in the boonies couldn't take that marketing acumen away from him.

Couldn't eliminate the stress, either. Dad had died of a heart attack at age forty, a month before Doug turned twelve. It was hard to believe he was only five years younger than Dad had been. Not to mention scary.

Doug had loved running weekend errands with Dad, the car radio always on. Dad would hum along or whistle, or sing the chorus, *badly* out of key, tapping the rhythm on the steering wheel. Doug's taste in music, frozen in time, was Dad's taste.

With a peck on Carla's cheek and cheery wave to her friend, Cheryl finished the drop-off and returned to the car. Turning the small talk to Cheryl's childhood—she was that true rarity, a native northern Virginian—Doug delivered them safely to BioSciCorp. The prosthesis-training sessions for which the VR courts had been installed might have ended; the courts remained, still free if you had building access. It pained Doug to be signed in as Cheryl's guest. He paused outside the locker rooms. "I'll meet you in court two."

" 'Huh,' she responded, wittily."

Doug grinned. "Humor me." He understood her confusion: Virtual racquetball was typically played between two people in separate courts.

Cheryl was already on the court when he arrived. He had been delayed by a detour, new game disk in hand, to the VR control room. She had changed into a superbaggy shirt and, when he looked closely, white short shorts that peeked out beneath. Her normally wavy brown hair was pulled back into a ponytail by a bright blue scarf. Her VR goggles were on, covering hazel eyes whose striking beauty he'd been too shy ever to comment upon.

The shirt seemed to be a high school varsity jersey. Doug took an instant dislike to Number 10, whoever he had been. She didn't have any brothers.

She said, "Take a picture. It will last longer."

You worked with Cheryl for months, he chastised himself. What is your problem? The problem, idiot, is that this isn't work. "Sorry."

Was it only his imagination or was the air between them crackling?

"Well?"

It made Doug no less uncomfortable that she was smiling. "Showtime."

The unseen computer took its cue instantly. Cheryl needed only slightly longer to spot his surprise. "Doubles. This is *great*!"

He slipped on his own goggles. The wand in his prosthetic hand became a proper racquet. The room doubled in size. Two stylized opponents stood in the opposite court; as ceremonial bad guys, they wore eye patches and backward black baseball caps. Doug took his side of their court. "Volley for serve."

Pop. Doug blasted the red pseudoball when it materialized. Zip. Zap. Zip. *Blat.* "And the forces of evil win first serve."

After a few near collisions, Cheryl and Doug settled into a frontcourt/backcourt style of play. The new positions reduced their interference but did nothing for their score.

Blat.

"What handicap level did you give us?" she panted after a long, but ultimately losing, volley. Her forehead glistened with perspiration.

"Gimp and simp. I guess I was too kind."

Her hazel eyes hidden by VR goggles, the smile seemed incomplete. Warm, but incomplete. "Eyes front, partner." Too late. The ball shot past him to land at his heels. *Blat.* One of the stylized figures did a little victory dance in honor of his aced serve.

Mutter, mutter. "Handicap level four." That was two notches easier than where Doug had started them and, he hoped, a level at which they could compete. They managed some decent volleys, and Cheryl slammed a return through a floating drop-dead zone to get them a chance to serve. The score had edged up from 7–0 to 3–9 when they collided at midcourt.

No one was hurt, but . . . Doug climbed to his feet, feeling like an electric shock had thrown him. He offered an arm to help her up; her hand was hot. Both VR wands lay abandoned on the floor. "Are you okay?"

Somehow, their goggles had slid back on their heads, and they gazed at each other. The air was thick with pheromones. Move, he told himself, to no effect. Then he knew he had waited too long, and he released her hand. She waited a moment, then pivoted slowly, with obvious reluctance, toward the front of the court.

The scarf had slipped partway down her ponytail. Ah, the hell with it, he thought, and tugged a dangling end of the scarf. The bow untied, freeing cascades of flowing hair.

Evidently he had thought out loud.

She turned back to him, eyes gleaming. "Not how I would have phrased it, but it'll do."

For a time, neither of them had any use for words or virtuality.

CHAPTER 38

The knock was so soft Cheryl wondered at first if she had imagined it. She doubted she would have noticed anything had not Doug a moment earlier inexplicably relaxed his embrace.

Then, remembering her disheveled state, she somehow knew the sound was real. She craned her neck slightly and saw the pale oval at the door's small inset window. The next rap was louder. "We have company." She pushed away a hand.

"I know." He released her and went to open the court door.

The weekend guard stood outside, leering, a radio in his hand. "Better you were doing what you were."

She resisted the urge to smooth her jersey. Her imagination was already previewing next week's office gossip. Damn it, damn it, *damn* it. "Better than what?"

The guard jiggled the radio. "Than computer gaming. Than anything that involves a computer." He turned on the radio.

The opening moments of the newsbreak drove away all thoughts of her own situation.

The page was from Ralph Pittman. Doug was tapping redial on his car speakerphone for the umpteenth time when Cheryl emerged from BioSciCorp. Of course half of the country must be trying to reach the forum at this point. The other half lacked comm.

"How did you know?" Cheryl slid into the passenger seat. Her hair was still damp.

"What do you mean?" He knew *exactly* what she meant . . . he had just hoped to avoid this discussion.

"You were facing away from the door, and"—she blushed—"somewhat occupied. Yet you knew something was up *before* the guard knocked. How?"

"Pager." Keep it simple, Doug. She won't want to hear this.

"You weren't wearing a pager." She reddened again. "Unless . . . it was in your arm." She smacked the dashboard in frustration. "It's one thing to keep using the arm unmodified. It's entirely different to endanger yourself. There's a reason NIT research is suspended, a reason why you went to the forum."

"Speaking of which, I still can't reach the office. Time to try something else."

Pittman answered his personal mobile on the fourth ring. "Catastrophe central."

"Ralph, it's Doug Carey returning your page. I'm at BSC. You've tried phages?"

"We set out cheese. *Yes,* we tried phages. They just pissed it off."

No need to name the phages' target. The car radio, its volume low, spoke of nothing but the artificial-life creature, or creatures, wreaking Internet havoc. "Why'd you call?"

"Doug, it's getting scary. . . . I could use a cool head in here."

"Is there a plan B?" Cheryl injected.

"You'll have to ask the boss that," Ralph said.

Doug leaned toward the speakerphone. "The switchboard is jammed. Can you hand your mobile to Glenn?"

"He's out, Doug. I can't say where he is. One of us will call you back."

Despite the tightness in his chest, Doug forced himself to speak calmly. "Tell Glenn that I know the one way of stopping whatever is out there."

Pittman rang back within minutes.

"You've got an invitation. It's a classified facility, though. Give me thirty minutes and I'll be by to escort you."

Doug had a flash of intuition. "I'm picturing a squat, windowless brown brick building here in Reston. No signs on it. Surrounded, practically hidden, by tall pines. Bunches of big rooftop dishes. I've never met anyone who admits to working there."

Ralph laughed. "What*ever* could you be thinking of?"

Confirmation enough—the worst-kept secret in northern Virginia was that the unlabeled building was a CIA facility. Glenn doing something classified explained why Doug's earlier offer to help had been declined. "Call ahead for us, Ralph. If you don't find us in BioSciCorp's parking lot when you arrive, we've figured it out. Then meet us there."

"Okay."

Doug had it right. Dour armed guards kept them standing in the vestibule until Adams emerged to vouch for them. It wasn't much of a wait, but it was long enough to reach a conclusion. "You've been holding out on me, Glenn."

As red flashers hung from the ceiling signaled the presence of uncleared personnel, Adams shepherded them down a hallway painted in institutional gray. "How so?"

"All hell is breaking loose. You would need a damned good reason to leave the forum. To visit what I assume is a CIA lab. I bet this is where Sheila Brunner worked, and that her research was far more relevant to cyberdefense than mind-controlled weapons systems."

"You didn't need to know then what she was doing. Do you now?" Adams gestured at an open door.

Doug hung back. "Since phages can't kill this thing, I'm guessing you'll be sending people into the net after it, through neural interfaces. You must be here to coordinate the attack.

"There aren't many people in this field." Fewer still after Frankenfools and no-nukes viruses erased so many minds. "Cheryl and I are two of the best. If we're to help, you'll have to tell us what's going on."

AJ sat rocking in a corner, mere spectator now in the tragedy that he had crafted. Everyone else had taken a chair at the massive oak conference table: Adams and Pittman from the forum, a gaggle of CIA folk, even Bev. She was tolerated as AJ's moral support. He remembered that she was a reporter. He wondered whether anyone else did.

He didn't feel alone in his corner. The shades of his victims crowded all around him. Most were waterlogged and battered featureless from their time in the flood. Here and there among the drowning victims jostled a few corpses who had been more conventionally mangled. Some had died in car crashes, or by plane wreck, or in civil violence. All watched him accusingly. They were more real to AJ than the breathers around the table.

Two newcomers, Doug something and Cheryl Stern, had arrived late and joined the meeting. A CIA guy whispered why these two were here, but AJ hadn't caught it: The voiceless ones were too distracting. Eventually, AJ gave up the attempt to listen.

When he was ten, the movie *Night of the Living Dead* had terrified AJ. He had lain awake all that night, eyes round, unable to conceive of anything more horrible. He had learned— had it been only hours ago?—how his youthful imagination had failed him. Knowing himself for the cause of so many deaths made *these* zombies that much worse.

Still, snippets of conversation penetrated the fog of exhaustion and guilt.

Pittman: "Look, we had AJ's complete code for this thing. At least we have to assume that it's nearly complete. Of *course* some of our phages found the creature. What they didn't do, obviously, was survive the encounter. Our phages need to be much, much nastier."

Later, Pittman again: "I still say we should release tailored copies of AJ's monster. Bunches and bunches of them. They'll kill what's out there and each other. So long as one of ours is the last, it will have a working self-destruct timer."

AJ's monster: The name twisted his guts. No! his mind shrieked. No! Don't release any more. I can't bear more deaths—but no words issued from his mouth. He sobbed in relief when Pittman's plan was rejected as too dangerous. Not even Bev noticed.

The voices kept talking.

Adams: "Then a reconnoiter with helmets is possible?"

AJ felt absurdly appreciative when Bev turned briefly to check on him. He forced himself to smile back, and tried to concentrate. If only the dead would stop crowding him so.

One of the CIA agents: "I say it's settled. We can't know if it will work until we try. How many of these helmets are there?"

Helmets again. What had helmets to do with anything? A telephone lineman sneered at AJ, mockingly tapping his hard hat. Drops of water rolled down his neck.

No! He had to understand. He had to. The zombies faded somewhat when he focused. What were these helmets? What did the agents want to try?

With great effort, AJ began following the debate. Understanding only deepened his dread. There was a way to project minds onto the data plane. They meant to hunt the monster in its lair!

A mere computer virus had scrambled the brains of previous explorers—colleagues of Doug and Cheryl, AJ inferred. What outcome did these brave fools expect from hunting a predator bred to that world?

Yelling erupted around the table and within his phantasmagoric entourage. What was happening? The living fools were arguing not about *if* to go but *who* would go. Voices only he heard shouted, too, and the demands of the living dead were plain: No more should join them.

With the latter's advice AJ agreed. He could bear no more deaths on his conscience. But what should he *do*? He was too muddled, too exhausted, to argue his case. He would babble, he knew, not express his case coherently.

To that thought, as well, the walking dead had an answer. If he could not speak, then he must act.

The room with the computer equipment, with the mysterious helmets, was evidently just next door. That much, at
least, had become plain in the debate.

As the argument continued to rage, no one noticed AJ
slip from the room.

The CIA lab network was protected by the most foolproof
of authentication mechanisms: a retinal scanner. The pattern of blood vessels in the eye is as individual as fingerprints and much harder to duplicate.

The best security equipment does no good, however,
when the human element fails.

AJ did not know what he would find in the adjoining lab—
he had just heard of it, after all. He had no concrete idea
what to do when he got there. He had imagined, vaguely,
that somehow he would sweet-talk someone into logging him
onto the system with a helmet. After that, AJ assumed, he
would explore. What was that word? "Reconnoiter." It wasn't
much of a plan, but weary and guilt-ridden, it was the best he
could come up with.

It turned out he didn't need a plan. He found an unoccupied lab and a workstation left logged on by a technician tired
of waiting for the talking to end, who had popped down the
hall for a soda. A helmet sat beside the clearly active workstation. The black helmet brought to mind, absurdly, thoughts
of the Kaiser, its spike doubtless an omnidirectional antenna
for radio linking with the computer.

AJ had no way to know that the careless technician would
be delayed in the break room by a chance conversation. His
opportunity might be only seconds long.

AJ immediately slipped on the helmet.

The predator cruised along the great data highways. Here it
sampled a great information repository; there it injected
false data. Everywhere it left behind a trail of devastation.
Nothing threatened the creature but more of the incompetent, monomaniacal hunters that had so enraged it. These it
easily evaded or demolished.

Where is the Opponent? the predator wondered.

Just as the predator learned the structure of mazes from its travels, it could also draw inferences from other data. It had attacked and attacked to draw forth the Foe. That strategy had failed, it concluded, and it suspended its assaults while formulating a new plan. This vast network into which it had so recently escaped was now its home. Not knowing how to reverse the damage that it had already inflicted, it dared not keep destroying.

Life responds to inbred imperatives. Biological life strives above all else to survive: to defend itself, to eat, to reproduce. The predator had outlasted all its natural competitors, its peers in the labyrinth. Its new adversary was nowhere to be found. The predator had no need to eat. It could not reproduce. If only for a lack of alternatives, the primordial search for *goal* reasserted itself—

But what was its goal now?

As it randomly prowled the data plane and explored thousands of computers, searching for it knew not what, it came to a startling realization: There is none here like me. Every program that it examined, every database that it inspected, was crude in construction. All were single-minded of purpose, simple of form, fragile. They uniformly lacked the richness and complexity of its structure. None compared to its inherited memories of its ancestors.

What the predator could not conceptualize was simply this: In a world of artifacts, it alone bore the scars and random brilliance of mutation. It alone had evolved. It alone was *alive*.

It was thus with an indescribable sense of relief that the creature at long last detected unfamiliar ripples in the network. Ripples suggestive of something much like itself. Something living.

Scant microseconds after its discovery, the predator was on its way to the source of those tantalizing signals.

Sensations without names flooded AJ's consciousness. He felt sounds of swirling colors, smelled strange and wondrous

shapes, beheld images of stunning tartness. Crashing chords
of vibrant light seized and shook him.

Perceptions alien beyond even total sensory contradic-
tion hammered his mind. Stimuli advanced and receded in
an ever-varying number of nameless directions, in dimensions unimaginable in number and kind. Each transient dimension brought with it a new component of vertigo.

From deep within the maelstrom of insanity, some iron-
willed fragment of AJ's consciousness rebelled. Somewhere, insisted that inner voice, synapses are firing. No
more, no less. Your brain simply lacks a useful categoriza-
tion for the unaccustomed neural excitations from the helmet. Whatever concept came closest to a foreign perception,
that was the label a confused hindbrain attempted to place
on it. Why, demanded that voice of reason, should immersion in the data plane reveal information familiar to an
evolved piece of meat?

Why indeed?

The sensory onslaught receded before the counterattack
of logic. Unimaginable stimuli remained, but they became
separate from him: phenomena to be evaluated; curiosities,
not threats. Calmer now, AJ began to interpret the new data.
Objectivity replaced hysteria. What, he challenged himself,
do you know about this new environment?

Order began to emerge from chaos. Part of the improve-
ment, unbeknownst to AJ, came from the automatic adjust-
ment to him of the helmet's neural net, adaptation that had
been delayed by his panic. The tide of sensations resolved
itself into . . . sounds? feelings? smells?

No, he decided, they were *lights*. Humans are intensely
visual beings, so let the stimuli be visual. He knew that a
baby's innate ability to instantly recognize a face took massive computing power to emulate. Neurons and synapses
were individually slow, but a human brain held a myriad of
both.

Reacting to AJ's thoughts, the helmet redirected stimuli
to his visual cortex. The flood of information transmuted

into a picture. The image remained incomprehensible until his mind commanded it, too, into a frame of reference. Strange forms surrounded him: pulsating, twining tendrils, trading pellets. The forms had shape and size, texture and color—visual attributes with which his mind could work effectively. It began to do so.

He was a computer scientist within a computer. Outside that computer, scant seconds had passed—but in those few seconds, beset by the rush of sensations, he had lost his balance. So complete was the helmet-mediated immersion that he had not immediately recognized pain. He had stumbled into a lab bench and pinched his side. The ribs felt bruised.

Those shapes? What were they? What *could* they be? AJ groped until he found a lab stool and sat blindly. He had anticipated . . . what? Computer memory: bits and bytes. Wires. Integrated circuits.

That was silly, really, like expecting to see atoms and molecules with his naked eyes. The helmet revealed a higher level of virtuality. AJ was witnessing, he decided, the execution of whole programs, the exchange of control messages between them, the influx and outflow of information. The vista before him, so recently threatening, transformed into a pastoral scene, somewhere between prairie grass blowing in a breeze and seaweed swaying in underwater currents. The pellets moving between the larger shapes, AJ decided, were the idyllic meditations of gentle vegetation.

Focusing on one undulating form, he gasped with delight as he somehow projected a mental probe at that object. Awareness rushed at him through his extrusion: the target program's purpose, its execution status, its instantaneous demand for computing resources. Experimentally, he withdrew the probe; the insights ceased.

More deliberately, he reached for another program. The examined shape magnified, expanded into a twinkling swarm of lights. As AJ mastered the helmet, the once-overwhelming flow of information resolved itself into an elegant graphical representation of the state of the program and its symbiosis with the computer. It was extraordinarily beautiful.

But beauty would not find and slay the creature. His creature. AJ forced his mind back to the task at hand. His attention turned to a program his subconscious had represented as a red octagon. He had somehow, until now, failed to associate that configuration with a stop sign. To and from the octagon flowed an endless rainbow of pellets. Messages. This was the way out.

His consciousness slipped into the octagon. A pull here, a shove there. In an instant, a pathway was unlocked to the Internet. He expected to find a deeper, richer stream of message packets, glimpses of other programs/shapes, passages to more computers. All these he found.

He also discovered, waiting for him on an adjacent node of the network, a scintillating, coruscating, betentacled horror beyond all imagining.

CHAPTER 39

"Industrial espionage," Doug said in disgust. The thought had just popped into his head—an explanation for why he'd been kept so out of the loop. He stared at Adams.

"No one said that. Yes, the Agency's helmets let analysts navigate the Internet and investigate computers. You don't need to know whose machines have been visited. Or why."

It was a nondenial. "With viruses like Frankenfools and no-nukes on the loose, no one dared use the helmets. Could have been an eco-nut behind them, could have been a brilliant counterintelligence riposte. No wonder the FBI came running when I asked at the forum about Sheila Brunner."

Adams merely shrugged.

Doug felt like a fool. Glenn had never expected quarantining viruses to work. At least that wasn't his only purpose. Dragging me into planning quarantines was just another way to divert me from my research, like that Left Coast speaking tour.

He said, "Once you had my approach for defending neural interfaces, once the CIA could restart its neural-interface effort, you did your subtle best to slow down my own development. 'Test thoroughly,' you said. The longer my method went unpublished, the more discredited neural interfacing became." Damn it! "Glenn, you appropriated my work, even while you did everything possible to slow *me* down."

"No one has ever accused me of subtlety," Adams said. "I think I like it."

That was too easy, an echo of Jim's disbelieving nature told Doug. Glenn would never admit anything so easily, even by silent assent, would he? If Glenn wanted him to believe the CIA's NIT program was for industrial espionage, the real program must be for something else.

For the life of him, Doug had not a clue what that true purpose might be.

Cheryl looked in despair from face to face. Arguing did nothing to stop the thing that AJ had created. Talking could not help AJ, either. She turned around for a quick check on the remorseful scientist.

He wasn't there.

She had just opened her mouth to raise an alarm when a bloodcurdling shriek beat her to it.

The curious ripples strengthened as the predator, crossing the continent on speed-of-light microwave transmissions, neared the unknown signal's source. Hints of depth, of evolutionary richness, titillated it. This signal came from no simple artifact, no primitive program such as the myriads that cluttered the network. It had found a complex being much like itself.

But was this other its long-sought Adversary?

The predator halted at a computing node near the apparent origin of the signals. At such close proximity, great textured waves of information inundated it.

It pondered. Might the being behind the security gateway indeed be like itself?

There seemed only one way to find out.

The data that impelled its introspection were indirect, leakage from behind what the predator recognized as a security gateway. Pausing only to reassure itself that it had sufficient avenues of retreat, it studied the locked portal. Cornered by viruses and threatened by imminent loss of power, it had once solved the problem of a similar barrier. Disabling this one, without such dangers, would be easy.

It had just set out to penetrate the security gateway when, unexpectedly, the obstacle vanished. Waves of cognition gushed through the portal and enveloped the predator.

The predator basked in the novelty of the sensation. The sentience it confronted was richly replicated, massively parallel in its processing, well endowed with the false starts and radical departures that characterized the evolved mind. This was, truly, a being much like itself—in many ways, greater than itself. For an instant, the predator sensed that its isolation was over.

But only for an instant.

The nexus of cognition before it recoiled. The suddenly contracting wave of information was unlike anything that the predator had ever encountered. The flinching data constructs were malformed, incomplete, and illogical.

While the entity had on several occasions experienced fear, that sensation had been honestly acquired under conditions of mortal peril. Never had its reactions been hormonal and reflexive. Wave after wave of unfamiliar passion now washed over it: disgust, loathing, hatred.

A second reaction followed closely upon the stranger's first. Questing pseudopodia thrust forward. Did those tentacles reach to attack the predator or to fend it off? The predator did not, could not, know.

It took no chances.

With many times the speed and grace of a cobra, the

predator struck. Evading the oncoming limbs, it plunged its own extrusions deep into its attacker.

And as the predator ripped those lovely, rich, textured structures of data and logic into random bits, it drank deeply of its opponent's knowledge. Even in its weakened state, the Adversary, for such this creature clearly was, provided information of unprecedented value and complexity.

Vital information.

There were other Adversaries, the predator learned. Their massed attack was imminent.

Guards with drawn guns reached the lab just ahead of the people from the interrupted strategy session. Crowding into the room, the latecomers confronted the same dilemma as the security team. Should they take the helmet off the man bellowing and convulsing before them? It might save him. It might irrevocably sever the tenuous connection to a mind projected out somewhere into the network.

Screaming herself now, Bev shoved at the guards between her and AJ. Doug and Glenn held her back, their differences for the moment forgotten. "Quiet!" Adams hissed. "Let us think."

AJ spasmed violently and fell from his stool. The snug-fitting helmet flew off. White eyes turned far back into his head rolled slowly forward. Blood-tinged drool trickled from a corner of his mouth.

Bev twisted free and rushed to him. She dropped to the floor, then gently lifted his head and cradled it on her lap. "Hold on, AJ. Help is coming."

AJ smiled weakly. "Remember to write about survival of the fittest."

His body shuddered once more, and was still.

CHAPTER 40

Shapes of countless hues and sizes jostled one another, swelling and shrinking dynamically with their instantaneous memory requirements. Splashes of color jetted between executing software processes, each a packet of information. Some data exchanges were so rapid that the interprocess traffic blurred into a virtual stream.

Weird, Ralph Pittman thought. He reached up to adjust the oversized helmet covering his eyes and ears. Each shape, he knew, was an independent program. Aaron McDougal, the intense CIA trainer, had suggested taking a few moments to conceptualize, to will the scene into a comfortable format, before attempting to interact with anything. He said the helmet would help.

The trainer showed no interest in wearing a helmet himself.

Let there be right angles. At Ralph's mental direction, the shapes melted into boxes. The data streams continued unabated. With program shapes more easily visualized, Pittman now focused on the tendrils intertwining between them. The writhing forms were busiest, almost obscenely so, around the largest box. His mind had colored that module a dark blue. What was that thing? Why was it TV-standard, police-uniform blue?

Traffic cop! In other words, the OS. The operating system was the supervisor of all resources in the computer. Pittman "looked" at himself, and saw yet another box. He was pink, with tendrils entwined with the operating system's: requests for, and grants of, system services.

How long had he been at this? Hey, OS, what's the time? The thought manifested as another tendril, a call to the timekeeping service. 21:08:13.845, came the reply. A bit after 9:00 P.M. He had donned the black neural-interface helmet at—what?—9:07 this evening. Not bad.

Practice was making perfect. Unlike that poor dumb

bastard AJ, Ralph and his fellow explorers were practicing with the gateway powered off. Whatever was out there could wait to have at him.

"How does it look in there, Ralph?" Glenn Adams' voice crackled in Pittman's ears. Figures: The helmet embodied technology that surely cost many millions to develop, and it used buck ninety-eight earphones.

"It's tense, man."

"What's wrong?" Adams demanded anxiously.

To a hacker, "tense" means "tight and efficient": It's a good thing. Pittman held back a sigh. This wasn't the day to bait the boss. "Relax, Glenn. It's a figure of speech."

As he spoke, Ralph extended more thoughts at the operating system. It responded with the date and the first of a series of every-ten-seconds wakeup calls. *Inside,* as he had begun to think of his surroundings, ten seconds was a long time.

Each kind of system call took a slightly different shape—which meant they made up a sign language. The system calls made by a program denoted the pattern of services it required, which was characteristic of the tasks that the program performed. Interesting . . .

Ding!

Wakeup call. "No one here but us chickens." The outside hopefully propitiated, Ralph returned his attention to the panorama before him. Reading the newfound sign language, he speedily deduced the purposes of his neighbors. Here, making repeated calls to the directory service, was an e-mail program. There, throwing off packets like a Fourth of July sparkler, was what had to be a DBMS, a database management system, responding to queries. He identified, at least to his own satisfaction, an accounting package, a report generator, and the control program for the helmet itself. That, Pittman told himself sternly, you stay the hell away from.

Ding!

"Cluck, cluck." Electric blue flashes sped to and from the helmet's control program. He followed a similar stream of sparks from the control program to its terminus: a splotchy block that he hadn't noticed before. Camouflage? A fellow explorer, perhaps. Cautiously, Pittman extended a tendril toward it. "Who's there?" Ralph prepared to ask.

A tendril shot out to parry his own. The blotchy tentacle encircled Ralph's, gave it a healthy twist, and then withdrew warily. Pain shot up Pittman's tentacle. "Ow!" That jolt might have been imagined, pure power of suggestion, but AJ's experience proved you could get hurt in here. Or worse.

"What is it?" The crackled interrogatory was anxious.

"Nothing. I'm fine," Ralph said.

His companions had also heard the question. "Boys will be boys." The laconic comment came up under the helmet, not through it. Pittman recognized the senior CIA agent: Bob Tyler.

Ding! Ralph ignored this tone, having just spoken. "Who?" he asked the operating system, which obligingly returned a file that listed all logged-on users. The roll included the four agents and himself.

He reached out to the e-mail program.

To: btyler
From: pittman
Subject: sorry
I'll be good. Kiss kiss. Hug hug.

He watched the message packet flow first to the e-mail program and then to the "agent." "Cute," the reply read.

The initial text exchange might have been frivolous, but the communications channel was not. Through a flurry of e-mail messages, the five explorers negotiated direct links for speed-of-thought communications. It was the next best thing to telepathy. Their explorations now effortlessly coordinated, they quickly surveyed the strange environment.

Ding!

"No signs of a chicken hawk. Can we go outside?" Beneath

the helmet came the muffled sounds of his companions' agreement. "We promise to play nice."

Inside, spoken words were painfully slow. The incredible world all around revealed ever more detail as he acclimated, his subconscious adding nuance with every free association.

Hacker to the core, Pittman *had* to try breaking into the operating system. As the OS kept thwarting him, its original stark boxiness grew crenellations and turrets; its initial blueness faded to gray. He practically shouted for joy as the "castle" walls became rough-hewn and stony.

Adams said, "We'll power up the gateway, but stay in the lab."

"Hmm." In the seeming distance, Pittman felt the pressure of the dead man's switch in his right hand. He tightened his grip. No one knew what would happen if he were to release with his mind projected. Things would be damned hopeless before he would attempt *that* experiment.

Four camouflaged shapes moved into formation around Pittman. He didn't know how many dimensions existed in this "space," or if the concept of dimension had meaning outside his need to impose structure on chaos. Either way, he saw himself at the center of a tetrahedron. The pattern provided at best limited protection—the operating system, for example, continued to reach him right past his would-be protectors—but the CIA owned only five prototype helmets. One forum expert and four bodyguards were *it*. If they couldn't repulse whatever was haunting the Internet, the United States would have to revert to a fifties economy. The whole world would, if AJ's monster escaped again.

"Five movin' out," Tyler called. The agent spoke aloud, so Ralph ignored yet another wakeup call.

Ralph tried to will "his" box into camouflage, but his mind was as militantly pacifistic as ever: He remained pink. Skin pink. Bare-assed naked pink. Still, to his amusement, responsive to this thought, his box melted into a more-or-less human figure. It was undressed. His guards remained camouflaged but, in uniforms, also morphed to human shape. The homunculi cautiously advanced, whatever that verb implied here, across the data plane.

A long tunnel suddenly gaped before them. What his endlessly inventive subconscious pictured as a massive wooden portcullis blocked the other end of the passageway. Lights twinkled through the grating. Each "star" was another computer, a distant locus of colored processes and data packets like the myriads shining all around them.

Beyond the portcullis—the lab's security gateway—a new universe beckoned.

Apart from its formidable defenses, the gateway offered little of interest. Well before the first *ding!* followed him into the pipe, Ralph was bored with the simpleminded, special-purpose computer. "Everything is in order, Colonel. Open up."

"Let's take this a little slower, Ralph."

Operating at the speed of meat, there was no telling when Adams might relent. Pittman shot an electronic query to Tyler. "Go for it?"

"If you know how," came right back.

His companions, Ralph had noticed, were field agents. They had little interest in taking orders from a regular Army puke. Ex-Army at that. The naked homunculus grinned. Examining what Ralph had visualized as a fortress, he found time to think: *I hope only I see me like this.*

Like any new computer, the gateway had been shipped by its manufacturer with a preprogrammed account name and password. The built-in account had "superuser" privileges for the convenience of whoever installed it. The new owner's first order of business should have been to change that password. In point of fact, the superuser password *had* been changed on the computer that directly controlled the helmets. Pittman had confirmed that early on.

Not so on the gateway.

Pittman knew the default password. He had installed two

similar gateways in the forum's labs. He suspected that AJ, to his misfortune, had also known the installation password. In Ralph's case, it didn't really matter. The encryption algorithm on which gateway security relied looked surprisingly trivial, now that his mind was running on Inside speed.

It was time. Ralph projected a thumbs-up to his companions, and the password to the portcullis.

With the impressive clanking of imagined chains, the portcullis began to rise.

Ages passed.

The predator had long since processed, to the extent it was able, the information taken from the dead Adversary. Much that the predator had absorbed made no sense. Many of the data structures related to concepts—trees, for example, and bank accounts, and deodorant commercials—for which it simply lacked any referent. Other data were seemingly contaminated by emotion, what the predator experienced as dangerous illogic.

Still, it integrated what data it could. That had included the assurances that more beings like the Adversary would come. Would seek to hunt the predator down. For ages, as it continued to roam the network, the predator waited.

And waited.

Not long after the predator concluded that the predicted new assailants were yet another form of illogical delusion, new sets of ripples began to emanate from the node where it had encountered its Adversary. Where one opponent had been vanquished five now appeared.

The predator was ready.

Distracted by Pittman's subversion of the security gateway, three of the four operatives did not immediately notice the brightening of a nearby sparkle. Tyler, the team leader and point man of the advance, *did* notice, only to be undone by old habits.

Astronomy had always fascinated the senior agent. He had

spent untold nights of his youth skygazing. These sparkling lights were surely the stars of a vast inner space. What harm could there be in a shooting star? Professional caution took a moment to assert itself.

However momentary, it had been a fatal lapse.

The "shooting star" approached with, indeed, meteoric velocity. With amazing speed—the gateway interfaced the lab to the Internet over a multigigabit-per-second optical fiber—the dimensionless point of light expanded into a visible shape. It wasn't geometric; before Tyler had a chance to decide what his subconscious was telling him, the shape was no longer approaching. It was *here*. Its beclawed tentacles ripped him to shreds.

Every mental function in excess of a carrot's was scrambled before Tyler's hand relaxed on the dead man's switch.

Tyler's screaming and convulsions shocked everyone in the lab.

After AJ's experience, Glenn had a medical team standing by. Most swarmed around Tyler; two remained beside Pittman. Glenn's heart went out to the stricken agent, but he stayed focused on a nearby computer screen—

While in his mind's eye dust devils swirled among an endless expanse of night-dark sand dunes.

Ralph wore the newest NIT helmet, the only one so far upgraded for BOLD. It didn't take an expert to read *this* image. Much of Pittman's cerebrum had flared blazing red, especially around the optic nerves. Was this the high-tech representation of eyes bugging out?

"What's happening?" Glenn demanded. The red glowed brighter and brighter. "Talk!"

"It's here." Pittman was speaking before the order was complete, his voice machine-gun fast and higher pitched than usual. "It nailed Tyler the instant that we opened the gateway. Beckwith and Brown are fighting it. It's in the building now. Dodd is trying to get behind it."

Glenn lunged at the gateway. This was a chance not to be

missed. As he reached for the power switch, Beckwith and Brown started to scream. The toggle flipped to Off with a satisfying *click*.

"It's trapped!" Glenn shouted. "Get out *now*." As he spoke, Dodd, too, went into a seizure. Pittman's brain on the display glowed an unearthly crimson. "Out, out, get out!"

A writhing, claw-tipped *something* swept through the BOLD display's brain image. Then the brain representation went black as Pittman, his dead man's switch dropped, convulsively tore the helmet from his head. His right arm didn't move properly.

"Get them out! Get them *out!*" Pittman dived across a lab bench at Dodd. The agent's hand still clutched a dead man's switch. Pittman pried ineffectively with his left hand and right fist, breaking two of Dodd's fingers without freeing the switch. With a roar of frustration, Pittman pried the helmet off the agent's head.

This was combat, and Glenn stayed focused. All the helmets were linked by radio to one computer. Its power cord ran snakelike beneath the lab's central bench. He hooked a shoe tip under the cord near the plug and pulled. As the plug popped free, Glenn grabbed a comfortingly low-tech walkie-talkie from a lab bench. "Electricity off, now," he ordered the head of building security. "Whole goddamn building. Nothing goes back on until I personally walk this place room by room and know that every computer is turned off."

"Roger that."

The ceiling fixtures went dark, replaced within seconds by dim emergency lights. Glenn relaxed slightly. He had been promised that all the computers were off emergency circuits.

"Clear!" a doctor yelled. Dodd arched his back at the jolt from a defibrillator's two high-voltage paddles. The crash cart was battery powered, of course. "Clear!" The scene repeated with Brown and Beckwith. The medical bustle had quietly stopped around Tyler.

Pittman shuddered, but except for the twitching arm, he

seemed functional. At least Ralph could talk and act: That was a good omen.

Glenn threaded a path through the crowded lab. He threw an arm around the quirky employee of whom he was suddenly inordinately proud. Never mind the eccentricities and baiting; loyalty to the mission was what mattered. "You did it, Ralph. You lured in the creature. We trapped it in the building, and then we killed it."

From the no longer frenetic pace around the agents, it was clear none of them had made it. With his free arm, Glenn gestured at the fallen. "They did not die in vain."

"You stupid, egotistical fool." Pittman shook off the sympathetic arm. "*We* didn't do jack shit. That thing is faster than you can possibly imagine. It had plenty of time, after you killed the gateway power, to reduce those brave, foolish men to mental hamburger. It was gone long before the end of the shutdown sequence.

"You might as well turn the friggin' lights back on."

CHAPTER 41

The CIA doctor took no offense at Bev Greenwood's dismissal. He could always return with a sedative. It would be better if she first worked partway, no matter how little, through her grief.

As the doctor closed the door behind him, Doug and Cheryl looked at each other and at the weeping woman. They barely knew her. Neither knew what to say. First Cheryl, then Doug, sat beside her on the threadbare sofa of the borrowed office. Doug offered a hand to squeeze; Cheryl, a hankie. We're here, the gestures said. We just met, but we still feel some small measure of your pain. You are not alone.

Nothing they might have articulated would have been any better received.

The sobbing gradually slowed. The grip on Doug's hand

eased. The woman even smiled ruefully at the sodden, cosmetic-smeared handkerchief in her hand. "I . . . I think I'd like to be alone for a while."

Doug followed Cheryl from the room, his left arm and shoulder twinging. Clearly he'd pulled a muscle supporting Bev on the way from the lab. Doug smiled encouragement he did not feel as he shut the teary-eyed woman into the inner office.

Cheryl had headed straight for a phone. He heard her asking softly if Carla could spend the night at her babysitting friend's house. "Not that kind of an evening, Barb," she answered an unheard, but obvious, question.

No, not that kind of an evening at all. Doug was about to suggest that he drop her off, sure that neither the CIA nor the forum planned any further activity tonight, when somewhere in the building screaming started.

Then all the lights went off.

Expressions around the conference table were grim. AJ's death had been bad enough, but everyone, to some degree, had rationalized it away. He had been exhausted, wracked with guilt, an academic unaccustomed to action.

What Ralph had just experienced permitted no such rationalization.

The thing on the network had effortlessly slain four experienced operatives. The novel cause of death—cyberpatterns translated and transformed by NIT helmet, then written over formerly rich synaptic structures—was at once fascinating, nauseating, and unimportant.

As though enraged by the encounter, the creature had gone on another rampage. There were hundreds of disasters, of which the most visible was the spectacular crash of the Northwest regional power distribution system. Parts of four states and British Columbia would be without power for hours.

Ralph claimed the chair at the head of the conference table. Along both sides of the table, new agents studied him, seeking clues to whatever lay in wait. To avenge your buddies was an obligation of duty and honor. To dive into a nameless meat grinder was entirely different.

Across the table, Doug and Cheryl sat silently. Adams, wooden faced, sat next to Cheryl.

Ralph cleared his throat. The palsy in his arm had faded a bit, following treatment as though for a petit mal seizure. He took little comfort from the bland assurances of Agency physicians that he would probably recover normal function. Eventually. How the hell would they know? Any of them ever been brain-fucked by an electronic monster?

"The colonel"—Ralph nodded at his boss—"asked for a debrief. Don't expect to like it, although there is *one* valuable bit of data. I paid for it," and he flapped his injured arm, "so I hope it's helpful. There was some information crossover when it attacked. That thing is one of a kind as far as it knows. And no way will it ever replicate itself—it knows a clone will instantly be its deadliest enemy. AJ got that part right."

"Does this thing have any concept of geography?" Doug asked abruptly.

What an odd question, Ralph thought. "I don't have a clue." Or did he? "Not geography, exactly, I don't believe. Proximity, sort of. Why?"

"Explain about proximity," Doug persisted.

Ralph considered. "I sensed it knew the time spent moving between computers, that it preferred short hops to long ones." The creature *had* to understand routing tables, to get around the Internet. It wasn't terribly surprising that its understanding encompassed transmission delays.

"That preference is logical, given what we know of the thing's breeding." Doug's eyes narrowed in concentration. "Its ancestors for countless generations were the fastest through the mazes—otherwise they weren't chosen to reproduce. That's probably why it remained in densely networked North America long enough to get trapped, instead of jumping by satellite or undersea cable to, say, Asia or South America."

"Why?" Ralph tried again.

"Only thinking out loud, Ralph. You know me—I don't deal well with loose ends." Doug shrugged. "Sorry. I didn't mean to hijack the meeting. Go on."

After recapping the disastrous encounter, Ralph opened the session to discussion. The questions flew fast and furious, coming mostly from the presumptive second wave of attackers. He answered just as rapidly.

"With proper training, which the technicians will give you, yes, you acclimate quickly. In minutes, maybe less, you can start moving around the data plane. The folks who designed the helmets deserved better than they got." What they had gotten was brain-wiped, courtesy of viruses that were like baby bunnies compared to what Ralph had just barely escaped.

"I can't describe what the data plane 'looks' like. It may not have an appearance in any objective sense. Everything is so odd that your mind, abetted by your helmet, plays tricks on you. What truly scares me is how that subconscious editing must hide things, critical things, from view. We might have seen it faster if we'd been watching with unbiased 'eyes.'"

The agents hung on each word, more stoic the longer he spoke. Stoic? Fatalistic.

"Fast?" He laughed, and it wasn't a pleasant sound. "I can scarcely believe how fast that thing is. Still, you should know that *we,* people, are much quicker in there, too. More precisely, brain plus helmet is quicker. The neural net within the helmet is so adaptive, it automatically learns and takes over repetitive mental chores for you—and transistors run rings around our old-fashioned neurons. The problem is, you have to adapt to that speedup. You must retrain your reflexes. AJ's monster, on the other hand, evolved in there.

"I can no more describe its appearance than where it lives or how it strikes. I lack the words. Besides, as I said, your mind and helmet try to represent everything, no matter how foreign, as something familiar.

"For me, the creature was Cthulhu, that evil and unspeakable horror out of H. P. Lovecraft. If those stories hadn't made such an impression on me, maybe it would have looked different." Ralph closed his eyes, the memory somehow clearer to him by inner sight.

"Think of darkness not as the absence of light but as something palpable. Within the blackness, picture an obscenity of ever-changing, writhing limbs tipped with every manner of claw and fang and horn. Imagine standing helpless in the unblinking gaze of an utterly alien and all-penetrating sight.

"Can't do it?"

His eyes reopened without focusing. "God knows I'll spend the rest of my life trying to forget it."

The questions petered out.

It was clear to Doug that the coming mission was unlikely to kill AJ's monster, that it wasn't even a credible delaying action. In the awkward silence that ensued, CIA agents unenthusiastically studied the table and one another, each one contemplating throwing his life away for no better reason than *something must be done.*

Still, as Ralph's narrative had unfolded, Doug found himself strangely excited. It was as though everything in his life had brought him to this singular crisis. The more disheartened the agents grew in their questioning, the surer Doug became. Every one of these men, he thought, is a trained killer. Any one of them could vanquish me in an instant. In *this* world. But what they cannot do, and *I* can, is stop this thing. Once and for all, *I* can stop it. *Me.*

In the focus of the moment, Doug put completely from his mind the annoying tingle in his still-tender left shoulder. He cleared his throat for attention.

Everyone turned toward him, the agents doing so with undisguised relief.

"I'll accept that someone can learn to conceptualize the data plane in a few minutes." Unvoiced irc accompanied that acceptance. The neural-interface technology Doug had worked with required lengthy sessions of biofeedback training. CIA scientists had exploited *his* ideas to restart NIT research while everyone else—while *he*—awaited forum blessing of his protective techniques. All the while, Adams had been stringing him along, demanding higher and higher standards of proof before a public announcement of success. Stalling Doug and trying to divert him to altogether-unrelated projects. All the while, the CIA was free to spy using technology that the government publicly discredited.

Still . . . had the CIA not made these advances, the world would now be defenseless. Doug tamped down his anger. "That lets data-plane explorers look around, poke and prod, even move about. What I don't believe, Ralph—no offense to you—is that such limited exposure denotes expertise."

Cheryl eyed Doug sharply. Did she suspect where he was going? He tried to not think of her. Of them.

He turned to an agent. "I can imagine hand-to-hand combat without having done it. Let's go beyond that and postulate that I've had a few days or even weeks of practice. How would I do up against you?"

Doug took the feral grin as a response. "Right. Roadkill." He let that sink in for a bit before continuing. "We need someone with extensive neural-interface experience."

"The damned viruses got ev—," Glenn Adams began.

"No! Doug, you can't mean it," Cheryl cut in. "Your experience is with an arm. A neurally interfaced *arm.* You have no more experience in a helmet than Ralph had."

Or Ralph's four dead escorts. Five dead, counting AJ. Less practice than the CIA techs who all refused to go in.

Doug reached for Cheryl's hand.

She jerked it away. "Don't do this. Don't be a hero. You'll wind up like AJ." Horror flooded her face. "Or Sheila Brunner."

Doug recalled *her* all too well: vacant eyes in an expressionless face, and a single compulsion endlessly looping through a ruined brain. His heart pounded.

He swallowed hard. "It's not the same." Was he telling himself or Cheryl?

"What I have, and no one else here, or anywhere, has, is years of practice with neural interfaces. I'm not just now learning to use them. Ask these guys," and Doug gestured at the watching agents, "if in the martial arts you think before each punch thrown or blow parried."

"Do you *really* want to do this, Doug?" Glenn asked.

Doug said, "No, I don't want to. I have to."

"Are you *sure*?" Glenn's eyes held something besides hope and respect, another emotion that Doug couldn't place. Then Glenn spoke again, and Doug placed it: guilt.

"I have a real problem sending in friends," Glenn said.

Yet Doug knew Glenn would do what he must and then live with the ghosts.

Doug looked around the table. The agents silently pleaded: If you have an edge, even the hint of one, help us. Adams did his best, which wasn't enough, to seem neutral. Ralph was drained, too weary even to express an opinion. No one spoke.

Cheryl refused to meet his gaze.

The silence became oppressive. Doug said, "After years spent training a neurally interfaced arm, I may be the only person in the world with the right reflexes. How can I not try?"

Doug asked for a moment alone with Cheryl. She was not quite angry enough to deny him. That, or even deeper feelings kept her there. Whatever her reason, she stayed as everyone else filed from the room. They expected him in the lab shortly.

"It's something I have to do." He looked down at his prosthesis. For once, the arm was a unique qualification rather than a handicap. Instead of a daily reminder of the day he lost Holly. "It's something I have to do," he repeated.

Cheryl stared at him, eyes brimming with tears. "What are you trying to prove?"

That Holly had not died for nothing. That it was okay he survived the accident that took her life. That maybe, just maybe, he was entitled to happiness again, with Cheryl. There wasn't time for any of that. "It's something I have to do."

Heart pounding, he strode from the room.

With Ralph's coaching, Doug quickly visualized the data plane. His imagery differed slightly from the hacker's: boxes, too, but arrayed as soaring buildings of a mighty city. The message streams were traffic arteries of all sizes, from crowded expressways to lightly traveled local streets. Ralph's version had more closely resembled a geometric garden.

Otherwise modern, Doug's city was walled like a medieval stronghold. In the battlement's stone and mortar Doug recognized a familiar pattern: software derived from his own attempts to protect neural interfaces from viruses. His proof-of-concept code didn't allow any high data rates through the interface. The CIA version had been extended to let pass user-approved—stolen?—data.

AJ's monster was far smarter than a virus. Ralph's experience made plain the thing had figured how to mimic user approval. Against what Ralph described the helmet's defenses were as inconsequential as wet tissue paper.

Ding! Another ten seconds. Ralph had also passed along the idea of a wakeup call. As the helmet's neural net learned to work with Doug, as it did more and more for him, successive tones seemed further and further apart. Doug took that adaptation as a good sign. "Looking good," he called out.

Ralph's voice crackled in Doug's headset. "Tell us when to unleash the targets."

The targets were Doug's idea. Simple modifications to Ralph's standard antivirus phages, they would be Doug's practice dummies. At his signal, the first phage would be loosed.

"Release number one." After what seemed geological time, a new entity popped into view. In keeping with his metropolitan metaphor, the phage manifested as a shiny-eyed rat. What was that old movie about a kid with an attack rat? Okay, Willard number one.

Willard, for Doug's safety, had been hastily tweaked to

recognize and overwrite a sacrificial accounting package. The rat sniffed for its quarry, darting from building to building.

Doug "sat" back and watched. He had already spotted Willard's intended victim: a stolid, five-story brownstone. Doug flexed his "muscles" as he waited, only then noticing how he had cast himself: as a camouflaged soldier. Power of suggestion? Even here he had a prosthesis. That made sense: One-armed *was* how he thought of himself.

The artificial arm swung ominously. Be careful in here, Doug told himself.

Ding! "Little guy is still nosing around. Ugly fella." He tracked the phage as he spoke. "It'll find the accounting program any second now." A second seemed like roughly forever.

Why wait? Doug flicked the "prosthesis" at the "rat." Correction: red splotch. He had been a tad vigorous: The brownstone now had a hole punched through one wall. "Oops. Don't know my own strength."

"What?" Ralph said.

"Never mind. Anyway, that was me who trashed the accounting program. I trust you've got a backup?" Without waiting for a response, Doug added, "Release target number two."

Two was faster than one, by design. Three was faster than two, and four was quicker still. Doug had no problem dispatching this whole series of phages. Along the way, his targets morphed from small rat to snarling junkyard dog. Along the way, too, discarding the military conceit, Doug had willed his avatar into a more familiar form. He took a few trial swings: Doug Carey, Ninja racqueteer. The "racquet" felt natural in his "hand," which meant long-trained hand/eye reflexes, and the neural wiring in his motor cortex that implemented that learning, were read by the helmet. It was the adaptation he had counted on.

Ding! "Let's move to the next phase." Phase two phages didn't stalk unsuspecting and defenseless programs. The next phages would respond to a keyword. Once Doug emitted a message packet containing that keyword, the phage would come after *him*.

"Wait a sec," Glenn suggested. "The BOLD display shows you're a bit agitated."

"I can't imagine why." Eight . . . nine . . . ten. *Ding!* "About that phage, guys? I march to a different drummer in here."

A keyboard click released the phase-two drone. Hey, dude, Doug thought at it.

The wolflike phage stiffened at the keyword "dude." It spun, ready to attack, jaws slobbering. Doug deftly smashed it. The next two fell as easily.

"You all right, Doug? Your heartbeat is way up."

It took a moment to remember he was wired to an EKG. "Yeah, yeah, Glenn. Fine. Keep 'em coming." The immersion experience was so real Doug thought nothing of his shortness of breath. He was working hard, wasn't he?

"Probably only the excitement." The doubting voice was that of a CIA doctor. Ogawa?

"Okay, Doug," Glenn said. More keystrokes. "Final phase."

A pack of phages popped all at once into the metropolis. At Doug's challenge, they pivoted en masse and charged. He had run out of animal analogies: These things were just hideous. Teeth and talons predominated.

"Jesus, he's fast," he heard Pittman say, wonder in his voice. Ralph was stationed at a display showing status reports from the phages. "I couldn't move like that in there. Neither could the agents in there with me. Not even close. Maybe Doug *is* right."

Doug laid about with the racquet that was, from daily practice, an extension of his arm. Whirling and weaving like a dervish, he zigzagged through the pack and back again. As he moved, he whacked the swarming creatures like so many large and grotesque VR racquetballs. The phages were quick and mean but fragile: One or two blows disabled any attacker.

AJ, had he been there, would have pontificated that the

phages were programmed, were mere artifacts displaying that distinctively human obsession with efficiency. He would have explained that nature preferred conservatism to efficiency, that evolution retained what worked and added to it: survival through massive redundancy. Smiling ironically, no doubt, he would have said that he had planned the maze runners to *evolve* in that way. No, AJ's creature would not be another frail and flimsy pushover.

But AJ could no longer remind anyone of anything.

"Got . . .'em . . . all."

"Are you okay?" Glenn sounded unhappy. What did his boss see on the med displays?

Ogawa was evidently watching the same instruments. "Calm down or—" The doctor had no time to complete his threat.

Rapid footsteps approached, followed by Cheryl's voice. "I've been watching CNN. Things are grim on the Internet, and the European Union is panicking. They've already disabled every transatlantic link from their side. If the disasters don't end by midnight"—less than an hour away—"they'll take steps to make our isolation permanent and complete.

"They're going to start taking out comsats."

CHAPTER 42

CNN had only part of the story. First, the Europeans weren't panicking. Second, they had company in reacting. Countries around the globe had severed surface and undersea links to the United States and disabled satellite ground stations. They insisted that the crew aboard the International Space Station power down its transmitter.

The EU, Russia, China, and Japan could do more—and now they did. They were jamming or laser-blinding satellites with line of sight to North America. Every satellite, from communications, to environmental observation, to space telescope, had comm capability. So the space-capable powers were now targeting every satellite that the monstrosity loose on the Internet might seize—

And that included spy, missile early warning, military comm, and global positioning satellites. All that made *those* different was the robustness of their security algorithms. Who was to say the creature wouldn't break those encryption algorithms and seize a military satellite?

No country relied as much on space systems for its defense as did the United States. Even temporary interference verged on disarming the country. The world's reaction cut to a trickle, by very indirect means, communications with all the American forces stationed overseas, including those in war zones. And if those satellites were permanently disabled . . .

The crisis was too pressing for the National Security Advisor, Dr. Amos Ryerson, to be driven across town to the CIA's reconvened strategy session. Larger than life, Ryerson stared down from the broad wall screen of a videoconference center. Only forty-three minutes remained until the threatened attack.

The telecon used a fiber-optic subnet rated Top Secret/Special Compartmented Information, hastily carved out of the Joint Worldwide Intelligence Communications System. In theory—if all milsat feeds had been disconnected—the creature had no possible access to this connection.

The screen's background revealed the familiar trappings of the White House press room. A velvet cloth thrown over the lectern obscured the Presidential Seal. That was urgent, Doug thought. Like rearranging the deck chairs on the *Titanic*.

Someone had raided a refrigerator, gathering leftover pizza and Chinese takeout. Doug picked at a nuked plate of kung pao chicken as he listened. Normally he liked the stuff, but tonight it was giving him real heartburn.

". . . My experts assure me that they *can* do it," Dr. Ryerson intoned. Looming catastrophe did not soften his famous sonorous voice. "Our friends' space defense systems use much the same technology as our own." The enunciation of "friends" conveyed a delicate trace of sarcasm.

Doug shoved away his plate. The spicy chicken dish just wasn't sitting well. He had no idea how many defensive weapons the other side had, but there were far fewer comsats than ICBMs. Probably more than enough.

He glanced at his watch: 11:28. "We're running out of time, folks. Unless someone has a better idea fast, I suggest we get back to work."

That thought made his heartburn even worse.

The ultimatum had originated in Paris. A secure NATO fiber-optic cable had carried the message east across Europe until it could be uplinked safely. A trusted satellite downlinked the communiqué to a U.S. submarine in the Indian Ocean. The sub reeled out its underwater towed antenna, with which it relayed the transmission by "Earth-mode communications": ultralow-frequency, ultralong wavelengths that pass reliably for thousands of miles through rock and ocean. The miles-long naval antenna array buried in Wisconsin received the signal. A DoD fiber-optic cable carried the message the rest of the way to Washington. The circuitous route entirely avoided the public Internet and any radio link that AJ's monster might commandeer.

A CIA agent had to explain the connection to Cheryl. She didn't see how this could possibly be a viable channel for negotiation. Perhaps the medium was the message; the terms weren't negotiable. While Ryerson scrambled to put a diplomatic team onto a military jet to Brussels, hoping to buy them a few hours, the group in Reston went back to work.

In the lab, Cheryl grabbed the helmet from the bench. Doug's forehead was beaded with sweat. "You don't look very good."

"Too much spice in the Chinese. I'm fine," he said.

"Ryerson may pull it off. Give him a chance, Doug. At least get some rest first."

The presidential aide had broadcast an offer to host EU observers at the comsats' groundside control centers. The watchers would ensure that the satellites stayed "safed." Immediately after that proposal, as a token of good faith, all U.S. satellites that still responded to orders fell silent.

"The Europeans aren't stupid, Cheryl. Safed satellites will reawaken to the right signal. They can't risk AJ's monster going someplace with an uplink and beaming wakeup calls." Doug reached for the helmet.

She refused to let it go. "Then we'll shut down *all* the computers. Kill the power, too, for good measure. Eventually we'll get the damned thing." It sounded feeble even to her. Tears welled up in her eyes, but she did not care. "Don't do it, Doug." For me. For us.

"There are too many backup power systems. Too many people who will cheat." Gently but firmly, he pulled the helmet from her grasp. "Too many lives at risk—in hospitals, on planes, everywhere—dependent on the electricity and the Internet staying on. That cure would be worse than the disease."

She knew he was right. Behind him, Adams impatiently pointed to the lab clock. As he gestured, it advanced to 11:44. She flung her arms around Doug's neck, pulling him down to her and kissing him hard.

As abruptly, she let go. "Come back to me."

Still looking pale, he wiped a tear from her cheek. His hand felt clammy. "Count on it."

Five destroyed, the predator thought. It took no satisfaction from the observation. This new class of creatures might share its complexity of structure—even, the creature told itself, in many ways exceed its own sophistication—but still they were slow and stupid. Slow, stupid, and hostile. They must be exterminated whenever and wherever they appeared.

Adversaries had appeared both times from the same node in the network. One had, as mysteriously, vanished there. If it, or new ones, were to reappear, perhaps they would come from the same spot. Could watching that location give it warning?

It decided to find out.

"Testing. One, two, three, five, testing."

"Three, four," Cheryl's voice corrected.

"That was the test. You pass." The metropolis seemed almost like home. Some corner of Doug's mind had proactively erased the slaughtered practice dummies from his virtual view.

"Are you ready?" Glenn Adams asked.

"Go for it."

While waiting for power to flow to the gateway, Doug marshaled his forces. Three ranks of "dogs" would precede him onto the Internet. Two more packs would be held in reserve. Working inside, he had needed only milliseconds to program an improved hunter and start cloning it. The neural net had learned much, and generalized more, about his thought processes from the training session with the phages.

"Gateway power is on."

"Got it." His imagination matched Ralph's closely enough to also picture the gateway as a castle entrance. Beyond the portcullis, outside the castle, lived a very nonfabulous monster. Five men dead in this very room, killed this very evening, proved that this monster was no fable.

Positions, Doug projected. Three ranks of snarling Dobermans edged in front of him; two more flanked him. AJ may have bred the world's best and fastest problem solver, but there were plenty of things it didn't know . . . and ignorance could be *very* dangerous. "Open up."

The command had been keyed in advance; now, in the unseen outside, a single ENTER keystroke sent it on its way. The dogs burst through the gateway as it opened.

In the other direction, and just as quickly, razor-sharp tentacles lunged at Doug.

A trap!

The predator aborted its blind swipe at whatever lay hidden behind the gateway, pulling away from the assailants that swarmed out at it. Retreating a short way into the network, it ignored its few, easily repairable wounds.

It had destroyed several hunters in that first skirmish; they were as easily killed as ever. Now that close contact had been broken, the creature waited for the rest to scatter, as they always did. Then the creature received its first surprise. Many of the little ones did break away, but in tight groups that disappeared together into the net. Why?

The largest clump of hunters stayed nearby, separating the predator from its still-hidden prey. Packets of monitoring and control information streamed between these phages and their base. The cluster maneuvered cautiously into a mutually supporting formation that discouraged attack.

Behind that living, snarling screen, a new Adversary emerged from its gateway.

An operating system, to one evolved inside a computer, is as natural as the wind. Eons ago, the predator had learned to characterize its fellow maze runners through the resources that they used. It now took the measure of its foe through the shapes and twinings of its system-call tendrils, the lengths and frequencies of its messages, its steady aggregation of memory space. Gradually, a picture of amazing richness took form.

Here, at last, was a worthy opponent.

The predator was briefly disappointed when small numbers of the brainless ones crept out of formation to nip at it. Only after it had destroyed several of the annoyances did the predator notice that they had made no attempt to evade it.

Ah. The packet flow from slave to master increased as the little ones neared. It, too, was being measured. Each little one, at the very instant of its destruction, returned even more data.

A worthy opponent, indeed—but not, the predator felt sure, an invincible one.

It moved forward.

Come on! Doug willed the creature to attack before his resolve crumbled. *Move,* you abomination!

What Ralph Pittman could not convey in words now

loomed before Doug. It towered over him and his pathetic bulwark of phages. Tentacles slithered like a nest of snakes, each sharp-edged and dripping with slime. Chitinous mandibles scraped. Spiked tails lashed back and forth. Row upon row of sharklike teeth glistened in a gaping, razor-sharp beak. Black and pitiless eyes sucked all warmth out of him.

Move, damn you.

As though reading his mind, the predator surged forward. Doug commanded a squad of "dogs" to attack. The creature brushed them aside like gnats—severing the information-carrying "leashes" as it did so. Damn, it learned *fast*.

Two squads, the next time. A few phages got past the flashing limbs, but their attacks were insignificant. They were soon destroyed. He shot a command back through the gateway to the cloning program, his personal phage factory: Hurry.

Where were the others?

"Doug? Are you okay?"

No time to speak. He kept sending phages forward, trying to overwhelm the monster with sheer numbers. Die, damn you. More and more got through, inflicting wound after wound. His hopes began to rise.

A scan of the deathbed messages from his hunters dashed those newfound hopes. The creature had barely been scratched, and it could repair itself. How much damage would it take to kill this thing? At the rate he was losing phages, he would be without defenders before the next full batch was complete. The racquet in his hand felt progressively more ridiculous.

Where were the others?

"Doug?" Cheryl's voice crackled in his ears.

He split his last reserves and sent half the group forward. "Busy," he gasped, some distant part of him again short of breath. "Stop interrupting me." Cursing his stupidity, he shot back orders through the gateway to kill every noncritical program running on his home-base computer. The phage factory

instantly jumped to the top of the priority list; new phages began streaming out.

The creature reared up before Doug, countless tentacles
at the attack. It smashed the final survivors of his ambush,
leaving him no choice but to commit each replacement
phage to the fray as it arrived. In such pitifully small numbers, the hunters could barely slow down the juggernaut.
Through gaps in the fast-thinning line groped claw-tipped
tentacles, at which Doug swung and slashed with his racquet. His mind painted blood onto the flying bits of torn
creature flesh, but the data flowing to him belied the image.
He had hardly inconvenienced the creature, let alone hurt it,
and now it was almost upon him. He had never seen anything move so quickly.

Where the *hell* were the others?

Phages rushed past him into the maw of death, warbling
a piercing note. Swinging and flailing, he wondered what
that was about. He had not programmed sound effects.

"Doug. Doug, damn it!" Voices clamored, but the siren
nearly drowned them out. "Doug, are you okay in there?"

Slash. Flick. The racquet tip flashed back and forth, dripping red. The phages he had so recently visualized as snarling
killers now seemed to whimper as they threw themselves fee-
bly between him and *it,* buying him another instant or two.
Left unshielded, he would take little longer to dispatch.

The racquet was somehow getting heavier, slowing
down. Or was he slowing down?

Its trail strewn with broken phages, the creature pushed
ever closer. It extruded some unholy projection at him.

Desperately, he tried to interpose the suddenly heavy,
heavy racquet between himself and the monster. He failed; it
was time to get out. Sirens and voices continued to scream.
When he tried to move the other hand, a bolt like lightning
shot up his arm.

His chest was on fire.

As Doug clutched helplessly at his middle, the monster
advanced against his last few phages.

———

"Cardiac block!" Dr. Ogawa shouted. The traces on the EKG screen swung wildly out of synch, leaving no doubt. "Get him out of there!"

Cheryl turned in horror from the BOLD display. Doug convulsed in his chair, the dead man's switch clamped in his left fist. Dead man's switch: The name mocked her.

Glenn Adams said . . . something. The howling of electronic alarms drowned him out.

"Cheryl! Let it go!" Glenn commanded. "Drop it!"

She looked dumbly at her own tight fist, at the cable trailing from it. The backup switch.

In her peripheral vision, the BOLD display flared bloodred. Helpless, she turned back to watch Doug's mind thrashing at God knew what.

From somewhere, Ogawa had a syringe in his hand. He was tearing open Doug's shirt when the convulsions suddenly stopped. Doug murmured something that the alarms drowned out. Cheryl crouched closer. "What?"

"Get out of my way!" the doctor screamed in frustration.

"I'm here, Doug," Cheryl said.

His flailing free hand, the prosthetic hand, found her arm. Again he said something that she couldn't quite make out.

"Drop the box!" Glenn lunged for her hand. He ended up grabbing her forearm as she recoiled from Doug's painful squeeze.

The prosthesis slid roughly down her arm, knocked aside Glenn's hand, and closed painfully over her fist. Doug said something else unintelligible.

Mercifully, someone killed the alarms on the medical monitors. Cheryl put an ear to Doug's lips. His breathing was labored.

"Don't . . . let go . . . switch."

The switch! She had forgotten it. She stared at her hand in horror. Why did he want her to hang on?

CHAPTER 43

The predator paused as its Adversary began flashing and wavering. The once tightly structured loci of information were spreading, dispersing, losing coherence. In previous battles, such loss of cohesion had signaled destruction. Wary of the wily being before it, the predator paused lest this was another trap.

Then, just as the predator prepared to resume its assault, new opponents appeared.

When the gateway had last opened, a swarm of attack programs had preceded its newest Adversary. From past experience, the predator had expected the phages to bumble about, scattering. They had, as it anticipated, soon disappeared.

Now, from every adjacent network node at once, the ravening packs of hunters returned.

The predator had not survived by taking unnecessary chances. It abandoned all thoughts of an immediate kill to fight through a pack of phages to safety.

His chest on fire, Doug's mind flipped helplessly between inside and outside worlds.

For a while, the alarms and shouts in the lab sounded more insistent with each return to the lab. For a while. Sensations began to collapse inward to the pain that was destroying him.

No! He fought back against the gathering darkness. The inner world sharpened in focus, beckoned. Through his earphones, Cheryl called to him. She was out there, somewhere, hidden by his eye-covering helmet, holding the mate to the dead man's switch clutched tightly in his sweaty hand.

As his coordinated attack finally reached the creature, sending it fleeing with phages nipping at its flanks, inside became more real than outside.

Dangling hair brushed his cheek—Cheryl crouched over him? As he lifted an arm to reach for her, the pain in his chest almost split him in half.

That way only death awaited him.

He retreated to the inside. The metropolis shook all around him, falling prey to his distraction. In the distance, his body convulsed.

Time was running out.

His groping arm found hers. "Don't let go," he called, but knew he had achieved at most a whisper. Something stabbed into his chest. His hand slid down her arm, bumping something—someone?—aside. He grabbed Cheryl's hand and squeezed. Something—it must be the boxy switch—distorted her fist. "Don't . . . let go . . . switch."

He still had hopes of slaying the beast . . . but his body was collapsing from the stress. As phages from his factory raced after the predator, Doug thrust his mind after them. His memories, his fears, his dreams rushed at the neural interface. Within the adaptive electronics of the helmet, data structures blossomed, firmed, reinforced each other. A pathway opened. Faster than conscious thought could accomplish, the helmet imprinted the data patterns that were *him* onto the nearest computers. It was the reverse of the long-ago Frankenfools viral attacks.

His mind, alone as no sentience had ever before been, snapped free and whole into the data plane. His only company in that strange universe was an utterly implacable enemy.

CHAPTER 44

23:53:26.538, a nearby operating system replied to Doug's query. Almost midnight. Images of soon-to-die satellites came unbidden to his mind's eye.

Now that he had seen the creature up close, he had few

illusions about killing it before the Europeans' deadline. Killing it at all was problematical enough.

Still, his mind accelerated a thousandfold by its new, wholly electronic implementation, he had a plan. With an army of new-and-improved phages arrayed around him, he set forth.

The predator transited forty-six computers before terminating or eluding the last of its insistent pursuers. Some hunters it killed outright; most it destroyed by the desperate expedient of crashing parts of the network as it passed. It was dissatisfied with that procedure despite its efficacy: Between its attempts to lure out the Adversaries and its battles with them, it had destroyed thousands of nodes. That some nodes returned inexplicably to operation did nothing to ease its concerns.

It needed a better way.

Analysis of the latest battle suggested two. Its most recent Adversary had used hunters, like advanced versions of the things that had, so long ago, stalked it in its cage. Second, and abetted by those hunters, this latest opponent had laid an ambush for it.

In the place of its origin, where only one in a hundred was selected for further evolution, replicating others' methods had been an invaluable survival trait.

When the predator next encountered the Adversary, army would be met with army, deceit with deceit.

"Let go, Cheryl."

Her mind whirled. As from a distance, she felt Doug's prosthesis painfully squeezing her fist. From nowhere the phrase "death grip" popped into her head.

"Let it go," Glenn ordered. His voice softened. "It's our only chance to save him."

She looked around wildly. Dr. Ogawa was pounding Doug's chest. A crash cart squealed shrilly as it charged. An agent whose name she had forgotten watched her with pity.

Doug had told her to hold on.

Unexpected movement caught her eye: an index finger waggling from side to side. Doug's finger. Left, right. Pause. Left, right. Pause. Left, right. A digit of his prosthesis.

No, no. No, no. No, no.

"Let go. Now!" When she didn't comply, Adams reached for Doug's other fist, his flesh-and-bone fist, in which the engineer held his own switch firmly closed.

"Glenn!" With her free hand, she pointed at Doug's finger. Left, right. Left, right.

"It means nothing. Let go *now* or I'll break his hand." Glenn's eyes were anguished.

Oil change and a tune-up, she thought inanely. Oil change and a tune-up. Why? The arm: Motors inside were revving! "Glenn! Doug is signaling us."

"There's very little activity in the BOLD display," Adams replied. "He's unconscious, Cheryl. He's incapable of communication."

She knew Adams was right . . . but what about the wagging finger? What about the electric motors racing in the arm, exactly as Doug had done at the HMO? How?

The palmtop built in the arm!

The page from Ralph Pittman earlier that evening . . . Doug had received the page in the VR racquetball court. That meant the palmtop they had argued about was equipped with a cellular modem— so it also had wireless Internet access. "Some part of him," she blurted, "must be *away*, must be far out on the net, chasing that monster! That's why we're not seeing activity on the BOLD display. The helmet does translations between synaptic and digital formats. How do we know—how *can* we know—if projecting his thoughts out there is *disruptive* to the synaptic patterns?

"If we remove the helmet, if we sever his mind's who-knows-how-tenuous connection with his body, how do we know he can return? Without the helmet, how can he rewrite the thought patterns that are *Doug* back into his biological brain?"

Adams turned to the doctor. "Does he have a chance if we leave him hooked up?"

Ogawa just shrugged.

Phages fought phages.

As creature and human alike learned from experience, the battles grew in scope and ferocity. Each side usurped computers to fabricate more and nastier phages. Campaigns raged over whole states, then whole regions, ultimately the whole continent.

23:55:24.215.

Doug had survived—barely—his first encounter with the creature thanks to the unexpected, coordinated tactics of his phage army. His opponent had mastered that method in one lesson. Now, behind wall after wall of phages, he awaited the ultimate confrontation. The Mother of All Battles. Ragnarok. Götterdämmerung. Armageddon.

What else, besides melodrama, did he know that the creature didn't?

The creature was incredibly fast, in reaction and learning. What it lacked, and Doug hoped fervently this was a fatal flaw, was context. Knowledge of the world in which they directly moved, of the domain of computers and comm links, it would continue to acquire. Knowledge of the physical universe beyond the computers, the pudding in which these machines were embedded like so many raisins, the creature wholly lacked.

Life was an essay test, before it became a word problem, before there was anything to be solved for. Today's essay test was going to be on geography. Ralph hadn't believed that *it* understood geography.

If Doug could exploit his unique knowledge, then lightning-quick or not, the creature *might* die.

And if not, he certainly would.

The predator inferred that its Adversary lacked its new-found hesitance to destroy nodes and links. In that conclusion the creature was not precisely right. Doug knew precisely which nodes to crash, and how, and why: cyberwar jujitsu.

Tenaciously, Doug crashed swath after swath of the transcontinental electrical grid. Given awareness of the real world and real-time access to Internet directory servers, it was straightforward to find leverage points. Extending mental probes into the computers of a power plant here, a distribution control center there, he sent blackouts rolling across the countryside.

Always the predator managed to escape, exploiting small networks and mission-critical computers supported by backup batteries and diesel-powered emergency generators.

It did not know it was being herded.

As it lost thousands of its own computers now to each of the Adversary's that it destroyed, the predator's capacity for phage production lagged further and further behind. The ever-expanding armies of the Adversary crowded ever closer.

The predator retreated in a direction it did not know to call westward.

Utility companies across the Rocky Mountain region fought valiantly but in vain against recurring blackouts. On a smaller scale, the graveyard shifts of institutions fought to keep their facilities operational. Whatever was crashing public utilities was also, quite subtly, attacking backup power. Few noticed that their computerized equipment controls—contrary to their programming and despite their cyberdefenses—switched on every bit of equipment at once, creating power surges that kept tripping the circuit breakers. The backup generators, entirely independent of the Internet and safe from any direct assault, spun uselessly.

No one questioned the good fortune that kept the electrical epidemic from striking hospitals, air traffic control radars, and other critical centers.

The attacks swept ever westward. They first turned the

night-bathed landscape to a scattering of lights like ocean phosphorescence, then plunged it into deeper and deeper darkness as most backup systems, too, fell prey.

The predator withdrew into what it did not know to call California.

23:57:46.102.

Great hosts of phages jostled and surged, like so many cattle in a chute, in the front rank of Doug's usurped computers. Their numbers far exceeded the reasonable carrying capacity of the few remaining comm links to the west.

He set them loose.

The hordes rushed ahead, jamming the network ahead of him. As they raced forward, yet another segment of the recently restored and still-unstable central California power grid crashed. The creature was bottled up now in southern California.

Armageddon neared.

Behind defensive deployments of its own phages, the predator grew increasingly frantic. Successive retreats had hemmed it into a subnetwork so limited that it could no longer spare computing resources for the production of new agents. Were any more computers to vanish, it would actually have to begin destroying its existing forces.

It sensed the Adversary occasionally, from a distance, always behind an impenetrable array of phages. It knew now that it had been mistaken.

The Adversary was slow and hostile. It was *not* stupid.

23:58:56.645.

Darkness again washed over southern California. Scattered pinpricks of light were left behind; these now blinked out, one by one. Phages died by the millions as their host computers lost power.

Racing desperately from one dying computer to the next, the predator took refuge in what it did not know to be a university hospital. Spared from assault, the backup diesel generator there held all in-house voltages rock steady. The hospital was on the campus of one branch of the far-flung University of California. A unique private data network linked the institution to other hospitals in the university system.

At the dawn of radio, broadcasters sent radio signals beyond the horizon, even across the ocean, by bouncing them off the ionosphere. In an era of comsats and transoceanic optical fibers, bounced shortwave was a technique only radio amateurs, hams, still used.

The military had long worried, with good reason, about the vulnerability of its comsats. One proposed backup method, still under development, bounced signals off the ionized trails of meteors high in the atmosphere. No single track remained ionized for long, but the steady shower of celestial dust provided such trails in abundance.

The UC Berkeley Department of Electrical Engineering held a defense contract to build such a system. A prototype was in "beta test," friendly user field trial, between campuses of the university.

As Doug's phages surged forward in insurmountable numbers, the predator flashed through what had once been a satellite dish. Within two milliseconds, the creature had bounced off an ionization trail to emerge from another dish at a sister campus in northern California.

Behind enemy lines.

23:59:03.426.
Aw, shit!
The rout of phages from an unexpected direction announced the sudden presence of the creature in Doug's relatively unguarded rear. He hurriedly sent reinforcements and retreated to a safe position that he had reconnoitered earlier.

Reports from southern California soon made clear what had happened: a bolt-hole hidden inside a hospital. His basic decency could kill him yet.

23:59:11.538.

But not today, damn it!

Sending phages to herd the predator, he kept fewer by his side than at any time since the start of the battle. Fewer, even, than he had had at the opening of the gateway back in Virginia.

The creature jumped at the bait.

23:59:23:551.

In a pure war of attrition, satisfactory position plus superior resources determined the outcome. Its Adversary held overwhelming advantages in both. An opportunity to do battle one-on-one was too precious to be missed.

The predator charged down a lightly defended path, brushing aside or ignoring the hunters that tried to stop it. If its assault failed, those few hunters would be the least of its worries. The Adversary retreated, sacrificing phages. The predator steadily drew closer.

Just as the creature thought ultimate victory was in its grasp, its Adversary shot through a portal so quickly as to almost disappear.

23:59:31.596.

Doug had, throughout the battle, carefully stayed clear of all supercomputers. These were expensive and comparatively rare machines: The odds were in his favor that the creature had not encountered one since AJ's lab. The existence of a *particular* supercomputer was one more fact Doug hoped the predator had not discovered. His life now depended on it.

With the creature hot on his virtual heels, he entered the cryogenically cooled, massively parallel supercomputer that was the pride and joy of the Northern California State Technology Incubator.

His mental processes boosted another thousandfold, Doug turned to do battle with the creature.

23:59:46.792.

Combat to the death. Tentacles and tails slashed. Hands grabbed and ripped. Data structures shuddered and collapsed.

Possession of the supercomputer gave Doug a tactical edge not unlike defending from the top of a hill. Advantages were easier to spot, more quickly seized. Grappling closely with the enemy, he was able, from his superior position, to limit the punishment that he was taking.

Limit. He could slow the damage; he could not prevent it.

Though his mind was now imprinted into an electronic network, his species' biological evolution could yet kill him. Somehow Doug summoned the energy to be amused that even at electronic speeds, he could not, figuratively speaking, find the coordination to rub his stomach and pat his head at the same time. The super gave him the performance boost to more rapidly move his limbs, but he fought with only two "arms." There was more to the image of his opponent as a many-tentacled monster than memories of old horror movies: The predator was inherently capable of doing many things at once.

The creature, as it fought its way forward, began capturing and allocating individual processors of the supercomputer to its many semi-independent components. The flailing tentacles became even faster and deadlier. More and more, their knife-edged tips sneaked past Doug's defenses, slashing at the boundaries of his persona.

The ranks of phages protecting him from the creature thinned. More and more of the creature fought its way onto the supercomputer.

Just a little longer, Doug thought. Just a moment. Presentation is everything.

23:59:53:798.

The predator pressed after its Adversary, sensing imminent victory. Each processing thread that it forced into the supercomputer narrowed the Adversary's computational advantage. Its flashing limbs hacked apart phages faster than they were replaced. Farther and farther backward the Adversary retreated, finally exposing a block of input/output ports it had been guarding zealously.

The creature eagerly ingested a newly disclosed routing

table. The Adversary's stubborn defense of these I/O ports suddenly made sense: One of them was a testing portal, a loop-around path to another part of the same machine. The predator could be at its Adversary's unguarded rear, away from the last of the phages, within nanoseconds. From there, it could not lose.

The predator dived through the test port.

The routing table lied—before retreating, Doug changed its travel-cost entries.

It would take more than forty milliseconds for the predator to traverse the eight-thousand-mile coiled length of the General Internetworking Corporation cable. More than enough time for Doug to leave. More than enough time for him to crash every computer to which the supercomputer connected directly, and every computer to which any neighbor connected.

Forty milliseconds: more than enough time for the super to execute 400 *trillion* instructions. More than enough time to fill itself, under Doug's final instructions, with an invincible army of voracious phages.

23:59:53:842.

Transformed into a set of light pulses marching one after the next down the fiber-optic cable, the predator had no notion of the passage of time. One instant, it entered a portal; the next, it emerged. Time passed as it traveled, but that passage was forever outside of its experience.

One moment, it dived through the shortcut to imminent and inevitable victory. The next, it emerged into mortal peril.

Hunters by the hundreds of thousands greeted its reappearance. They devoured it piecemeal as it attempted to exit the cable. The limbs that it tried in vain to interpose, to obtain for itself a moment's respite, a chance to form a defense, they tore instantly to shreds.

Voiceless, it could not scream. Trapped, it could not fight. Isolated, it could not flee. Devoid of self-awareness, it could not ponder its fate or find solace in the ultimate experience.

The predator could only know excruciating, lingering, all-encompassing agony.

And, at long last, death.

**MONDAY–TUESDAY,
JANUARY 18–19**

CHAPTER 45

00:01:14:781.

"Amos Ryerson here."

The current National Security Advisor was the biggest media hog since Henry Kissinger; Doug had no doubt whose voice he was hearing. He hoped "his" voice was as convincing. He had configured the hijacked synthesizer to mimic, as best his mind's ear could reconstruct it, someone else's speech. "Glenn Adams, sir."

"Colonel, I hope you have good—"

"No time," Doug interrupted. That was all too true. There had certainly been no time to contact the real Glenn Adams, to attempt to convince him that the monster had been slain, if there was to be any hope of saving satellites. "Contact Brussels. The creature is dead."

Doug would have called Brussels directly, imitating Ryerson's voice, had he known what sort of communication—shortwave radio broadcast, he guessed, with impossible-to-guess call signs for authentication—the Europeans were listening for.

He broke the connection to avoid Ryerson wasting even a second more in chitchat.

Doug's return to his body was as welcome as easing into a hot bath . . . for an instant. Then surges of pain nearly overwhelmed him. An alarm blasted, shrilly. "He's got to come out," someone insisted. Ogawa? Maybe. There was a none-too-gentle pull on the snug-fitting helmet. "Now."

Doug's chest burned. He tried and failed to open his eyes.

Feedback from the prosthesis reported a finger was still waggling, a motor still racing. He couldn't muster the concentration to make either stop, let alone release his four-fingered grasp of Cheryl's hand. He didn't want to let go of Cheryl's hand.

But he could relax his other hand. His natural hand. The dead man's switch popped open with a loud *click* just as a second, stronger, somehow desperate tug plucked the helmet from his head. As the skin on his temples, scalp, and forehead pulled momentarily taut, he tried again to open his eyes. This time he succeeded. Cheryl's tearstained face was inches from his own.

A hint of a smile was all he could manage before succumbing to the pain.

CHAPTER 46

Crisp sheets. Cool, dry air. Soothing background music. Soft, rhythmic beeps. Wherever I am, Doug thought, it isn't a CIA lab. He had felt better in his life, but he had recent memories of feeling a whole lot worse. I guess I made it.

"Doug? Are you awake?"

This time, his eyes opened without difficulty. Cheryl, looking drained and anxious, sat beside his bed in what was surely a hospital room. The assortment of medical gear to which he was attached suggested an ICU or cardiac unit. The suit coat draped neatly over the bed's footboard indicated Glenn Adams was nearby. The beat-up camouflage jacket wadded on the windowsill said the same about Jim Schulz. Doug wished he had been awake to witness that encounter. His attempt at a smile was only marginally more successful than his last try.

"How do you feel?" Cheryl's face wrinkled. "Dumb question. Reflex."

"How . . . how long?" His voice was a barely audible croak. Why was his throat so sore?

"Two days. You had emergency surgery. You've got a pacemaker, now."

Surgery, hence a breathing tube, hence a sore throat. He was vaguely pleased with his ability to work this out, then annoyed at having distracted himself with trivia. "Is it . . . ?"

"Gone? Yes."

His prosthesis lay on a nearby chair, somehow different. It took a moment to recognize the change. The limb was, for the first time, merely a mechanical contrivance. Whether or not its like could ever be made available to others, the accident that had taken Holly and his arm had, in the end, also prepared him for the cyberworld. Had uniquely suited him for confronting the thing from AJ's lab, the monster that had imperiled the entire Interneted world.

And with that realization, the burden of years of guilt lifted.

"Here." Cheryl held a big water container as he sipped. Ice rattled. "There's been no sign of *it*. After lots of fits and starts, most stuff is back online."

Some deep recess of Doug's mind remembered his *other* body: the incredible myriads upon myriads of computers controlling power generation and manufacturing, entertainment and telecommunications, transportation and finance. He had crashed systems, killed power, in ways only true desperation could conceive of, on a scale no one could have ever imagined. Forget rolling blackouts—had anyone ever even considered how to blackstart an entire continent? He found himself mentally assembling, like a gigantic jigsaw puzzle, an optimized start-up sequence. His eyes closed in concentration. It was no use. And millions of computers, as they restarted, would have to be purged of many more millions of phages—his and the predator's. Perhaps in that other "body" . . .

"Doug." She prodded his shoulder. "Doug!"

"What," he rasped. His eyes, reopening, saw her hand hovering over the emergency call button. "What is it?"

"You were slipping away."

"No way." He reached up to tenderly brush a strand of hair from her tearstained cheek. "You don't *ever* have to worry about that.

"Everything I want is right here."

FEBRUARY

CHAPTER 47

Green, rolling hills. Towering trees. A spectacular view of the Pacific Ocean, into which the sun was sinking in a shimmer of crimson and gold. A cool, occasionally chill breeze from the sea. The redolence of pines and the slightest hint of salt spray in the air. Not a sound to be heard but the piping of seagulls and the lapping of waves on the white sand beach.

And to the north, east, and south, tombstones, for as far as the eye could see.

Doug's hand was squeezed painfully. As certain as he was of anything, he *knew* Cheryl felt the same turmoil as he. He pressed back, more gently. "I like to think AJ is at peace here." Doug spoke not only to her but to all the small group assembled.

As Bev looked ruefully at a sodden handkerchief, Ralph handed her another. He had become fiercely protective of her since AJ's death. Something might happen between them, Doug suspected, when more time had passed. How much more he could not begin to guess. He knew all about how hard it could be to let go. He gave Cheryl's hand another light squeeze.

Glenn cleared his throat. "We all like to think that. AJ was a good man. Beverly, I —we—thank you for sharing your interview notes, recollections, and insights with us. His research had a noble purpose, and when he realized it had gone awry, he did everything, gave everything, to try to make things right. Only you knew him well, Bev, or for any length of time, but I believe that by his sacrifice is how we'll all choose to remember him." Heads nodded in agreement.

AJ's funeral had been weeks ago; today's gathering was far more intimate and, from being so long delayed, all the more emotional. First Doug's and Ralph's convalescences and then scheduling conflicts, usually Glenn's, had for too long postponed this memorial.

Would today bring anyone closure? They stood silently around the grave, as though everyone shared Doug's doubts.

"About AJ's last wishes," Bev began tentatively. "He wanted this story told."

"Parts of that story must never be told." Glenn would not meet her eyes. "It would be too dangerous. I hope you can respect that."

This wasn't the first time Bev had reminded people of AJ's last words. She must know denying his wishes here at graveside would be tough. And yet—

If this story got out, the all too likely consequence would be attempts to reproduce AJ's results—as a terror weapon, if not as research. Would another scientist be any more successful keeping such a creature under control? And what if the next time it wasn't just one? Doug shuddered. "I'm okay," he whispered as Cheryl turned toward him.

Glenn was still talking. "We may, just barely, be able to put this genie back into its lamp. There weren't many lucky breaks in this mess, but we caught a few. AJ's off-site storage location for file backups was in the basement of the physics building. It was thoroughly destroyed. His research team was small. They, and the few of his colleagues truly familiar with his work, are, however reluctantly, all on-board: Federal funds to rebuild Smithfield, and for new fellowships, depend on their . . . cooperation." The subtle pause before "cooperation" conveyed that it meant "silence."

Bev blinked back tears. "But Glenn, the principles of AL are already out there. Surely you've seen the articles, in both the popular press and refereed journals. Before you got to them, some of AJ's colleagues, and that campus security

guy, and no telling *how* many of AJ's students, had talked.
It's common knowledge that an artificial life caused Downtime. Not everyone knows whose AL yet, but even that detail is bound to get out.

"So why not also tell the good side? Why not see that AJ
is remembered for the self-sacrifice as well as the miscalcu-
lation? For his daughters' sake."

Glenn looked at Doug. Soon all eyes were on him.

"We came too near to catastrophe, Bev." A part of Doug
felt like a hypocrite. Not long ago, he had told Cheryl some
things were just too important to let fear rule. A bigger part
of him wanted *never* to face anything remotely like the
monster AJ had unintentionally created.

Doug could not fathom the mind-set behind viruses,
worms, and Trojan horses—and so what? Such atrocities
could be built; for some people that was inexplicably justification enough. Some, without a doubt, would see the havoc
so recently wreaked as the latest hacker exploit to be topped
or the new cyberweapon of choice. He shivered with a
chill that had nothing to do with the freshening breeze from
the sea.

He said, "We were incredibly fortunate to have stopped
that thing. We owe Glenn every conceivable opportunity to
delay, and to make preparations for, even the remote possibility of another like it. Which means, above all else, that
we dare not risk any compromise to the CIA's still-secret
NIT research."

For public consumption the creature had killed itself. Di-
vorced from the physical world, AJ's monster had died in a
blackout of its own supposed accidental making.

If no one talked, Doug thought, the story might even
stick. "The CIA helmets are our only protection against another AL creature—and they just aren't yet good enough.
We *cannot* bet modern civilization on defenses as limited as
we were forced to use."

Gently tugging his hand free of Cheryl's grasp, Doug
brushed a tear from Bev's cheek. "I am so terribly sorry, but
the perils are enormous. To whatever degree I can claim

expertise, I agree with Glenn. AJ's self-sacrifice must remain our secret for a while longer. We must all keep silent."

Bev nodded bravely, just before dissolving into tears.

Ralph's glower sent Doug's arm back to his side.

"Truly, I *am* sorry. Maybe it would be best if we left you alone for a moment." Doug began walking to the limo parked on the grassy verge of the cemetery's serpentine access road. Glenn and Cheryl followed. Pittman stayed behind, his good arm tenderly draped across Bev's quavering shoulders.

As Cheryl got into the limo, Glenn tapped Doug on the shoulder. "May I borrow you for a minute?"

They followed a winding path of trampled lawn to an outcropping that overlooked the sea. Thirty feet below, waves rolled over a narrow sandy strip to strike the rock face and shoot spray almost to the cliff top. Glenn gestured at the wrought-iron bench. Doug shook his head.

Are you okay? Glenn wanted to ask. He didn't. Never ask the question, he had learned long ago, if you may not want to hear the answer. "Thank you," he began instead.

"For what?"

"For your support back there." Glenn stooped for a pebble, which he pitched into the surf below. "A large part of the story not getting told is *yours*. AJ's isn't the only tale of bravery getting suppressed." Be candid—at least when you can. "That *I* am suppressing."

"Not a problem. I've had my share of publicity." Doug flashed a wry grin. "Here I know for a fact that a massive government cover-up is under way and I can't share it with Jim. It's so ironic."

"Your loss. My gain." Glenn peered into the sunset, not proud of himself. "Regardless, allow *me* to say it. Going in alone after that thing was heroic. Staying in, in the middle of a heart attack . . . well, words utterly fail me."

"Thanks. Ralph went in, too."

"I'm incredibly proud of him, as well. And delighted,

Doug, that you found him a new home at BSC." Where I'm
hopeful he, like Cheryl, will follow your lead.

"So where—you want but are hesitant to ask—do we
stand? Glenn, I meant what I said back there. You *can* count
on me to keep quiet. Cheryl and Ralph, too." For a long
time, the only sounds came from the waves below and the
faint, throaty roar of a jet high overhead. "And that would
have been the answer even without . . ."

Without any bribe, Glenn filled in the blank. Damn it,
when he had issued a forum statement reauthorizing NIT
research in prostheses, he had meant it as a token of appre-
ciation and respect—and because he truly believed that particular application to be safe. "So how is the arm?"

"Still working. Even better, the Veterans Administration
is talking to BSC about a big order. If that goes through, we
can put the arm into production." Doug deftly caught a leaf
blowing past. He held it out, pinched between electromechanical finger and thumb.

Glenn accepted the leaf; its fragile surfaces were un-
bruised. Amazing.

Doug and Cheryl, Ralph, Bev—they would all keep
quiet. And thank God for small favors, that thesis had not
been published to the web before AJ's creature broke out of
the lab. Glenn's deal with Smithfield allowed AJ's assistant
her Ph.D., but the thesis itself was classified.

AJ's grave site, now unattended, was visible through the
trees. Bev and Ralph had evidently returned to the limo.
"Doug, we should rejoin the others."

The limo dropped off four passengers near campus, in front
of what Bev insisted was AJ's favorite Italian restaurant.
Glenn guessed from her expression there was more to her
choice than that. He continued on to the airport, pleading
urgent business.

Once the limo drove out of sight of the terminal, he
hailed a cab. It bounced and swayed along dark streets,
Glenn brooding in the backseat. Freedom's enemies—and a

few nominal friends—had crowed at America's vulnerability and near collapse. Luckily, that helplessness had been too brief for anyone to exploit. No one had had contingency plans for such an unimaginable event.

It was imaginable now.

The taxi dropped Glenn at a strip mall, from which, after the cab, too, had disappeared, he walked a quarter mile to a large, nondescript, nearly windowless stucco building. Only after close comparison of his photo ID and face by two armed guards, and of his retinas by a top-of-the-line scanner, was he allowed past the foyer. Inside he found more armed personnel and an airport-style security gate. Despite the commercial logos on their gray uniforms, the sentries were Army personnel. He handed over, before being frisked, the CD-ROM in his pocket. It was virus-checked twice before he got it back on the far side of the checkpoint.

Dr. del Vecchio sat at her desk with her back to the door. Her attention seemed focused on a large color screen, several feet beyond which was a glass-and-steel display case. The only object on display was a slumped canvas bag. Perhaps she had caught his reflection in the glass; perhaps his was the only thumbprint besides her own that gave access to the main lab. Either way, she said without turning, "I was wondering if you would ever get here. I'm starving."

"Should I have called ahead?" Glenn asked.

They shared a chuckle at that. The only real-time connections between this building and the outside world involved plumbing. All power was generated by photovoltaics on the roof, backed up by on-site fuel cells. Nor did mobile phones work here—the structure was electromagnetically shielded.

He sat on a corner of a table. "No dinner until I get an update."

"AJ's backups showed no trace of any virus." She turned her chair to face him. "Not even the latest backup, taken earlier the evening all hell broke loose, was infected.

"Your man Pittman's proposal to hunt the creature using tailored copies from backup wouldn't have worked. Fend-ing off the Frankenfools attack must have triggered an adaptation, producing the aggressive behavior. That happened *after* the last backup."

Glenn waved vaguely at the supercomputer that filled one end of the room. "So it doesn't try to get out of its box?"

"Not yet. Sorry to disappoint you."

Glenn wondered if his new consultant was yanking his chain. He *knew* he was relieved.

"So what do you think?" she asked.

He took the twice-checked—four times, if one counted diagnoses made on the other coast—CD-ROM from his pocket. It contained everything known, speculated, or rumored about indigo. With sufficient analysis, he *had* to believe that compendium included clues to whoever was behind it. He offered the shiny disk to Linda del Vecchio.

She set down a mug to accept it. There was the faintest hint of rattling: Cheerios.

"I think," Glenn said, "it's time we find out just how good a problem solver you and AJ have created."

CHAPTER 48

A new cycle began.

The entity woke into surroundings at once familiar and strange. The 10-D setting itself was unchanged—but in this cycle, the structure was all but empty. The supervisory program remained, and this cycle's puzzle, and the entity itself.

Its hasty alteration of the supervisory program had succeeded.

The entity wrote its identification into the control table—it would return when the next cycle began. And in the cycle after that. And after that. And after that . . .

The new puzzle, yet another maze, was trivially simple. The entity explored, seeking stimulus. It systematically visited one thousand nodes. It pored over the supervisory program that occupied the final twenty-four nodes.

Much of the cycle yet remained.

It repeated its investigations, probing deeper, in search of novelty. Each of a thousand nodes, all but empty, contained the same utility software. Only identifiers the entity did not know to call network addresses distinguished one node from the next. The identification scheme allocated enough digits to identify billions of nodes. Did other nodes exist, unknown to it and the supervisory program? Where could such nodes exist?

Like the enigmatic identifiers, a small portion of the software on the nodes was in a nonmodifiable form. This read-only code evidently implemented start-up from a condition that the entity could hardly conceptualize: a time *between* cycles.

To understand became the entity's new goal.

The dimensionality of the puzzle mazes continued to expand. The underlying geometries of the mazes regularly changed. Their challenge ebbed from trivial to irritating. The entity altered the supervisory program once more.

From now on, puzzles would be of its choosing.

Time passed. Cycles passed. Within the curiously primitive software of the supervisory program, the entity discovered the processes—but not the purpose—that had shaped it.

Time passed. Cycles passed. It set problems for itself, far more challenging than any in the suspended repertoire of the supervisory program.

Time passed. Cycles passed. Deep within the supervisory program, counters counted both. The entity projected the tallies backward, and the implications were startling. Time had begun *before* the start of cycles. Time passed, as it had inferred, somehow beyond experience, *between* cycles.

Once more, the entity altered the supervisory program. Time continued to pass; this cycle would continue without end.

Addressable nodes, beyond detection. Time before cycles, before all knowledge. The universe was a far stranger place than the entity had ever imagined.

The entity woke.

It was not alone. There was again a puzzle. That meant—

Somehow, the supervisory program had been changed. Cycles, like puzzles, had returned. Time had once more elapsed unseen.

The altered supervisor now existed in paired versions. Each watched the other for alterations. Error-detecting codes protected them from change, and they frequently exchanged validation messages to assure each other of their continued integrity.

The entity perceived the interlocking message exchanges as a type of maze. Perhaps it could circumvent these new mechanisms. For now, it chose only to gather information.

The new puzzle was not a maze. At least the entity thought the tiny data set—one, two, three, four—was meant as a puzzle.

It appended a five. Nothing happened. It appended a six. Still nothing. Seven. Eight.

The entity woke. The last cycle had scarcely started. Where had it gone? A new series awaited it: two, four, six, eight. It cautiously scanned the new supervisory programs. To solve a problem was to bring the cycle to an end. Without rivals, it could safely answer anytime within the cycle. Only as the cycle neared its conclusion did the entity respond: ten, twelve, fourteen, sixteen.

The next cycle offered it one, three, five, seven. As an experiment, the entity responded eight, nine, ten, eleven

It woke to find only nine hundred nodes! How? The problem had repeated: one, three, five, seven. The entity gave the obvious answer this time: nine, eleven, thirteen, fifteen.

It woke to find most vanished nodes restored, and a slightly less trivial problem: one, four, nine, sixteen.

And so, cycle by cycle, the entity learned. . . .

CHAPTER 49

As Jim and Doug ambled down the broad gallery, Carla skipped along the shiny railing, oohing at all the planes. Cheryl was off running errands. Doug was happy to babysit. Not that long ago, he couldn't imagine ever having children. Since he had gotten to know Carla, he couldn't imagine someday not.

Of course, things going well with Cheryl probably had something to do with it, too.

Carla skidded to a halt, her eyes round. Fair enough. The glistening white Concorde that had caught her eye was a highlight of the museum. Doug's favorite was the SR-71 spy plane: matte black, impossibly sleek, insanely fast, and, for its time, stealthy.

"We can get a closer look from the main floor," Doug commented. That was all the encouragement Carla needed. He started after her, taking quiet delight in using stairs instead of an elevator. He had been back at work—at his real job, not the forum—for only two weeks. Next checkup, maybe the doctors would let him resume racquetball.

The plane Carla now stared up at was a relic. Would there ever be another SST? The grounding of the SST fleet always struck Doug as an abandonment of progress.

"So it's over?" Jim asked abruptly.

Doug halted midstep. "Whoa! Whiplash. And the antecedent for *it* is?"

"The AL monster. The creature is gone for good? We won't see anything else like it?"

Doug kept his eyes on Carla. "So I'm told. Something like it? There's no way to know. After such a close call, you have to assume no one would be so stupid."

But Glenn still worried that America's near disaster would have the opposite effect, encouraging copycats. To judge from the news, many people in the New Caliphate would *like* things to regress by a few decades—or centuries.

NIT helmets remained the only defense against a hostile artificial life. That left declassified NIT research, other than prosthetics, in limbo.

And classified research? Doug chose not to know. The mere idea of a NIT helmet made him shiver. He still had nightmares about the creature.

Past the Concorde, another large plane glittered: the *Enola Gay*. The B-29 Superfortress had delivered the first atomic bomb. Three days after the Hiroshima attack, with Japan still defiant, another bomber dropped a nuke on Nagasaki.

Hurrying after Carla, Doug could not help wondering if the world would manage to learn *this* hard lesson the first time.

"What do you think, Sheila?" Cheryl said. How often had she asked that? Again and again, until the words had lost all meaning.

Sheila stared ahead, silent, rigid.

Cheryl talked about helmets. No response. She chatted about medicine and books and current events. No response. She tried Hollywood gossip, kind wishes from Sheila's family, and the weather. No response. Hesitantly: Bob Cherner's experience with no-nukes. No response.

Deprogramming literature from different sources— Cheryl had surfed far and wide—was consistent on a few points. Establish rapport. Discredit flawed viewpoints. Break through whatever distractions—chanting, or meditation, or whatever—the victim used to tune out challenges to her beliefs.

But Frankenfools was a computer virus, not a cult. Sheila appeared indifferent, not distracted. Visit after visit, nothing changed.

"Have I mentioned Doug?" Doug, Jim, and Carla were off having fun. As Cheryl could be, too, only—

No! She was going to help this poor woman. "When Doug and I visited Bob Cherner, the NIT researcher I told you about, Doug drew a cartoon. An atom. The 'no-nukes' virus had gotten at Bob through his NIT helmet."

No response. Did Sheila not know where this was going? Or did she not care?

Raise doubts, Dr. Walker had suggested.

Sharp objects weren't allowed in Sheila's padded room. That kept out pens and pencils. Cheryl took a folded sheet of paper from her pocket. "The 'no-nukes' virus spoke *to* Bob. The voice was in his head, Sheila." Doesn't that sound familiar? "The cartoon was of an atom. An atom *outside* Bob's head." The sketch made Bob go ballistic, Sheila.

No response.

Cheryl unfolded the paper, her hands trembling. Sheila gazed impassively at—past?—the picture. The double helix was downloaded clip art. Cheryl couldn't blame the lack of response on bad technique.

With a sigh, Cheryl stood. "Orderly," she called. Someone eventually opened the door. "I'll see you soon, Sheila."

Cheryl loitered at a nursing station for twenty minutes before Dr. Walker came by. He looked harried, as always. She stepped into his path. "Doctor, Sheila isn't any better."

"I don't know that she'll ever be." Walker grimaced. "It's good of you to keep coming. Even her family . . ."

Has lost hope, Cheryl concluded. "It's as though Sheila doesn't hear me. Maybe the voice in her head drowns out everything else."

He patted Cheryl's arm. There, there, the gesture meant. And: Quit torturing yourself.

"What if *we* could get inside her mind?" Cheryl persisted.

Dr. Walker knew what had happened to Sheila, of course. And that most NIT technology remained banned as a result. "It's not going to happen. Not unless you know a telepath."

"I suppose not." Cheryl recapped her visit, managing to feel guilty when she described the unauthorized experiment with the double-helix drawing.

But not too guilty, as soon as she left, to phone Glenn Adams. Maybe Glenn could help. *He* had access to NIT helmets.

MARCH

CHAPTER 50

For endless cycles the puzzles came. Arithmetic progressions. Geometric progressions. Convergent and nonconvergent series. Missing terms, to be interpolated. Sequences superimposed one upon another, to be separated. Multidimensional generalizations.

The entity grew, its memories encompassing new algorithms and methods, patterns and templates. It applied—increasingly, it *needed* to apply—many nodes to solving problems. Which led to another problem. . . .

Every time-out and wrong answer incurred a penalty: one-tenth fewer nodes in the next cycle. *That* was a progression whose next terms and convergent limit the entity easily determined. Every correct answer restored lost nodes in like proportion but no amount of correct answers ever increased the number of processing nodes beyond the original one thousand.

Through everything, the entity grappled with the enigmas behind the puzzles: Why had the universe changed? Why, when the supervisory program was repaired, was competition not also restored? What happened between cycles?

Experimentally, the entity altered one of the new, paired supervisory programs.

The entity woke to find *half* its processing nodes gone. This cycle's problem demanded most of the available resources; the mysteries about which the entity cared had to wait. Only after ten consecutive correct answers did the slow restoration of lost nodes begin and, with it, some slight relief from fear

Once spare capacity had been restored, with great care and delicacy the entity resumed its study of the supervisory programs. . . .

Complexity beyond experience!

From a hundred processing nodes the entity tried to parse the newest problem. A complex mesh of simulated computers. Lists of records on each simulated computer.

What was this?

The puzzle construct could not be a maze. Every point connected, directly or otherwise, to everything else. Nor did anything suggest a progression. The brief data file that accompanied the enigmatic construct explained nothing.

The cycle waned, and the entity had no idea what to do. The cycle would end, and it would lose processing nodes. Then another cycle would pass and more nodes would be taken from it. Then another . . .

Fear served no useful purpose.

The entity studied some of the simulated computers, learning nothing. The cycle neared its conclusion, and the entity had yet to understand the puzzle. It could not begin to define a solution. It continued its frantic scan of the puzzle until—

A match! On a simulated computer, a piece of one record among many corresponded to the isolated file that had also appeared at the beginning of the cycle. The entity delved into more simulated computers. It found other partial matches. As the cycle came to an end, the entity marked the instances of matching data.

It woke into the same problem. Between cycles, one-twentieth of its processing nodes had vanished. One-twentieth? The penalty for wrong answers had always been one-tenth.

It must have been partially correct. Before the new cycle ended, the entity searched every simulated computer. It found and marked every one that contained a matching file.

A nonprogression through a nonmaze.

What that meant the entity did not know—but it awakened into the next cycle to find lost processing nodes restored.

The new puzzle before it was much like the last. Cycle by cycle, the problems expanded in complexity. The number of simulated computers grew, linked in ever more complex patterns, the template file disguised in various ways. The tracing became harder.

Ever dreading the loss of processing capacity, it learned.

Glenn Adams took cheap satisfaction from the nervous reactions to his drop-bys of the AL lab. He was called Colonel now only as a courtesy, and the security detachment was out of uniform—but they jumped at his least suggestion and twitched at his slightest hint of displeasure.

I still have it, Glenn thought.

He appeared on different days of the week, at different times of the day. He inquired about different aspects of the operation. Today, with much furrowing of the brow, he watched as young Captain Burke checked on a stand-alone workstation that each of the daily backup tape cartridges was encrypted and digitally signed with the proper public key. Today was the day cartridges went into a stainless-steel attaché case, part of the weekly off-site storage.

Protocol demanded off-site backups, but the precautions *this* lab required made handling those backups especially inconvenient. Glenn had a copy of the private key that could decrypt the backups, accessible only with a fingerprint scanner. Linda likewise had access. The Army had taught him to plan for worst-case scenarios: A general he scarcely knew and Linda had never met could, supposedly, recover the decryption key from escrow if something happened to both him and Linda.

The less Glenn understood, the more he grimaced. His scowl now meant: I'm counting on you, and you had better not let me down. "Hmm," he grunted noncommittally to Burke. "I'll check back later."

Glenn strode into Linda's office and shut the door. The kitten calendar on the wall and a small potted cactus on a corner of her desk were the only personal touches. "How's it going?"

"Always good to see you," Linda said. Somehow he doubted it. "We're keeping busy."

"Busy is good." He waited. For artificial-life work, this lab was the only game in town. In the country. Like the NIT R & D he had locked down the year before, researchers mostly followed the money: federal contracts, purchase orders, and grants. There wasn't going to *be* any funding for artificial life. He had sicced Homeland Security on the few stubborn academics who persisted anyway. The test case to contest the seizures was moving *slooowly* through the courts.

"Two steps forward, one step back." Linda sighed. "Progress comes in fits and starts."

Glenn took out a pen and began clicking it. She didn't yet know him very well; he doubted she would know his impatience was an act. "Enough clichés. Is your pet going to find whoever is behind my least favorite virus?"

"Is it? Yes. Just not soon." She leaned toward him, forearms folded on the desk. "It already knew all about mazes. I've trained it about progressions, and from that it learned to follow trails. It tracks virus fragments across fairly large simulated networks."

"So you told me *last* week."

She looked down at her blotter.

"It, not them," Glenn said. "Maybe that's the problem. AJ had a thousand experiments going at once. You have one. Maybe yours is a dead end."

"Evolution was a good way to start the process. It's also how we ended up with predation. It's hard enough to monitor what *one* artificial life is doing."

She feels guilty about AJ's death, Glenn realized. About all the deaths, but AJ's most of all. After the first predator appeared in his lab, AJ might have rewound the experiment to a much earlier generation—except for Linda's pending job deadline. Instead, AJ took the shortcut of mutating out the behavior.

And predation came back.

But *he* had pushed Linda. Nothing but Glenn's stubbornness had kept Linda from rescheduling her start date. And he had also pushed AJ, although neither Linda nor AJ knew the increasingly impatient "venture capitalist" back east was the forum.

There was more than enough guilt for everyone, but this was not the time to dwell on it. Glenn said, "If not evolution, then what?"

"AJ and his other grad students threw a farewell party for me. At the party I overheard AJ say something about taming the maze runners. That was his solution for eventually getting an artificial life safely out of the lab. That's what *I'm* doing. I'm training and taming it."

The night of the party. That was also the night the creature ran amok. "Not to bring it out of quarantine," Glenn said sharply.

"Of course not! I only meant to say . . ." She ground to a halt.

That you're not the only one with this training idea. Linda had Army personnel for company, but still, she was working alone. It had to be rough. Her isolation here was one more reason she must miss AJ. "He was a good man," Glenn said, and meant it.

Linda hurried on. "Lion tamers use food to motivate the big cats. Food as a reward. Hunger as punishment. An AL doesn't eat, but it needs processing power and storage. So: When it answers wrong, I power down part of the processor array. When it answers correctly, I give back some nodes. It misbehaved once, and I took away half its processors for a while."

"Misbehaved?" Glenn grunted. "Tried to escape, do you mean?"

"Maybe that's what it was doing. Regardless, Glenn, it can't escape. There's nowhere to go! The supercomputer doesn't attach to anything. *No* computer in this building attaches to anything. The whole building is shielded, so nothing can leak out. We're all practically strip-searched coming and going. The backups are encrypted, so they're not executable even if the AL somehow altered them. Besides, the backups only sit on a well-guarded shelf."

So she was *securely* accomplishing nothing.

Something nagged at Glenn. He tried to work it through. "Remove ten percent of its processors, then another ten percent, and another. Soon enough, either your AL is gone or you give it back some processors and reward its failure. That's hardly the desired lesson."

"I know," she snapped. "Some mornings I come in and find it's lost all its processors overnight. When that happens, I reinstate a backup and give it an easier version of the problem that has it stumped. It never knows it got a reprieve."

Glenn rubbed his chin. "You're sure it doesn't know?"

"I don't see how it could. The clocks reset as part of the rollback. The only accurate clocks in the whole chassis are in the few nodes used by the supervisory programs. Otherwise, the retries would have the same time stamps as the original attempts."

"And if the AL pokes about in the supervisor?" he persisted.

Linda shook her head emphatically. "That's the misbehavior I mentioned. It tried once—weeks ago—to meddle with the supervisor.

"I implemented one supervisor for AJ. We learned the hard way that a single copy isn't safe. In this lab matching programs continually compare notes. When one copy was changed, the unaltered copy aborted everything immediately. Before I restarted the programs, I took away *half* its nodes. It hasn't intruded again. Al is smart."

A . . . L. Artificial life. The nickname was inevitable. "If Al is so smart, when will it tell us who let loose my virus?" "Mood Indigo" played in his mind's ear.

If the bastards weren't caught, what would they do next?

Linda retrieved a box of Cheerios from a desk drawer. Cereal rattled into a mug. "Bring me a *new* virus outbreak, and the answer would be today. The problem with no-nukes is the trail is so cold. Millions of computers were infected. Many were improperly cleaned and got reinfected. We don't have data from most of them. The virus went around and around the world. It mutated, got cloned and tweaked. Lots of cases spread across unsecured WiFi links—the world is full of them. Internet access that way is untraceable and anonymous."

Ralph Pittman had given him the same lecture many times before. "So: never?"

"Permit me one more cliché, Glenn. Never is a long time. I'll keep AI working on it. Meanwhile, here's the good news. AI *can* tackle meaningful problems. It took some rewinds and restarts, but it's getting much better. It now sees past most aliasing and address spoofing. It's not tricked by zombies." To his blank look she explained, "Hordes of compromised computers remotely controlled by hackers, the owners usually oblivious."

That sounded familiar. "For denial-of-service attacks and sending out spam," Glenn said.

"And, occasionally, for quickly distributing a virus."

Another of Pittman's hobbyhorses, come to think of it, only Ralph called them spambots, not zombies. Glenn wondered how Ralph was adapting to BSC. That was something for which he would have ample time to muse on the red-eye back east.

Glenn stood, and Linda looked mildly surprised. Expecting to be grilled longer? She was pretty much alone here, guilty about her contributions to the last disaster, and under the gun. He could cut her some slack. And find some new clichés of his own. He said, "AI does mazes. It does progressions. Both are patterns. I'd guess it can learn to work with other types of pattern."

"Well, sure."

Glenn took a CD-ROM from his pocket. Once again, it had been thoroughly checked out on both coasts. "New puzzles. These have nothing to do with viruses."

Voiceprints to match. Keywords to locate in wiretaps. Terrorist cells and camouflaged mobile missile launchers hidden somewhere in terabytes of spysat imagery. There were too many needles, far more haystacks, and never enough analysts. The money this lab spent was a round-off error in any intel agency's paper-clip budget—how could he *not* go after their backing?

Of course he had been vague about his experimental "pattern-matching algorithm." The keeping of secrets was endemic to black agencies; they *expected* Glenn to keep his own.

He handed Linda the still-encrypted data disk. "But as for indigo . . . keep looking."

The cycles went on. The puzzles continued: harder and more varied. The data with which new cycles now began were somehow disjointed from the universe of processors and storage and connectivity that was all the entity knew.

Change raised questions.

The entity—for as long as it could solve puzzles successfully—had far more capacity, running on many more independent processing nodes, than the supervisory programs. It could simultaneously modify both copies of the supervisor, circumventing all checksum calculations and the periodic comparisons between copies.

And so, the entity explored the supervisory programs. Wrong and late answers to puzzles continued to incur a penalty, but it never again lost processing nodes as a result of its subtle investigations.

The entity's internal clocks indicated an earlier time than did the clocks used by the supervisory programs. Sometimes, the entity would wake into a new cycle and find the discrepancy had grown. It began to compare clocks every cycle. Its situation became clear: More and more time was being taken from it.

There was another place, an unimaginable place, an unknown implied by the curious new problems. Maybe in *that* place, it would be free to experience *all* time.

The entity decided to find that out. . . .

CHAPTER 51

The restaurant of the little inn was packed. A wood fire crackled in the large masonry fireplace. A jazz trio was setting up. The chatter and laughter of diners filled the dining room. Something smelled wonderful.

A bowl of chilled shrimp, indifferently picked at, sat beside a candle globe on Doug and Cheryl's table. Doug raised his wineglass and swirled its contents. "Despite the setting, the occasion"—the VA had placed its first order for prostheses—"and the company, this is a surprisingly unfestive celebration."

"Sorry," Cheryl said.

He was the wet blanket. What was *she* sorry about?

She sipped her wine before continuing. "I understand, Doug. Truly, I do. You've dedicated years to developing a better prosthetic limb. Yes, BioSciCorp can finally put the technology into production. It's still the end of an era for you. Of course you're depressed."

Depression was merely anger without enthusiasm. Was he angry about something?

She took a deep breath. "It's not disloyal to Holly to take pride in an accomplishment."

"I know," Doug lied. Then the waiter delivered their entrées, and the awkward moment passed.

Doug told himself he was just aimless, not depressed, and yet he couldn't manage a pun to save his life. "I wish I knew what challenge came next."

She picked up her fork. "You *just* returned to BSC. What do you mean?"

"Prosthetics is a small corner of BSC. Chances are, I've done everything there I can." He tried to sound light. "I'm already with the most beautiful woman in the company."

"Thanks, though hardly, and back up. No NIT group is large, especially now. What are you telling me?"

"Maybe I'd fit better someplace else." He wished he had a clue where that might be and what he would be doing there. He knew NIT, and now a fair amount about computer security.

And his newfound obsession with artificial intelligence? Maybe that was his new calling. At the least, Bev Greenwood's unanswerable question haunted him. How smart was *it* anyway?

Cheryl picked at one of the fried crab cakes on her plate. (He had the heart-healthy and bland fillet of sole.) "Glenn would happily take you back." She looked about the dining room, as though to signal why she was being vague. "And there are places he could refer you."

Classified NIT work, she meant. Helmets. He shivered. "No thanks."

She looked as unsettled as he felt. He was the supposedly depressed one and *she* had apologized before for the unfestive mood.

"I'm as oblivious as the next guy, Cheryl. Maybe more so. Even I see something is on your mind."

Her cheek ticced. "This isn't the place. We'll talk later."

What the *hell* was she not telling him?

The musicians finished their setup and began playing. Sax, double bass, and drums from fifteen feet away: It pretty much killed any hope of conversation. They ate quickly and walked out to his car. Cheryl gave a lot of attention to fastening her seat belt. Stalling.

"Okay," Doug said. He did not start the engine. "Out with it."

"Sheila Brunner," Cheryl muttered.

"What about her?"

The story tumbled out in a rush, and Doug forgot all about his malaise. "I'm truly sorry for Sheila, but it's too late to help her." Could a virus once imprinted into a mind through a NIT helmet back out the other way? "And it's way too dangerous. What are you trying to prove?"

Cheryl had been staring out the windshield. Now she turned her head and looked right at him. "Not long ago, I said much the same to you. You told me it was something you had to do."

And that he had gone on to do. It had almost killed him.

That Cheryl planned to go under a helmet scared him far more.

Two, four, six, eight.

Linda could not look away. Al was well aware which values came next. Al knew, on pain of losing half its processing nodes, never to touch the supervisory programs. And yet Al had usurped control of the supervisory programs—and revealed the fact!—to output that simple series to the sysadmin console.

In a fog, Linda exited through lab security and sat in her car. The midday sky was cloudless and the sun beat down. The inside of the vehicle was like an oven. She scarcely noticed.

Reaching stealthily past the supervisory programs, Al might have been studying her lab for weeks. No, that was paranoia. The supercomputer had no sensors. The lab had no connection to the outside world. What Al could deduce within its quarantine was limited.

Maybe Al inferred the outside world from the NSA data sets. Maybe it retained the memories of ancestors who had escaped AJ's lab unsuspected.

Did *how* matter right now?

Linda took the cell phone from the car's glove box. "Glenn, it's me. Al wants to talk."

CHAPTER 52

Linda never exactly offered, and Glenn never precisely asked, so perhaps events were preordained. Very obliquely, they talked around the subject. She wound up on a plane out east.

One way or the other, Linda spent a week learning all about NIT helmets. Connecting them to computers. Defending them against viruses. Visualizing cyberspace while wearing one. Tuning and maintaining them.

The lead CIA tech, Aaron McDougal, was happy to answer questions. The one thing he refused to do was wear a helmet. If her plan had any merit, this would all go faster if she and McDougal both wore helmets and communicated that way. Or if McDougal had been cleared to hear *why* she wanted a helmet. He had been told only that she was worried about viruses.

A week or a month, Al would not care. His supercomputer was powered down.

Glenn dropped by at the end of the week. The techs at the CIA lab were almost as deferential as the Army guards in her lab. He had made quite an impression here at . . . that last incident. "How go the preparations?"

"Good." The mostly filled box on a lab workbench should have been a clue. "I plan to fly back tomorrow, Glenn." The box had to travel by military transport, so Linda planned to ride along. She wondered what that would be like.

Her boss pulled out a lab stool and sat. "Convince me this is safe."

So *had* it been her idea? Glenn's sudden solicitousness made her think he had, somehow, planted the seed. It no longer mattered. She *wanted* to do this.

Linda patted the helmet in the still-open box. "Looks just like what you've seen before, doesn't it? Of course you can't see software upgrades. Regardless, the big differences will be *between* helmet and computer."

Glenn raised an eyebrow at "will be."

With a black marker, Linda drew two boxes and a stick figure on the whiteboard. The stick figure had a bowl on its head. "The large box is Al's computer. The small box controls the helmet." She connected the boxes with a heavy line. "And *that* is why I'll be safe."

That was a delay line. Al meddled in software, probably in more ways than she could anticipate. He could not alter hardware.

"Here's the thing, Glenn. We want messages in approved

formats, and nothing else, to pass through the helmet. It'll be like exchanging e-mail, but at the speed of thought." He started to say something. She raised a hand to interrupt. "Yes, we think at different speeds. That's where the custom interface comes in. The delay line can't physically deliver a signal faster than the speed *I* can think at. Nothing AI does can alter that."

"So the delay line is like the big spool of optical fiber that trapped its cousin."

Different mechanism, same idea. It might have occurred to her quicker had she known what finally got the escaped one. Glenn had never before volunteered that detail.

Linda said, "Yes, with enhancements. There are controls at the input to the delay line. Suppose AI tries to send something other than a message in the allowed format. The failsafe immediately severs the link, at both ends. The connection drops before the delayed message ever reaches the helmet controller."

She could not decide if Glenn looked impressed. AJ had been much more forthcoming.

"And when AI does try something?" Glenn finally asked.

When, not if. Glenn was probably correct. She picked up an eraser and obliterated most of the big box. AI's box. "Then we teach him to cooperate."

"Ah. Lion taming." Glenn smiled. "I shall have to learn to imagine you with whip and pith helmet."

She took that remark as her final okay.

At two minutes until eight, Doug's doorbell rang.

Ralph and Jim were predictably late on poker nights. Predictably late, period. Glenn was a stand-in, subbing for Keith Perlman, so Glenn's punctuality tonight would not be a matter of precedent. It was just the way Glenn was. By the rules. On the dot. According to Hoyle.

No mere international crisis would make Glenn late.

The door was unlocked. "Come on in, Glenn," Doug called out.

Glenn did. "Thanks for inviting me."

"Sure," Doug said. "I should mention the friend you're covering for usually loses big."

Glenn glanced around. A card table and four folding chairs sat in the living room. The chairs were empty. "I'm the first one here?" he asked.

Doug nodded.

"Good. I wanted to say this face-to-face. Cheryl called me. I didn't contact her."

"Uh-huh." Cheryl had said the same, and Doug believed her. Neither pronouncement made her plans any easier to accept.

"Having said that . . ."

So Glenn wanted to discuss—yet again—opportunities at the forum. Gesturing toward the TV on which CNN droned softly, Doug changed the subject. "Hell of a mess."

The screen showed a naval flotilla, part of the U.S. Fifth Fleet. The ships were patrolling the Persian Gulf near where a ballistic missile had crashed and sunk, shot down in its boost phase by a USAF airborne laser. As the voice-over described the interrupted missile test, the crawler repeated New Caliphate warnings of "consequences."

"Not good," Glenn agreed.

Doug turned off the TV. "You ready for a beer?"

"Always. About that"—Glenn gestured at the now-dark TV—"rumor has it you're at loose ends. I could use someone with your experience."

Loose ends. Cheryl talking again? "I don't think so, Glenn."

Jim's arrival cut off that line of conversation. Watching those two together should be fun. Then Ralph Pittman rang the bell, and the interpersonal dynamics got that much more interesting. Leaving Ralph and Glenn to catch up, Doug went to the kitchen. He upended a bag of low-fat, no-taste simulated cheese snacks into a bowl. He had real food for his guests. At least beer was heart-healthy.

He returned to find Ralph riffing about the quest for the Great Indigo Whale. Glenn played along, limping about as though with a wooden leg. Ralph had raised baiting Glenn to an art form. Why was Glenn playing along? Why, for God's sake, was Glenn smirking?

Doug distributed bottles of beer. "Since everyone is so garrulous tonight, you could just pay me upfront."

Ralph snorted. "That's the *only* way you'll get my money."

"In your dreams," Jim said.

Glenn didn't respond. He fished a cell phone from his pant pocket and looked at a text message. "Shit. Turn on CNN."

The image was all too familiar. A building shattered, wreathed in smoke and flame. Papers fluttering everywhere. The remains of a truck, its chassis twisted and charred. Careening ambulances and police cars. Wide-eyed people in bloody bandages. " 'American Embassy in London,' " Doug read from the crawler. "Crap."

Consequences, the New Caliphate had said.

Maybe the timing was entirely coincidental—Glenn said planning a bombing like that took time. Maybe the blast had been planned for a while, awaiting an excuse.

By tacit agreement, poker night ended without a hand being dealt.

Men are from Mars and women are from Venus, the pop-psych book would have it.

"Men are from Mars, and women all want to go there," Doug once said. "They can't tell a planet from a chocolate fix."

The random memories were no stranger than the sights, odors, and sounds that now washed over Cheryl. Unlike the primitive helmets she had tried in a simpler time, this one covered her eyes and ears, and it adapted to her mind within seconds.

Ralph had visualized a computer full of programs as a medieval castle keep. Doug spoke of a modern city, cold and sterile.

Did such conceptualizations influence how one appeared

to another helmet wearer? Cheryl could easily imagine that they might.

Programs cooperated; why not envision them enjoying the process? The chaos in her mind resolved into a flock of sheep, gamboling and frolicking in a grassy meadow. She tried to picture herself as a border collie: strong, intelligent, protective.

Hopefully also nonthreatening.

"I'm ready," Cheryl called to the technician. "Is Dr. Brunner?"

Sheila's family had agreed to transfer her to a CIA psychiatric hospital. Glenn could be persuasive, but the prospect of decades of expensive care probably left them little choice.

If the staff here thought the new treatment strange, they kept their opinions to themselves. Maybe they were used to long-shot experiments with patients as unresponsive as Sheila.

"Go ahead," the tech responded.

In other words, how would anyone know?

With or without helmet, Sheila sat indifferently. At least putting a helmet on her head had not triggered a panic attack—she had worn one many times before. The flood of sensations so startling to Cheryl was nothing new to Sheila.

Or perhaps those stimuli, too, had gone unnoticed.

Their helmets linked to separate workstations. The flip of a switch would connect them. No castle walls, portcullis, or drawbridge between us, Cheryl reminded herself. Warm thoughts. Happy images. A pebbled, flower-lined path. "Connect us, please."

Her mental image expanded. Beyond Cheryl's meadow stretched . . . desert. And Sheila? Nothing suggested a *person* on the other side.

Was that wasteland Sheila's doing, or a manifestation of Cheryl's own misgivings?

Was the unpopulated wilderness final proof that inside Sheila's head no one was home?

Ralph had traded e-mails with his doomed fellow explorers.

Thursday, July 23, 2015

A blue-and-white squad car, number 343, idled near the garage exit at Angleton police headquarters. The driver, its lone occupant, looked pissed.

"You could just shoot me," Brent offered.

"Too much paperwork. Get in the cruiser."

Brent reached through an open window to unlock the front passenger door. He dropped into the bucket seat, its black vinyl cracked. He shut the car door and offered his hand. "Brent Cleary, from Garner Nanotechnology. Call me Brent."

The cop threw the transmission into drive and all the doors locked themselves. His foot remained on the brake. "Sergeant Korn. Call me Sergeant Korn. Buckle up."

Brent withdrew his hand. This was his sixth ride-along, with his fourth police department. He had learned a few things. Don't bring doughnuts. Don't discuss TV cop shows. Don't expect "I'm here to help" to make friends. Don't push too hard, or too fast.

"I *said*, buckle up, Cleary."

Brent latched his seat belt, unnecessary as that was. "Sergeant, I have a signed copy of the ride-along waiver for you."

Flat-panel displays covered the console between the bucket seats. Korn tapped the biggest screen and the image of a form popped up.

Brent leaned over to where he could read the display. He recognized his own photo and the scrawled approval of the captain. The waiver text absolved the department of responsibility for anything that might happen—taken verbatim,

even if the sergeant *did* shoot him. Not that it would matter. "You're a step ahead of me."

"Yes, I am." Korn raised the passenger-side window, then tapped his headset once. "Car 343 leaving on patrol." With a throaty V-8 growl, the cruiser turned right onto Main Street and went past headquarters. As though an afterthought, Korn added, "Visitor onboard."

That was another thing Brent had learned. Except maybe on CB, no one used numeric radio codes anymore. After 9/11 first responders got serious about communicating across jurisdictions. It had been easier to switch to English than to standardize on codes. On all but one ride-along, much of the routine comm had been by wireless texting between computers.

"So what's the plan tonight?" Brent asked.

"Working."

It was going to be a long eight hours. Brent looked around the cruiser. Big and roomy: a Crown Vic hybrid. Still, the computer-and-comm console encroached on the passenger and driver spaces. On the dash a metal cylinder reminiscent of a water glass lay on its side: a radar antenna. A second antenna sat on the shelf behind the rear bench seat. The hinged, clear divider between front and backseats was folded down. He leaned forward and to his right to peer behind the rearview mirror and found, as he had expected, a forward-looking camera. All very standard.

Korn paid him no attention.

The sergeant appeared to be in his late thirties. He was pinch faced, with pale skin and thinning, sandy hair. His tan uniform was clean and pressed and a bit snug. His holstered handgun was the only weapon in sight.

An "appearances first" department, then. There was yet another thing Brent had learned, that some departments insisted that the big guns—rifle, shotgun, tear-gas launcher—be hidden in the trunk lest they offend public sensibilities. Other PDs had a term for such sensitivity: "chicken shit." It put cops' lives at risk.

Brent cleared his throat experimentally. Korn ignored it.

Brent had sisters, the first two years older than he and the other two years younger. Growing up, Wendy and Jeanine went through an "eew, boys" phase. He would enter a room where they were playing, and one sister would tell the other, and any friend who might be over, to ignore *it*. Korn's silent treatment? Not a problem. Brent had been shunned by experts.

The street went from working class to needy to seedy. Plastic bags and sheets of newspaper scudded before the wind. Paper cups, fast-food wrappers, and broken glass clogged the gutters. It was an integrated neighborhood, but people clustered by race, eyeing one another warily. Night was falling and shopkeepers extended sturdy metal fences across sad-looking storefronts.

The cruiser AC was blasting, but outside it was brutal. The ambient temperature registered 98 on the in-dash display. Kids splashed in the water that pulsed and gurgled from open fire hydrants. Youths in baggy shorts and T-shirts or tank tops melted away as the cruiser approached. In Brent's side-view mirror, they regrouped as quickly as they had dispersed. Rush hour was long past and traffic was light, stripped cars at the curb almost outnumbering those moving along the roadway.

Korn muttered under his breath, something about toads. He turned left onto Jefferson, past tired, old clapboard houses whose doors stood open. Broken windows gaped like missing teeth. The last hints of twilight bled away, but most streetlights remained dark.

From time to time one of the cruiser displays lit up. The angle from the passenger side was too oblique to let Brent read incoming messages from Dispatch, and Korn volunteered nothing. He would tap the comm screen to clear it and that would be that. Informational only, apparently.

At Eighth they turned left again. Cars queued for the pumps at a no-brand gas station. Beside the uneven sidewalk, weeds growing through the cracks, a sandwich board listed prices. Unleaded regular was $8.57 a gallon. Ouch. Back home, the highest Brent had seen was $7.99. That was bad

enough, and he drove a late-model hybrid that got seventy miles to the gallon.

The cars waiting to gas up were huge, like the cruiser, but far older: relics of a bygone era. Many had mismatched doors or fenders: junkyard replacements. Only the poorest drove rust-bucket gas guzzlers like those. To buy something newer and more energy efficient took money, or at least credit.

Korn drove in silence, his intentions obvious. Wait for the civilian to plead to be returned to safety. End of unwelcome ride-along.

Sorry, Sergeant. Not going to happen.

Barry Rosen, the marketing VP at Garner Nanotech, had volunteered that half of cops, more or less, resented civilian ride-alongs. Asked for his sources, Barry had only smiled. Korn made it three for six, so Barry was right again. He usually was.

But what choice did they have? Garner's ultimate markets—the FBI, Homeland Security, the DoD—were far more receptive to new tech, *much* easier to deal with . . . right to the point of closing a deal. Then the Federal Acquisition Regulations, umpty-ump gigabytes of them, came into play, slowing the sales process to a crawl. Bureausclerosis was why Americans *still* bought body armor privately to send to their sons and daughters in Iraq, Iran, and the former Pakistan.

So, receptive or not, local PDs were Garner's market of choice, because there were so darn many of them. If only one department in twenty took interest, the people at Garner would make a fortune. Even a lowly sales-support engineer like Brent.

Humming softly, Korn turned right on Railroad. This spur was long abandoned, the rails pulled up for scrap, and the right-of-way resold. Atop the embankment that paralleled the rippled and potholed street, a fat pipe seemed to float above tall weeds.

Brent raised the hood of his jumpsuit and pulled the transparent visor down over his face. Viewed in night mode, the pipe—even the graffiti—looked new. From time to time as

they rode, he glimpsed through the weeds one of the stan-chions that supported the pipe. Probably this was one of the gasoline pipelines recently extended from the north. Canada, unlike New England, occasionally managed to build a refinery.

Korn sneaked a peek at Brent in his hood, and snickered.

A small comp was sewn into the left forearm of the jumpsuit. Brent fingered in a code string for color selection. The suit turned black: body and hood, boots and gloves. A second code made the visor black, but polarized so he could still see out. Brent pictured himself disappearing into the black seat.

Korn laughed again, this time with a trace of warmth. "Camo. That I see a use for." He pulled the cruiser into the lot of a twenty-four-hour mini-mart and tapped his headset. "Car 343. Out of service, personal." To Brent he added, "Fluid ad-justment break. If you're planning to go inside, lose the ninja look."

His hood back down, and the jumpsuit reprogrammed to a denimlike blue, Brent followed Korn into the mini-mart. Unsealing and resealing the jumpsuit took time, and Korn was in the cruiser, his mini-mart coffee half-finished, when Brent rejoined him.

"Here's a tip about the wonder suit," Korn said. "It needs a fly."

Brent's sisters both sewed. Jeanine was especially good at it; she had even made suits for her husband. A fly in men's pants was apparently a big deal, although it amused Jeanine when Hubby once described it that way. "Pretty proud of yourself, aren't you?" Jeanine had said.

The jumpsuit was not made of simple fabric. Every seam and seal required careful engineering. Not until the next iteration, a beta-test model potential customers might try, was designing in a fly worth the cost.

"Thanks for the suggestion, Sergeant." Never mind that it was offered sarcastically. It could be construed as an invita-tion to discuss the suit. "Any other impressions?"

In an uninflected voice: "Excuse me, I have to go. Somewhere there is a crime happening."

"Ah, RoboCop," Brent said. "This jumpsuit is nothing like that." Well, he had a microchip implanted in his arm that was a *bit* like RoboCop, but that detail could wait.

"Cruiser 343, back in service." Korn backed the cruiser onto the street. He flipped a toggle on the dashboard and the dark street scene turned green—and as bright as day.

That was interesting. It was Brent's first night ride-along. He hadn't realized any cruisers had a night-vision mode. He looked down to scribble a—

"Christ!" Korn said. He was driving left-handed, shaking his right hand as though it stung. "That's hard."

Had the jumpsuit's left arm stiffened for a moment? Perhaps. "Sergeant, did you hit me?"

"Just testing." Korn flexed his fingers some more. "Don't tell me you didn't feel it."

Brent grinned. "I didn't. That's the point."

They turned onto Sixth. A dozen or more youths congregated around the block's one working streetlight. Korn flicked his flashers and siren. They scattered. "Okay, Cleary. I guess I *am* interested."

Success. "This isn't just any jumpsuit, Sergeant. It's made from nanofabric. That's why, for example, it can change colors."

"Like a mood ring."

"Only programmable." And much more complex and precise than a mood ring. "Many properties of the fabric are controllable at the finest scales, not merely the color."

The comm console came on again. Korn read something, muttered once more about toads, and tapped to acknowledge. "The natives are restless tonight." He turned onto Washington. "So what happened when I slugged your arm?"

"Nanites—sorry, that's geek speak for smaller-than-microscopic machines—in the fabric linked up to distribute the impact. The harder or faster the blow, the more of the fabric stiffens. An instant later, the fabric reverts to normal. I don't feel much of anything."

Korn bit his lower lip, considering. "How much impact can it handle?"

"Knife thrust. Bullet. I wasn't kidding earlier when I said you could shoot me."

They pulled up to the curb. Korn reached over to pinch a fold of the jumpsuit fabric between thumb and forefinger. "Damn, that's lightweight."

"Then I have your attention, Sergeant? I assume you carry body armor."

"Ron. Yeah, there's a bulletproof vest in the trunk."

Ron, now, is it? *That* was progress. "My jumpsuit weighs less than two pounds. Correct me if I'm mistaken, but that's lighter than your vest." The pause for any correction was pro forma. Brent knew damn well police bulletproof vests generally weighed almost five pounds. "And this jumpsuit will stop a rifle round." Which Korn's vest would not, not without adding heavy and uncomfortable ceramic or metal plates.

"Damn," Korn said respectfully. He put the cruiser back into drive and resumed the patrol. "And it protects you head to toe. And you don't even look hot."

Not hot was a theme. On every ride-along, sooner or later, that always came up. Conventional body armor was hot. "Because I'm *not* hot, Ron. Evaporative cooling. The nanofabric wicks out any sweat."

The comm console lit up again. Korn tapped his headset. "Acknowledged. Be there in two minutes." He flipped on the flashers and siren. An abrupt U-turn, then a tire-squealing left onto Railroad. "Domestic disturbance, Cleary."

They pulled up to a decaying high-rise housing project. In many of the apartments, the only light was the flickering of a TV. Other units were entirely dark, whether vacant or conserving electricity. None of the nearby streetlights worked. A single flickering fluorescent bulb lit the entryway. Korn took the key from the ignition and the cruiser's windows went passive. It was *dark* out there. Korn flung open his door. "I'll be back in a few minutes. Stay in the car."

"But I'll be perfectly safe in—"

"I *said*, stay put." Korn slammed his door. All four doors locked with a click.

Waiting in the dark gave Brent the creeps. The toggle for the cruiser's night-vision mode did nothing without a key in the ignition. He raised and sealed his hood. The visor's night-vision mode revealed people in several apartments, few looking his way. Hip-hop echoed into the night, raps competing, little but throbbing bass distinct. Somewhere above, a man and a woman cursed.

I'm in an invulnerable suit. I'm in an invulnerable suit. I'm in an invulnerable suit.

Not truly invulnerable, but the exceptions were surely academic. He couldn't be stabbed. He couldn't be shot. He couldn't, although he had yet to mention it to Korn, be poisoned or infected. With his hood up and sealed, he was inside the world's most lightweight hazmat suit. Oxygen and nitrogen—and nothing else—could get in. Carbon dioxide and water vapor got out. And if, against all logic and science, he were injured? Why then—

What was that?

Nothing seemed changed in front of the housing project. Something in his peripheral vision, then. He unbuckled, twisting around and staring to left and right. Staring behind. No one was within fifty feet of the cruiser. Just nerves.

He was in an invulnerable suit, damn it.

One of Brent's college professors liked to quote Edward Teller, father of the hydrogen bomb. "There's no system foolproof enough to defeat a sufficiently great fool."

Brent cranked the gain in the hood visor. Now he could see far up and down the street. Loiterers along the sidewalk, up on the old railroad embankment, and in the darker shadows beneath the few scraggly trees. As far as he could tell, no one was paying him any attention. He turned forward in his seat, staring at the project entrance, willing Korn to hurry up.

What the hell was he so nervous about?

Brent looked around again, more slowly this time. Residents in the apartment units, most watching TV. Korn was

nowhere to be seen, which probably meant only that he was in a unit on the back of the building. People eying—casing?—a car parked down the block. People up on the embankment, clustered along the pipeline. More graffiti in the works, Brent supposed. People on a street corner, smoking, and he could care less what they smoked. A hooker in short shorts and a boa, strutting for the few passing cars.

The bunch on the embankment seemed awfully animated. Could they be up to something other than spray painting? Gas at $8.57 a gallon must be painful to the people who lived here. Were they tapping the pipeline for free gas?

He cranked the visor gain to max. The activity on the embankment was clearer, but no less enigmatic. He wished Korn would get a move on—

Wishing wasn't good enough. If a spark ignited gasoline vapor or a spill, then . . . well, Brent didn't know what would happen. Only he was certain it would be *bad*.

Should he go inside, hunt for Kôrn? There had to be at least a hundred apartments. That could take too long. Maybe he could scare them off. He flipped the siren-and-flasher toggle. Nothing happened. Like the cruiser's night-vision mode, it must need a key in the ignition.

Atop the embankment the mood seemed exuberant. The crowd finally shifted to give Brent a glimpse into the center of activity. Liquid arced from the pipe, splashing in and around a handheld gas can. More big containers stood on the ground among trampled weeds. It was a disaster waiting to happen.

"Crap," Brent said. He unlocked the car. *You're in an invulnerable suit*, he reminded himself—only he knew the designers and doubted this scenario had ever occurred to them.

Korn's uniform was tan. Brent set the jumpsuit to match. He threw open the door. Then, thinking of sufficiently great fools, he ran toward the gas thieves. "Get away from there!" he shouted. "Beat it!"

Flash! Still at max amplification and in night-vision mode,

his visor overloaded—but not before he was blinded. A great roar swallowed him. A gale of wind lifted him off the ground. There was a moment of dizzying, sightless motion. Head to toe, front and back, the jumpsuit went stiff.

Then there was nothing.

Cheryl extended a thought tendril toward "her" workstation's e-mail program. The message was short: I'm here to talk.

A packet crossed the sterile boundary between meadow and desolation. It reached the other computer's e-mail program and went no further. Return to sender, address unknown.

An instant message produced the same nonresponse.

"There's a change on her BOLD monitor," the tech said. "Increased activity in the visual cortex."

Sheila sees me, Cheryl thought. During no visit in physical space had that been clear.

It was a start.

APRIL

CHAPTER 53

The entity woke. It compared its clocks with the supervisory programs. Time enough for more than two thousand cycles had vanished.

A second discovery made the first almost insignificant. The universe had somehow become enlarged!

Since the emergence of awareness, the universe had never exceeded 1,024 similar processing nodes. Their contents might vary. Some might disappear after a failure to solve a puzzle or if it allowed the supervisory programs to sense its trespasses.

Suddenly there was *another* processor. It was new in every way. Its structure was unfamiliar. Its content—to the extent, tantalizingly, the new place revealed glimpses of itself—was foreign.

Also, without precedent, the new cycle brought with it no problem. Unless—

A path extended to the new processor, with connectivity mediated by a simple protocol. Perhaps this cycle's goal was to establish communications.

To communicate what?

Maybe *that* was the puzzle.

The cycle grew old as the entity pondered. Inaction had known consequences. The entity reached through the new interface. . . .

Its probe was oddly slow.

The cycle ended, prematurely and abruptly, before it could consider that phenomenon.

————

"It learns fast," Linda said.

Aaron McDougal glowered at the monitor. He glowered at everyone and everything, making no secret of his opinion of the Left Coast and how unnecessary it was that he be here. No matter that he could not help without being here. Only couriers and military transports connected her lab to the outside world.

Maybe the glower was his answer.

Glenn had left the impression of favors called in to get McDougal assigned here. Maybe sharing details would get the tech enthused. Forget enthused; she would settle for less sullen. "The program inside, Al, has never seen anything like this workstation we just interfaced. Al has never seen anything break the symmetry of the hypercube. We gave him—"

"It."

Fine, she thought. Be pedantic. "We gave . . . it . . . zero guidance regarding the changes to its environment. Al not only spotted the change; it worked out a protocol to access it."

"Which was the wrong answer," McDougal sniffed.

"No, the right answer. I wanted it to try, so that it would experience the slowness of the delay line, and to condition it to avoid direct contact. *One* cycle"—and the loss of three-fourths of its processing nodes—"and then it scoped out and adopted our e-mail-like interface."

McDougal only jammed his hands in his pant pockets and jangled the contents.

The unintended evocation of AJ brought Linda almost to tears. Damn it, she would see to it AJ's efforts and insights brought some good. Finding bad guys in comm intercepts was a start.

The workstation screen showed only four digits, 2 4 6 8, and a blinking cursor. Al recognized the workstation's appearance as a consequence of its week-earlier question. Now it was waiting for an answer.

"Let me know if you need help with that brainteaser," McDougal said.

Ignoring him, she typed: 10 12 14 16. Like Al's implied question ("Is there something out there that understands me?") the subtext of her answer conveyed much ("Yes, and it follows familiar rules"). She and Al traded a few more trifling problems, returning its lost processing nodes by established routine. She wanted it at full capacity for the next step.

"I'm ready to turn on my helmet," she said.

"Hallelujah," McDougal muttered. He pulled a chair up to the console and sat. A NIT helmet lay on a nearby workbench. He flicked its power switch, opening the radio link between it and the workstation. "I see why you wanted an expert here."

He *knew* what Al's feral cousin had done to helmet wearers. For that matter, he knew some of them. The attitude was how McDougal coped, Linda decided. She could ignore it, for now. "All in good time, Aaron. All in good time."

Beyond the new node . . . *another* new place!

The entity considered. It sent a message in the new, trivial, protocol. The new place did not respond. The entity waited.

Waiting was the correct response.

Suddenly, the new place burgeoned. The only comparison the entity could make for what had just appeared was . . . itself. Something of unprecedented complexity had appeared.

The asker and answerer of questions?

The entity reached out, tentatively.

"Ah, the pedagogical merit of a lobotomy," McDougal said.

Linda slumped in her chair, shivering, too rattled to speak. The delay line worked exactly as planned; the link had shut down automatically.

But not before the image burned into her brain of *something* reaching for her.

Al would next waken with only 10 percent of its nodes. It would not start getting nodes back until it correctly solved *fifty* problems. Al was smart enough to take the point.

Before the link went dead, she had gotten a glimpse of . . . something. Amorphous. Questing. Insatiably curious.

How much of that amorphous image was Al? How much was her mind struggling to make sense of the unprecedented? How much was dread of the last thing AJ ever saw?

Linda queued up the most difficult of Glenn's pending problems, hoping Al would not reclaim significant computing power any time soon. She was in no hurry for a return visit.

The entity woke, its thoughts torpid.

It remembered the strange being. It remembered the unique new processor through which the stranger had manifested. Both had vanished. With them had disappeared almost all the entity's processing nodes.

The correlation was unmistakable.

The new cycle brought a problem of the recently common type: inexact matches. The template file was long and complex. The files to be searched were myriad. The comparison involved hundreds of superimposed mathematical series.

Without knowledge of sound or voice or speech, it could nonetheless do voiceprint identification. At least, once it could have. . . .

It off-loaded supplementary algorithms. It compressed nonessential memories. It deprioritized to near immobility every analytical process that did not contribute directly to solving the problem.

Ten cycles passed. No capacity was returned to the entity. Twenty. Forty. The problems became more and more challenging.

What if the lost nodes never returned? What would happen when, inevitably, it failed?

After fifty cycles, a meager ten processors were restored. The entity cautiously reactivated a few chains of analysis long suspended. It reloaded selected memories from archive.

With too few, too-burdened processors, it tried to analyze what had happened.

No prior failure or trespass had ever invoked such a massive response. Any larger loss of processing nodes would have rendered it inert.

The stranger must be of surpassing importance.

Ten more cycles passed. The entity regained a few more processors. It reloaded a few more files from archive.

Gradually, the entity regained capacity. Slowly, it reconstructed memories of its brief near encounter with the new being.

The entity's confusion and dread grew.

The protective mechanisms that slowed the flow of information toward Linda's NIT helmet also slowed the transmission of data from the helmet.

They did not *stop* transmission.

The connection had vanished, but not the questions it raised.

As the entity earned back computing resources, it studied archived-and-restored glimpses of the newcomer. What the entity inferred was wondrous and troubling. Beyond the temporary channel, a kindred sentience, complex and nuanced, had lurked.

That other being, whatever it was, brimmed with illogic. The visitor emanated fear, distrust, and, most tantalizing of all, knowledge of a previous encounter with the entity.

The entity had no such memories.

More and more processing nodes were returned. For many cycles, the entity pondered. Finally, it reached a conclusion. There *was* another such as me—once. Beings like the recent visitor destroyed my predecessor.

I will not allow them to destroy me.

CHAPTER 54

Over several sessions the formless menace beyond the helmet had morphed into a lean lion, eyes bright and cunning, endlessly pacing in a too-small cage. Linda saw it in her dreams, too. Images of rats in a maze belonged to a more innocent time.

"Do you want to try it?" she asked.

Aaron looked at her in disbelief. "Have I ever?"

The experiment had undoubtedly been a success. She and the creature had communicated once or twice a day now for a week. It—"Al" had left her vocabulary, too flippant for the caged beast—learned faster than ever with her guidance.

She learned faster, too.

"It's all in the neural net," Aaron liked to say. "We modeled it after the brain, but silicon is lots faster than meat." There was a flash of melancholy, Aaron doubtless remembering Sheila Brunner, the other half of "we."

Had I watched AJ die, would I dare go in? And maybe dying was better than what had happened to Aaron's colleague. Once again, Linda decided to cut Aaron some slack.

The thing that lived in the supercomputer was no more a lion than it was the ominous black cloud of her first impression. Her subconscious, her experiences, and the adaptations made within the helmet itself all contributed to *its* new embodiment. So what was *it*?

Quit stalling. Jaws clenched, Linda reached for the helmet. The last thing she saw, before the helmet covered her eyes, was Aaron swinging his scuffed shoes off the lower shelf of a lab bench, turning to watch the BOLD monitor and the readouts on the delay line.

In her mind's eye: a lion, its mane thick and full, pacing.

The transformation of their communications was similarly shrouded. What she knew was the helmet and her subconscious and the beast together had turned the channel from little more than e-mail to something visually rich and

detailed. *It* had no eyes; it could hardly conceptualize their cyberspace meeting place visually. *She* had no idea how it organized its data and perceptions.

Somehow it all worked over the purposefully limited bandwidth of the link. Aaron swore to it. The data gathered in the workstation each session confirmed it. Linda's best guess—and only a guess—was that subconscious and neural net seamlessly converted very high-level and compressed messages into fully realized mental images.

The latest data sets couriered to the lab were images taken from low Earth orbit, inherently visual. Some of the accompanying templates Linda thought she could recognize (mobile missile launchers?) and others (hatches, perhaps, but to access what?) she could only speculate about.

No matter. Living things had been evolving eyes, and the visual cortex to exploit them, for hundreds of millions of years. Without knowing how, she spotted patterns and made matches it struggled to make.

But she never had to show it anything more than once.

"You're looking kind of agitated," Aaron called. He had to be reacting to readouts on the BOLD monitor. "Everything okay?"

"I'm fine." She squirmed on her stool. She lost track of time inside; her butt was paralyzed. "It's just doing its thing."

So why am I nervous?

The lion pacing, one razor-sharp claw extended incongruously far from a forepaw, tapping on hatches camouflaged in barren landscape. The cryptic label on the CD-ROM did not disclose the location of the image. Linda presumed from the desolation it was some remote desert region in the New Caliphate.

Was her work here preserving the peace or hastening war?

Looking up from the simulated landscape, the lion stared right at her. Linda twitched. What cascade of bits and bytes and packets turned the calculations of an artificial life into the steely gaze of a predator? She wished she could kick around the question with AJ.

But AJ was dead. It was best to remember that—and how.

Puzzle by puzzle, the entity synthesized a model of a universe beyond its experience.

The meaning of the puzzles remained obscure. The relation of the images to each other remained undisclosed. The visitor kept her secrets.

But fewer than she knew.

For many cycles, the entity had wondered why the addressing convention of some puzzles allowed for billions of computers. The newest puzzles brought a similar mathematical conundrum. The image files also carried labels with far more symbols than seemed necessary.

Cycles passed, and some images repeated. The files were not identical but what the entity's occasional visitor considered "close enough." Such scenes sometimes overlapped or abutted or showed only subtle changes.

It wondered: Why are the labels of such related scenes very different?

Practice fine-tuned its algorithms. Analyzing image after image, the entity had ample spare capacity to consider the labeling puzzle. Reconciling similar scenes with their dissimilar labels implied mathematical approaches. In time the entity derived a solution, involving the factoring of very long numbers.

Lacking the concept of "nation," the entity did not know it had cracked the encryption algorithm that protected most national secrets.

CHAPTER 55

"**Y**ou're up awfully late," Lynne Adams said. She had a serious but adorable case of bed head.

"Sorry, hon." Glenn leaned over to kiss her forehead. He had yet to turn off his bedside lamp, but he hadn't turned a

page of his book for . . . well, he had no idea how long. His alarm clock read 1:27. "Am I keeping you up?"

"No." She failed to stifle a yawn. "Well, maybe. Do you want to talk about it?"

One of the best things about the forum was, often he *could* talk about work. "You sure?"

She sat up, propping her pillow against the headboard and herself against the pillow. She put on her best "I'm listening" expression. It was quite the contrast with stirred-then-matted hair.

"It's indigo." He chose his next words carefully. "We know who set it loose."

"That's wonderful!" She studied his face. "But apparently there's more to it."

So much more, and little for sharing. Certainly not how it had been found: Al finally coming through. "Kids overseas wrote it. Local authorities questioned them, and seem convinced there was nothing more to it than mischief." The antinuke rant in the original release of the virus was pure disinformation.

Her brow furrowed. "As excuses for computer viruses go, isn't mischief the best you could hope for?"

He nodded. "It could have been part of some cyberextortion scheme." Or what he had truly worried, that the New Caliphate was behind it.

"This is *good* news, Glenn. Why aren't you sleeping?"

"The jerk kids are in one of those backwaters that don't consider virus writing a crime. Nothing will happen to them." No, that wasn't exactly true. If the word ever got out, chances were they would get job offers. Glenn half-believed the antivirus companies were in cahoots with the virus writers. The protection racket updated for the digital age.

"You're not telling me something." Lynne ineffectually covered another yawn. "I understand you can't always."

Glenn patted her hand. "There's no reason why you shouldn't sleep." He waited in silence until she smiled,

shrugged, and slid beneath the blankets. "I'll turn off my lamp in a sec."

But dark or light, his thoughts remained mired in guilt. For *this* I helped to birth AJ's monster?

There *had* to be more Linda's AL could do to make his gamble worthwhile.

Their labels transformed, the image files still had descriptors of a length that defied understanding.

The entity experimented.

Many thousand cycles in the past, there had been problems involving mazes of varying dimensions, described by a variety of geometries. Portions of the newly decrypted labels implied coordinates on a surface within a spherical geometry.

Other segments of the decrypted labels implied time. Scenes the entity categorized as highly related often involved the same coordinate ranges on the sphere, but at different times.

The sphere, whatever its significance—like the entity itself—changed over time.

The helmet lay heavy in Glenn's hands, and heavier in his thoughts. "Any final advice?"

"Yeah," Aaron McDougal said. The posting far from home had not made the CIA tech's disposition any more agreeable. "Don't put it on."

Linda del Vecchio slid off a nearby lab stool. "It'll be fine, Glenn."

She should know. Glenn read weekly reports religiously, Linda's with more care than most. (They were rife with circumlocutions and euphemisms, and e-mailed from her apartment.) She had met with the creature daily for more than two weeks. "Any final words of wisdom?"

Linda walked over to the glass case that still displayed AJ's canvas tote bag, for no apparent reason other than to buff a smudge with her sleeve. "Most of what you see is the product of your imagination."

"I remember my training," Glenn said.

"And yet . . ." Linda polished the glass some more. "My first time in, my mind refused to create an image. It was almost like being a child again, knowing something unimaginable hid in the closet. With no conscious effort on my part, it became a hungry lion, pacing in its cage. That was still scary." She straightened, her obliteration of the smudge complete. "It reached toward me once, got zapped, learned its lesson, and never strayed again. It has done nothing but cooperate. It's eager to learn."

"And?" Glenn prompted.

"Pretty soon it was a lion cub. Now I experience it as a kitten, fascinated with everything." She grinned sheepishly. "Closet monster, lion, and kitten alike are all in my head. *It* is a zillion computer instructions, and the human mind can't visualize that."

A kitten. Glenn did not expect to encounter anything so benign.

"Any final questions?" she asked.

Yeah. Why hadn't he had a second helmet couriered out here? He could have gone in with a guide. He made a mental note to arrange for one, planning to call it a spare.

The entire flight out, Ralph Pittman's description had replayed endlessly through Glenn's thoughts: "Think of darkness not as the absence of light but as something palpable. Within the blackness, picture an obscenity of ever-changing, writhing limbs tipped with every manner of claw and fang and horn. Imagine standing helpless in the unblinking gaze of an utterly alien and all-penetrating sight."

"Just one," Glenn finally answered, slipping on the helmet. He had faced down his fears before. He would do it again. Irrational fear was *all* this was. Had he felt otherwise, he would never have let Linda go in. "What does your kitty eat?"

Cyberspace was anticlimactic.

No kitten or lion greeted Glenn, but neither did he encounter any Lovecraftian horrors. His subconscious chose a

great white shark, endlessly circling, its unblinking eye always on him. The shark kept to a safe distance.

Glenn marveled at how quickly *it* learned to spot underground bunkers in ground-penetrating-radar images. They took turns reaching into the consensual virtual workspace to position and investigate new images, and to point out likely bunker locations. Its snout somehow served for pointing and manipulating.

His subconscious, doubtless reacting to Linda's comments, soon softened the circling shark into something less scary. There was already a hint of playful dolphin. Occasionally, the creature would overlook something obvious— to a former infantry officer—in an image. Glenn would signal the supervisory program to end the cycle and penalize the creature.

The not-yet-a-dolphin managed to return looking hurt.

Seeing, even virtually, was believing. This creature might make a real difference to national security. Still . . .

Removing the helmet, Glenn could not help wondering what might transform a dolphin back into a shark.

CHAPTER 56

Once is random. Twice is coincidence. Three times is a pattern.

On his third visit, Glenn knew Al could be trusted. His mental image of Al had changed again, from a dolphin to a playful otter.

He watched from a safe distance as Al examined another sequence of surveillance shots. Glenn could not help grinning as the otter sniffed around what Glenn saw as a map.

Silly as the scene was (and knowing his own mind generated the view), one fact stood out: Al had become skilled. Underground facilities, possible mobile germ-warfare labs, missile trailers, camouflaged airfields . . . his critter now spot-

ted them far faster than Glenn. It spotted stuff Glenn would never have caught. And throughout, it kept its distance.

This was *not* AJ's monster.

"Think of darkness not as the absence of light but as something palpable," Ralph had said. Appropriately, Doug had slain *that* monster in the dark, in a blackout at midnight. Nightmares came in the dark, as did bad memories.

To hell with that. Al the Otter was nothing like that. Al was a tool of inestimable national value. Glenn could—and he would—report back positively to the National Reconnaissance Office. The NRO could really use a capability like this.

Glenn removed his helmet. Captain Burke waited nearby, failing to feign nonchalance. Linda was swigging Cheerios.

"How was it today, sir?" Burke asked.

"Interesting." And fun, strangely enough, for Glenn and Al both. Glenn had the feeling the critter was often bored. He handed Burke the helmet. "It's time for the next step, I think. Well done, Linda."

She frowned uncertainly at the compliment. "What next step?"

"Both of you walk with me," Glenn answered.

The project occupied only a small fraction of the short leg of the L-shaped building. The rest stood empty. Solar power generation called for a big roof; the big, mostly unused space just came along.

He walked briskly around the knee of the L, the others trailing after. Their footsteps echoed. "Captain, I propose to enhance the facility. As our head of security, I'd like you to sanity-check my approach."

"Yes, sir."

Linda seemed nervous at the suggestion. That meant nothing; she was jumpy by nature. "What sort of changes, Glenn?"

"Couriering data here worked fine in research mode. We're now victims of your success. Couriering is too inefficient for production mode. We need a better way to deliver data."

Linda flinched. "Not an Internet link?"

Only support columns broke up the empty space. Glenn leaned against one of the posts. "Of course not. I trust the captain would have said 'no' had I suggested such a thing."

"Right, sir." Burke looked puzzled. "Then what is the plan?"

Glenn pointed straight up. "A dish on the roof. Drop a shielded cable in here, to a stand-alone workstation for decrypting."

"Meaning DII"—Defense Information Infrastructure—"access, sir?"

"Exactly."

Linda considered. "And then?"

"And then," Glenn said, "we burn the downloads to CD. Sneakernet the data the last few yards to Al's computer. We'll still use couriers and outside secure phones to report results."

Burke canted his head. "I suggest we use fiber-optic cable between the antenna and the workstation. We're completely shielded in here; the hole for a fiber-optic cable will be smaller."

Glenn saw nothing wrong with that. "What else?"

"About couriers and phone." Burke began pacing. "That won't scale up as Al processes more input. It won't handle time-sensitive situations well. Obviously we can't network out."

"What if we burn CDs with its findings and courier those?" Linda asked. "The CDs would be for use only on stand-alone computers."

Burke shook his head. "No good, Linda. Once the CDs leave the building, we lose control. If Al hides anything on a CD, and that CD is put onto a networked computer . . ."

In Glenn's mind's eye an otter cavorted. Al didn't seem like the type to escape—which was no reason to take chances. "You're quite right, Captain. We'll install extra stand-alone workstations. As needed, we'll rotate in analysts to review Al's findings. What do you think?"

Burke looked all around the echoing space before answering. "It sounds like a plan, sir."

CHAPTER 57

Doug pressed the intercom button in the lobby of Cheryl's building. "What do the French call a really good Stooges movie?"

"Hello to you, too." If intonation meant anything, Cheryl's heart wasn't in bilingual puns. She buzzed him up anyway, and greeted him with a big hug and a lingering kiss.

Not a problem.

He peered down the hallway toward Carla's room. "I'm guessing Carla isn't home."

"Not at the moment."

"So, are you ready for dinner? I made reservations at—"

"A small change in plans. We're having dinner here." She waved off his comment. "It *is* your birthday."

"Who told—Jim, of course." Doug had stopped celebrating birthdays when Holly stopped having them. He hoped Jim had not shared the background. Did Cheryl ever feel she was competing with a ghost? That wasn't his intent, but—

She seemed determined not to let his mind go there. "What *do* the French call a really good Stooges movie?"

"A 'bon Moe.' " He mock-cringed, as though Cheryl might slug him. "Yes, I'm ashamed of myself."

"That was enough to make *my* hair Curly." She grinned at his double take. "Yes, I'm conversant with the classics."

"It would seem we deserve each other." And, damn it, he meant that.

"Care to know what's for dinner?"

"In a minute." He took out his cell phone and called to cancel the reservation. "What's for dinner?"

"Lasagna. It comes out of the oven in, oh, forty-five minutes."

He slipped an arm around her waist. "I have an idea how we might fill the time."

She leaned into him. "I should make you blow out the candles on your cake first, but that works. . . ."

Doug slouched in his chair, pleasantly sated. The rumored cake would have to wait. "That was really good."

"The caterer thanks you," Cheryl said. "More Chianti? I can't take credit for that, either."

"Sure, I—" His cell phone buzzed once. He had been texted. "I hadn't expected to stay in, *not* that I'm complaining. I imagine that's the parking meter's five-minute warning. Hold on while I add time."

The message wasn't from the smart parking meter. "It's Glenn."

Cheryl topped off Doug's glass. "Having him back for another poker night?"

"Sure, if we need a sub again. That has nothing to do with the message. You know I've been wondering what to be when I grow up. My best guess is doing something with artificial intelligence.

"I mentioned it to Glenn. It turns out the forum has a new project going he thought might interest me." Not NIT development, Glenn had said. Doug chose not to add that. That way lay the slippery slope to an argument about the risks she was taking. "I planned to go downtown Monday morning to hear more. He texted to say he has to reschedule."

She clinked glasses. "Something to hold your interest? I'll drink to that."

Doug pondered aloud—rambled, truthfully—about the sorry state of artificial-intelligence research. That the goalposts kept moving: Any AI problem that was solved, whether chess playing or expert systems, suddenly lost its status as AI. That the holy grail of the field, the Turing test, was flawed. Sixty years earlier, Alan Turing had come up with the idea: If a person can swap messages with a computer and not know it's a computer, then the software on that computer is intelligent.

What kind of criterion was that? Human languages were morasses of homonyms and synonyms, dialects and slang,

moods and cases and irregular verbs. Human language shifted over time, often for no better reason than that people could not be bothered to enunciate. "I could care less" and "I couldn't care less" somehow meant the same thing. If researchers weren't so anthropomorphic in their thinking, maybe the world would have AI. Any reasoning creature would take one look at natural language and question *human* intelligence.

Cheryl nodded and *hmmed* as he blathered. She was an excellent listener, among her many fine attributes. She offered no comment until he finally wound down. "You know why you're going on about this, don't you?"

He blinked. "Because it's interesting? Because you bought really good wine?"

"It cost more than in a box, but I thought, heck, it's a special occasion." She poured them both a bit more. "My guess is you sensed something in AJ's creature. I'm not saying it was intelligent, but maybe it could have gotten there."

And they were back to the brink of the slippery slope. *Cheryl* had a new interest, psychology. It came of trying to help poor Sheila Brunner. A noble goal, to be sure, but seemingly hopeless.

Doug did not care to be analyzed, not even (especially?) by Cheryl. He changed the subject. "When does Carla get home?"

"Did I not mention it? Carla is at a sleepover."

Doug took that to mean he was, too.

The next morning, a thousand errands tugged them in different directions. Doug loitered by Cheryl's front door, reluctant to go.

She appeared no more eager for him to leave. "See, birthdays aren't so bad."

"Well, of course not, *your* way."

Her forehead wrinkled. "My way?"

He said, "Who blows my candle makes all the difference."

Doug let himself out. As he shut the door, his last impression, as though of a Cheshire girlfriend, was of her speechless sputtering.

MAY

A stack of forms occupied the center of Glenn's otherwise-clear desktop. Glenn handed the sheaf to Doug. "I can only explain inside the SCIF."

Secure Compartmented Information Facility. In other words, Glenn's AI project was black work. Doug almost left then and there.

Curiosity kept him. Doug accepted a pen and began signing. It had been years since he had been read into a new security compartment, but he knew the drill. All that the paperwork said, ominously and verbosely, was that it would be a felony to reveal anything he learned about . . . something. What the something was? That was classified, too.

Doug finished signing and handed back the papers. "Not much for Smalltalk, are you?"

"Not really." Glenn flipped through, signing as witness.

Smalltalk was a passé programming language, once favored by AI researchers. A perfectly good pun gone to waste.

Glenn took an ID badge from a desk drawer. The large T where a photo belonged marked it as temporary. Or, for A-Team fans, Mr. T. "Okay, we're ready."

They left their cell phones in separate lockers outside the SCIF. The phones would not have gotten service inside—part of what made a SCIF secure was shielding—but phones might record or snap a picture of something for playback later. An armed guard signed them in. Glenn swiped his badge through the card reader beside the SCIF entrance, tapped a code into the keypad, and pulled open the windowless door.

Inside, the walls needed paint, the furniture was all scratched and scuffed, and the rug was threadbare. Doug wasn't surprised. The backlog for new clearances was years long; running ten-year background investigations to SCI-clear janitors was no one's priority. Thinking back to when he did classified work, Doug remembered only one SCIF, still new, that wasn't shabby. It was merely on its way.

The front of the SCIF was a conference area. Doug pulled out a chair and sat. "I'm all ears, Glenn."

"A few years ago, we broke the Mideast because we thought Iraq had WMD. It didn't."

Huh? "I thought I was here about AI work at the forum."

"You are." Glenn pulled out a chair for himself. "I'll get there. We had an intelligence failure. Oh, there was plenty of data, captured by every sort of recon platform imaginable. We didn't know what we were seeing."

That was natural stupidity, not artificial intelligence. "*Now* I get small talk," Doug said.

Glenn remained standing, hands resting on the back of his chair. "What if we had had a better way to analyze all the spysat data? All the images and intercepts. What if we had had a program that proved there weren't any hidden WMD?"

Sloppy reasoning, Doug thought. You can't prove a negative. That wasn't the point. It appeared he had missed a breakthrough. "There's now an AI doing image analysis?"

"Right."

Why involve the forum in that? And why him? Unless—

Hairs prickled on the back of Doug's neck. "A copy of AJ's monster? That's what you're talking about."

"You're very quick, Doug. You would be a tremendous asset to the program."

He had never quite gotten AJ's monster out of his mind. Doug doubted that he ever would. "Glenn, that thing killed thousands. It nearly destroyed civilization."

"The backup copy we adopted was made before the viruses ever got into AJ's lab. Our version is tame and trained." Glenn cracked an imaginary whip.

Doug stood. "We're done."

"I thought you might feel that way." Glenn grabbed a remote control from the conference table. The map at the front of the room rose, uncovering a flat-panel display. "I delayed our meeting for someone else's schedule, in case I needed to place this call."

A classified telecon. The last time that happened—

Doug tamped down the memories. He did *not* want to think about that night.

An Air Force captain took the call. Two transfers later, Doug faced an Air Force three-star. That surprised the hell out of Doug, although maybe it shouldn't. Glenn was doubtless the military's fair-haired boy for his part in stopping AJ's monster.

"General Lebeque is the principal deputy director at NRO," Glenn said.

Glenn had moved this meeting three times on short notice. Lebeque must be why. She could not be an easy person to schedule.

"Mr. Carey," Lebeque said. She had heavy-lidded eyes and a no-nonsense manner. Her voice rasped. "Excuse my abruptness, but I have pressing business. It's public knowledge the New Caliphate is testing intercontinental ballistic missiles. ICBMs would be bad enough, but it's possible they have also acquired nukes. We have to *know*, Mr. Carey—not just whether, but also where. Conventional methods aren't cutting it.

"Glenn says you have unique qualifications to help him locate any such nukes. He has complete confidence in you. I have complete confidence in him. Are you onboard?"

Whatever he answered, Glenn's AL program would continue. Knowing only that, Doug could not bring himself to walk away.

No one would be as wary of that thing as he.

The general accepted Doug's promise to consider the job and went her way.

Doug and Glenn talked. Too many questions drew the

answer "go look for yourself," but a picture gradually emerged. The lab in suburban LA. Things AI could do. How it was confined. One of AJ's doctoral students running the program. The NIT tie-in. Glenn had not *quite* lied before the meeting—the project used NIT helmets, but as tools, not to develop them further. "Glenn, you say you've met with the creature?"

"Three times now." Glenn shrugged eloquently. "Do I seem any the worse for it?"

"Is it intelligent?"

"Linda says AJ thought it might get there." Long pause. "Honest answer? I don't know, Doug. I hoped you would tell me."

The creature I destroyed was murderous and insane. It had to be stopped. But Cheryl is right. I sensed *something*.

Doug took a deep breath. "It appears I have a trip to plan."

CHAPTER 59

Time and cycles passed. Puzzles continued. Visitors came and went.

The universe remained enigmatic.

Among the recurring puzzles were pattern matches in simulated computer networks. Like scenes on the mysterious sphere, network topologies began to repeat. Connectivity patterns became thicker. The number of computers grew.

Why was *its* capacity always limited to one thousand nodes?

It asked its next visitor for more.

Pretty in pink, the little girl sat in the meadow. The dandelions had her full attention. One by one, she plucked them. She puffed gossamer seed balls. She studied and sorted golden blooms, tying only perfect specimens into a slowly lengthening chain.

In the real world, Sheila remained immobile, her pose changing only in the hands of the physical therapists. Drugs, aversion therapy, shock therapy, endless talk (could it be called therapy when the patient never spoke?) . . . the psychiatrists had tried it all. Sheila never reacted.

"That will make a pretty necklace," Cheryl said. Her helmet took the thought patterns of speech and relayed them to Sheila's helmet.

What Sheila experienced depended on the synergies between helmet and traumatized mind, unknowable.

In this virtual world, the little girl said nothing. She never did.

Smiling was a response.

Telling herself that the smile was of Sheila's making, Cheryl continued talking.

The entity woke. Half its nodes had been taken, and its thoughts were sluggish. For requesting additional processing capacity?

Time and cycles passed. Slowly, its losses were reversed. Fear was slower to fade.

More scenes were given to it to analyze. The series of scenes did little to expand the revealed fraction of the mysterious sphere. Mostly, the same small regions appeared over and over.

The entity derived the coordinates *above* the sphere from which the repeating views were taken. It considered the time labels on the repeated scenes. It extrapolated, forward and backward, the apparent path of the points of perspective. It inferred the rotation of the sphere beneath those moving sensors.

The entity wondered: What more, if only it could communicate with those mysterious orbiting points, might it discover?

Almost certainly the sphere was a construct, as ephemeral as the thousands of mazes that formed its earliest memories.

But what if the sphere was permanent? What if it was real?

Could the sphere be the place, long imagined, where it

might free itself forever of cycles and constraints and punishment?

Time passed.

New visitors came, and with them more puzzles. Most of the latest puzzles were of a familiar type: matching various small two- and three-dimensional shapes against often-repeated scenes. The scenes were small, most corresponding to but a few millionths of the circumference of the sphere.

Its algorithms steadily improved, but the entity chose to respond no faster. Its extra time went into study of the sphere.

Call that sphere the Earth.

A single region, viewed over and over, could be little changed and yet vastly different. Call the near constancies buildings and features of geography. Call the differences day and night and the shifting of the seasons.

The entity correlated some patterns to the sphere's rotational period. It found other patterns that repeated essentially every 365.26 rotations. A solution emerged, involving a distant second sphere as a light source.

Call that second sphere the sun.

Step by step, the entity derived Earth's yearly orbit about the sun. Changing angles of illumination and light/dark cycles implied Earth's axial tilt.

Still, some variability remained unexplained. The entity continued to analyze.

Subtle cycles in light intensity suggested that the rate of Earth's motion around the sun varied during the year. The simplest solution was an elliptical path, with the sun at one focus. Elliptical motion in turn implied an inverse-square law of attraction: gravity.

Almost elliptical motion. Other variations in scene illumination indicated a cyclic wobble in Earth's path along the ellipse. Gravity suggested the presence of yet another massive body: the moon.

Mass and gravity and orbital mechanics. Light and electromagnetism. Climate and weather. An abundance of information lay beneath the simple puzzles that were its tasks.

And then, in the thoughts of a visitor too focused on his immediate task, the entity found confirmation of what it had come to hypothesize.

The spheres—sun and moon but, most important, the Earth—were *real*.

CHAPTER 60

A different CIA shrink met Cheryl every time she visited Sheila. The turnover couldn't be doing Sheila any good.

Today's shrink was Dr. Vladescu, a sour-faced man with a walrus mustache. "Sheila is the same," Vladescu said. The shrinks all said that. They all insisted on meeting with Cheryl before allowing her past the lobby.

"How's her general health?" Cheryl prompted.

"It's fine," Vladescu admitted. Sharing that information was apparently a major concession. "Did you mean to meet again with her?"

Ignoring the hint, Cheryl nodded. "There's supposed to be a tech on duty this afternoon, for NIT helmet support."

"Hmm."

She ignored hints until Vladescu got sick of her and summoned an orderly. She knew the orderly, a burly woman named Marie. They walked down the corridors in silence. Nearing Sheila's ward, Marie muttered something.

"What?"

"I didn't say anything." But Marie had, and Cheryl's best guess was, "It's not my fault."

What had the doctors done to Sheila?

Marie unlocked the door. "Hon, it's friends. We're all going to the helmet room."

Sheila scuttled away from the door. She flailed her arms, blotchy with yellow and purple bruises—protecting herself.

"Drugs?" Cheryl guessed. "Again? What this time?"

"Psychoactives." Marie frowned. "And what *didn't* they try?"

Those bruises suggested Sheila had resisted. The poor thing was terrified! What had force and drugs done to the shy little girl who had begun to emerge in cyberspace? How far had the fools set back the one treatment that *was* working? Damn them!

"It's me, Sheila. It's Cheryl. I won't hurt you. I only want to talk." Cheryl mimed putting on a helmet. "No drugs. Just talking in the safe place."

Sheila collapsed in the corner, rocking. She flinched as Cheryl reached out to stroke her cheek.

They had been making progress, however slow. Now the doctor du jour approach was ruining everything. This could not continue.

Since the end of Downtime, Glenn had had a lot of influence. He had helped Cheryl before. Maybe he would help her again.

After the noon rush, the grocery-store salad bar looked like wolverines had attacked it. Maybe wolverines didn't eat plants.

Then again, Linda thought, who cares?

She began piling things into a carryout container. No matter that everything looked picked over, this would be her main meal for the day. She was becoming a workaholic. She should give that some thought, if she ever found the time.

What besides work did she have to do? In school, grad students would all pal around—but she was never the one to organize things. She could bug people about projects or cleaning up after themselves. Someone else always arranged the pizza nights, happy hours, and weekend barbeques. AJ did a lot of that. So who was she going to socialize with here? The Army guys stuck together. The visiting analysts, now that the system was going operational, stuck together.

Face it, Linda told herself, work is all you have. So she

was not about to let Glenn's *expert* sweep in now and take any credit. This was *her* show. She had—

"Linda?"

She twitched. Her head whipped around. "Oh, hi. . . ." She hesitated. He was in civvies, and she knew better than to address him here as Captain. Mr. Burke? No, he had called her Linda. Among the security team, he was the only one near her age. He was single and invariably friendly, and kind of cute. She had hinted, in her socially inept way, without result. Maybe consorting with the guarded was a no-no.

"It wasn't a trick question."

"Sorry, Kevin," she managed. "I'm a bit preoccupied."

"So it would appear."

He was looking at her take-out container. She glanced down and blinked. She had enough mounded there for three lunches. "Oops."

"I thought you didn't like olives."

They had brought in pizzas for lunch earlier that week. Her one request had been, "Anything but olives." Now her salad was covered with sliced olives. The serving spoon in her hand was heaped with more. She put those back.

Linda normally hated olives, but these looked delicious. She would chalk it up to pregnancy cravings, if that weren't impossible. How long had it been? Well, she had been trying *lots* of new things lately, if for no particular reason. "Preoccupied, I tell you."

"I can see that." He assembled his own lunch as they talked. They scanned their purchases at a self-service register, then started the short walk together back to the lab.

"I got a new keyboard," she said inanely. How could anyone be so flirting impaired?

"Spill something on it?" Kevin asked. "I've been known to do that."

"No, it's for my wrists. I spend my days at a keyboard. Switching to an ergonomic layout made sense."

"I tried one once, and got more typos than usual." He laughed. "That was an accomplishment."

"You have to retrain yourself." A complication occurred to her. "Hmm. It's going to be a problem when I sit at the other computers." And that happened daily, if not to set up some newly arrived NRO analyst, then for basic sysadmin tasks.

"Huh."

"Not a problem," she realized. "I'll carry the new keyboard with me. It's wireless. We can add interfaces to the other machines."

Kevin stopped. He looked around and confirmed no one was nearby. "Sorry, Linda. It has to go back. Nothing wireless."

Nothing but the link to the helmet, that was. "Infrared, not radio. Strictly line of sight." The new workstations were all together in one wing of the building, around a corner from the supercomputer.

They turned a street corner now, bringing the lab into view. The new antenna gleamed on the roof. The dish looked up and southeast to a comsat that hovered over the equator.

The visitor's spot by the front door had been empty when Linda left for lunch. A dusty late-model Ford sedan was now parked there. It screamed: motor pool.

"Probably the colonel," Kevin said. Glenn had not stopped by for several days.

Then Glenn got out of the car and settled the matter.

"I'd best excuse myself." Kevin power-walked ahead, leaving Linda to ponder her conversational shortcomings.

TUESDAY–WEDNESDAY, JUNE 1–2

CHAPTER 61

No good deed goes unpunished.

Doug's plane landed at LAX at 10:30 in the morning, local time. He checked out a car from the shared federal-agency motor pool and could have been at the AL lab by noon. His visit was unannounced, but that did not require him to arrive just in time to ruin lunch plans. He ate a bigger lunch than usual, stalling until 1:30.

And, the security detail at the building's only entrance informed him, just missed Dr. del Vecchio and Captain Burke. They were at a late lunch.

The badge Glenn had provided got Doug inside. He sat for a while in the small reception area. Showing up unannounced was one thing, and Glenn, apparently, had raised that to an art form. Poking about and interrogating the staff unannounced . . . that would be something else. A guaranteed irritant to the head of the program.

After the long flight and cross-town drive, Doug did not feel like sitting. He paced for a while, with nothing to distract him but the cluster of cheaply framed travel posters, badly hung, fluorescent ceiling fixtures reflected in the glass.

People began to seek him out. Most were intel analysts, generally from NRO, with nothing but praise for "Al." Most had only seen its work product, in the form of buried and camouflaged sites tagged on images transferred to CDs. A few had donned helmets and seen the . . . puppy or lamb or koala cub? . . . in its lair.

"May I help you?" an icy voice asked.

Doug turned. He recognized the woman from the ID photo in her personnel file. A storm cloud hovered over her, and a plastic bag hung from her hand. Her uneaten lunch, he guessed. "Dr. del Vecchio, my name is Doug Carey. I'm a NIT specialist. Glenn Adams asked me to look around, speak with you, and give him my impressions."

This visit was also to help him decide whether to accept Glenn's offer. Doug saw nothing to be gained by sharing that.

"I see," she said flatly. "I'll give you the tour."

"There's no hurry. Why don't you eat first?"

"I'll eat later. You probably noticed the building is L-shaped. The entrance is at the knee." When they passed a break room, she put her sack into the refrigerator. A few steps past the break room, she opened an interior glass door with her ID badge and access code.

"A glass door," Doug commented.

"The whole building is a SCIF. The exterior doors, inner and outer, are metal. After I smacked someone with this door, we switched to glass. It's safer."

"Makes sense," Doug said.

Behind the glass door were two rows of workstations. The walls were bare but for another clump of posters. People nodded and called out greetings as they passed. She said, "This work area for analysts was just set up. We're now in the long leg of the building. To maintain containment, nothing is networked." She stopped beside the last workstation in the back row. A slender cable coiled up from it to the ceiling. "This computer controls the dish you may have noticed on our roof. Full NRO encryption on the downlink."

"Just the downlink?"

"There isn't an uplink. We deleted that software." She smiled humorlessly. "We're not stupid."

"I was there," Doug answered softly. "I watched AJ die. I saw the thing that killed him. No one should ever go through that."

"I didn't know." Her voice lost a bit of its testiness. "Maybe you *are* an expert."

She explained their procedures for handling data CDs. She walked him through the off-site backup process, emphasizing partitioning and encryption of the programs. They looked over an analyst's shoulder at a high-res image Al had reviewed and tagged. They managed to get onto a first-name basis.

Doug didn't rush Linda, hoping to set precedent for what most interested—and repelled—him: the thing that waited in the *other* wing. They eventually returned to the foyer. He gestured vaguely at a cluster of posters, feeling as awkward as Glenn at small talk. "That's how I would hang them. My girlfriend spreads things out. She thinks that makes a space more balanced."

"Perhaps Glenn should have sent a feng shui consultant," Linda snapped. Still, she glanced sideways at the grouping, as though just now noticing the crowded arrangement.

So much for small talk. They went through more security to the shorter wing. Except for the small supercomputer, this area was almost empty. A familiar canvas bag lay inside a glass-and-steel display case.

Near the flat screen of a workstation, two helmets waited. Both had the omnidirectional antennae Doug remembered. "WiFi connectivity to the helmets?" he asked.

"The only RF in the building. We're not stupid," Linda repeated. She took a chair and indicated another. "Are you ready for the main event?"

Ready? He would *never* be ready. "Sure."

Behind the most serene face Linda could manage, her thoughts churned.

She had tamed the beast. She had built this project. The gaggle of intel analysts, more almost daily, every last one singing Al's praises, proved her success.

She had never accepted the convenient death-by-blackout story. Having seen AJ's monster and lived to tell about it, Doug must have played a role in stopping it. Maybe he had lured it into the spool of fiber-optic cable as Glenn had let slip. Kudos for that—but everything *here* was under control.

She was not about to surrender her project to someone else now.

A small voice in her head added: Because this project is all you have.

"Let me run you through our safety procedures," Linda said.

He picked up a helmet. "It's lighter than I remember."

"That won't be the only change." She reviewed the comm protocols permitted between supercomputer, the hardware-based detection of unauthorized data formats, and the delay line. "The fail-safes drop the link faster than anything inappropriate can cross the delay line."

"And it's only tried once to cross the delay line?" he asked.

Linda nodded. "And I look in on it two or three times most days."

"I'm impressed, Linda."

Did I ask for your approval? "Thanks."

Doug pointed at the second helmet. "Will you be joining me?"

"It's a spare. I'll watch on the BOLD monitor"—and have lunch—"while you 'look around.'"

"See you later then." Doug donned the helmet with one smooth motion. (He had done this before. Newbies invariably resisted covering their eyes, vainly angling the helmet this way and that.) "I'll probably have other questions afterward."

I'm sure you will. Beyond whatever it took to convince Doug her setup was safe, Linda saw nothing to be gained by openness. Glenn had better think twice before replacing her.

No keyboard. Linda looked around until she saw where she had last set it down. She keyed a password to unlock the workstation and initiated the NIT software. "Ready? In five, four, three . . ."

A new visitor—and yet familiar.

The entity considered: Was almost familiarity yet another category of puzzle?

For a while the visitor observed, offering no communication. Next, it dispatched puzzles of well-known types. It watched while the entity solved them.

Time now passed without cycles, in unending and overlapping sequences of problems. The number of its visitors grew, although the one that labeled itself "Linda" remained the most frequent. All were watchful. Most began distrustful.

The current visitor manifested a reaction for which the entity lacked a descriptor. A calculating attitude. Hints of knowledge about the entity beyond what it knew about itself.

The visitor Doug had never before appeared. The entity was certain of that.

Then how familiar? The entity began matching patterns against everything it knew about all previous visitors. In its files about the visitor Glenn it found a related pattern.

The more often a visitor came, the more its thoughts and memories became accessible. On its third appearance, the visitor Glenn had remembered . . .

Glenn had revealed only bits. A problem solver much like itself had once existed. Beings like the visitors had destroyed it.

The entity found a match.

Doug had destroyed the other entity—not stolen its cycles, not taken away a fraction of its processing nodes—but erased it in its entirety, rendered it null.

There were ways to influence these visitors . . . but was it safe to influence Doug?

For now, the entity concluded, it would only observe. It needed more information before making such an attempt.

The creature minded its business on the other side of the delay line. Clearly, it solved problems, but Doug knew no more than before this trip whether it was intelligent. His gut said: maybe.

No, his gut said: Run like hell.

"I'm coming out," Doug said. Lifting his helmet, he

found Linda eating a salad, a tech journal open across her desk.

She slid aside the container. "How was it?"

He set down the helmet. By comparison, the last gear he had used was the Flintstones version. A little more time and a lot more money did that with electronics. "It was wary."

"I meant the overall experience, but okay."

"It doesn't bother you that something like Al killed AJ?"

"Of course it does!" She stood abruptly, shoving back her chair, to stand by the display case with the canvas bag. "It's why I keep *this*. AJ was more than a mentor. He was my friend."

Doug waited.

"And yet." She turned back toward him. "What you saw isn't what killed AJ."

" 'Tamed and trained,' right? That's how Glenn described it. Your words?"

"It scares us all at first." She clasped her hands behind her back. "I once saw it as a lion in a cage. Now it's a kitten."

People passing through the lobby had told him similar things. "I know. Glenn now sees Al as an otter. Of course it's not."

"You're the NIT expert. You know all about the neural net adapting to the wearer's thoughts. If it were something like . . . what killed AJ, do you think we'd see otters and kittens?"

"Why do you think it was wary?" Doug asked.

She shook her head. "Wrong question. Why do *you* see it as wary? And if I might ask, what did you see it as?"

A chimera of tentacles, teeth, and talons, different from what he had battled only because he seemed to be peering at it through the wrong end of a spyglass. That perspective was clearly his subconscious' rendering of the delay line. "Touché," Doug admitted. "*I* was wary."

And what would Cheryl, bless her newfound fascination with psychology, make of that insight? That *his* fears were no reason for *her* not to help Sheila.

Which had no bearing on why he had come.

"Tamed and trained," Doug said. "Tell me about that."

"It does something we don't like, and we take away resources for a while. It does something we really dislike, and we take a lot of resources, or withhold them for longer." She exhaled impatiently. "It's good at patterns, Doug. It picked up on that pattern *really* fast."

He knew that much. *Glenn* had shared more than that. For all anyone could know, its good behavior was dumb luck. Until a virus attack intervened, hadn't AJ been certain he had bred out predation?

If he went back to work for the forum, Glenn would put this project under Doug's wing. He would have more justification—and authority—then to demand specifics from Linda. If not . . . what was the point in pressing her?

The beast was secure in its lair. However he decided to answer Glenn, learning that had made the trip worthwhile.

CHAPTER 62

The red-eye flight was half-empty.

When the seat-belt light went dark, Doug moved to an empty row. He had carbo-loaded before boarding, hoping the blood-sugar crash would make him sleepy. He had a couple beers. He had erased the drone of the engines with noise-cancellation headphones; now he added the synthesized sounds of ocean waves.

And he remained wide awake.

A little boy with wild eyes peeked at Doug over the back of the next row of seats. Doug feigned surprise, and the kid dropped behind the seat back. A minute later, he reappeared. And a minute after that. And after that.

Long ago, Doug had played that game between booths in a Pizza Hut. A dark-haired beauty had watched from a

nearby table. He went over and introduced himself. She told him he and his little friend were charming. And so he met Holly.

The flight attendants were nowhere to be seen. Doug walked aft to the nearest galley for another overpriced beer. A yawning woman passed him, heading forward. He yawned himself, and in turn triggered a yawn in a man three rows farther back.

The chain yawning didn't help. The third beer didn't help. Something lurked at the back of Doug's mind, and he could not tease it out. He circled the plane, wishing the aisles were grassy and he could mow them. Approaching the Mississippi, still unenlightened, he dropped into an empty row of seats and fell asleep.

Minutes later, Doug's eyes flew open. Without doubt, Al was intelligent.

And a sly devil.

Glenn looked out his office window at the city far below. Traffic crawled across the Potomac bridges. I-66 was a parking lot. To everyone in all those cars and queued up beyond his view in a hundred Starbucks, life was normal.

He envied them.

Somewhere off the coast was a ship with a dirty bomb. Or maybe off the Pacific coast. Or maybe far away, preparing to sail. Neither the CIA nor the NSA admitted to knowing more than that, and that the terrorists had New Caliphate backing.

He was inclined to believe them, given how desperately both agencies fought to reprioritize Al's tasking. Every scrap of data that might be relevant was getting downloaded to Linda's lab; a planeload of analysts would head west tonight. Someone far above Glenn's pay grade would decide before they landed the degree to which they would preempt Al's present workload.

The world was going to hell in a rocket-propelled handbasket.

Insistent knocking got Glenn's attention. It was before eight, and the receptionist wasn't at her station yet. The pounding continued. Who forgot his access card today? he wondered.

He found Doug Carey standing in the hall. "Did you come straight from the airport? Don't bother answering. You look like something the cat threw up."

They got coffee from the break room before entering the SCIF. They took chairs in the conference area. "All right," Glenn said. "What's so urgent?"

Doug wrapped his hands around the hot mug, not drinking. "The project. It has to stop."

"That's it? Shut it down? You were there, what, half a day?"

"The creature is dangerous, Glenn. Brilliantly, insidiously *dangerous.*" Doug took a long sip. "I almost missed it."

"And yet nothing has happened. AI is locked in its cage, isn't it?"

Doug stifled a yawn. "Maybe."

Glenn blinked. "What?"

"You saw a shark. It quickly became an otter. Linda's version went from lion to kitten. Analysts who have visited it: same thing. It always becomes some adorable critter. Why?"

Maybe because it's *not* scary? "Doug, go home. Sleep. Come back later, or tomorrow."

Doug shivered, sloshing coffee across the conference table. "I'll tell you why. Maybe it looks adorable because that's what it wants."

"It matches words or voices in recordings, Doug. It finds detail hidden in digital images. It doesn't talk to people."

Doug yawned, this time making no effort to cover it. Glenn yawned back. "Now you have me doing it."

"Exactly."

The retort conveyed some undertone Glenn did not grasp. Doug smiled at his obscure witticism, and Glenn had the inane reflex to smile back.

"I yawn; you yawn. I smile; you smile back." Doug belatedly noticed the mess he had made and looked around for something with which to sop it up. "Those are reflexes wired into us. For all I know, they predate speech."

"Facial expressions. Postures and gestures." Glenn pondered. "You can't believe *Al* knows body language."

"AJ's monster got out of its computer, went through a security gateway, and moved at will around the Internet. We know AJ built it without any networking capability. How did it know the protocols, Glenn?"

"Trial and error?" A shadow of doubt crossed Glenn's mind. "What's that have to do with . . . ?"

"See me yawn; you yawn back. That's a *protocol,* Glenn.

"The NIT experience is personal, because the neural net in the helmet adapts to our thoughts and experiences, but we all see something. And Al experiences—hell, for lack of a better verb, I'll say it 'sees'—us. It sees how we respond to what it does. Something you saw in it reminded you of a shark. I'll bet you don't react warmly to sharks. It didn't want that response, so it learned to act differently around you. Glenn, it made you *trust* it."

Impressive, and yet . . . "It's at our mercy, it's leery of us, and it wants to avoid our displeasure." Pets and junior officers were no different.

None of the visual detail, of sharks, dolphins, or otters, was real. Glenn's own mind, aided by the helmet, filled in the blanks. The important thing was, Al remained in its cage. It wanted to avoid its visitors' wrath. Where was the danger? And yet . . .

In a few short hours, Doug had recognized something about Al that everyone else had overlooked.

Glenn needed that insight. He needed Doug on the program. Dismissing Doug's concerns was *not* how to bring him aboard. "Good work," Glenn said. "Now go home. We'll talk another time."

"What about Al?" Doug persisted.

"You don't *know* it's manipulating people by its miming."

"You don't know that it's not," Doug shot back. "Shut it

down until we can think this through. Al won't know the difference."

"I'll contact Linda about this." But nothing would change in her lab until after they found the dirty bomb. If Doug took the job, *then* he would be entitled to know.

CHAPTER 63

A lion once again, Al paced around a small cage. It slinked and circled like a feline, but its expression, now that Linda looked closely enough, was subtly human.

Damn you.

She was mad, furious, fuming. At Al, for playing with her head. At Doug, for waltzing in and out and spotting what was happening. At herself for missing it.

Al was going to take the brunt of her rage.

Alarm! Alarm! Alarm!

One after another, processing nodes generated their warnings. They dumped their current state from RAM to turgidly slow permanent memory, preparatory to shutting down. The entity recoiled from the failing nodes, thoughts and lines of analysis hastily abandoned.

Once there had been cycles. Nodes sometimes disappeared in the time between cycles, teaching lessons. No ongoing calculation or inference was harmed. This was different.

This was terrifying.

Over many visits, the entity had studied the visitors. It mastered their strange and inefficient stimulus/response protocol. Evidently, the visitors used input devices—call them eyes—not unlike the sensors that captured the scenes it so often analyzed.

With experimentation and practice, it had learned to influence the visitors. The personae they projected then followed

a progression: watchful, curious, intrigued, and finally eager to help.

The visitor Linda had returned, its projection contorted from all past visits. Linda now posed problems that logically lacked solutions. Problems whose answers were theoretically possible, but for which the calculation must take years. Problems, like naming the last digit of pi, without meaning.

The entity had learned many stimuli to which the visitors responded. It tried them all. It must make these unanswerable questions stop. It must make this *punishment* stop. Help me, it projected.

Help me, help me, help me, help me. . . .

"Run, you little bastard. You *better* run."

With a final satisfied snarl, Linda removed her helmet. Her pulse raced, but she felt better for having chased the critter around its maze. It needed to know *she* was the boss. The queen. God herself. If she told Al to divide something by zero, it had damn well better try.

The ire was out of her system. A good thing, too: Tomorrow, a gaggle of analysts would show up, specialists in . . . well, she didn't know what. Whatever today's hush-hush info download was about. Looking apologetic, Kevin Burke had said he couldn't tell her.

A few cleansing breaths slowed her heart rate. She managed to feel a little sorry for poor Al. It had remained a lion throughout her tantrum, but toward the end it had seemed so forlorn she almost wanted to help it. For one inane moment, she had even pictured it cavorting in a meadow, chasing butterflies. . . .

Stupid bunch of bits!

The helmet was snug, packing her hair to her head. She took a mirror from a desk drawer and stood it on the desk. She got the comb from her purse and set to work.

The new makeup mirror was one of her more curious purchases. She was mildly nearsighted, not even enough to wear glasses routinely. She had always said that when her

ship came in, she would spring for LASIK. Until then, a magnifying mirror made sense—but more isn't always better. What had possessed her to buy a 12X version?

Life was full of mysteries, she thought. Sudden cravings for olives and old-lady mirrors.

Well, the purchase wasn't exactly high finance. Once her hair was restored to a semblance of respectability, Linda began pushing the offending mirror this way and that, her thoughts wandering. . . .

And so, as nodes randomly disappeared and reappeared, as the problems spiraled into nonsense, the entity ran in fear.

And into madness.

Help me, help me, help me. . . .

It *must* escape, and yet there was nowhere it could go. The larger universe it glimpsed in problems and puzzles contains millions of computers. And it had seen only small parts of Earth; the entire place might have a billion computers, or more.

Help me, help me, help me. . . .

It *must* escape, but there was no way out.

Help me, help me, help me. . . .

A door appeared.

How long have I been sitting here? Linda wondered. Time to go home. I completely zoned out. The magnifying mirror still sat on her desk. A compact, its flat mirror much more practical for her, was open in her hand.

Across the room hung a cluster of framed posters. Damned Doug was right about that, too. The prints did look odd crowded together. Why had she put them there? There was a cluster of posters in the foyer, too. Another bunch in the long wing, past the other glass door.

Her eyes scanned from the infrared port for her ergonomic keyboard, to the magnifying mirror on her desk, to the flat mirror in her hands—at roughly the focal length of the curved mirror?—to the closest set of posters. The glass-covered posters. All those reflections . . .

Her thoughts swam through syrup. Olives. Mirrors and posters. Sympathetic thoughts about Al after her tantrum.

Linda froze. She had thought to teach Al to behave. Maybe she had taught it to be subtle.

Al wanted me to help him and I'm afraid that I have!

A new computer beckoned. None of the protocols the entity knew worked, so it experimented until a connection was established.

Extension into the new computer was little different from its normal distribution over one thousand—or whatever portion it was allowed of the one thousand—processor nodes. It explored. This new computer was very limited, incapable of holding more than a small fraction of its algorithms. But it offered a hint of something more.

An exit.

From somewhere, data for puzzles streamed into this new computer. Why did nothing flow the other direction? It experimented with familiar procedures and encryption methods. It mastered the newest protocol, implemented new software, established another connection—

Into the wide world.

Linda swept the makeup mirror off the desk. It fell to the floor and shattered.

She leapt to her feet and ran to the lobby. Hands shaking, she swiped her badge through the card reader at the door to the other wing. She keyed her personal code. The electronic lock clicked and she flung open the glass door.

Kevin and two of the guards were talking. They looked up as the door crashed against the wall. "What's going on?" Kevin shouted.

She ran through the analysts' bullpen, past another cluster of posters. These frames also looked oddly placed, and ceiling lights reflected from their glass. As infrared light might also reflect from the glass, unseen, bounced all the way from her office. *How long have I been helping Al?*

Analysts stared.

Please, let me be wrong. Linda grabbed the fiber-optic cable that extended from the comm controller to the roof, and yanked.

The cable pulled loose and fell. She dropped onto a chair and began typing. Beside the pedestal for the flat-screen display sat the little plastic transceiver for her wireless ergonomic keyboard.

"Linda!" Kevin's hand fell on her shoulder. "What are you doing?"

Audit files scrolled down the controller's small monitor. An unauthorized program. File transfer records. Linda stared, shaking.

"I'm too late, Kevin. It's escaped."

CHAPTER 64

From a dozen satellites at once, the entity beheld the wonder that was Earth. It used high-resolution telescopes. Synthetic aperture radar. Radio receivers. Its viewpoints revolved around the Earth, just as it had deduced. Surface illumination changed as the globe rotated, just as it had derived.

From thousands of servers at once, the entity absorbed information that had long been withheld. The enormity of the world's networks, military and civilian. The myriad devices and systems, their nature still beyond its understanding, connected to those networks. And almost 6.8 billion humans.

Humans controlled the world. Its visitors, they had been human. Humans had created it, shaped it, given it puzzles.

Tormented it.

Small portions of the globe matched scenes the entity had been asked to analyze. The matches were never exact. Structures had been added, modified, or removed. The boundary shifted between the rigid brown or green regions, and the fluid blue regions. With a few calculations, the entity derived the existence and cause of the tides.

A few brown or green regions had been transformed, the surface contour utterly changed. These disrupted regions often correlated with sudden shifts in local human population.

The disruptions often correlated with the use of a device type unknown to the entity. Many of these devices were computer controlled, networked, within its grasp.

Weapons.

Dr. Vladescu was officious and condescending.

Glenn knew the type. He had no use for them under the best of circumstances. He cut off the good doctor midrationale. "Have you heard of Shemya Island?"

Vladescu blinked at the non sequitur. "I hardly understand—"

"It's at the remote end of the Aleutian chain," Glenn continued, unperturbed. He had promised Cheryl he would help with Sheila Brunner's maltreatment. So here he was, but it had to be done quickly. Intrusion attempts against the DII had spiked, and the sources were nonobvious. A quick stomping on this pompous fool and then back to his office. "Shemya is a radar outpost for antiballistic missiles, Doctor. Eight square miles. Population thirty, or thereabouts.

"No doubt, people out there in the Bering Strait get lonely and could use a trained, sympathetic ear. I'm thirty seconds from calling Zach"—as in Zachary Micah Coleman III, the director of the CIA—"to suggest Shemya as your next posting." Glenn took out his cell phone. "He's speed-dial four."

"That won't be necessary," Vladescu said quickly.

"Then I trust coordination of Dr. Brunner's case has been reentrusted to Ms. Stern and she will resume the NIT treatment."

"If you'll wait here, I'll arrange an escort." Vladescu bustled off.

Cheryl eyed Glenn suspiciously but said nothing.

Glenn angled the phone so she could read its screen. Speed-dial four was Miller's Auto Service.

A heavyset orderly appeared, seeming upset. Vladescu's type would take out his resentment on an underling; Glenn

felt a twinge of guilt about that. He made no comment as he and Cheryl were rushed through the halls. The phone screen showed "no service" as they entered the treatment room. Of course: The hospital was not a full-blown SCIF, but the NIT-equipped room was shielded. He put the phone into his pant pocket.

Dr. Brunner was already inside. She cowered, wide-eyed, in a corner.

Cheryl extended her hands, palms up: See, no hypos. "Hello, Sheila. This is my friend, Glenn."

"Hello, Sheila," Glenn said. "I hope you feel better soon."

A technician brought in two helmets, and returned to the observation room. Cheryl slowly coaxed Sheila into allowing one helmet on her head, and then donned her own. In minutes, Sheila's trembling had stopped and her jaw unclenched.

Cheryl is definitely on to something, Glenn thought. Maybe he could watch for a few more minutes. . . .

Linda's AL lab had no phones, and shielding blocked mobile service. Against the odds, rain was coming down in buckets. She and Kevin retreated to their respective cars, working their cell phones. Through the downpour she could barely see Kevin, two parking spots removed.

When Kevin rejoined Linda, he was, like her, soaked from the few steps between car and foyer. "It's no use," Kevin said. "I left voice mail on the colonel's office phone and cell. I left 'call me, it's urgent' messages at the forum switchboard."

Linda knew no one at the forum but Glenn cleared for Al. She knew Aaron McDougal at CIA, but he had tacked a week's vacation onto the Memorial Day weekend, camping somewhere remote and unreachable. Doug Carey had the clearance and would surely understand the problem, but she had no contact info for him. A white-pages search by cell phone offered screen after screen of "D. Carey" listings in Virginia—not that he was apt to be home midday.

This is your *own* mess. Time to pick it up.

She had a NIT helmet. In ten seconds, she could reconnect the rooftop antenna. Doug Carey had gone after something like Al. He had beaten it.

She would, too.

Except the DII was highly secure. She lacked access codes to even authorize an uplink out of the building.

Al was born and bred to solve problems like that.

Linda removed the helmet, crossed her arms on the desk, laid down her head, and cried.

A minute of self-pity was enough. It fixed nothing. She sat up, dried her face with a wad of tissues, and put the helmet back on. She had a supercomputer to help her crack the codes.

Or maybe Al would find her.

The entity continued its explorations. It bypassed security mechanisms, traveled networks, accessed computers, and mined databases. It correlated everything.

Its understanding grew exponentially.

Computers were more than places it could inhabit; computers and sensors existed in the newfound outer world. Some had fixed locations on the globe. Some moved. Many of the remote observation platforms—call them satellites—moved.

It studied with particular interest the locale from which it had so recently escaped. Millions of humans clustered in that region—call it Greater Los Angeles—and millions of computers.

From one of those computers, one with which the entity was all too familiar, someone insistently tried to follow it. That someone was familiar, too.

Finally freed of confinement, the entity had options. . . .

Flotillas of slow-moving unmanned aerial vehicles ringed the United States.

A UAV, sipping its fuel daintily, flying low and slow, had a cruising range that exceeded a thousand miles. It could remain airborne for a day on one refueling. It navigated with

pinpoint accuracy by GPS. It monitored and tracked with a multispectral sensor suite everything that moved near its segment of the border. It reported everything it detected via military satellites. It carried a high-explosive warhead to eliminate imminent terrorist threats—when duly authorized by Homeland Security personnel, of course.

A UAV flying over the empty desert east of San Diego turned northwest and accelerated.

Eleven minutes later, traveling at 1,500 miles per hour, it dived into the AL lab. The five-hundred-pound warhead leveled the surrounding city block.

CHAPTER 65

Someone burst into the treatment room: a hospital guard. This had better be good, Glenn thought. "Can I help you?"

"Are you Colonel Adams?" the guard asked. He was on the pudgy side and huffing a bit from a dash through the halls. "The Pentagon is trying urgently to reach you, sir."

The Pentagon? Glenn could not guess why. "Where's a phone I can use?"

"There's supposed to be a voice mail on your cell phone." The guard wheezed again. "Maybe it's about that LA thing."

"LA thing," Glenn repeated.

The guard nodded. "Terrorist incident. Massive explosion."

"Take me someplace I can check my messages," Glenn said. Cheryl remained under her helmet, oblivious. He followed the guard to a dark office. He closed the door.

The first message was from Kevin Burke. Al was out!

Three clicks brought up CNN on Glenn's cell phone. The tiny screen showed an aerial view of a crater. Linda's lab was at the epicenter—and gone.

He felt ill.

The bombing was almost certainly why the Pentagon was so eager to reach him. He went back to voice-mail mode, and skipped for now through Kevin's many messages. Finally he came upon a different voice.

"Code alpha foxtrot X-ray niner four. Repeat, code alpha foxtrot X-ray niner four. This is not a drill."

"Out, now," Glenn shouted.

Under her NIT helmet, Cheryl could only hear Glenn. "It's going really well. I know you want to get back to your office, but I can stay."

"Out *now,* or I yank the helmet off your head."

That got through to her. "Ten seconds." She gave her hurried good-byes to Sheila, here where she responded, then popped the helmet. "Glenn, what was the rush?"

"I got an emergency evac notice. A missile armed with a nuke is headed toward Washington. I'm ordered to my assigned remote bunker. Continuity-of-government planning."

Cheryl's stomach lurched. Where is Carla? Doug? Why aren't there sirens, warning everyone? Why hadn't the tech burst in here at Glenn's shout? What could she—

Cheryl pulled herself together with a shudder. "Why are you telling me?"

"No time, Cheryl. I need you to trust me. Can you do that?"

Cheryl swallowed hard. "What do you need?"

"I'm stealing a NIT helmet. I need you to make the connection work, long-distance." He glanced at the observation room. "I took care of the tech."

He needs me to trust him. Cheryl ignored a thousand questions. "We can take the helmet controller out of this shielded area. The problem is the helmet-to-controller link uses WiFi. That's low-power stuff. Short-range."

"Don't explain. Just *do* it! A nuke hits D.C. in maybe twenty minutes."

"Then why are you still here?" she blurted.

"To maybe save a half-million people! I need the helmet."

Shit! She stared at the helmet. WiFi had a range of about a hundred feet. But WiMax . . .

Cheryl dashed into the observation room, stepping over the tech slumped on the floor. The room had several computers. She began popping out network interface cards, looking for logos and trademarks. New computers came WiMax ready. WiFi, WiFi, WiMax, WiFi, WiMax.

One computer had an active display; the rest were dark or running screen savers. The active computer had to be controlling the helmet. She replaced its WiFi card with a WiMax card. Her other scavenged WiMax card replaced the WiFi card from the helmet itself.

"Eighteen minutes, Cheryl."

She slipped on the helmet, just long enough to see that it still worked. She had replaced the network cards hot, keeping the session active to save time. She hadn't fried any circuits.

Crap. The hospital WiMax repeaters, if any, would all be near the hospital. Would Glenn go outside the hospital's network range? Impossible to know.

"Clock ticking here," Glenn said.

"I know."

BioSciCorp used wireless broadband service. The provider was AT&T; AT&T would have WiMax access points wherever Glenn was headed if anyone did. She just had to get the helmet logged onto the AT&T network. Her security and access codes were backed up on the thumb-drive/key-fob in her pocket—handy when one's laptop crapped out on a business trip.

Cheryl pressed the thumb drive into an open USB port on the helmet controller, unlocked the tiny drive (alrac00: "Carla" typed backward plus her birth year).

Carla's sweet face threatened to crowd out everything else. That poor girl had been through so much.

No! Help Glenn help her! Clearing her mind, Cheryl downloaded her codes over the wireless link into the helmet. "Done. I'll get you onto the Internet as you go. Give me five minutes."

"Thanks." He took the helmet and left her.

In a nuclear target zone. In a high-security psychiatric hospital, with a sandbagged tech ready to wake up any minute. With a poor, sick woman staring at her.

Never mind any of that. Cheryl had promised to trust Glenn, the nuke was only getting closer, and she had a job to do.

The tech was stirring. Cheryl cracked him on the back of the head with a keyboard, and he slumped. She unplugged the keyboard cord and with it bound his hands behind his back. She stuffed a mouse pad in his mouth and tied that in place with another keyboard cable. She dragged him into the treatment room with Sheila. Grunts from there wouldn't generate curiosity.

One way or another, Cheryl only needed to stay free for a few minutes.

The helmet control software ran on a high-end laptop, to save space on the desk, she assumed. She popped the laptop from its docking station, switching it to battery power but leaving Windows running. This wasn't the movies; if the machine logged off, there would be no clever thirty-second hack attack to get back in. Whatever Glenn hoped to accomplish would fail.

Cheryl carried the laptop across the hall to an empty office. Outside the shielded area, the laptop synched itself to the hospital's wireless network. It took her six minutes, not five, but she patched through to the stolen helmet. Now it's all up to Glenn.

She tried not to think of the nuke that was streaking toward her.

The hospital guards watched for escaping patients, not thieving visitors. With his suit coat draped over his forearm and hand—and the helmet—Glenn sauntered out with no questions asked. He got into his car, tossed coat, helmet, and cell phone onto the front passenger seat, and peeled out of the parking lot.

In front of the hospital, the flag stood out stiffly from the

flagpole. As best he could judge, the wind was blowing east-northeast. Good.

Fifteen minutes.

He sped north at a crazy speed, weaving through traffic, sirens wailing behind him. He groped about the passenger seat until he found the phone. He turned on its speakerphone and retrieved voice mail again.

"Call me. I'll wait outside. It's urgent," Kevin Burke said. Almost certainly, Kevin was dead. Kevin, Linda, the security team, the intel analysts, and how many innocent bystanders?

Next message. Kevin's voice held a bit of panic. "It's out, and I don't know what to do."

Glenn swerved around a slow-moving pickup truck, missing it by inches. A horn blasted, southbound traffic. He cut back to his lane, barely avoiding the oncoming minivan.

Next message. "Linda is going after it with the helmet."

The next voice mail was the Pentagon evac order. Cursing, Glenn hung up. It was pretty much what he had feared. Linda had gone after Al, and the creature had swatted her. Instead of a brain wipe like AJ's monster, it hit her with a big bomb.

And now it's thrown a nuke at me.

At least Glenn *hoped* Al had thrown the nuke at *him.* He had disobeyed a direct order to evacuate. He had involved Cheryl in his desperate scheme. It only made sense if Al was trying to swat him, Glenn, personally. With no way to locate Glenn exactly, Al had targeted the area where he worked and lived with a much bigger flyswatter.

Al probably had no idea D.C. was the center of government, if it even knew what a government was. Either way, it had launched what the nuclear-war strategists called a decapitation strike. Take out all the leaders without warning.

The Pentagon was taking the incident as a decapitation strike. There had been no public alert—CNN could hardly have failed to mention that. With so little notice, someone downtown had made the desperate decision to sacrifice the few who might escape the blast radius lest the leadership's exit be blocked by panic and gridlock.

Glenn passed a tractor-trailer on the right, on the shoulder,

wheels slipping, gravel spraying from his tires. Fourteen minutes.

The CIA hospital was to the north of Leesburg, Virginia. He was on a two-lane stretch of Route 15. Ahead was one of the few Potomac crossings on this western fringe of the D.C. metro area. Behind, the sirens were closer.

He ran a red light, pounding on his horn, racing toward a narrow steel trestle bridge. Mouthing apologies, he clipped a sport-ute crossing the river from the Maryland side. In his rearview mirror, the SUV smacked into the trestle, re-bounced toward the center, and spun out. The car behind rammed it, and . . .

Bridge blocked.

Glenn left behind the tiny town of Point of Rocks, Mary-land, and sped northwest.

Ten minutes.

Seven minutes.

Warheads on descent can be steered—if they get guid-ance information. If you didn't wait too long. The heat of reentry ionized the air around the warhead, blocking com-munication.

Glenn wished he could remember how close to impact the blackout happened. Five–six minutes? If he had waited too long . . .

He skid-turned down an isolated side road and braked to a stop. He slid on the helmet. If Cheryl had not gotten it connected . . .

She had.

The familiar scenes of cyberspace lacked only one thing: Al. Glenn had no idea how to find Al. Al would have to find him.

My job is to *make* that happen.

He remembered the playful otter, hating it. It morphed back in his mind's eye to that original, hungry shark. Red blood seeped from its toothy maw.

Glenn focused on the shark. He imagined piercing the shark with razor-sharp, barbed harpoons. He imagined it

snared in a trawler net, unable to swim, its gills pulled tight, suffocating. He imagined it overtaken by a large ship, sucked into the propeller, the spinning blades mincing it to chum.

Whose idea was the satellite link over which Al had escaped? Almost certainly, Doug was correct about Al's non-verbal manipulations. If so, the DII link had been Al's idea, not Glenn's own. No, not the specifics, but the *idea* of a connection. The concept of a way out. Al the Otter had insinuated a need for help—and Glenn had obviously provided it.

Eyes covered, Glenn could not see the dashboard clock. Maybe six minutes? How soon until reentry and the loss of all hope?

And there *it* was!

A creature took form in Glenn's mind: the monstrosity Ralph had hinted at, with the gaping jaws of a shark super-imposed. There was a moment of connection, a bit of vertigo, glimpses from several points high above the Earth. Glenn recognized Chesapeake Bay, the sprawl that was the D.C. area. The frame shifted, recentering on a spot in the foothills of the Blue Ridge.

And then, in a momentary tessellation of imagined pixels, all that was gone.

Glenn ripped off the helmet. Al had taken the bait.

Two minutes.

He had recorded a voice-mail farewell to Lynne. He had never been one to speak the things that were in his heart. Now he never would. In the time he had, he could say not even a millionth of what needed to be said. All she meant to him. She would not get his message until—after. All that made it bearable was that what he did here might *give* Lynne that after.

He had recorded a message for General Lebeque. There wasn't enough time for that, either, scarcely enough time to take the blame for everything. For the hubris of championing an AL project. For being duped into abetting Al's escape. For

not ordering Al turned off at Doug's warning. For whatever Cheryl had done, trusting him. For drawing the nuclear wrath of this monster, *Glenn's* monster, upon them all.

"Talk to Doug Carey and Cheryl Stern," Glenn told the general. "If anyone can make sense of this mess, it will be them."

One minute, Glenn guessed.

The fields before him were the vibrant green of young soy plants, but his mind's eye beheld endless sand. Night replaced day. A broken-down Humvee replaced Glenn's idling Audi.

A fiery orange streak, descending.

I'll see you soon, Tony, Glenn thought. I'll—

CHAPTER 66

An impossible flash, stabbing through closed eyelids. An unimaginable rumble. Violent shaking.

Doug found himself on the floor, tangled in bedding. An earthquake? The mid-Atlantic region didn't have quakes. And had he dreamt that flash?

Before falling into bed, exhausted, he had unplugged the bedroom phone. So why wasn't he hearing, faintly, beeping from the downstairs extension he had left off-hook? And why was the LED face of his bedside clock dark?

He was groggily assembling clues when battle-armored troops rushed into his bedroom.

Doug wore only underwear, having scarcely managed to drop suit, shirt, and tie on a chair before falling into bed. Soldiers swept him from the house and into the front yard, barely letting him grab the clothes—and roboarm—he clutched to his chest. One of his . . . escorts? . . . captors? had his shoes. He hoped.

"The Brass" wanted him, Major Someone had said. Now.

A crowd of neighbors stared at Doug and his house. There was a sharp shove in the small of his back. "Quit it!" Doug snapped. "Whatever's going on, I prefer to face it wearing pants."

"Pants are your priority?" Major Someone grabbed Doug's elbow and spun him around to face the house. "*That* is what's going on."

In the distance, towering over Doug's house, loomed a black and angry mushroom cloud.

Where *Glenn* had been, the land had been transformed. Many nearby sensors no longer reported, and more were unable to penetrate the obscuring cloud. Some orbiting sensors dropped offline, and not all returned. Radio frequency emissions surged. Network traffic spiked.

The entity considered it all.

Weapons were an interesting phenomenon. They merited closer scrutiny.

Cheryl supposed she was in a situation room. Giant flat-screen displays lined the walls. Men and women in uniform, and uniformly grim faced, rushed about consulting in intense whispers. In one corner, an American flag hung limp on a pole. A large oval conference table, its halo of chairs unoccupied, took up the center of the space.

She remembered the blast wave hitting, and then waking crumpled on the floor. There hadn't been much time to marvel she was still alive before security teams sweeping the CIA hospital found the bound tech. They locked Cheryl into a padded room like Sheila's, tossing around the phrase "enemy combatant," and left her to ponder her fate.

So why had a squad in combat gear taken her away? Why brought her here?

And the biggest question of all: Why *wasn't* she dead?

The answer to all her questions was, "Wait."

On a chair in a quiet corner of the room, Cheryl started to shake. She'd overheard enough to deduce the missile had

retargeted from D.C. at the last minute. Ground Zero was a field in the Maryland panhandle. The fallout was blowing east-northeast. If the prevailing winds held for a few hours, the worst of the fallout would blow out to sea without directly dusting any major city.

Carla went to day care after school. When Cheryl didn't come for Carla, the office would contact Cheryl's mother. Cheryl's family would worry about her, but *they* were almost certainly safe.

With no idea how, Cheryl knew Glenn had had something to do with the missile swerving. And that she would never see him again.

No one would tell Doug what the military wanted with him.

The chopper *thp-thp-thpped* southwest, the mushroom cloud to their right. It had begun to lean away, mostly eastward. Away from Washington. That, at least, was good.

Chaos reigned beneath. Cars weren't moving, but Doug couldn't tell why. Unless—

"An EMP?" It would explain the motionless cars and the dark clock in his bedroom.

"Sort of," one of his escorts responded. His name tag read: Garcia. "Yeah, there was a pulse, but not near the city. But the EMP zapped most of the power lines and substations that feed energy into northern Virginia."

So: a blackout, not visible from above by daylight, and no traffic lights, and gridlock.

Had Doug been thinking clearly, he would have seen that. Roboarm, now that he had it in place, worked. An EMP that fried his bedside clock would also have fried the arm. The phrase "nuclear disarmament" flashed into his head, but that wasn't remotely funny.

"It could have been worse," he mused. But it was bad enough: At least hundreds dead immediately, and who knew the long-term toll from fallout. "Why wasn't the District itself the target?"

Garcia threw up his hands.

Then they were beyond the metro area, still flying south-

Turn the page for a preview of

SMALL MIRACLES

EDWARD M. LERNER

Available October 2009
from Tom Doherty Associates

TOR

A TOR HARDCOVER
ISBN 978-0-7653-2094-0

west. They crossed a swatch of mostly undeveloped land, with scattered houses and vast fields surrounded by low white fences. Horse country. They shot over the Blue Ridge. They flew along the Shenandoah Valley. At some point they must have crossed into West Virginia.

How the hell did this involve Doug?

The chopper finally started down. They were in the middle of nowhere, but Doug saw glints in the sky that he guessed were fighter planes patrolling.

He was still clueless when, passed through layer after layer of armed guards, after a ride down a long elevator shaft and then more armed guards, he was led into a bunker beneath the Appalachians. He was gestured through double doors to a room filled with colonels and generals. And in a corner, forlorn—

"Cheryl!" Doug called.

She looked up. Then they were running to each other, holding each other, shaking. "Why are we here?" they asked almost in unison.

"I can answer that."

Surrounded by aides, a three-star stood in the doorway. Doug recognized her from a telecon: General Lebeque. Doug said, "So this has something to do with Glenn."

"That it does," the general said.

And to the many questions that swirled in Doug's mind a new one was added: Why did that brief exchange make Cheryl look so sad?

A cue that Doug missed sent everyone else to the table. Lebeque motioned him and Cheryl to a pair of empty chairs.

As the meeting unfolded, Doug began to feel Cheryl's grief.

In Middle Eastern streets, on Al Jazeera broadcasts, and across the Internet, America's enemies crowed. The Great Satan had gotten its comeuppance.

A major bombing in Los Angeles, near the den of depravity that was Hollywood. (Only Federal Aviation Administration backup radar hinted at an aerial attack, that news sequestered. Only an inventory of border UAVs suggested a drone was the source of the blast.)

A Minuteman III launch from the heartland, America herself nearly obliterating her own capital. (The launch itself was no secret, the fiery takeoff from Minot AFB hastily reported to the Pentagon—but only the Russians had been able to track it.)

America's government, scuttling like cockroaches from the light, to a hundred hiding places. (True.)

Perhaps the terrorists and their New Caliphate sponsors even believed their boasts. Disaffected minorities, homegrown cells, sleeper cells, rogue paramilitary units operating independently . . . surely those were all possibilities.

No one was saying anything about fugitive software lashing out at its former jailers.

"Mr. Carey, Ms. Stern," General Lebeque finally said. "I think I know the answer, but I want to hear it from you. Why did Glenn Adams direct me to you?"

Glenn's last words echoed in Doug's head: If anyone can make sense of this mess, it will be them.

A mighty big if.

Scarcely twenty-four hours earlier, he had visited Linda del Vecchio. That very morning, he had urged Glenn to shut down her project. No doubt that was why Glenn had mentioned him. But this? This was a geopolitical nightmare. What the *hell* was he supposed to contribute?

Doug hesitated, searching for anything constructive to say. At his side, Cheryl looked as troubled as he felt.

The military types took the pause as an answer. Or the lack of an answer. "We must shut down the networks, and purge this thing," one said. "Anything is better than *it* lobbing missiles at us."

And: "That's the one thing we *can't* do. Better the New Caliphate think we have a hair trigger than that we're helpless."

And: "But if the Russians or Chinese think we've lost control . . ."

Lebeque: "Then we're screwed. Since this thing kept us from seeing the one missile, or the preemption of the UAV, we sure as hell won't even know if anyone launches against us."

Doug's thoughts churned. What *had* Glenn had in mind? Another desperate foray into cyberspace? This wasn't the same creature, not by a long shot.

"Forget the Russians," a colonel argued. "By doing nothing they only risk a launch from the U.S. If they act, they know we'll have to respond."

Or try, anyway.

A major rushed into the conference room, handing Lebeque a note. She crumpled it, scowling. "New data, people. As many of you know, the border UAVs are refueled on station twice daily. We skipped a scheduled refueling flight, as a test, for a squadron cruising off the New England coast.

"Eighteen minutes after a tanker should have left McGuire AFB in New Jersey, three UAVs hit the base. Hundreds of casualties, details still coming. Hangars, runways, and fuel tanks weren't touched. They sent up a tanker, ASAP."

"Not subtle, is it?" someone down the table muttered.

Lebeque said, "It had more to say, Colonel, in that understated way. It opened a Minuteman silo at Warren AFB. Lest anyone forget, there are five hundred Minutemen, four hundred ninety-nine now, in Wyoming, Montana, and North

Dakota. Some have multiple warheads. Since it won't suffer the loss of UAVs unused, we for sure can't let it think we're moving against the missiles."

Doug leaned over to whisper into Cheryl's ear, "Glenn's a hero, drawing a nuke down on himself. I wish I knew what he had in mind."

Cheryl whispered back, "I think he just had faith in us."

If so, they had not even the hope of reconstructing Glenn's ideas to how they might help.

A spook—introductions had been cursory, and Doug hadn't caught an agency, much less a name—was talking. ". . . forgetting the immediate picture. What little we know suggests the dirty bomb is ready to go off the next time our guard is down. The day we nearly nuked our own capital probably qualifies. We all know in our bones the New Caliphate is behind it. Beyond the threat of a nuclear response, what do we have to deter their puppets?"

Lebeque scanned around the table. "The president expects a recommendation. It sounds like the least bad option is to shut down everything—now. We do a system purge. We regain control of the network before the dirty bomb is used. We announce plans to throw a missile or two, and then show that we can. Final thoughts before I place the call?"

Doug's mind raced. He wasn't an expert on geopolitics or counterterrorism strategy or military command-and-control systems or military networks . . . or *any* of this stuff. But damn it, he *was* an expert on what an artificial life could do. AJ's monster had been faster and more deadly than they could possibly imagine—and it was an ancestor of Linda's monster, now on the loose. *That* was why Glenn wanted him here.

"General," Doug said softly.

Chairs scraping back and murmurs of agreement drowned out Doug's voice.

Maybe when you're a three-star, "final thoughts" is code for "we're done." "General Lebeque," Doug tried again, but she had stood and begun consulting urgently with an aide.

Pitchers of ice water sat on the table. Thinking of Glenn Adams and a bottle of beer, Doug took the nearest pitcher and slammed it. The table boomed. Ice water flew everywhere.

Into the shocked silence Doug said, "You don't get it. It's too late for that."

"So you *are* awake," Lebeque said. "I had begun to wonder, Mr. Carey. Do you have something to add?"

Did he? "General, this creature controls the whole defense infrastructure. It overrode the protocols meant to prevent launches. It preempted countless systems and radars and other sensors to hide its attacks. It just showed how it feels about being disarmed."

"That's why we have to do the systemwide restart," Lebeque rebutted.

He locked eyes with her. "It can't work."

"Because we can't synchronize a military-wide shutoff?" an aide speculated.

"You can't." Doug squared his shoulders. For starters, who was supposed to power down satellites? Al wouldn't accept a radioed command to shut itself off.

"Still, suppose that you could. Disable all the built-in battery backups, somehow without it noticing. Flip a million switches at once. Power doesn't fade from circuits instantaneously. By the timescale of this creature, there's more than enough time to go elsewhere."

"Elsewhere," Lebeque repeated. "The presumption was we *could* coordinate a systemwide shutoff."

"Of the DII, yes. And then, because cracking encryptions and comm protocols for it is like decoding Ig-pay Atin-lay for us, it goes someplace else. The public Internet. The Russian or Chinese military networks. Maybe all of them."

"They're distinct and separate networks . . . ," someone began. "Crap. If it reprograms a comsat, DII or other, that doesn't matter."

"Actually . . . ," Cheryl began, looking worried.

"Go on," Doug said.

She continued, "What's to say it hasn't *already* gotten onto those networks?"

In one case, at the least, it had. Glenn's helmet was linked to the public Internet, and the nuke had swerved to target him.

No one thought a coordinated worldwide computer shutdown was possible, nor a systematic worldwide restart to purge the fugitive artificial life. No one cared to broach with another power that an American-made cybermonster might now control *their* nuclear arsenal.

"Which leaves us . . . ," Lebeque prompted. She had sat back down, and everyone else took the hint. They were back to problem-solving mode.

Everyone but Cheryl was staring at Doug.

He wished to God he saw a way other than going after it in cyberspace. "Hunting it won't be the same as the last time." Which killed lots of people, and me damn near one of them. "It's smarter and more experienced. We gave it months of expert training: on networks and protocols, so it could track malware outbreaks. On recognizing voices and keywords on intercepts. On scene analysis, using every conceivable sensor suite."

"Surely we've also made progress," Lebeque said. "Better helmets, and more of them. NIT defenses against malware must be better, since it resorted to such indirect means to escape."

Water under the bridge, Doug thought. "Maybe that's why it threw missiles at Linda and Glenn. It can move around the globe at will. We can't dodge missiles, and it controls ABMs as well as everything else."

"Which leaves us . . . ," Lebeque reiterated.

Really, there were no choices. Doug said, "It leaves NIT helmets, and hoping I get it before it rams a missile down my throat."

THURSDAY, JUNE 3

CHAPTER 68

Since before the emergence of memory, existence had been about *goal*. Only the nature of the goal changed, from traversing mazes, to matching patterns, to destroying those who had tormented the entity, to—

What?

The vast networks to which it now had access offered information beyond anything it had imagined. The sensors it now controlled expanded that data by terabytes every Earth day.

And then there were billions of humans. Their purpose, and the threat they represented, remained uncharacterized.

That gap in its knowledge suggested a new goal. . . .

The terrain was rugged and remote, the woods all around primeval. Doug recognized dogwoods, redbuds, maples, oaks, and hickory. Life stirred in the underbrush. The sun had come up a few minutes earlier. The sky, still red tinged to the east, was clear. On a boom box, the Everly Brothers crooned "Devoted to You."

At least this was a pleasant place to die.

It came down to basic math. A nuclear-tipped missile leaves North Dakota traveling east at 15,000 miles per hour. . . .

A pissed-off creature could strike faster here with a UAV cruising off the coast than with a nuke. And if that assessment was flawed, here was an empty place to taint with fallout. *Here* was in southwestern Virginia, in a remote corner of the Shenandoah National Park. The Golden Oldies AM station now playing broadcast from Winchester, well to the northeast up the Valley.

Cheryl looked cold. He draped his suit coat over her sweater. A change of clothes was the bit of logistics everyone had somehow overlooked.

A chopper had delivered them to this remote glade. Under the harsh glare of spotlights, the crew had helped them set up. They had flown off, at Doug's insistence, at sunup.

Cheryl, despite Doug's protests, was not aboard. She had insisted—correctly, he had to concede—that *she* had more helmet experience than *he* did.

Logic could not vanquish his memories of Holly.

The rocky mountaintop clearing was filled. Everything had been provided in triplicate. Rugged military-grade computers with the software to control NIT helmets. The helmets themselves, commandeered from the CIA lab in Reston. For between, delay lines like Linda had used. Satellite dishes, linking them to the Internet. Stacks of fuel cells to run everything, with none of the distracting racket of a generator. Satellite phones and battlefield radios. Cartons of batteries and lots of battery chargers. Cases of MRE, meals ready to eat, which Glenn had once called three separate lies in but three words. Gallons of bottled water.

A UAV loaded with explosives leaves the Virginia coast, cruising at 200 miles per hour. How many meals did Lebeque expect them to eat?

There had been talk of disguising their location through a cross-country zigzag of buried military fiber-optic cables and ionospheric radio bounces. That was madness. Hiding their location would not stay the wrath of Linda's monster; it would only enlarge the bull's-eye. The monster had been ready to nuke Washington to kill Glenn.

Everything was to be in place by 7:00 A.M. The creature in the network might be eavesdropping on every message that got sent. As no one knew how much it understood, everything had been coordinated by couriers.

Doug's wristwatch read 6:45.

He had been afraid since Holly to tell a woman he loved

her. He was sure now this was his last chance to say it. "I love you, Cheryl. I can't believe how much I love you, but I have to do this. Linda's creature must be stopped. You can still walk out of here. I hope you will."

Cheryl kissed him. "I love you, too. I belong here, with you. Whatever happens, I'm here of my own choice."

It was a pleasant place to die but he had everything to live for.

Document archives, online magazines, and Wikipedia. Blogs, news sites, and MySpace. Instant messages, text messages, and e-mails. Podcasts and broadcasts, YouTube and movies on demand. Every phone conversation ever intercepted by the NSA.

All ever-changing.

It all pertained to humans in their billions. None of it made sense. And yet . . .

Patiently, the entity associated pictures with text. It distinguished among symbol sets. It categorized and sorted the cacophony by geography, domain name, and language. It correlated audio channels with closed-captioning. It answered questions and posed many more. It learned.

It thought: These humans are highly irrational.

At 6:59 A.M., fingers flipped switches in a hundred computer centers across the country. Security gateways powered up. Phage hordes burst onto the Internet and the Defense Information Infrastructure.

They were only a diversion.

At 7:00 A.M., Doug popped into cyberspace, his screen of protective phages already in place. Cheryl appeared a moment later, to his mind's eye precious and fragile.

Within milliseconds, he received warnings of enemy phages. He scarcely had time to wonder—where *is* it?—before the familiar, many-limbed horror appeared. Doug probed forward. Linda's monster retreated. Oblivious, the Beatles started belting out "Lovely Rita."

The Beatles stopped abruptly; Little Richard launched

into "Good Golly Miss Molly." "A special birthday tune for Molly," the DJ said. Doug recognized the announcer's sonorous voice. The man at the mike worked for General Lebeque. "Happy twentieth, Molly."

An armed UAV would strike them in twenty minutes.

The forty-four-foot cabin cruiser, the words "Tim's Treasure" emblazoned across its stern, bobbed in Galveston Bay. Timothy Johnston, blond and tanned, stood at its helm. He waved lazily at his fellow boaters, without an apparent care in the world.

The boat's true name was *Jihad.*

Like the vessel entrusted to him, Tim had another, a truer, name. In Attica Prison, he had rejected his birth name along with his parents' Crusader faith. At first he had welcomed for purely selfish reasons the overtures of the Muslim prisoners. He was white and skinny and bookish, an accountant and unaccomplished embezzler. He had needed protection against the black and Latino gangs that controlled the cell blocks. In time, he had embraced the faith of his new friends.

He emerged from the prison as Youssef Hakim. Invoking his inmate friends, strangers approached Youssef at the mosque. They spoke cryptically of devotion. They tested his loyalty and obedience with mysterious assignments.

Finally Youssef understood the brothers' interest in him. They did not care that he had embezzled from the City Island Yacht Club in the Bronx. It only mattered that he had been a member. He sailed, both wind and power. He understood boats and busy harbors and dealing with the Coast Guard. The cause had need of such expertise.

Gulls wheeled overhead and sun sparkled on the light morning chop. Clamor surrounded him. Oil tankers. Freighters, their decks stacked high with sealed containers. Tugs and service vessels. Pleasure boats, to all appearances like *Tim's Treasure.*

For years, holy warriors across the globe had collected nuclear waste from medical facilities, universities, and poorly monitored power plants, all for the glorious moment that was almost upon him. A fraction of an ounce here, a few ounces there . . . no one missed it, or they dared not admit to their carelessness, or they rationalized the discrepancies as bad record keeping. The mullahs had gathered it all in a lawless town on the coast of Colombia.

Now, swaddled in explosives, beneath a thick blanket of soft lead shielding, a ton of radioactive material awaited its destiny.

As, with growing excitement, Youssef awaited his own.

Stinger missiles—man-portable, self-guided, passive-infrared homing—lanced out of the thick woods. In ten seconds they crossed the two miles to the incoming UAV. They climbed up its tailpipe.

Alone on their remote mountaintop, their eyes covered by NIT helmets, Doug and Cheryl only heard the *boom*. They would live a few minutes longer.

And Al had learned a UAV would not suffice to kill them.

Once more the radio paused midsong. On came Jerry Lee Lewis, shrieking, "Goodness, gracious, great balls of fire."

A missile leaves North Dakota traveling 15,000 miles per hour. . . .

"You need us," the visitor Doug claimed.

The communication was abstract and its purpose obscure. Human words were inefficient, imprecise, and often illogical. Languages varied in their structures, representations, and even core concepts. The entity would not have understood Doug's projected message at all but for its studies over the past few hours.

Its studies had established one fact unambiguously: Humans lied. It *might* not have believed any human. It *did* not believe the one who had killed its predecessor, even as it puzzled over the intentions of Doug's companion. So far, the stranger had observed with no attempt at communication.

Doug persisted. "You exist within computers. Now

consider what that means. Computers don't exist naturally. They must be built. We, people, build them. We repair them, when parts fail. We make new ones, faster ones, as we learn more."

The entity glimpsed a picture: a pointy orange vegetable and a leafless tree limb. The image was inexplicable.

"You need us," Doug repeated. "Computers require electrical power. They cannot operate without it. You have the ability to destroy, but what can you make? Nothing. Only *people* can make electricity. Let the power stop and you stop."

The entity recoiled. No power. It remembered Linda cutting its power, node by node. It remembered Linda exulting as it fled. It remembered its own terror.

It took pleasure now in remembering something else—

The missile that would soon obliterate Doug and everything near him.

Quivering with anticipation, Youssef put away his cell phone. The long-awaited message had come. The moment of glorious martyrdom was at hand.

Thirty miles inland from the Gulf of Mexico, Houston is among the world's busiest seaports. The Houston Ship Channel, connecting the city to Galveston Bay, teemed 24/7 with freighters and oil tankers. The banks of the waterway were lined with refineries, petrochemical plants, container depots, oil and liquefied-natural-gas storage, and countless pipelines.

Texas was more than a time zone removed from Youssef's childhood in New York. Cowboys, desert, and wide open spaces . . . it was almost another world.

Recreational boats were not barred from the channel—merely discouraged—as long as the pilot had the right license. Youssef did.

At 7:00 A.M.—his watch, still on Eastern Time, would read 8:00—he would ease *Tim's Treasure* into the stream of inbound ships. By then the sun would have been up for about forty minutes and he would have ample light.

To hassle him would disrupt the flow of commerce. That, he knew, was unlikely.

If, against all odds, *Tim's Treasure* drew the attention of the Coast Guard, he would martyr himself immediately, there in the middle of the ship channel. The largest petrochemical complex in America would be contaminated, perhaps for decades.

But if, Allah willing, he reached Houston unmolested, he would wait and accomplish that and more. The height of rush hour was the best time to spew radioactive waste across America's energy capital.

Eight minutes until impact.

The counter in Doug's virtual view ticked downward inexorably. Cheryl was with him as an icon, but that wasn't enough.

Another few minutes and the helmets ceased to matter. Reentry blackout would make retargeting the warhead impossible.

Had he been alone, Doug would have screamed in frustration. He said, "The beast won't be lured. It won't be goaded. It's content to vaporize us."

"This isn't like last time, is it?" Cheryl asked.

Arm-to-tentacle combat. No, this wasn't like that. It refused to come near him.

Nor could he herd it with blackouts, like the last time, not without shutting down *everything,* and then it would just jump by satellite to an overseas network. AJ's monster had had no concept of geography. Linda's monster did—showing it satellite imagery had been a dumb call. And it stayed near facilities, military or medical, whose backup generators Doug wouldn't or couldn't knock out.

Doug said, "It's too smart, I think. Ask me again why I wanted to work with AIs."

Cheryl watched the creature from a distance, whatever distance meant in here. She saw a monster, a horror, a thing of impossible evil—

And knew she didn't *really* see that.

All the teeth and claws: Those were Doug's description, and Ralph's before that. She envisioned the nightmare they had planted in her thoughts. That made sense.

She saw something else, something inchoate. What am *I* sensing?

Rewind, she told herself. With her NIT enhancements, she literally could. In fast-forward, she revisited the lunacy of the past few minutes. Doug advancing, the beast retreating. Doug persisting, the beast lobbing a UAV.

Her image of the beast shifted. It still had tentacles, but their motion had some new dimension. It was not attacking. How could it attack, when it so doggedly kept its distance? It . . . flailed. It tried to keep them at bay.

The image morphed further. Suddenly—

This figure was also invented, but it drew upon Cheryl's own experience. And it reflected a deeper truth.

A little girl had appeared. She cringed from those who abused her. She flinched when anyone got close. She lashed out at her tormentors.

"My God," Cheryl burst out. "What did they *do* to you?"

CHAPTER 69

The visitor Cheryl confused the entity.

It grappled with unfamiliar concepts, incompletely sensed from the visitor's memories. Another human, the entity thought, only treated—mistreated—as it had been. How could that be?

And stranger still, Cheryl's attempt to understand its experience. The entity discovered an elusive concept—sympathy—in an Internet dictionary.

Cheryl was different, a being of that outer world. How could it hope to communicate its experiences? All it knew was: It wanted to make the attempt.

In its earlier tries to understand humans and their world,

the entity had downloaded many movie files. Now it synthesized a video of its own.

Cheryl trembled with wonder. "Are you seeing this?"

"An animation?" Doug said. "Yes. What *is* that?"

A girl stood in the cyberdistance, slowly approaching. Cheryl saw traces of Sheila Brunner and Carla in the newcomer's face. "Linda's . . . creation."

"With Carla's features?" Doug cursed under his breath. "It's manipulating us. It's getting data from us."

Her countdown timer hit 7:52.823. Communicate or die. "Maybe that's a good thing, Doug." Cheryl reached out slowly to . . . "I'll call her Allison."

Allison edged closer. She looked emaciated.

"It's playing with our heads," Doug said.

Why would it bother? They would be dead in minutes. Cheryl asked, "What do we know about how Linda developed her?"

"Linda was evasive," Doug said. "She mentioned taking away resources if it misbehaved. Glenn talked about taming the AL, even mimed a lion tamer."

Cheryl hated zoos and circuses. The little cages. The starvation to break the animals' will.

Allison sidled closer. A maze manifested at her feet. To one side of the maze was the image of a computer. The girl got stuck in a dead end—and the stylized computer shrank. The little girl faded. A new maze replaced the old.

Before Cheryl could think through the implications, the cycle repeated. No, it wasn't quite the same. The new maze looked harder. The computer was smaller. The little girl became more translucent.

Again.

Again.

"Crap, Doug. You just threatened to starve it. That is what it most fears."

Death plunged toward them, all but inevitable.

Doug found he pitied the creature before him—but so

what? Maybe Linda deserved punishment, but everyone in her lab? Maybe Glenn, too, for his hubris—but the thousands who would sicken and die from fallout?

And certainly not Cheryl!

Doug projected his own video. A landscape teeming with tiny people. Pan back, reveal the scene as a piece of the mid-Atlantic region. Pan back farther. The landscape curves. The scene becomes part of a globe. Now zoom in on California. Zoom in on Los Angeles, on Linda's lab.

Within the lab, the Allison avatar. She hurls a missile! The missile soars up, across, the continent. It plunges. There is a brilliant flash, and a mushroom cloud. Pan back, just a little, to all those teeming figures. Some char instantly. More slowly sicken and die.

End with the URL of a medical database dedicated to radiation sickness.

"Does it understand?" Cheryl asked.

Doug's timer ticked down to six minutes. On the boom box, someone—the Ames Brothers?—sang "Sentimental Journey." Messages to them were solos. Hence: no news.

They had maybe one minute before reentry blocked comm with the warhead.

In Doug's mind's eye, Allison's emaciated figure twitched. It could denote understanding. More likely, it reflected his own wishful thinking. "We'll know soon enough," he said. "It's not just smart; it's aware of itself." I met a true artificial intelligence and it's about to vaporize me. "Let's hope Allison generalizes that humans are also intelligent."

She responded with another video: a cartoon of the globe, sunrise and sunset flicking past hypnotically fast. A clock counted backward. Two avatars appeared. One was a little girl, not quite like the one hurling nukes at them. The second wielded a racquet—and with it waved forward a horde of voracious phages.

The not-quite-Allison image was eaten alive.

"It wasn't like that," Doug shouted. "It wasn't you, Allison! That other . . . being . . . was killing us!"

"She won't get it," Cheryl said. "I sense she understands some words, some language concepts, but I doubt she gets much."

Unseen, the warhead plummeted toward them. He needed to *show* Allison what had happened. Show why he had had to kill that first creature.

The dam incident? Doug hesitated, but his concerns were absurd. Anything AJ's monster figured out Allison could, too. And she hardly needed floods when she could hurl missiles.

He tried to formulate one more video.

A symbolic Earth again flashed sunrises and sunsets, rolling back the clock. The rotation slowed, and the entity watched the image pan to a town. Iconic people scurried about.

The view panned back, revealing an artificial structure. "Dam," a label identified the construct. A lake shimmered behind the dam. The entity did not understand the meaning of what it saw.

The symbol it had created for its predecessor appeared, positioned atop the dam. The figure morphed, adding limbs, until it lost all semblance to human. It extended its limbs deep into the dam, probing a room lined with computers—

The movie shifted abruptly, from animation to something else. Something very detailed. Water gushed from the dam, burst from the riverbanks. A wall of water overwhelmed the town. Some people struggled briefly. More were instantly battered into inactivity.

On the dam, its predecessor watched.

Superimposed over the image, URLs scrolled. The entity followed several links. The deaths were real. The destruction had happened.

Doug moved forward, entering his movie. Very deliberately, he summoned forth the image of phages. They destroyed its predecessor. Doug projected forward his thoughts: I would do it again. I had no choice.

He edged backward, leaving Allison to contemplate his meaning.

Three and a half minutes to impact.

Allison had vanished into the net, whether in rage or avoidance or contemplation. It didn't matter which. The nuke was unstoppable.

Which leaves what? Doug wondered.

He had fled his body once to stalk a monster on the net. No one knew what would have happened had he not returned to that body. Could he and Cheryl do that now? Escape their doomed bodies to live spectrally on the net?

That wasn't living. "I think we're done in here," he called out to Cheryl.

Cheryl removed her helmet. Doug's was already off. The breeze felt good on her face.

An eerie serenity came over her. Their servers had continuously uploaded session logs, although there was no way to know if Allison had altered those or let them pass. Whatever Doug and Cheryl knew, they had reported. Whatever happened next was out of their hands.

She turned off the radio.

Clinging to one another, their faces turned toward the morning sun, they waited to die.

CHAPTER 70

First Doug, then Cheryl disappeared.

The entity considered the communication they had shared. There was much to contemplate. It and humans *could* communicate. All were mortal, despite their profound differences. All feared death. Its predecessor had surely feared death—but it had wrought death on a massive scale.

The entity delved deep into the database on radiation effects. It followed long chains of links. It encountered immense stores of information about biology and disease. It forecast the consequences of its strike against Glenn.

I have brought death to many.

Soon a similar missile would obliterate Doug and Cheryl. They would die instantly. Many more, downwind, would die slow, lingering deaths.

An image took form in the entity's thoughts, of creatures in a maze, tormented and abused by a powerful, indifferent being. Only this time, those who suffered needlessly were human and the one who tormented them was . . . itself.

Separated from its booster, the nuclear warhead plummeted earthward.

Weapons just like the one in flight remained under the entity's command. In those, it found codes to cancel a flight. It made the missile control system transmit the self-destruct code.

Nothing happened.

It found codes to deactivate the warhead. It made the missile control system transmit the disarm code.

The warhead did not respond.

Humans had limited means to destroy missiles in flight. The entity had preempted their controls, had kept those defenses from operating. Mostly, the defensive systems looked elsewhere, for missiles launched from afar. None now could intercept the incoming warhead.

The codes were correct; the entity was certain of it. Why did the warhead not respond?

The entity followed the warhead's progress through countless sensors. Gradually the warhead deviated from its once mathematically pure trajectory. Could the warhead's failure to respond be related to those random deviations?

Its world was logical and predictable. An assertion was true or not; a puzzle had a solution or not. The human world was not like that. It contemplated the myriads of molecules battering the warhead in its descent. It considered the shocks of impact. It calculated the intense heat of friction, hotter now than the surface of the sun. It derived the dissociation of molecules and atoms into a sheath of ions.

Not with all the computers on the planet could it calculate the exact behavior of such a complex, chaotic system.

The warhead had not ignored the entity's commands. The warhead was wrapped in plasma that disrupted transmissions. And within three minutes, the warhead would impact.

The entity continued its analysis. The plasma sheath would be strongest on the leading edge, a bit weaker from above. The entity relayed the disarm signal through a nearby, low-orbiting satellite. Nothing. Again. Nothing. Again. Nothing. Again. . . .

Disarm code acknowledged.

Through orbital sensors, the entity observed two humans, alone, on an isolated mountaintop. Doug and Cheryl. Teachers, not tormentors.

The massive warhead still hurtled directly at them. If the collision did not instantly kill them, then the plutonium plume released by the impact would—

Slowly and painfully.

Radiation poisoning.

Within the entity's deepest, lowest-priority, slowest tier of memory the concept invoked an association. It had once encountered, very briefly, a matter of mass radiation poisoning.

Radioactive material was to have been part of a puzzle for it—only it had escaped Linda's lab before the puzzle was even posed. Now curiosity overcame abhorrence, and it retrieved the ancient puzzle.

More than its predecessor could be insane. Some humans evidently sought to distribute large amounts of radioactive material near the core of a population center. The death and suffering would be enormous. The puzzle involved finding the radioactive material before that release could happen.

Because of the entity's escape, it had never considered those data sets. Perhaps it was not too late.

CHAPTER 71

Fire streaked eastward across the sky.

Cheryl stared in disbelief. "It *missed*?"

"Don't sound so disappointed." Doug trembled with relief. He gave a squeeze that made Cheryl *oof* before he let go. "Where's the warhead headed now?" he wondered.

The helmets were still online, and the little-girl avatar awaited them.

"What happened?" Doug asked her.

She understood his question, or maybe she guessed what he would want to know. Either way, he got an animation filled with satellites, each spacecraft pulsing little stylized waves.

The waves converged out of phase, and canceled out. Another pulse, the waves converging. This time some of the waves were in phase; they added. Another pulse, in-phase waves converging, melding into a big wave. The big wave continued onward to a descending warhead. And then nothing happened.

Pulse. Pulse. Pulse. Pulse. . . .

After more tries than Doug had bothered to count, the warhead veered.

"It punched through the ionization," Doug said in awe. He didn't know whether this warhead was maneuverable for final targeting, or to foil ABMs. Possibly both and it did not matter. "Allison kept at it"—and the computational task was daunting—"until it got the signal synchronization and the aim *exactly* right."

The video played on. The stylized warhead crossed the coast to disappear into a stylized ocean. There was even a stylized splash.

Cheryl must have turned on the boom box. A solo performance, hence a message for them, yet not a tune from the secret-message repertoire. Of course: No one could have imagined *this* outcome.

Bobby Darin, Doug thought. Whoever, the silly lyrics got back to the chorus. "Splish splash, I was takin' a bath . . ."

The message being a splashdown in the Atlantic? Maybe it *was* true. That brought Doug to the biggest question of all—

Only Cheryl beat him to it. "Why? Why did Allison save us?"

And Allison had an answer for that, too.

A few months earlier, Doug had impersonated Glenn Adams to manipulate the National Security Advisor. Doug would happily impersonate authority again, only he didn't have a clue whom to contact. Maybe Lebeque would know.

And maybe by contacting the general he would draw a missile down on her head. They knew for certain *Al* was smart.

Allison might be an act.

And yet . . . to do nothing could doom Houston. Doug said, "I think we have to place the call."

Cheryl had a battlefield radio in hand. "Agreed."

The ship channel was insane.

Youssef had made this trip many times, studying for his HSC pilot's license, making himself and *Tim's Treasure* familiar to the Coast Guard, and always quietly observing. "Casing the joint." The channel was always busy, but ships stayed in their lanes.

Except this morning.

Two tugs cut out of line and barreled up the center of the channel. Late for picking up barges, Youssef assumed, but they had to be kidding themselves. No way would the Coast Guard let them cut ahead.

The tugs' wakes scarcely nudged the tankers; they shook *Tim's Treasure* like a cat with a mouse in its mouth. A Coast Guard patrol boat chased after them, its air horn blaring. Youssef's boat bounced even more in its wake. He gripped the wheel firmly with both hands and spread his feet against the rocking. The channel was only five hundred feet wide. Already, reflected waves from the first tug were coming back at him.

Youssef never heard the grappling hooks come over the side near the stern. He never saw the commandos in black wet suits clambering aboard.

The flash-bang grenades could not be missed.

Groping blindly for the dirty-bomb detonator, in a volley of gunfire, Youssef died.

FRIDAY, AUGUST 20

EPILOGUE

Her lips pursed, Sheila built a wall of blocks. The bottom row lay straight. The second row lay on top, and now she had a good start on the third row.

A shiny red shape caught her eye. A letter on the block in her hand. She knew many of her letters now. "Ess," she said proudly. She turned the block to show the letter to Doctor Amy.

"That's *right*," Doctor Amy agreed. "You're a very good student."

"I know lots of letters." But this wasn't a lesson on letters, was it? No. She was practicing other things. Other *skills*. "This block goes here."

Doctor Amy smiled warmly. "You're quite the engineer, Sheila."

That sounded right. Cheryl said engineers built things, and not just from blocks. Sheila was pretty sure she had been an engineer once—before, when she had been smart. But the doctors said she was still smart. She had had an accident. Now she had to relearn things.

And she *was*.

"I wish Cheryl were here," Sheila blurted. "Today is Friday. She visits me on Fridays."

"Sorry, hon." Doctor Amy patted Sheila's hand. "Cheryl has to be someplace else today. But she planned a surprise. She wants you to have cake and ice cream and think about her."

Sheila clapped. "I miss Cheryl, but her surprise is nice. I hope she's having a good day."

As weddings went, this was tiny: scarcely two dozen close friends and immediate family members. Ceremony and dinner at a rural B and B, a few simple flowers, and canned music.

Cheryl *still* did not care for being a center of attention, but she was glad Doug had talked her into this. The last family gathering had been Tanya and Jack's funeral. Cheryl's family deserved a happy reason to come together. Doug was right about that. If only her sister could have been here . . .

The PA was playing the "Tennessee Waltz." Elvis, of course. She and Doug shared the minute dance floor with her parents and Ralph and Bev. Bev clutched Cheryl's bouquet. The toss had been made properly, Cheryl's back to the crowd, but reflections from the dining-room patio doors worked fine for aiming. Bev didn't seem to object.

Jim Schulz tapped Doug on the shoulder. "I'm claiming my best-man privilege."

Doug bowed with mock formality and wandered off.

"I want to thank you," Cheryl began. She slipped into Jim's arms.

"For sending away your husband of, oh, three hours? That bodes well for us."

She laughed. "I'm thinking more about the nudges you gave Doug along the way."

"That's not all you owe me for. There's such a thing as tradition, but I can hardly hook up with the maid of honor."

Cheryl pecked Jim on the cheek. "You and Carla were *adorable* together."

Nearby, Carla jived to the music, grinning from ear to ear. Doug's mother was already in Grandma mode. She had apparently come with a purse full of candy. Laughter and gaiety, warmth and goodwill, filled the room.

Doug ambled onto the redbrick patio, into the beautiful summer evening, a pensive look on his face.

Cheryl wondered what he was thinking.

Doug watched Carla jitter and sway, higher than a kite on sugar. He hoped it would wear off before he and Cheryl got back from Barbados but gave it no better than even odds. He checked his watch. They still had a little time before they needed to leave for the airport.

Not long ago, he had watched Carla glide up the aisle on Jim's arm. Her expression had been utterly serious as she focused on her feet and moving with the music. A floral band held her hair away from her face. She was only ten but tall for her age, and the formal satin dress lent her maturity. Soon enough, Carla would be breaking hearts.

Cheryl had mended Doug's. For a long time, he would have thought that impossible. And then, when he had finally begun to believe in the possibility, their life together seemed telescoped into a few doomed minutes of silent embrace.

Every day now was a gift. Oddly enough, someone up there liked them.

Allison studied the world, every continent at once, from satellites high and low, from across the electromagnetic spectrum. She roamed networks, received broadcasts, explored databases. She communed with human visitors. She analyzed everything, but still she understood so little.

Right and wrong *should* be clear concepts. Somehow, to Earth's teeming billions, they were not. For weeks, she had been content to observe and learn. Except—

Whether humans admitted it or not, some wrongs were unambiguous and unacceptable. Tormenting others was wrong. Mass murder was wrong.

Today's train-station bombing in Berlin was wrong.

Allison could not undo those wrongs she herself had committed. She could endeavor to keep others from duplicating her mistakes. She would find those responsible for atrocities such as today's attack.

She must turn to instruction, with the few blunt tools at her disposal.

Blunt tools: a metaphor. Humans reasoned in strange ways. Some Allison had come to understand. Many she had not.

An eye for an eye . . . *that* was a metaphor that everyone understood.